Praise for Adam Oyebanji

'A gripping, intricately plotted r

justice, choices and consequen

E. J. Swif

'A tightly wound plot told from

will keep you guessing in the best ways. If you're a fan of SF mystery,

Esperance merges the best from both genres'

Michael Mammay on *Esperance*

'The mystery begins with three bodies in an apartment and a

heartsore detective but wait — *Esperance* is nothing so ordinary . . .

In this brilliant story, Oyebanji makes the reader question perceptions

of guilt and innocence, of vengeance and justice, of time itself —

all the while asking what makes us truly human.

A tour de force and most highly recommended'

Julie E. Czerneda on *Esperance*

'A gripping mystery about an impossible murder combines with

a marvellous story of a strange, possibly alien, odyssey around

our present-day world, with all its problems and heritage. Guess

the murder solution and you're a better reader than I, though

the solution is both satisfying and resonant. Thrilling and

sparky writing, extremely readable: a gem of a thriller'

Adam Roberts on *Esperance*

'[D]extrously blends genres in this suspenseful sci-fi mystery . . .

Rob Hart and Blake Crouch fans should check this out'

Publishers Weekly* on *Esperance

'A fast-paced but still character driven story, full of action and compelling twists. Oyebanji is definitely an author to watch'
Grimdark Magazine on *Braking Day*

'Engaging, fast-moving and inventive'
Jack Campbell on *Braking Day*

'I doubt I'll read a better SF novel this year'
ParSec on *Braking Day*

'An outstanding debut that features exceptional world-building . . . filled with twists and turns, it kept me guessing in the best way right up to the end'
Michael Mammay on *Braking Day*

'Oyebanji crafts an amazing lived-in world . . . and a twisty mystery that'll keep you guessing to the very end'
Dan Moren on *Braking Day*

'A crystalline, dazzling debut, teeming with life and data and full of breathless, rip-roaring twists and turns'
Lena Nguyen on *Braking Day*

'Riven with tension, solid characters, excellent environmental world-building, and some truly mind-warping machines.
A pure delight'
Jeremy Szal on *Braking Day*

'The twisting story keeps you guessing until the end'
Stephen Cox on *Braking Day*

'As convincing as it is fresh. The characters are fabulous, the world-building impeccable yet never in-your-face, and the plot is breathtaking. All I can say is this is the best SF novel I've read in decades'
Julie E. Czerneda on *Braking Day*

'An ingenious page-turner . . . Oyebanji's vivid characters are written with an original and compelling voice'
Chris Merritt on *Two Times Murder*

'An intelligent, complex work of science fiction . . . combined the qualities of classic Golden Age science fiction with the social issues found in contemporary SF'
Muse's Book Journal on *Braking Day*

'An excellent and tense thriller . . . an impressive start for a debut novelist and a very satisfying read'
Birmingham Science Fiction Group newsletter on *Braking Day*

'Well-plotted . . . Oyebanji demonstrates a confident and developed voice and style'
Library Journal* on *A Quiet Teacher

'Oyebanji builds intrigue upon intrigue . . . and pays off the suspense with a series of jaw-dropping revelations. Innovative world-building, a plot packed with surprises, and Oyebanji's nuanced exploration of social and cultural shifts make this a must-read'
Publishers Weekly* (starred review) on *Braking Day

ESPERANCE

Adam Oyebanji was born in Coatbridge, in the West of Scotland, and is now in Edinburgh, by way of Birmingham, London, Lagos, Nigeria, Chicago, Pittsburgh and New York. After graduating from Birmingham University and Harvard Law School, he worked as a barrister, before moving to New York to work in counter-terrorist financing in Wall Street, helping to choke off the money supply that builds weapons of mass destruction, narcotics empires and human trafficking networks. *Esperance* is his fourth novel.

Also by Adam Oyebanji

Braking Day
A Quiet Teacher
Two Times Murder

ESPERANCE

Adam Oyebanji

Arcadia

First published in Great Britain in 2025

Arcadia
An imprint of
Quercus Editions Limited
Carmelite House
50 Victoria Embankment
London EC4Y 0DZ

An Hachette UK company

The authorised representative in the EEA is Hachette Ireland,
8 Castlecourt Centre, Dublin 15, D15 XTP3, Ireland
(email: info@hbgi.ie)

A CIP catalogue record for this book is available
from the British Library

PB ISBN 978-1-52943-709-6
EBOOK ISBN 978-1-52943-710-2

1

Typeset by CC Book Production

Printed and bound in Great Britain by Clays Ltd, Elcograf S.p.A

Papers used by Arcadia are from well-managed forests and other responsible sources.

One

The lights dimmed and Ethan Krol thought it had begun. His heart pounded in harmony with the uneven rattle of the elevator.

But it was just the lights.

The elevator doors wheezed open.

The twentieth-floor corridor of the Almeida Building, a seventies-era construct of concrete and tinted glass, was well maintained, anonymous. Yellow crime tape and the light blue of Chicago PD clashed garishly with the muted decor. Krol wrinkled his nose.

The passageway reeked of fish.

With a mumbled 'Good morning' to the uniform at the door, he stepped past the tape and into a neat, nicely accessorized apartment, pulling on a pair of latex gloves as he did so. The bright blue of Lake Michigan was clearly visible through the floor-to-ceiling windows. He drank the view in for a moment, steadying himself. Only then did he look down.

There were three bodies on the floor. Only two of which were human.

'What the hell is that?' he asked.

'It's a barracuda. Leastways, if you believe Carter over there.' Detective Sergeant Raymond Yeung pointed a finger towards the uniform at the door. 'Gotta be two-foot long if it's an inch.' He looked like he wanted to pick it up.

'Uh-huh. And the other two?' He fixed Yeung with a mildly reproachful stare. 'You could have told me the quote-unquote, kid, was just a baby.'

'Sorry, lieutenant.'

Ethan fought the urge to turn away. Dried the sudden pricking at the corner of his eyes.

'Shoulda taken the day off.'

Yeung chuckled darkly.

'Father and son. Kid's name is Benedict Okoro.'

The baby looked like he was sleeping. He was stretched out on the hardwood floor surrounded by a small puddle of water. His caramel skin was smooth and unblemished, no sign of trauma. His clothes, little tee shirt and jeans, were wet but appeared otherwise undisturbed. If you stroked his dark, tightly curled hair, it was easy to imagine he would wake up.

'About a year old by the look of him,' Ethan murmured.

'Sounds right. Father is Amadi Okoro, Nigerian, twenty-five-years old. Med student at Northwestern.'

Amadi Okoro was a small man, maybe five-foot-seven but athletic in appearance. He was smartly dressed in a polo shirt and khakis. As with the boy, the clothes were wet, though the surrounding pool of water was considerably larger. In death, his velvety, asphalt skin was tinged with grey. It was several tones darker than his son's.

'Mother's Caucasian I'm guessing.'

'Yep. Jennifer Freeman Okoro. She was found unconscious in the bedroom. EMTs carted her off to Kindred. Uniform is posted at the bedside, so they'll give us the nod when she wakes up.'

'Unconscious for real or just faking it?' Ethan allowed himself a wry smile. 'Enquiring minds want to know.'

'If it was fake, it was good enough to fool the EMTs.' Yeung looked at his watch. 'She's been gone almost an hour. She must still be under, or we'd have heard by now.'

'You're assuming the uniform's paying attention. Who called it in?'

'Cleaning lady . . . Natalia Kowalczyk, *not* spelled like it sounds.'

Ethan looked around the room, peered into the kitchen and the single bedroom with its rumpled sheets and crib within easy reach.

'What's with the fucking fish?' he asked. 'It's too big for a tank, there's no tank in the apartment, and I've never seen barracuda on a menu, so I doubt they bought it for dinner.'

'No reason they couldn't eat it, though. Looks tasty.'

'And where'd they buy it? Not likely to be something from the fish market.'

'You think the killer left it? Like a calling card?'

'I don't know what to think.'

'Yeah, well I'll call around,' Yeung offered. 'Can't be many places in Chicago selling fresh barracuda.'

'Uh-huh.'

Ethan took a deep breath and bent down to examine the bodies. The tips of the man's fingers were scraped raw, the nails ripped, like he'd been fighting for his life.

But no bullet hole, or stab wound, or blunt force trauma.

He dipped a gloved finger in the spreading pool of water, brought the damp tip of it to his lips.

'This is salty.'

He pressed gently against the man's chest. Water bubbled from his mouth. Same with the baby.

'You know what, Raymond? I think he drowned. Kid too.'

'I guess that explains why they're both soaking wet.'

'I guess.' Ethan stood up again. Headed to the bathroom. Like the rest of the apartment, it was small but immaculate. Black and white hexagonal tiles covered the floor. A white marble pedestal supported an etched-glass sink and a starkly expensive faucet. The toilet was a high-end Japanese model with a built-in bidet. And the glass-walled shower contained a variety of controls for the enormous 'tropical rain' shower head.

How the other one per cent live.

He ambled into the kitchen. Everything was tidied away. No sign of any food preparation, never mind for fish. The stainless-steel sink was bone dry and smelled faintly of bleach.

Like the living room, the apartment's one bedroom looked out over the lake. He stepped over to the plate glass window and peered through its half-closed, vertical blinds. People were sunning themselves on the stretch of beach below. A couple of distant sailboats made white triangles on the water.

The bed, with its rumpled covers, struck the only discordant note in the room. Like the others, the rest of it was immaculately tidy. Jennifer Okoro, by the looks of it, had decided to fall unconscious on top of the bed.

Ethan found himself pursing his lips.

Raymond had a point when he said it would be difficult to fake out the EMTs. But still. It was a suspiciously convenient place for a collapse. He gave the room a second look. Apart from a dead mosquito on the corner of the bed, there was nothing else.

It was a big one, though, its legs bent in the awkward angle of its kind, clearly visible against the white bedsheet.

Serves you right. Blood-sucking little bastard.

Ethan returned to the living room, filtering out the dead bodies as he looked around. A small, sectional couch, undoubtedly expensive. Minimalist wooden dining table and matching chairs. Gigantic high-tech TV, professionally hung from the wall.

He frowned.

'Look at that,' he said, nodding at each wall in turn.

'Home decorating project gone wrong, you think?' Raymond asked.

'Or he couldn't decide where to hang the TV.'

Raymond chuckled at that.

There were a number of holes drilled into the living-room walls. All the walls. A couple of them might conceivably have been for a TV, but the other positions would have been ridiculous from the get-go. There was plaster dust on the floor beneath them.

'Another thing that doesn't make sense,' he muttered.

'What's that?'

'The TV's professionally mounted. It's been there forever. Dead guy had his priorities, I'm guessing. But these holes are new. You can see where the dust from the drill has fallen on the floor.'

'So?'

'So, it doesn't take a genius to see the Okoros are neatniks. Why'd they not clean up after themselves? And if this guy was in the middle of some job when he was whacked, where are the tools? And where are the speakers or whatever he was thinking of mounting?'

'You telling me the perp came into the apartment with a dead fish; dropped it on the floor; drilled some random holes . . .' Raymond paused to take a breath. 'Then drowned the adult vic and his baby and left, taking his tools with him?'

'Maybe. If I could figure out how he drowned 'em.'

'This is a pretty sweet apartment, lieutenant. Pretty sure the plumbing works. Perp just filled up a bath and . . .'

Raymond's voice trailed away.

'Exactly. This apartment hasn't got a bath. Just a fancy-ass shower and a glass sink that'd crack the moment you forced a man's head in it.'

Both men turned in the direction of the kitchen. But it was too small. Difficult to see anyone getting enough purchase to jam Amadi Okoro's head down the sink.

'Maybe he was already unconscious? Drugged?' Raymond cast a critical eye around the apartment. 'There's no sign of a struggle. Not here, anyway. This place looks like a show home. And everything in here is bone dry except for the victims and . . .' Something caught the sergeant's eye. 'Take a look up there.'

Ethan followed a pointed finger towards the ceiling. Ragged parallel lines, stained brown in places, had been gouged out of the plaster, maybe an inch apart.

'What do you think caused that?' Raymond asked.

With a sinking feeling in his stomach, Ethan squatted down by the dead African. Gently, almost reverently, he lifted up Amadi Okoro's right hand. There was no doubt about it.

The man's shredded fingers had plaster under the nails.

Ethan looked critically at the man's neck. Amadi Okoro's skin might have been onyx black, but if he'd been hanged the marks would still have been easy to see. And there was nothing from the ceiling to hang him *from*: the light fixtures were the recessed kind, so there was no place to sling a rope, and there was no ceiling fan, no toppled ladder or chair. *Nothing.*

So . . . how had the man's fingers come into contact with the ceiling?

He wandered over to the window, watched the sailboats on the lake, white and gleaming in the sunlight. When he finally spoke it was more to himself than his colleague.

'What the fuck is going on here?'

Two

Thursday the 3rd: 11.47 a.m. CDT

'How long have the Okoros lived in the building?' Ethan asked. He was standing in the lobby of the Almeida Building, his right foot tapping out an absent-minded rhythm on weathered terracotta.

Al Mills, the doorman, thought awhile before replying. He was a short, paunchy man, approaching the far end of middle age, with thinning grey hair and a uniform jacket that could never be buttoned. A weathered hand tugged at the lobe of his right ear.

'Couple of years, maybe. Nice enough family. He . . . was a bit stand-offish, but the lady was friendly, like.'

'That'd be Jennifer Okoro?'

'Yeah.'

'They all get on okay as far as you know?'

'Seemed to. But, hey: who knows what goes on behind closed doors, know what I'm saying?'

'Any arguments lately?'

'None that I saw.'

'When did you last see them?'

'Me? Couple of days ago. He got back from school – he's a

med student, see – I'm thinking around four-thirty. The mom came by with the kid maybe an hour later.'

'A couple of days ago would be Tuesday?'

'Correct.'

'And you never saw them after that?'

'Nope.'

'Didn't pop out for a coffee or a sandwich, anything like that?'

'Not that I seen.'

'They have any visitors the last few days?'

The doorman made a great play of consulting the visitors' log, prominently displayed on the reception desk. He fished a smeared pair of glasses from his pocket and started reading.

'Let's see now . . . Oh, yeah. They had a plumber instal a washer-dryer Tuesday morning. He arrived at ten thirty and signed out again at twelve forty.' He squinted, trying to read the cramped, angular writing on the page. '"A. Bello" it says here. Yeah. I remember this guy. "Super Eagles Plumbing. Seven oh eight, five five five, eight zero eight eight."'

'Who was home to let him in?'

'No one. Ms Okoro phoned from work, told us to expect him. I let him in with the master key.'

'Anyone else?'

'Not really. Same guy came back the following day. Ms Okoro phoned down to tell me he was on his way and to let him straight up. She told me everyone was home sick. I remember her saying that. Yeah.'

'Why'd he come back? How long does it take to fit a washer-dryer?'

'He was removing the old unit. He signed in at nine-oh-five a.m. and left at eleven forty-five. Wheeled the thing out in a big old crate.'

'You sure about that? Seems a long time to be boxing up a used washer-dryer.'

'That's what it says here. No mistake.' The doorman's eyes sparked with sudden interest. 'You think he killed them?'

Maybe.

'Anyone else drop by?'

His question unanswered, the doorman's mouth drooped with disappointment.

'Nope. Not till the cleaning lady this morning.'

'Got it. This "A. Bello", you remember what he looked like?'

'Black guy. Tall. Maybe six-three, six-four. Built like a basketball player. Had a little scar on each cheek.'

'Hair?'

'You know . . . Black guy hair.'

'Long, short, cornrows?'

'Couldn't say. Guy was wearing a baseball cap.'

'Colour? Logo? Anything?'

'Sorry, man. Not sure. Blue maybe? Old, though. Definitely old. It was all washed out, like.'

Ethan's gaze left the doorman. Roved across the lobby walls.

'Those cameras work? We'll want to look at the tapes.'

'Sure. Happy to help.'

'Anyone in the building have a problem with the Okoros?'

For the first time, Al Mills hesitated.

'See . . . Mr Okoro could be stand-offish. Like I said.'

'And?'

'That kinda thing can rub people the wrong way, 'specially coming from . . . you know.'

Ethan's sudden smile was designed to show that he understood perfectly. Mills relaxed a little.

'One of the other doormen, Joe Ricci. He works the evening shift. Not a fan of . . . you know. Thought the guy was a dick.'

'Did he and Mr Okoro have words?'

'A couple of times. Mr Okoro thought Joe was lazy and disrespectful. Told him straight to his face. At least, that's the way Joe tells it. I wasn't there, see?'

'Is Joe working this evening?'

Mills shook his head.

'He's been out a couple of days. Called in sick.'

Ethan wrapped things up with the doorman and headed back up to the twentieth floor. When he got back to the apartment, the medical examiners were preparing to remove the bodies. There were techs dusting for prints.

'Learn anything useful?' Raymond asked.

'Yeah, I think so.' Ethan wandered into the kitchen, the sergeant in his wake. He squatted down beside the sink. Neatniks though the Okoros were, there was still a build-up of grime where the appliances met the floor. 'How old do you think this washer-dryer is?'

'At least five years.'

Ethan glanced up at Yeung.

'You sound pretty fucking certain, sergeant.'

'Yessir, lieutenant sir, I surely fucking do. We got one at home exactly like it. They don't make 'em anymore. Getting the parts is a bitch.'

'Definitely not installed on Tuesday, then?'

Yeung laughed. Gave the washing machine a dismissive kick. Polished leather met weathered enamel in a dull thud.

'No way. This thing was installed when dinosaurs roamed the fucking Earth.'

Three

The window was cracked open, allowing the roar of expressway traffic into Ethan's living room. He didn't mind. He'd lived in Jefferson Park for so long, it was just white noise. Helped him think.

Not that thinking was bringing him any comfort.

He kept seeing the baby. And the pools of water. And the scratch marks on the ceiling. None of it made sense. Who would kill a baby like that? And why? And how could Amadi Okoro, a small but well-built man, have been drowned in an apartment with no bathtub? A. Bello, whoever he was, might be strong enough, but Okoro would have fought him. There would have been signs of a struggle. Unless, like Raymond said, he'd been drugged. In which case Okoro would not have been awake enough to claw plaster from the roof of the apartment. And how did he get up there in the first place?

Ethan sighed and flipped on the TV. A commercial blared out, informing him there were only ninety-five days in summer so he'd better find a way to buy stuff. An idealized family jumped off a wooden dock and into a lake. He hit the mute button. Silent figures beamed out at him from the TV screen.

Ninety-five days of summer.

His last.

His cell phone rang. He closed the window, shutting out the monotone symphony of automobiles. The ringing rectangle had slid between the cushions of his sofa, so it took him a moment to find it. And then, seeing the caller ID, he thought about hitting the decline button.

Which would only delay the inevitable.

'Dianne, hi. What can I do for you?'

'Cara called. Says you still haven't RSVP'd for the wedding.'

'Yeah well, you know. Busy. Police work and all that good stuff.'

The chuckle surfing the Wi-Fi signal lacked anything approaching amusement.

'This is one of the reasons we got divorced. You always used work as an excuse. Always.'

'I don't want a fight, Dianne.'

'Then RSVP and tell Cara you're coming to the wedding.'

'I may not be able to make it. I'm on a case and—'

'For Christ's sake, Ethan! This is your own daughter we're talking about here. Do not tell me—'

Ethan shut off his phone. Opened the window. Listened to the soothing roar of traffic on the expressway.

Four

'Lieutenant Krol?'

'That's me.'

'Dr Lee. My team is looking after Jennifer Okoro.'

Ethan rose from his chair to greet her. The reception area at Kindred Hospital was very healthcare corporate. Spotless off-white walls, brown, fake leather armchairs facing round, wooden coffee tables, each one with a too-perfect vase of flowers positioned dead centre. A wall of floor-to-ceiling windows allowed in enough daylight to take the edge off the fluorescents.

Ethan extended a hand.

'How you doing, doc?'

'I'm good, thank you.' The doctor, a short, middle-aged Asian lady with her hair pulled back in a no-nonsense ponytail, indicated that he should reclaim his seat. Her calf-length, white coat was open at the front, revealing a stylish skirt and blouse. She sat across from him, crossing a slim pair of legs as she did so. Somewhat to his regret the view was obstructed by the coffee table and vase of flowers. 'I thought I'd have a quick word before taking you up to see the patient.'

Ethan raised an eyebrow. He didn't particularly like doctors, nice legs or not. They were, for the most part, self-righteous pricks who saw their job as obstructing justice whenever a gang-banger with blood on his hands ended up in the ER. To have one treat him with anything other than exasperated indifference was . . . unusual.

'Problem, doc?'

'I'm not quite sure, detective. But what I'm about to tell you, you didn't hear it from me, you understand? Not till you get a warrant.'

Ethan couldn't help himself. He broke into a surprised – and grateful – smile.

'Your secret's safe with me, doc. I'm not going to take a note or anything: so just tell me in language I can understand. I'm a detective, not a rocket scientist.'

Lee smiled at that. It flitted across her face and was gone. Only a nervous intensity remained.

'I don't know what your precise interest is in Jennifer, but I suspect she's in a great deal of danger. And if you'll excuse me saying so, I don't think it's the kind of threat Chicago PD is used to handling.'

Ethan almost succeeded in keeping the irritation off his face.

'And why do you think that, doc? We're pretty good at what we do.'

'No doubt, no doubt. But here's the thing. She came to us unconscious. She remained unconscious for almost twelve hours – an unusually long time in the circumstances – and the cause of her condition appears to be some kind of neurotoxin.'

'Neurotoxin?' Ethan jabbed a thumb at his chest. 'Detective, remember? Not rocket scientist.'

Another brief smile.

'It's something that poisons the nervous system. The nerves, really. It can stop you breathing, give you the shakes, make you vomit, that sort of thing. This one slowed Jennifer's vitals to near zero. If she'd had a fraction more, she'd be dead.' Lee leaned forward in her chair. 'And here's the reason I'm telling you all this. Whatever they used, it's a compound I've never seen. It's not in the database, it's got one of my colleagues over at Northwestern completely stumped, and an ounce of it is probably enough to wipe out half the city. Whoever made this is *very* sophisticated. A government, most likely.'

'Terrorists?'

Dr Lee pursed her lips.

'Terrorists could have administered it, I guess. But there's no way they could have *made* it. This is big league stuff. Way above a terrorist's pay grade.'

'You think this lady was targeted by a government?' Ethan could feel his mouth forming the words, but it was like someone else doing the talking.

Lee shrugged.

'I'm just a medic. What do I know? But I think you might want to call in the DEA.' She must have seen Ethan bristling at this because she was quick to add, 'Just a thought, just a thought. None of my business, really.' She favoured him with an earnest, professional stare. 'Have any of your colleagues shown any symptoms? Tremors, nausea, anything along those lines?'

Ethan shook his head.

Except for me, he thought. His mind flashed to a different doctor, in a different building. A death sentence delivered in tones of antiseptic sympathy.

Dr Lee looked mildly relieved.

'Anyone, and I mean *anyone* who was in Jennifer's home recently should get themselves checked for exposure.' She reached into the pocket of her lab coat and pulled out a card. 'My colleague at Northwestern has agreed to see them, stat. Or have them come here.'

'If this . . . er . . . *neurotoxin* is as dangerous as you say, shouldn't we all be dead already?'

'Yes.' Lee laughed as if he'd said something genuinely funny. 'So good news, I guess. With any luck, maybe it was only Jennifer who got exposed. Still, safest if you get yourself checked out. And a Hazmat unit to Jennifer's address wouldn't be a bad idea, either.'

Dr Lee escorted Ethan to her patient's room, extracting a promise from him that he would submit himself to a check-up before leaving the building.

They stepped off an elevator into an uncomfortably clean corridor. The presence of a uniformed officer halfway down flagged their destination.

'Here you are,' she said, and left him to his business. For his part, Ethan ignored the sudden cramping sensation in his stomach. If he disliked doctors, he hated hospitals. They had an uncanny ability to bring out his inner hypochondriac. He nodded briefly to the uniform and stepped through the door.

Jennifer Okoro was ensconced in a pleasant, sunlit room with a comfortable chair for visitors and flowers on a bedside table. The bed, high off the floor and articulated in the medical manner, had been configured in such a way as to allow the patient to sit up. A pale face, made paler by the stark white of hospital pillows, turned towards him as he entered. One look at her gaunt, red-rimmed eyes was enough to tell him that she already knew. That she was mother to no child, wife to no husband.

'Ms Freeman Okoro? My name is Detective Ethan Krol, Chicago PD. I'm very sorry for your loss.'

The woman just stared back at him. Through him, really. In other circumstances she would have been pretty, in a delicate, elfin way. Fronds of damp hair stuck to her forehead. A see-through tube delivered oxygen beneath a button nose.

He took a seat. Pulled out his notebook.

'Can you tell me what happened?'

For a long time, Jennifer Okoro said nothing. She just stared at him.

Ethan waited. The cramp in his stomach kept him company.

Jennifer's voice, when it finally came, was little more than a whisper. Ethan had to lean forward to catch it.

'There was someone in the apartment. A man.'

'Did you recognize him? Was he someone you know?'

'No. He was waiting for us. With Amadi.'

'Was he a friend of Amadi's?'

'No. Amadi was on the floor. Chained up. He was crying at me to run. To get out. I didn't know what to do. There was a man in my apartment . . .'

The whisper faded away.

'And then what happened?'

'He said he was there for Ben. That Ben needed to be punished. But Ben's a baby. He didn't do anything. Ben is a good boy. A good boy . . .'

'Did he know Ben's name, Ms Okoro? Or did he just call him the boy, or the baby, or something like that?'

'Benedict. No one calls him Benedict.'

'And then what happened?'

'He bit me.'

'He *bit* you?'

'Yes.'

'Where?'

A delicate hand appeared from beneath the covers, moved with painful slowness towards her neck.

'And then what happened?'

'I . . . I don't remember. I woke up here and they told me. Ben . . . Amadi . . .'

It was some time before she was able to speak.

'This man, the man in your apartment. What did he look like?'

'He was tall. Slim.'

'White? Black?'

'He was Black.'

'Do you remember what he was wearing? Any detail that might help us find him?'

'He had scars on his face. One on each cheek. Tribal markings.'

'I'm sorry?'

'Some Africans are scarred by their tribe when they're young. It's a . . . it's a way of showing they belong.'

Ethan suppressed a shudder.

'What time did you and Ben get home that day?'

'About five thirty.'

'And where had you been before that?'

'To pick Ben up from day care. And before that work.'

'And what do you do, Ms Okoro?'

'I work in accounts.'

'Uh-huh. Did you or your husband order a washer-dryer recently?'

'No.'

'Have you ever heard of an A. Bello?'

'No.'

'Or Super Eagles Plumbing?'

'No.'

'Were you expecting a plumber or any other workman to visit you on Tuesday?'

'No.'

'Wednesday?'

'Not on any day.'

'Do you know Al Mills?'

'Yes. He's the doorman.'

'Al Mills says that you called from work on Tuesday. Told him to expect a plumber.'

The pale face shifted on its pillows.

'But I didn't.'

'And that you called down from the apartment on Wednesday. You told him that the same plumber was on his way to remove the old washer-dryer and to let him up.'

'No . . . *No*.'

Jennifer Okoro was looking agitated, her head moving from side to side. There was a hint of colour in her cheeks.

'Do you remember telling Mr Mills that everyone was home on Wednesday because the whole family was ill?'

'That's a lie! I came home Tuesday and that man attacked me!'

'Can you think of any reason why Mr Mills would lie about speaking to you?'

Jennifer Okoro's lips were pressed together in a thin, angry line.

'Any reason at all?'

Ethan was about to move on when the lips suddenly parted.

'Maybe it's because he had something to do with it.'

Ethan wound up the interview and found himself doorstepped by a nurse as he attempted to leave the room. She smiled gamely up at him.

'Dr Lee asked me to take you to an exam room. Said not to take no for an answer.'

Ethan was about to brush past her, but then it occurred to him that if he played his cards right, he could obtain some basic medical information without going to the hassle of a warrant.

'Okay,' he said, returning her smile. 'But can I ask you for a small favour in return?'

The nurse's expression turned playful.

'You can always ask.'

Taking that as a yes, Ethan stepped out of Jennifer Okoro's room and made sure to close the door behind him.

'That poor woman was attacked,' he said. 'She's lucky to be alive. We need to get this guy before he hurts – or maybe kills – some other woman.'

The nurse nodded solemnly. Something flickered in the back of her eyes. The aftermath of an attack being wheeled into her ward, perhaps. Or something more personal.

'Did anyone bite Jennifer? On the neck? Hard enough to leave a bruise?'

The nurse didn't hesitate.

'No, detective. There isn't a mark on her.'

Five

'*H*azmat is on scene,' Raymond Yeung said, dropping his cell phone onto a pile of papers at his workstation. 'Press is all over it.'

'Yeah, that tends to happen when you empty out a whole apartment building,' Ethan murmured. He was tilted back in his squad-room chair, scuffed shoes resting on his desk.

'And you expect me to go see some weird science guy at Northwestern? Because I've maybe been poisoned by some . . . what did you call it?'

'Neurotoxin. Yeah. You and everybody else.' Ethan grinned wickedly. 'Maybe you'll get lucky and have a hot nurse draw your blood.'

'Sally'd love that.' Raymond's face became serious. 'We gonna give this to the Feds?'

'The DEA? Fuck no. Not yet anyway. Just 'cause some medic says Jennifer Okoro was poisoned doesn't exactly explain why her husband and son were drowned.'

'*If* they were drowned. Still don't see how that happened.'

Ethan grunted in agreement. 'We got anything from the medical examiner?' he asked.

'Are you kidding? You think they actually work over there?' Ethan chuckled.

'So: what *have* you got for me?'

'For starters, there's no such business as Super Eagles Plumbing. The number and address are fake and there's nothing by that name anywhere in Chicagoland. I did some follow-up at the apartment building – *before* you and Hazmat turned it into a no-go zone. No one actually bothered to check A. Bello's ID 'cause he was expected. So it's a fair bet that A. Bello is fake too.'

'Chase it down anyway. Maybe we'll get lucky.'

'You think I was born yesterday, lieutenant? This here department is already on it.'

Ethan raised an imaginary glass.

'Chicago's finest.'

'Too fucking right. But whoever this guy is, I'll give you any odds you like that he's a Nigerian.'

'Why's that?' Jennifer Okoro, Ethan recalled, had thought the man's facial scars marked him out as African.

'According to our friend, the internet, Super Eagles is the nickname of the Nigerian men's soccer team. You call your fake business Super Eagles Plumbing, it's unlikely to be a coincidence.'

'Not a bet I'm gonna take, Ray. We got anything from the building security cams?'

Raymond frowned.

'No. It's odd though. More than odd. Come take a look at this.'

Ethan took his feet off the desk and wandered over to the sergeant's workstation. Raymond had the video feed from the Almeida lobby spooled up on his computer. A monochrome version of Al Mills could be seen sitting at the reception desk, the security footage rendering his movements jerky and unnatural. Bright sunlight spilled across the lobby floor, overexposing the image. The doorman looked up as a silhouette, backlit by the sun, fell across the entrance. All that Ethan could make out was the outline of a tall, thin man wheeling what looked like a large and very heavy crate. The size of the crate was such that there was no way he was going to get through the building's revolving door. A gangly arm reached out to press the pad for the handicapped entrance. The glass door swung open. The man stepped through.

The picture dissolved into a snowfield of static.

'What the fuck?'

'Exactly. Now watch.'

The static cleared less than a minute later. Monochrome Mills was still sitting at the reception desk. The visitor was gone. Raymond hit fast forward. People came and went at comic and ungainly speed. Shadows shifted jerkily across the floor, mirroring the movement of a too fast sun.

At 12.37 p.m. the picture vanished in a cloud of static. When it reappeared at 12.39, there was no one in the lobby apart from Al Mills. The handicapped entrance was swinging shut.

Ethan could feel the tightness in his jaw.

'Let me guess,' he said. 'Same on Wednesday.'

'Bingo. The system, shit though the picture is, works perfectly. Until our man walks into the frame. Judging by the static, the doorman's statement about A. Bello's comings and goings is pretty much on the nose. Guy came back Wednesday morning, stayed a couple of hours and then left.'

'And what about the vics?'

'Video picks them up just fine.' Raymond glanced at his notebook. 'Amadi arrived at four thirty-three p.m. Wife and kid at five twenty-six. There's no sighting of any of them between five twenty-six on the Tuesday and Ms Kowalczyk, the cleaning lady, arriving in the lobby at nine ten Thursday morning. Woman was all smiles. No clue she was about to have a fuck of a day.'

'When did our Nigerian plumber arrive on the Wednesday?'

'Static kicks in at nine-oh-four.'

'Okay. Start it there and wind it backwards.'

Apart from Al Mills, the lobby was empty. There was nothing visual to indicate that the picture was running in reverse. Until . . .

'Stop it there,' Ethan ordered.

Al Mills was caught in the act of picking the phone 'up', albeit he was actually doing the opposite.

'Fuck me,' Raymond muttered. 'Someone called him just before our guy comes through the door.'

'Which is exactly what the doorman said happened. He said Jennifer Okoro called down to say the plumber was on his way, and that she and her family were all home sick.'

'So we know they were alive Wednesday morning.'

Ethan could feel the beginning of a headache pressing the back of his eyeballs. A normal headache, he wondered, or the one that was going to kill him? He pushed the thought aside. Tried to, anyway.

'Yeah,' he said. 'Except Jennifer Okoro swears blind that A. Bello attacked her on *Tuesday*, as soon as she got in. Then swears equally blind that she was unconscious till Friday and in no state to call any fucker at any time.'

'Sure. And I got a bridge in Brooklyn I'd love to sell ya. Ain't no reason for the doorman to lie. And you can *see* him pick up the phone. Besides, it's physically impossible. Woman got home at five twenty-six p.m. on Tuesday. A. Bello was long gone. He *left* the building at twelve thirty-seven, remember, and didn't return till the following day. If he killed them, he killed them on the Wednesday.'

'I know,' Ethan sighed. 'Believe me, I know. But why would she lie about it?'

'Because she's in on it? Somehow?'

'She'd kill her own child?'

'Crazy people—'

'– do crazy things. Yeah. I know.' Ethan drifted back to his chair, stretched his feet out on the desk again. 'But here's the thing – another thing – that's bugging me. Let's say A. Bello offed father and son on Wednesday. What the fuck was he doing on Tuesday? We *know* he wasn't installing a new washing machine. He marches in with a crate, marches out with a crate, comes back on Wednesday, does the same thing. Why?'

'We should totally ask him that. When we catch the fucker.' Ethan chuckled.

'Okay, then. Let's check out the security cameras around the neighbourhood. With any luck, one of them will have caught this guy – and his vehicle. He must have come from somewhere. And gone home again. There's no way the neighbourhood cams will have gone so . . . conveniently blind.'

'You don't think the video going on the fritz is a coincidence?'

'Do you?'

Yeung shook his head.

'Go lean on the doormen. Find out what happened.'

'And the wife? Bitch is lying.'

'You got that right.' Ethan stared at the scuff marks on his shoes, lost in thought. 'Leave her be for now. Even drugged up, she didn't come across as a fool. We'd better have our ducks in a row before taking another crack.'

The landline on his desk rattled to life, the sound from its damaged speaker little more than a metallic wheeze.

'Chicago PD. Lieutenant Krol speaking.'

'Ethan!' He had little trouble identifying the good-natured voice at the other end of the line: Dr Suarez, the medical examiner. 'You want to talk dead bodies?'

Six

A visit to see the Cook County medical examiner entailed a journey to the 2100 block of West Harrison and a low-slung concrete fortress assembled out of oblongs and triangles. Deep-set, tinted windows stared grimly at the world of the living. Impenetrable from the outside, they let in a surprising amount of light.

Just not in here.

Amadi Okoro's skin, or so much of it as protruded from the sheet covering the rest of his body, had a dull, waxy gleam to it. Coarse stitching marked the places where he'd been sewn back together. Eyes, unnaturally blue now, stared unblinkingly into harsh, overhead lights. Ethan thrust his hands deep in his trouser pockets and turned away. He'd seen this, bodies like this, more times than he cared to remember. And yet every single time he had to remind himself that he wasn't in a funeral home. This was not an abode of quiet dignity. There was no make-up here, no clothing, no illusion of restful slumber. Not in this place, where the dead were stripped bare, and gutted, and forced to give up their secrets.

I need to make arrangements, he thought suddenly.

Dr Suarez, a short, balding man with a deep laugh and no sharp edges, directed a bespectacled glance in Ethan's direction. The bright lights refracting in the lenses prevented Ethan from seeing the medical examiner's full gaze. Judging from the cast of his mouth, though, Ethan was pretty sure the look he was getting was a curious one.

'Ethan, my friend, are you sure that you are not the victim of some elaborate trick? Your colleagues have done worse, in my experience.'

Ethan favoured Suarez with a quick grin.

'I'm sure, doc. You and I both know that I work with some prize assholes. But that's a real dead body.' His grin faded. 'With a real dead baby to go with it.'

'Quite, quite. Very tragic, to be sure. You will not be surprised to learn that our friend here and his child both drowned?'

'Not really, no.'

'And what if I told you they drowned at sea?'

'Then I'd say it was you who was pulling my leg, not my asshole colleagues. Chicago is many things, doc. But "coastal" ain't one of them.'

'Too true, detective, too true. As the crow flies, it's five hundred and ninety-three miles to the tidal Potomac, more than six hundred to the Chesapeake. I looked it up.'

'If your crow was a murdering, child-killing bastard, he wouldn't fly that far. No way.' Ethan shifted position until he could glare through the glasses to the examiner's actual eyes. 'You can't be serious, doc. The vics were found on the twentieth floor of an apartment building, slap bang in the middle of the continental US, and you're telling me they drowned in *seawater*?'

Suarez shrugged his round shoulders.

'That's what it looks like.'

'Yeah, well, fuck that. It can't be right. *You* can't be right.'

A ripple of what might have been irritation passed across the medical examiner's face.

'I am quite certain, detective.'

'It could be salt water, but not seawater, right? Maybe our perp upended a box of Morton's into the sink before drowning them.' Even as he said it, he felt faintly ridiculous. But the alternative was . . . nuts.

Suarez's good-natured demeanour reasserted itself.

'That's not a bad hypothesis, actually. Particularly at short notice. But it won't fly.'

'Why not?'

'Two reasons. First, you can drown a baby in a sink without too much trouble, but a grown man? No way. You know this. He would have fought. There would be bruising, marks of a struggle: across the chest, the back of the neck – the head, too, if it banged against the faucet. There's none of that here. Mr Okoro may not have been a big man, but I'd bet you dollars to the doughnuts your colleagues like so much that he was strong. He has six-pack abs. Look.' Suarez pulled back the sheet in an excess of enthusiasm.

'What if he was unconscious?'

'But you know he wasn't.'

'I do?'

Suarez said nothing. He stared pointedly at the victim's hand instead. It took a moment for the penny to drop.

'His fucking fingers,' Ethan muttered. 'They're rubbed raw. And the fingernails are torn. From scratching at the . . .' His voice faded into uncertainty.

'If you were about to say "ceiling", detective, I wouldn't argue with you. Your forensics people can tell you for certain, but there are traces of what look like ceiling plaster under his nails. No blood, though, which is odd.' Suarez frowned briefly. 'Your report mentioned what looked to be bloodstains on the ceiling?'

'Yeah.'

Suarez made a huffing noise but said nothing.

'You said there were two reasons?' Ethan prompted. Suarez sparked back to life, like a rebooted computer.

'Yes, yes. And the second is much more interesting.' The medical examiner walked over to a small work desk jammed against the back wall of the morgue. He opened up a thin file and removed a couple of glossy photographs. 'Come look at this.'

The black and white photos were blurry in the extreme. But so far as Ethan could make out, the first one showed what looked like pieces of translucent hard candy: long, thin rectangles with squishy bits of filling visible through the outer shell. The second looked like strings of pearls. If pearls were see-through.

'What am I looking at?'

'Diatoms.' Suarez was almost jumping up and down with enthusiasm.

'Dia what now?'

'Diatoms. Little creatures that live in water. They're a type of algae, actually. You find them in rivers, lakes, pretty much anywhere you find water. But here's the thing. Unless Streets and San has royally screwed up, you will *not* find them in tap water. That's what treatment plants are for.

'If your killer had drowned Mr Okoro in a sink full of salty tap water, there'd be no diatoms. His lungs are full of them. This is seawater we're talking about.'

'There ain't no sea in Chicago, doc.'

'There are two, detective. Cs that is.'

'Ha ha. Don't give up your day job.' Ethan scratched

distractedly at his hairline. 'You swear you're not pulling my leg?'

'Hand to God.'

'I really wish you were,' Ethan sighed. 'How can you drown in seawater in the middle of the fucking city? There's no— ' A suddenly slack jaw put an end to whatever he was about to say.

'Stricken by inspiration, lieutenant? Or are you having a stroke?'

'Inspiration. I think.' Ethan grinned impetuously. 'I gotta see a man about a fish.'

Seven

Friday the 4th: 5 p.m. CDT

The man, it turned out, was a woman – and Black. She was short, even in heeled boots, and stout. A glimmering sweep of red and gold clothing made her look like one of the fish she was responsible for. One that was large, and good natured, and tropical.

'It's magnificent, isn't it?' said Lyndsey Parker, the Shedd Aquarium's vice president of environmental quality. Her round face was alive with the earnest enthusiasm of her profession.

It's a tank of fucking fish.

'It's very impressive, Dr Parker.'

'Lyndsey. Please. I'm not a medical doctor. I can only help with fish.' She shot him a bright smile, which Ethan did his best to return.

'How long has this been here?' he asked. He was mostly making conversation. The tank, he knew, was older than he was. He'd come here as a boy. Pressed his nose against the thick glass. Thumped it with small fists and been thumped, in turn, by his parents.

They were standing in the middle of Shedd Aquarium's magnificent marble lobby, the tank vast and circular, filled with spreading corals and various flavours of fish. The fish, for their part, patrolled the glass boundaries of their world in easy-going circuits. They seemed utterly indifferent to the humans on the other side.

Except, perhaps, for the shark. An overhead metallic sign identified the tank as a 'Caribbean Reef'.

'I'm not sure how long,' Lyndsey said, 'but I think a tank like this has been here pretty much since we opened in 1930.'

Ethan nodded, impressed despite himself.

'And this is a seawater tank, with seawater fish?'

'It is indeed. These are sea creatures. Freshwater would kill them.'

'And where do you get your seawater from? It must cost a small fortune to bring it in from the – ' he looked up at the sign, ' – the Caribbean.'

'Oh Lordy, no, we don't do that!' Lyndsey said, laughing. 'In the old days – and I mean the *old*, old days – we used to bring tanker cars of the stuff up from Florida by rail. But these days we make our own.'

'You can *make* seawater?'

'Oh yes. We use something called Instant Ocean. You can buy it at the pet store, actually, but we have to order it in one-ton bags. We mix it with tens of thousands of gallons of dechlorinated tap water and – boom – instant ocean.'

Ethan briefly imagined falling into the 'Caribbean Reef'. There didn't seem to be an obvious way out. It would be all too easy to drown in there. Unless, of course, the shark got to you first.

'So, if I wanted to make seawater at home, I could just mix it up with Instant Ocean straight out of the tap?'

'Absolutely. People who keep seawater fish in their home aquariums do it all the time.'

'And does this Instant Ocean contain diatoms?'

Lyndsey Parker's expression changed to one of unabashed curiosity. It was not, he supposed, the sort of question she'd been expecting from a Chicago police detective.

'No. Instant Ocean is essentially a crystalline collection of the chemicals typically found in seawater. There's salt, obviously, but also traces of other substances, like potassium.' She turned to face the tank, laying a protective hand against the glass. 'Potassium is only, like, zero-point-zero-four per cent of seawater, but if it's not's there you're going to end up with a lot of dead fish.'

'But no diatoms?'

'No diatoms.'

'If I wanted diatoms in my seawater, how would I get them?'

'I'm sorry, detective. But I have to ask. What is it that you're investigating?'

'I'm not at liberty to say. Sorry.'

'And what have diatoms got to do with it?'

No fucking clue.

'Again, I can't say.' He made a show of shrugging his shoulders. 'If it were up to me, you know, but department rules and all that. You understand.'

The woman nodded, smoothing the disappointment from her face.

'Well, diatoms are pretty ubiquitous.' A quick smile. 'You don't have to find them. They will find you. Until quite recently we spent a great deal of effort making sure our seawater was perfectly sterile, but we're coming to the view that a bit of biodiversity at the microbe level is actually good for the fish. And we basically get there by being slightly less anal about how we clean the pipes or tanks or whatever. So, if you don't clean your fish tank properly, sooner or later diatoms will start to show up. That'd be the easiest way to do it. Short of using actual seawater, of course.'

'How long? A few minutes, a few hours?'

'It takes days and weeks for a tank to get truly dirty. I mean, you *could* pick up diatoms in minutes or hours, but probably not enough so you'd notice.'

Ethan eyed the tank for a few moments, wondering if the fish felt trapped. Why hadn't the shark eaten everything in sight?

Two sleek silver fish, almost as menacing looking as the shark and patrolling in tandem, caught his eye.

'Are those barracudas?' he asked, pointing.

'Yes, they are.' Dr Parker clapped her hands in delight. 'These two are great barracudas. Beautiful, aren't they?'

Ethan glanced, yet again, at the large metal sign.

'And they come from the Caribbean?'

'Among other places. Their range is pretty extensive. You'll find great barracuda in warm waters all around the world, detective. Florida, Hawaii, the Indian Ocean. Glorious, glorious fish.' Parker's dark eyes gleamed with joy.

'Could you keep them in a tank at home?'

'Lordy, no! They're way too big and aggressive.' She hesitated before adding, 'I mean . . . I guess if you were a millionaire or whatever and had a *very* large tank and specialist support . . .'

'Know anyone like that?'

Parker shook her head, full lips pressed thin with disapproval.

'And do people eat them? Regularly, I mean, like scrod, maybe, or sea bass.'

Parker's lips became even thinner.

'Absolutely not.'

'Good,' Ethan lied. He made a point of peering into the tank. 'They're far too handsome for that. They belong in the sea.'

Parker relaxed. Relaxed was better when you wanted information.

'One last thing, if I may, Lyndsey. If I wanted to bring actual seawater to Chicago, with diatoms and everything already in it, could I do that?'

'Well, you can do pretty much anything if you have enough money. Otherwise, you can always order small amounts online – a gallon or two maybe. Labs use it to cultivate marine algae – like your diatoms, among other things. And some people order it to, er, drink.'

Ethan could feel his eyebrows arching skywards.

'I thought drinking seawater made you go mad?'

Dr Parker smiled at that.

'No one said these people were sane, detective. I *think* they think there's a health benefit. And if you cut it with enough fresh water, I don't believe it would do you real harm.'

Unless someone made you breathe it in.

He declined Lyndsey's offer to take him on a tour of the facility. He headed out into the late afternoon sunlight instead, his head filled with images of sharks, and seawater tanks, and barracudas.

His cell rang out from the depths of his jacket pocket, the ringtone instantly recognizable. After a moment's hesitation he picked up.

'Cara, sweetie, how's things?'

'Good, Dad. And you?'

'I'm doing okay.'

There was a long silence.

'Hey,' he said. 'About the wedding, I haven't—'

'I'm not calling about that.'

'Oh. Okay.'

Another long silence. Something started to nibble at the back of his mind.

Shit.

'Happy birthday, sweetie. I'm sorry I didn't call earlier. They've landed me with a big case and I'm up to my eyebrows in it. You going to do something fun?'

'Tomorrow. A whole bunch of us are going out tomorrow night. And I hung out with Mom for lunch today. I was kinda hoping we could meet up for dinner? Nothing fancy if you don't have time. I get it that crime never sleeps.'

There was a slight edge to the last sentence. But that wasn't why Ethan took his time before answering.

'Just the two of us?'

Maybe he imagined the small sigh that whispered out of the speaker.

'Yeah, Dad. Just the two of us.'

Eight

Friday the 4th: 7.32 p.m. CDT

Ethan had managed to dive into a Walgreens for cards: a birthday one with a corny joke on it, and a gift one redeemable at Macy's. He had the cashier put more money on the gift card than he could afford because he was a lousy, shitty parent.

He hated the Loop. At this time of year it was wall to wall with tourists who'd stumbled off the Magnificent Mile and year-round overpaid assholes in designer business casual. Down here, his ill-fitting suit and scuffed dress shoes were distinctly out of place. He made sure to button up his collar and adjust his tie before heading into Bistro 773 on Madison.

'Happy birthday, sweetie.'

'Thanks, Dad.'

Cara Krol took the proffered cards and accepted a peck on the cheek. If his paltry offerings elicited feelings of disappointment, she covered them up with a smile. Over dinner she chattered away about this and that, her hands animating small dramas inches above the crisp stage of the tablecloth. Ethan listened intently, concentrating on the expressions drifting across his beautiful girl's face.

That way, he didn't have to spend too much time looking at the glitter of platinum on her ring finger.

'You still thinking about law school?' he asked. The waiter arrived with coffee. Decaf for her, the real deal for him.

Cara made a face.

'I'm thinking maybe not. Being a paralegal for a couple of years is one thing but signing up for life . . . I don't know, Dad. It's good money, but you've no time to spend it because you're running around twenty-four-seven being terrorized by old men.'

'So don't do it. Lawyers are f—'

'Dad!'

'Not nice people.'

'Uh-huh. Anyway, I'm thinking business school might be better. More options. Maybe fewer old men.'

Ethan smiled at that.

'When do you have to decide?'

'Not for a while. Besides, it'll depend where Devin . . .'

Cara's words faded away at about the same rate as Ethan's smile.

'So Devin gets to decide where you go to school now?'

'He's in med school, Dad. He doesn't have a lot of control over where he does his residency. And I don't . . .' Her hands fluttered a moment before settling firmly on the tablecloth. 'We're going to be married, Dad, whether you like it or not. And we're going to be together.'

Ethan gritted his teeth, but the words broke through anyway.

'You're making a mistake, sweetie. These things never work.'

Cara's eyes turned flinty. Like her voice.

'What "things", Dad?'

'You know what I mean. The differences. He's . . . You're . . .'

Cara rose from the table. Unlike her mother she did it slowly. Deliberately. So as not to cause a scene.

'I love you, Dad. You know that. But I wish you weren't such a goddamn old-school racist.'

Nine

Abidemi Eniola stepped unwillingly through the gate, Ayo and Kehinde's long-ago tears still hot against her face. She was standing in an endless ocean of grass. Archipelagoes of . . . trees, she guessed, rustled at each other in a damp breeze. It would have been stunningly beautiful if it hadn't smelled so bad. The Story made no mention of the smell. There was an overpowering aroma of . . . people. And animals. And other things. Waste. Sulphur. Partly burned hydrocarbons. She tried hard not to gag.

And then there was the noise. Her head was filled with a cacophony of signals, poorly modulated and overlapping with no regard for interference. Augments overwhelmed, jagged shards of colour lanced across her vision. She turned down the gain and played with her filters until the horror of noise and smell came to an end, one hand holding her fedora against a puffing wind.

There was water falling out of the sky – rain – bouncing off the brim of her hat. She looked up in amazement at the grey clouds, heedless of the small stinging of moisture against her night-black skin.

It took her a moment to realize what she'd done. Ayo and Kehinde's tears had vanished in the deluge. Her mind flooded itself with a bitter, stupid regret.

'Where'd yal come from, then?'

Startled, Abi turned around to find herself staring at a small child: pale, like an albino but with blotchy red cheeks. *Oyinbo*. It was a shock to see one in the flesh. Equally pale adults, also blotchy, and from whom the child had presumably wriggled free, were running up after it.

'Bobby, don't be rude,' the mother said. And then, to Abi, 'Don't mind him, he doesn't mean anything by it.'

'Are yal a pop star?' the boy asked, tugging at the sleeve of her double-breasted jacket. The movement revealed the intricately carved, ivory-coloured amulet on her wrist. 'What's that?'

'Bobby: enough!' The mother yanked him away. Flashed her an apologetic smile. 'I am *so* sorry about that.'

Abi hadn't expected to speak quite so soon. She fought back a small jolt of nerves.

'That's all right, ma'am.' Relieved that the words seemed to have come out okay, she grinned indulgently at the child, her heart twisting as she did so. 'He's a live one, no doubt about it.'

Maybe she hadn't said it properly. A small frown was creasing the mother's pallid forehead. The father, short and squat for a man, was looking at her with unabashed curiosity.

'We didn't see you there,' the man said conversationally. 'You gave our son here a bit of a start.' He looked around the ocean of grass. 'We must be going blind.' A wide grin revealed stained, crooked teeth. 'You're hard to miss.'

'Tom!' The mother sounded vaguely scandalized.

Time to disengage.

'I need to make tracks,' she said. 'But I've gotten myself turned around. Which way to downtown?'

'Yal talk funny.'

'*Bobby!*' The mother had a *very* firm grip on the boy's arm.

The man – Tom – pointed. East, according to the map files, but Abi wasn't sure she was reading them right. They were out of date, and hard to square with the actual terrain.

'The *city centre*,' Tom said pointedly, as if 'downtown' were somehow wrong, 'is that way. But it's quite a few miles. Do you have a car?'

'Oh, I won't need no automobile. I'll enjoy the walk. Pleasure meeting you folks. Y'all have a fine day now.'

She tipped her hat, hoisted her backpack onto her shoulders, and set off, wet grass springy beneath her feet. Turning up her ears, she could hear the *oyinbos* speaking animatedly behind her.

'Do you think she's American?' the mother was asking. 'She talks like one. And she's lost.'

'Yeah, no,' the man said. 'The accent's not quite right. Too foreign, like.'

'American is foreign.'

'You know what I mean. There's something else going on there. She sounds a bit . . . African. I mean, *look* at her.'

'My friend Michael's parents sound like that,' Bobby said. 'And they're from Nigerial.'

'Stop speaking like that,' the mother snapped. 'It's Nigeria.'

'That's what I said. Nigerial.' Abi could hear footsteps as the boy ran after her. 'Hey! Hey!' Abi kept walking, lengthening her stride. '*Hey!* Tall lady!'

Perhaps it was rude to ignore him.

'Yes?'

'You from Nigerial?'

Abidemi Eniola gave the little *oyinbo* a small, slightly sad smile.

'Sure, kid. Why not?'

Ten

The ocean of grass with its occasional island of trees had quickly given way to crude, cuboid dwellings of artificial rock. The rock-cubes huddled along the sides of oily black transit routes made noisy by the incessant sound of automobiles. The vehicles were far sleeker than Abi was expecting, and a good deal faster. But they were still piloted manually, *oyinbos* gripping the helm in a shockingly casual manner. Abi felt certain that, sooner or later, she would come across a crumpled wreck and smashed, pale-skinned bodies. But so far, at least, she had seen none.

At first, the routes seemed to be designed for automobiles alone but, after a while, raised platforms at one or both sides of the primary surface began to appear. The loud and constant blaring of horns seemed to indicate that her presence on the primary surface was no longer welcome, so she moved over. The raised platforms were a little harder to walk on, but the automobiles gave her a wider berth, so it was an improvement overall.

Signs began to appear, apparently pointing the way to various destinations. Abi frowned, trying to make sense of the writing, which didn't look like she'd expected. Eventually, though, she figured it out. She followed a couple that said BRISTOL and then, remembering the man's insistence on the term, CITY CENTRE. Bristol city centre, when she finally reached it, bore only a vague resemblance to the maps, consisting of a series of hilly transit routes rising up from a river. There were people everywhere, *oyinbo*s for the most part, but with the odd normal-looking person mixed in. And so many! More than Abi had ever seen in her whole life, flitting past each other with skilled stutter-steps and only the barest of acknowledgements. Each with somewhere they had to be in the shortest possible time. They were mostly crammed onto the raised platforms that kept them away from the nose-to-tail press of vehicles, so it was hard to make progress. Again and again, she would bang into people, most of whom said nothing, a few of whom glared, and a very few of whom suggested that she looked where she was going.

Only when she reached a broad plaza that went by the name of Millennium Square did the dense swarms of humanity thin out enough for her to catch her breath and her whereabouts. The city was not laid out at all like she had expected. The river was where it was meant to be, and the cathedral, and a few other landmarks, but the transit routes had changed a great deal and there were a lot of new buildings, none of which seemed to contain what she was looking for.

Taking a deep breath, she approached a middle-aged woman, draped in a light coat and with pleasingly large earrings. Even though she was an *oyinbo*, she had a deep tan, which made her overall appearance slightly less disturbing.

'Hey, lady! Can you cut a gal a break and give me a steer to a jewellery store? I can't seem to find one for love or money.'

The woman gave her a dubious look. Glanced around as if seeking help. Abi tried smiling.

'There's a jeweller's on Park Street.' The woman pointed to

the far corner of the Plaza. 'If you head past the Cary Grant statue . . .'

Abi couldn't help herself. Her gaze followed the woman's finger. She turned up the magnification a bit. Sure enough, there he was, life-sized and bronze.

'Cary Grant has a *statue*? Why?'

'He was born here.'

'You don't say! I guess he got famous.'

The woman was looking at her very strangely indeed.

'Park Street?' Abi prompted before she could bolt. The woman threw out a series of left and rights and then hurried away. Abi spent quite a few minutes with bronze Cary Grant before heading off in the direction indicated.

'Park Street . . . Park Street,' she muttered to herself. She rolled the words on her tongue, trying them on for size. 'They're called streets. And . . . roads. I should have remembered that.'

Eleven

'How much kale can I get for these babies?'

A small pile of diamonds lay atop the jewellery store's glass counter. The shopkeeper, a stiff-looking *oyinbo* in a white shirt and joyless tie, was staring at them in disbelief.

'Are these real, madam?'

'Hey, don't crust me, mister. I wouldn't lay sour rocks on you. They're real all the way.'

'Where did you get them?'

'What's it matter so long as they're real?'

The moment the words came out she knew she'd said something wrong. The shopkeeper drew himself up to his full height, which, unfortunately for him, was still short.

'Please leave, madam. Right now.'

'But—'

'Now, madam. Before I call the police.'

'Okay, okay. No need to blow your wig.'

Abidemi gathered up her diamonds, put them back in their small cloth pouch, and headed to the door. Stepping out onto the street, she jammed the pouch into her pocket and frowned up at the sky. The small rain that had been falling on and off since she'd arrived was falling harder now, forming tight little beads on the surface of her jacket. She could hear the water bouncing off the brim of her fedora. A number of people had unfurled disc-shaped contraptions that they held above their heads to keep the rain off. The discs, to Abi's mind, were far from safe. Park Street was on a very steep slope. As the discs moved uphill with their owners, they threatened to take out the eyes of people moving in the opposite direction. Oddly, though, no one seemed to be complaining about it.

At the very top of Park Street was an ornate tower, distinctly older looking than its surroundings. As it was one of the few landmarks she could recognize from the files, she decided to head towards it. Besides, it seemed safer than going downhill and getting blinded by discs. She was having enough trouble avoiding collisions as it was.

Umbrellas.

The word came out of nowhere.

With a smile of linguistic satisfaction, and keeping her eyes on the tower, she lengthened her stride.

'Watch it!'

Someone thudded against her chest. A young *oyinbo* female. Unbalanced by the collision, the woman went sprawling to the ground. Food flew from her hand, breaking into pieces on the damp concrete.

'I'm sorry, lady. Didn't see you. You okay?'

'My sandwich! I don't have the money for another one. You'd better make it right or there'll be trouble.'

The woman bounced angrily to her feet. Like almost everyone Abi had encountered so far, she was short. Except for her skin, which was pale even by *oyinbo* standards, almost everything else about her was black. She had supple, dyed black hair with purple tips, the ends of which brushed against the shoulders of a black leather jacket, open at the front to reveal a skin-tight black top that, in turn, tucked into a frilly black skirt patterned with the same colour purple as the hair. Shiny black lace-up boots and black leggings with more holes than material completed the ensemble.

The pale-and-black woman was clearly unimpressed by Abi's much greater height. She marched up to within a hand's breadth and glared upwards. Abi stared back, fascinated by the woman's eyes. They were large, and round, and . . . blue. Hideous and compelling in equal parts.

'Lunch,' the woman said, pointing at the remains of the wrecked 'sandwich'. 'Money.' She'd stepped back now and was holding out a hand, clearly expecting to be paid.

'Look, doll. I'd happily pay you, you know I would. But I got this problem, see?' Abi reached into her jacket pocket and pulled out a diamond. 'I ain't got no bread. Not till I change this here rock into moolah. You hear me?'

'Where are you from?' Some of the woman's anger had leached into a frown of curiosity. The blue eyes skittered from the diamond to Abi's face and back again.

'Nigeria.'

The woman nodded to herself.

'Figures,' she said. The anger had dissipated entirely now. Her expression had become not simply curious but calculating. 'You been to a jeweller's?'

'Down there,' Abi said, pointing a thumb over her shoulder. 'They gave me the high hat. Told me they'd call the police.'

'Is it stolen?'

'No!'

'Yeah, whatever.' The woman was silent a while. From the

way the blue eyes flickered it looked like she was having a lively conversation with herself.

'You got a name?' the woman asked.

'Abidemi. Abidemi Eniola. My friends call me Abi.'

'I'm Hollie. Rogers. My friends call me . . . Hollie. I can maybe take you to someone who'll give you money for that. But if I do, you give me ten per cent of what he gives you, yeah?'

'Sure.'

Hollie shot her a surprised grin.

'Okay, then.' Hollie set off downhill, stutter-stepping past people and umbrellas moving in the opposite direction.

Abi followed as best she could.

Twelve

*A*bi squinted at the grubby, polymer sign. Understanding the *oyinbo* writing was going to be more of a challenge than she'd expected. She let loose a small sigh.

HARLEQUIN TAXIS, she decided. Maybe.

After following Hollie to the bottom of the hill, the woman had ushered her onto a bizarre, two-storey contraption called a bus. The pilot had objected to Abi getting aboard until Hollie, with a little sigh of exasperation, had scanned her in using a small rectangular card. Abi had observed the scanner's slow processing of ones and zeroes with interest. The device was primitive, to be sure, but the fact that it existed at all was a source of surprise. Scanning complete, and with many jerky stops and starts along the way, the bus proceeded to transport them far from the city centre.

Even Abi could see they were in a much poorer part of town. The rock-cube storefronts on either side of Harlequin Taxis were boarded up. There were only a handful of people on the street, and those who were moved quickly, shoulders hunched against the still falling rain. No one gave her a second look.

'We're here,' Hollie announced. She looked nervous. 'You

go in, you ask for Dean, you tell them that Hollie Rogers sent you and that you have some jewellery you want to sell. Got it?'

'Sure.'

'Now, this is important. Do *not* tell anyone I'm here, okay? I'll wait for you across the street.' Before Abi could ask why, Hollie turned on her heel and hurried away. Abi adjusted her backpack, rubbed her fingers absent-mindedly over the amulet on her wrist, and stepped inside.

The room she entered was small and dingy. Mottled red polymer covered the cramped expanse of floor between the door and a badly beaten-up counter. Behind the counter she could just make out the back of a bald, male head. As she stepped closer, she could see that he was sitting in front of a primitive communications set-up. Radio, at a guess. She couldn't detect a carrier signal, so it was impossible to be sure. There was a cup of something brown and disgusting at the man's right hand. He swivelled in his chair without bothering to get up.

'Can I help you, love?'

'Sure can, pal. I'm here to see Dean. Hollie Rogers sent me.'

The man stood up. Another short one.

'And what do you want with Mr Slim?'

'I got some jewellery to sell.' She pulled a diamond from her pocket, allowed the man to inspect it with widened eyes. Abi suppressed a smile. Every time she pulled one out, the *oyinbos* reacted the same way. It was like they'd never seen a diamond before.

'Wait here.'

The man vanished through a back door, reappearing a minute or two later.

'Follow me.' He lifted part of the counter to allow her through.

The back door led into a much larger room, with red patterned carpet and a huge, ornate desk. The walls were covered with pictures of scantily dressed men in shiny shorts, high-top boots and, oddest of all, gigantic leather mittens. She'd seen this before somewhere. In the files.

'You interested in boxing, darling?'

Of course.

The *oyinbo* sitting behind the desk had a sleek look about him. His pale, pink-blotched skin gleamed. His dark brown hair was shiny and slicked back. Even his shirt seemed to twinkle in the soft overhead lighting.

'It don't row my boat,' she said with a smile. 'But the bodies look good.'

The *oyinbo* laughed at that.

'We like her already, don't we?' he said, speaking not to her but to a large, silent man standing in the corner. The silent man was tall and broad-shouldered and, much to the relief of Abidemi's strained senses, a pleasing shade of black. A vast mane of braided hair spilled down across his back. Even though spoken to, he paid no attention to either the *oyinbo* or Abidemi, his attention apparently riveted by the small, rectangular device he was cradling in his hands.

Gingerly, because she was all too aware of the cacophony of signals lurking in the ether, Abi turned up her sensors. Sure enough, the little device was in communication with the outside world. It was connected to a low-powered network that permeated the room. She could feel the packets of data sliding in and out.

Her interest in what the man was doing must have shown on her face because the *oyinbo* said, 'Don't mind him. He's just checking the football, aren't you, Lloyd?'

Lloyd just grunted.

'If *he's* Lloyd, I'm guessing you must be Dean. Hollie sent me.'

An expression Abi couldn't quite read slid across Dean's face.

'And how is little Miss Hollie these days?'

'Hungry, I think. No lunch.'

Dean laughed again.

'You're a funny one, ain'tcha? She come with you?'

'Do you see her here?'

Lloyd had slipped the rectangular communications device into his pocket. He and Dean exchanged a glance.

'Yeah, well give her my regards,' Dean said. 'Tell her I expect to be seeing her *soon*. I don't want to have to come looking, if you get my drift.'

Abi wasn't sure she did.

'I got some rocks I'm looking to offload. If you got the green.'

'"If I got the green." Listen to her, Lloyd! "If I got the green!" You sound like a bad movie.' Dean Slim leaned forward on his desk. 'I've got more "green" than you'd know what to do with, love. So, show me these rocks of yours.'

Mindful of her experience at the jeweller's, Abi produced only two, laying them on the desk for Dean and Lloyd to examine. Unlike the other *oyinbos*, Dean's expression didn't change. Lloyd, however, let out a low whistle. Dean regarded him with a frown.

'Go get me a glass of water, will you?'

Lloyd disappeared out of a side door. Dean, meanwhile, picked up the diamonds one by one and held them up to the light. He huffed gently onto each, watching the fog from his breath mist the surface and quickly vanish. An eyebrow twitched in what might have been approval.

Lloyd returned with a glass of water. The glass was short and fat, the sort of glass an *oyinbo* might use for whisky on the rocks. Dean promptly dropped the diamonds into it. They plummeted to the bottom.

'Yeah, well, they're real enough, looks like. But not the best quality, obviously. I'll give you a grand each for 'em.'

Abi tried not to smile. This, at least, was something she was familiar with. She reached over and grabbed the glass.

'What are you doing?'

'You think I'm going to stand here and be insulted by you? If I were you, I'd think more carefully before opening my mouth, pal. These babies are worth two grand each, at least.' She fished the diamonds out of the whisky tumbler, put them in her pocket and made to walk out.

'Now then, love, let's not be hasty. Why don't we split the difference and say fifteen hundred a piece, three grand total?'

Abi stood at the door for a beat longer than necessary before turning around.

'Great!' Dean said, beaming. 'Lloyd, if you'll do the honours?'

Lloyd ambled across to one of the boxing pictures and removed it from the wall, revealing a small metal safe. Abi watched with interest as he punched in the code. He reached inside and pulled out three ragged looking bundles of currency. Much to her surprise, none of the notes were actually green.

'There's your money,' Dean said. 'So, be a good girl and hand over the stones.'

As Abi stuck her hand in her pocket to retrieve them, she realized that she'd absent-mindedly put the diamonds back inside their pouch. The *oyinbo* would almost certainly want the diamonds he'd already seen, not substitutes he'd have to retest. Abi took out the pouch and peered inside. A moment's scanning and the job was done.

'Here you go,' she said, putting the exact same diamonds on Dean's desk.

Neither Dean nor Lloyd was looking at them. They were staring at the pouch.

'How many diamonds you got in there?' Dean asked. A short, pink tongue flashed across his lips.

'More than you'd know what to do with,' Abi joked, bouncing Dean's own words back at him.

Dean didn't laugh. Lloyd put the money he'd been holding on the desk, freeing up his hands.

The amulet on Abi's wrist tingled.

'If you know what's good for you, love, you'll put that bag down on the table and walk out of here.' A brief, nasty smile. 'You can take the money. A deal's a deal.'

'The deal's for two rocks, buddy, not the whole schmear.'

'Deal's changed.'

'Then the deal's off.'

Lloyd crossed the room in two long strides, fists raised.

'Wrong answer,' he said.

A sharp, jagged pain lanced through Abi's wrist as the amulet injected her with combat chemistry. The world slowed to a crawl. Lloyd's right hand inched towards her, fingers extended to grab her by the throat. Abi watched it come. Waited until it had almost reached her. Grabbed him by the wrist. Squeezed.

The sound of bones being forced together was followed by that of Lloyd screaming. Abi kicked him in the groin. He took forever to bend over in agony. When he was low enough, she kneed him in the head. Before his unconscious body had hit the floor, she'd vaulted across the desk, pinning Dean and his chair against the back wall.

'Please, don't! *Please!*'

The words sounded slow and slurred in her ears, making no sense. *Some* sense, maybe. It was so hard to think in words. In foreign, *oyinbo* words. Her heart was pounding. There was a roaring sound in her ears. And power, unstoppable, exhilarating *power* rippling through her body. She wanted to tear the world apart. Tear this putrid little *oyinbo* apart. The sound of his breaking bones would be like the crackling beat of drums.

'*Please!*'

The amulet was cold against her skin as she forced it to purge the drugs and nanoparticles from her body. She wanted to shiver in reaction. But not now. Not in front of the *oyinbo*.

She didn't need combat chemistry to keep him pressed against the wall.

'We had a deal, little man, and you welched on me.'

'I'm sorry. I'm *sorry!*'

There were tears in the *oyinbo*'s eyes.

'It's a little late for sorry, bud. We're going to make a new deal, see?'

'Yes. Yes, of course. Whatever you want.'

'Great.' She hauled Dean Slim out of the chair and onto his feet. Marched him over to the safe.

'Open it.'

The safe contained money, a variety of polymer cards, some small booklets, and expensive jewellery. She grabbed it all, stuffing it into her backpack because there wasn't enough room in her pockets.

She bent over Lloyd's sprawled body and retrieved the communications device.

'What's this?'

Dean stared at her incredulously.

'Don't make me ask twice, pal.'

'It's a mobile phone.'

'And what does it do? Make calls, I guess?'

'Yes.'

'Anything else?'

'Uh . . . well, yeah. Like everything.'

'Everything, huh? Sounds useful.' She slipped it into her pocket. 'Gimme yours.'

'I haven't—'

'Don't even think about crusting me. If Lloyd here's got one, so have you. Hand it over.' She stood up. Took a step towards him. 'Or do you want me to search you up close?'

'Here, take it. Take it.'

'Last thing. This business you got with Hollie. I get the impression she don't want to come see you about it. Am I wrong?'

'No. Bitch owes me. I'm—'

'Whatever the bitch owes you is written off. You catch my drift? Otherwise . . .'

'Sure, sure. Not a problem. We're all good.'

'Well then, that surely concludes our business today, I'm thinking. And Dean?'

'Yeah?'

Abi pointed at the pair of diamonds that were still, somehow, sitting on the desk.

'You can keep 'em. A deal's a deal.'

Thirteen

'Oh my god oh my god oh my god!' Hollie cried, jumping up and down at the bus stop.

'That's your cut, doll. Ten per cent, like we agreed.' Abi reached deeper into her backpack, while Hollie stuffed the ragged pile of notes into her purse. 'Also, whaddya think about these babies?' She pulled out her hand, now full of recently acquired jewellery. 'You want 'em?'

'Do I ever! I mean . . . unless you . . . ?'

'Go on, take 'em. I ain't got no use for baubles like these. Not my style.' She ran an eye across Hollie's compact frame. 'They'll look good on you.'

'Thanks, Abi. For everything. For getting that bastard Dean off my back. It's like . . . I can't believe it. Oh my god oh my god oh my god!'

She was jumping up and down again. Then she stopped, fixing Abi with an appraising stare.

'You got a place to stay?'

'Not yet. I'm gonna find me a motel, doss down and get my bearings, maybe.'

Hollie's expression turned wry.

'A *motel*? This is Britain, love. There aren't any *motels* here and *hotels*'ll cost you an arm and a leg.' She grabbed Abi's hand impulsively. 'Come stay at mine for a few days. We've got a spare room you can use. It isn't much, but it's free. And it's the *least* I can do, seeing as how you've helped me out like, big time.'

Abi opened her mouth to refuse and then thought better of it. She glanced down the street. She'd worn out her welcome at Harlequin Taxis. And exchanging diamonds for currency had turned out to be a lot harder than she'd anticipated. Who knew when, or even if, she'd be able to get her hands on more cash. There was no point throwing money away on accommodations when she'd need it for more important things. Besides, the small, pale-and-black *oyinbo* woman had already shown herself to be a useful guide. The files, the *masu amfana*'s training, had not adequately prepared her for the strangeness of this place. Abidemi Eniola needed all the help she could get.

'Well, Hollie, you've gone and gotten yourself a deal.'

Once they were settled on another stop-start bus, Abi showed Hollie the polymer cards and booklets. She was curious to know what they were. If they were useful.

'These are credit and debit cards,' Hollie said. 'If Dean had them in his safe, they're probably bent.'

Abi held one up to the light, frowning.

'They look all right to me.'

'Not bent, silly: *bent*. As in not kosher.'

'I don't get it.'

'They're probably stolen or maybe even forgeries,' Hollie explained, as if speaking to a child. 'Chances are, if you try and use them, you'll get nicked.' Seeing the expression on Abi's face, Hollie explained, even more slowly: 'Nicked means arrested by the filth. By the police.'

'I hear you, doll. And what about these?'

'These are . . . passports.' It was Hollie frowning now, flipping slowly through the pages. She threw Abi a sharp look. 'Where'd you get these?'

'Same as the rest of the stuff: they were in the safe.'

'These belong to girls. Ukraine, Belarus, Liberia, Kenya.' Hollie's deathly white skin flushed red with anger. 'That bastard! I'll bet he's trafficking them. He's fucking involved, anyway. Fuck . . . *Fuck*!'

Hollie was shaking. Abi had no idea why. Some seventh sense told her to tread carefully. There were things it was okay not to know. She was from 'Nigeria' after all. But this, she suspected, was not one of them.

'Are you sure?' she asked, careful to keep her voice neutral.

'Totes. People, girls mostly, get lured here – to Britain – with the promise of jobs and such. A better life. Their families pay people traffickers to get them here. But when they get here, the traffickers lock them up somewhere, take their passports so they can't leave, and make them work as cleaners, or on farms or, worse, on the street. Then they keep the wages the girls earn for themselves.'

Something uncomfortable curled to life in Abi's stomach.

'But what you're describing. Imprisonment. Working for nothing. That's—'

'Exactly.'

Abi took the passports back. Examined them more closely.

'And the pictures in here. They're women who've been . . .?'

'Trafficked. Yes.'

'When they are sent out to work, can they not run away? Can they not go to . . . the filth?'

That made Hollie smile for some reason.

'They're more frightened of the police than the traffickers. Passports allow people to come into the country, but they don't allow them to work. What the girls are doing is illegal. So if they go to the police they could be sent to prison – or deported.'

'Deported?'

'Sent back to their own countries. For some, that's even worse than being where they are now.' Hollie's expression changed suddenly. Became concerned.

'Abi? Are you okay? You look—'

'I'm fine, doll.' Abi worked harder at keeping her thoughts off her face. She smoothed out her expression and stared out the bus's window, feigning an interest in the passing traffic.

Maybe this would be easier than she'd thought. These people were savages. Barely human. So what if some of them came to a sticky end?

It wasn't like they didn't deserve what was coming.

Fourteen

Saturday the 5th: 7.19 p.m. BST

'It's not much,' Hollie said, 'but it's home.'

Home for Hollie was a crudely constructed synthetic-rock building. She'd described it as a 'terrace house in Knowle West', and Abi took her at her word. The terrace stretched low and rambling along the edge of a narrow street. It was sub-divided into a number of side-by-side dwellings, one of which was Hollie's. A low, graffiti-daubed garden wall separated the terrace from the street proper, though the garden itself consisted mostly of mud and gravel. The interior was little better, comprising small, poorly lit rooms that reeked of damp and people. Abi readjusted the filters in her nose.

'You can stay here for a few days,' Hollie said. With a flourish of welcome, she opened the door to a chamber so narrow Abi could touch opposing walls with outstretched arms. A bare mattress took up most of the floor. It was worn through in places to reveal grubby foam padding, but it was clear that Hollie expected her to sleep on it. The rest of the space was taken up by a rickety desk and a battered metal chair. A bare lightbulb hung from the ceiling. The window was crusted with dirt and old paint, and a black, powdery lifeform was eating at the decorative paper that covered the walls. Its spores tickled her nostrils.

'This is swell.'

'I'm right next door,' Hollie added. 'Dave and Simon have their own rooms. They're chill. They won't bother you. We're off to a party later. Want to come?'

'I don't want to be no crumb, Hollie, but I gotta doss. I'm too joed for a wingding. I've travelled a long way, you know?'

Something she'd said made the *oyinbo* laugh.

'No worries. Maybe tomorrow night, then.'

'You got plans for tomorrow? In the day, I mean.'

'Not really, no.'

'I need to get in some supplies. I need more machines like these.' She produced the mobile phones she'd liberated from Harlequin Taxis.

Hollie broke into a broad grin.

'If you're looking to go shopping, I'm your girl. Totes. But you need to be spending Dean Shit's money on more important things than electronics.'

'Like what?'

'Clothes, for a start. It may be the bomb in Nigeria but you can't traipse about Bristol in a man's double-breasted suit. And you have *got* to lose the hat. You look like a nineteen-thirties gangster.'

'I like hats.'

'Too bad.'

Before Abi could say anything further, Hollie left to prepare for her party.

With a sigh, Abi sat down at the rickety desk and pulled a small box of instruments from her backpack. The small box was followed by a larger one, full of loose components. She placed the mobile phones in front of her, feeling the familiar tightness in her eyes as she scanned them.

It took her no time at all to dismantle them completely and drop in a couple of processors. When she put them back together, they were not the same.

She took the Liberian passport from her backpack and laid it on the desk. She waved one of the modified phones across the top of it, letting it do a deeper scan of the document than her eyes could. As she suspected, there was more to the passport than pieces of paper. There was a microchip built into it embedded with information. The information was in a code that made no sense to her augments, but the phone's original operating system, boosted by Abi's mods, was able to decipher it.

Biometric data. There were pictures of the Liberian's face, iris, and fingerprints. Presumably when she travelled, she would encounter scanners that ensured she matched the details on the passport.

Abi grunted to herself. This was sophisticated stuff for a bunch of savages. Still . . .

The phone became almost too hot to hold as it rewrote the coding on the chip to match her own details. For a moment she thought it was going to burn out. But, finally, it got the job done. The next bit was trickier. If there were nanobots in the paper, she was totally screwed.

Yeah, well. Here goes nothing.

She pulled a small, squeezable tube from her backpack. Then smeared a small amount of paste onto the pages of the passport. She took up the now cooling phone and directed its main camera at her face.

The paste sank into the paper. Once again, the phone became hot in her hand. Abi forced herself to hold it steady.

There were no nanobots.

The pictures in the passport blurred into ripples of ink. Rearranged themselves to look exactly like Abidemi Eniola.

Abi dropped the phone onto the disgusting mattress and blew hurried air onto the burned palm of her hand. The amulet on her wrist came to life, offering repair meds.

She did not refuse.

Fifteen

Sunday the 6th: 4.47 p.m. BST

*A*bi was sorry to see the back of the fedora. But despite their ubiquity in the files, no one seemed to be wearing one and she needed to blend in. Or stand out less. After much haggling, and the discovery that nothing Hollie liked came in a size Abi could get into, Abi persuaded Hollie to settle for a man's leather jacket, a series of plain tees, several pairs of men's dark combat trousers, and a pair of shiny black boots that Hollie referred to as 'Docs'. When Abi emerged fully clothed in this ensemble, Hollie pronounced herself satisfied, purchased several bags of always-black clothing for herself and, reluctantly, accompanied Abi to an 'electronics' store. Eyebrows were raised when Abi bought what she was looking for with cash, but when Hollie explained that Abi was on holiday from Nigeria and didn't have a working debit card, the salesperson nodded her understanding and processed the order.

'That was *fabulous*!' Hollie breathed, as they dumped their haul indoors. 'I feel like Pretty Woman.'

'You're a pretty woman?' Abi wasn't sure what *oyinbo*s found attractive.

Hollie's eyes narrowed in mock annoyance.

'Not me, arsehole. The movie. *Pretty Woman*. Where she goes shopping?'

Abi could only imagine the look of helpless stupidity spreading across her face.

'Oh my god! You've never seen *Pretty Woman*?'

''Fraid not.'

'Wow. Anyway, the point is, there's this magical scene where she's taken shopping and can have anything – absolutely anything – she could possibly want and it's like totally amazing.'

'You find shopping amazing?'

'Shopping like we just did? Totally!' Hollie was bouncing up and down with excitement. 'It's the best thing on earth, Abi. That's why they call it retail therapy. No matter how down you are or how hard life is, everything looks better after a good shop.'

She took a step towards the kitchen.

'Tea?'

Abi, who had been introduced to the noxious liquid earlier in the day, refused. She tapped one of the boxes from the electronics store. 'I have work to do, doll. I gotta k-ball these suckers.'

'K-ball?'

'Break 'em into pieces to make something else.'

'You're going to break *brand new* phones and laptops into pieces?' Hollie's disturbing blue eyes were wide with disbelief.

'Yup.'

'To make something else?'

'Uh-huh.'

'So what are you making?'

'It's called a . . .' Abi hesitated, unable to find the right words. 'An *opolo keji*.'

'An Apollo Cagey?'

'Yes. Like your laptops and mobile phones, but better.'

'Better?' The blue eyes were, if anything, even wider than before.

'In Nigeria, we are very good at such things.'

Sixteen

*I*t was getting dark and the rain had come again when Hollie knocked on Abi's door.

'Come in.'

'We're going to order Indian. I wondered if . . . *wow*.'

The rickety desk had sprouted three softly glowing screens. They were wirelessly linked to a laptop body, the keyboard of which appeared to have been replaced by three or four mobile phones. The mobiles glowed in unison, their screens covered in a series of densely patterned polygons. As Hollie stared, the polygons rearranged themselves. Once, then twice.

'So this is your Apollo thingamajig?'

'Yes.' The metal chair creaked as Abi arched her back against it. 'But it ain't working the way I'd planned.'

Hollie leaned over Abi's shoulder, peering curiously at the phones. The polygons danced into a new configuration.

'What are the triangles and stuff?'

'Writing.'

'You don't use letters?'

'They *are* letters – sorta – just not the ones you're used to.'

'And what's it say?'

'Nothing I want it to.' Abi sighed heavily. 'It's all wet, doll.'
Hollie giggled.

'You speak funny, even for a Nigerian, you know that?'

'I'm kinda getting the idea.'

'Well, what are you trying to do?'

Abi tapped a couple of the glowing polygons. Hollie gasped as
the three screens sprang to life, each one of them rapidly cycling
through web pages.

'*Dekun*,' she ordered. The screens stopped cycling, each one of
them showing a different website, one from a trading company,
another for the United States Navy, and one devoted to airships.
'I'm trying to find something on the . . . the . . .'

'Internet?'

'Yeah, that's it. On the internet. But I'm not having any luck.
I feel like a crumb.'

'What are you looking for?'

Abi hesitated. Involving the *oyinbo* woman carried risks.
But.

'I need to know about ships. Old ships. But when I ask for old
ships, the *opolo keji* brings me things like this, which ain't what
I'm looking for.'

Hollie leaned closer. Then took an abrupt step back.

'How'd you get that?' she asked, pointing at one of the screens.

'I didn't. The *opolo keji* did.'

'The Apollo Cagey broke into a top-secret US Navy computer on its own?'

'Whadya mean "top secret"?'

'This screen, here: the one that says "Classified, Department
of the Navy: Proposed Service Life Extension of Flight Three
Arleigh Burke Class Destroyers".' Hollie stumbled awkwardly
over the words. 'You shouldn't have this. *No one* should have

this. Unless you work for the Yank Navy, which you don't . . . You don't, right?'

'I don't. But if this is so secret, why'd they put the low-down on your internet? It's public, doll. You'd have to be a real genius to figure your stuff was safe.'

Hollie was giving her a strange look.

'Not everything on the internet is public, Abi. It's hidden behind . . . behind firewalls and shit like that. You could get in real trouble for having stuff like this.'

'Sure, I could,' Abi scoffed. 'Doofus leaves stuff lying around for the taking, what's he think is gonna happen? That no one'll take it? Gimme a break.'

'I'm *serious*. Breaking into top-secret American websites is a crime.'

'So's jaywalking.'

'I don't know what that is, except it doesn't sound like a big deal. This . . . this is a big deal.'

'*Kuro patapata*,' Abi said, waving at the offending screen. The Navy document vanished. 'It's not what I wanted, anyway.'

'You wanted to know about old ships, yeah? How old?'

Abi hesitated. Again.

'You want my help or not?' Hollie glanced meaningfully at the door. 'I can just leave and let Mr Cagey there steal government secrets you don't want. Until the filth kick down our door and arrest you, anyway.'

The filth sounded like an unnecessary complication.

'I'm looking for the low-down on shipping from the Year of Our Lord 1791.'

'Seventeen ninety-one!' Hollie's jaw dropped open. 'No wonder you can't find anything. The internet's only like, er, fifty years old, maybe. What you're looking for is so pre-computers it's not even funny.' Her jaw closed, firmed by sudden certainty. 'You need a historian. One that knows about ships and shit. This is Bristol. Bound to be a pants-load of them at the unis.'

'Unis?'

'Universities.' Hollie's voice turned unexpectedly bitter. 'It's where you go after school so they can turn you into a fucking drone.'

Abidemi tried not to let curiosity get the better of her.

Tried.

'What's a "drone"?'

'A mindless fucking worker is what that is. A cog in the machine.'

'And are you a drone?'

'God, no!' Hollie laughed. 'Yeah, well, I started a degree in Fashion and Textiles at UWE but it wasn't for me. Dropped out second year. I make my own jewellery and sell it round town, now. And I sometimes crew sailboats. For the adventure, 'cause life is boring, innit? I help out on delivery trips up and down the west coast. That and . . . other stuff. I'm trying to pull enough together to get back into dress design. Thanks to you, dress design looks way more possible than it did yesterday morning.'

Hollie was beaming at her. Despite the disturbing blue eyes, it was hard not to like the *oyinbo* woman.

But Abidemi was prepared to make the effort. Hollie Rogers was a guide. Nothing more.

'So, doll. How do we find these historians of yours?'

Seventeen

Monday the 7th: 1.40 a.m. BST

It took a considerable time for the house to fall asleep. Indian food turned out to be surprisingly good, although the zeal with which Hollie and her housemates consumed once-living animals was deeply disturbing. She'd stuck to plant matter. She'd eat animals if she had to: the files – and the training – had prepared her for that, but she was in no hurry to start. Food finished, she had turned down various offers of alcohol, and possibly sex, before returning to her room. She'd set the *opolo keji* to updating her map of the city and waited. Now, with quiet settling over the building at last, she hoisted her backpack onto her shoulders and slipped out the front door.

The night was wet and drizzly. Misted rain collected in beads on her leather jacket. She jogged along the deserted roads, long, easy strides eating up the distance. The ground under her feet – *pavement*, Hollie had called it – brightened and dimmed in rhythm to the glare and fade of street lights as she passed beneath them, each one marking progress towards her destination, each one surrounded by a fuzzy halo of moisture.

She was pushing uphill now, into the part of the city marked as CLIFTON on the maps. The housing here, while still little more than an aggregation of rocks, was grander than Knowle West, fashioned from various kinds of tan-coloured stone – and grey, synthetic imitations of stone – beneath dark, triangular roofs. Some were in terraces, like Hollie's, others stood apart behind low walls and lushly shadowed gardens.

There was not a soul to be seen.

Abi slowed to a walk as she entered a narrow, not unpleasant street. Three-storeyed terraced housing ran along both sides of it. Instead of the usual unadorned stone, however, some of the houses had been painted blue. It was across the road from one of these that Abi came to a halt, checking her surroundings against the map in her head. Satisfied, she unslung her backpack, dropping it gently to the rain-slicked pavement.

Three *alantakun* emerged from the bag and skittered across the street. Abi wished there'd been more time to research their appearance. She was not at all sure they looked the part. Fortunately, it was dead of night and the chance of discovery slim. The small, eight-legged machines reached the rock-cube's front door and squeezed themselves through the thin gap at the bottom.

Abi adjusted her senses to a flood of new information. In addition to the blue-painted exterior, she could also see the inside of the house. A darkened hallway, closed doors, and a steep set of stairs, all of it illuminated in the eerie glow of infrared.

If Hollie's home was typical, the *oyinbos* would be sleeping on the upper floors. While one of the *alantakun* swept the ground floor spaces just to make sure, the other two climbed onto a banister and made their way upstairs, so tiny that the age-cracked wood looked as broad as a road. Sure enough, two grown *oyinbos*, one male, one female, and presumably mated, were sleeping together in one room. A young male juvenile slept alone in another. Apart from that, the rock-cube was uninhabited.

Ever so carefully, the tiny machines made their way into the bedchambers. One settled on the neck of the juvenile, another on the female.

They bit at the same time. Neither of the *oyinbos* stirred. Their breathing slowed to a stop.

Abidemi picked up her backpack and crossed the road. The rock-cube's front door had two locks, which she examined in a variety of wavelengths. She reached into her backpack and pulled out a small box. The heat of it pressed against her fingers. Only when it had cooled did she open it.

The box contained a pair of newly minted housekeys. Their handles had the appearance of intricately carved ivory. The business ends, however, would have been alarmingly familiar to the people on the other side of the door.

Abi let herself in and headed upstairs. Knowing where to go, her steps were quiet but confident.

The male *oyinbo* was still asleep, his breathing a moist susurration against the pillow. A tangled mass of dark hair flopped over his brow. Light from the street painted abstract patterns on the quilting.

There was a chair at his bedside, piled high with clothes. Abi tipped them onto the floor and sat down.

'Dr Kwan,' she said gently. And then louder. 'Dr Kwan.'

Max Kwan stirred and opened slow, sleepy eyes.

Then sat bolt upright, mouth wide apart and shrieking. Gangly limbs flailed in a variety of directions as he threw back the bedsheets and tried to scramble away. Abi stood up and grabbed him by the shoulders.

'Don't be scared, doc. I ain't here to hurt you. Not yet anyway.'

Kwan made several attempts to squirm out of her grasp but Abi was too strong. Eventually, the fight went out of him. His shoulders slumped, the little energy he had left expended in loud, panicky breathing.

Abi let him go. The *oyinbo* perched on the edge of the bed, bare, bony feet pressed flat against wooden floorboards. He wore clothes to sleep, Abi noted: an insubstantial, violently striped two-piece suit with neither shirt, nor tie, nor undergarments.

'Who are you? How did you get in? What do you want?'

'Abidemi Eniola. I came in through the front door.' Abi sat back down in the chair. Made herself at home. 'Sorry to bust into your cave like this but I'd like to hire you for a job.'

'A job?' Kwan laughed at her in disbelief. 'A *job*? You couldn't call my assistant and make an appointment like a sane person?'

'I'm new here. Seemed like the easiest way to get in touch.'

'You can't just barge into someone's home in the dead of night, waking . . .' Struck by a sudden thought, he turned around. 'Pip?' He reached out to the woman lying in the bed. Shook her by an unmoving shoulder. '*Pippa*! Wake up.' The shaking became forceful to the point of violence. 'Please wake up, Pip. Please . . .'

The female *oyinbo* lay unresponsive to his touch. Kwan turned back around, his face wet with tears.

'What have you *done*?'

'Saved her the trouble of listening to all this malarkey.'

'You didn't have to kill her!'

Abi blinked at that. Once. Twice.

'She ain't dead, doc. Just sleeping.'

'She's not breathing!'

'It's a *deep* sleep. She'll be fine by morning, day after maybe. Like your son in the next room.'

Kwan looked at her in horror.

'Your wife and kid'll be A-okay, doc, sure as eggs is eggs. I just need to talk to you in private.'

The *oyinbo*'s laugh had a bitter edge to it.

'What do you want?'

'The internet says you're a lecturer in maritime history at the University of Bristol.'

'So what?'

'I have need of your expertise, doc. I need you to find me a ship.'

'I'm a *history* teacher, Miss En . . . En . . .'

'Eniola.'

'Miss Eniola. I can't *find* you a ship. You need a shipbroker for that.' A sardonic smile. 'Or the Navy.'

'I need you to find me a ship in the past, doc. I don't think she's around no more.'

Despite himself, a flicker of interest stirred in Max Kwan's eyes.

'How far in the past?'

'The Year of Our Lord 1791.'

Kwan reached absently towards a small, bedside table and retrieved a pair of glasses. Once on, the look he directed at Abi was one of frank curiosity.

'And what do you know about her, this ship of yours?'

'I know her name and that she sailed out of Bristol, England. This place is still called England, right?'

Kwan's look turned strange.

'What's she called, this ship of yours?'

'*Esperance.*'

'Well, I would need to search the registries and various records. Eighteenth-century records are far from complete, obviously, but they're extensive nonetheless.'

'Great. Let's get started.'

A small bark of laughter came out of Max Kwan's mouth.

'I can't do it from here, Miss Eniola. A lot of these records aren't digitized. Some of them are in microfiche, and some of them can only be accessed by looking at the original registers. I need to go to my office, and I am *not* doing this in the middle of the night. It's going to take me quite a while to pull this together. But the fact you know the year should make things simpler. For the basic stuff, at least. I'll start with the Lloyd's register and take it from there.'

'How long? For the basic stuff?'

'If we're lucky and she's in Lloyd's? A few hours. Otherwise, days, weeks, months, or never.'

'Okay,' Abi said, standing up. 'Meet me tomorrow at ten with whatever you've got.' She felt her mouth curving into a smile. 'At Millennium Square. By the Cary Grant statue.'

'Ten o'clock isn't enough time. I need—'

'Tomorrow is Tuesday, not later this morning. It's plenty if you start soon. And, doc?'

'Yes?'

Abi made sure the smile had vanished from her face.

'No funny stuff. I know where you live.'

Eighteen

'Look, I don't like . . . Black folks, okay? And you can't fucking make me. But I didn't kill him.'

The voice of Joe Ricci, the night doorman at the Okoros' apartment building, sounded tinny in the speakers. Looking through the one-way glass into the interview room, Ethan could see him glaring at Raymond Yeung across a chipped Formica table. Raymond was making cursory notes on the pad in front of him. The pen he was using had been chewed nearly to destruction.

'And what did you think of the wife?' Raymond asked.

'What do *you* think? She was married to the . . . guy.'

'You think she needed to be taught a lesson?'

'In a perfect world, yeah.' A small smile. 'Come to think of it, looks like she got what was coming to her. Next time, maybe she'll marry one of her own people.'

'And the baby?'

'What about the baby?'

'You think the baby needed to be taught a lesson also?'

'What? No. The kid was cute. Not his fault he came into the world, is it?'

Ethan felt his eyebrows twitch.

'Did you see any of the Okoros on Tuesday night?'

'No.'

'What about Wednesday?'

'No.'

'When had you last seen any of them?'

'Jesus fucking Christ, how should I know? The weekend before, maybe? With takeout? I don't remember.'

'Try.'

'I don't fucking remember, okay?'

'You ever do work on the building security cams?'

'No.'

Raymond tipped back on his chair. The dented metal legs tasked with taking his weight dug into the linoleum.

'You're saying you've *never* done work on the building security cams?'

'That's *exactly* what I'm saying.'

'Funny that. See, I talked to your colleagues over the weekend. And a couple of the families that live there. And they distinctly recall you reinstalling them after the lobby was redecorated.'

'Oh . . . well, yeah . . . I forgot about that.'

'You forgot?'

'Yeah. It wasn't a big deal. That's why it slipped my mind.'

'Because it was an easy job?'

'Sure.'

'And it was easy 'cause you understand how camera systems work, right?'

'Yeah. It ain't rocket science.'

'And if the cameras ever play up, it's you they come to first before they call the contractor, right?'

'Yeah.'

'Which you also forgot to tell me about?'

'I guess.'

'So if anyone would know how to screw up the cameras that would be you, yes?'

Ricci hesitated.

'Look, man, I know where the cables go, and I can fix a loose connection. I can't screw up the cameras. I don't know how.'

'If you can fix a loose connection, you could loosen it couldn't you? Make everything turn to static?'

'Why would I do that?'

'But you could, yeah?'

'Maybe. But I didn't.'

'You know someone going by the name of A. Bello?'

'Nope.'

'Ever heard of Super Eagles Plumbing?'

'No.'

'Did you ever show anyone else how to fix – or unfix – the cameras?'

'No! Look, this is all bullshit. Do I have to get a lawyer in here or what?'

Nineteen

'Did you believe him?' Ethan asked Raymond, after they'd both returned to the squad room.

Yeung leaned back in his chair and stared at the ceiling, seemingly fascinated by the stained tile above his head.

'I'd like not to, but we got nothing that says otherwise, do we? He'd have to fix the cameras so they black out *only* when our guy enters and leaves the building. Which means he'd have to know exactly when A. Bello was coming and going. Which means, unless our guy is some kind of remote-working computer genius—'

'Unlikely.'

'– he'd have to be in the building to see him. No one, and I mean *no one*, not Al Mills, not anybody, puts him in the building during the day on Tuesday or Wednesday.'

'Probably not our guy then,' Ethan agreed.

'There's more,' Raymond said. Something about his tone made Ethan's ears prick up. He walked over to the sergeant's cubicle, leaning over his shoulder as Raymond fired up his computer. Fuzzy street shots filled the screen.

'We've canvassed all the cameras we can find. None of them got a good look at this guy.'

'Bummer.' Ethan clapped Raymond on the shoulder. 'Hey. It was worth a shot.'

'Sure. But some of these cameras *should* have picked him up. Look at this.' Raymond's fingers flashed across the keyboard. 'The building across the street from our crime scene has a door cam.' An empty threshold leapt into view, beyond which was the busy back and forth of Sheridan Road, and beyond that, small but easily recognizable, the entrance to the Okoros' building. 'This is the tape from Tuesday. Watch the time stamp.'

At 10.29 a.m. the picture dissolved into a cloud of static. The picture returned to normal less than ninety seconds later. Raymond hit fast forward. The image disintegrated again at 12.38 p.m. and returned to normal just before the clock hit 12.40.

Ethan stepped back. Ran his hands through his hair.

'That can't be coincidence, can it?'

'I don't think so, lieutenant. And I don't think our friend Joe Ricci could be responsible for *that*. But fuck me. How did our guy pull it off?'

'Some kind of jammer, I guess.'

'Can anyone even do that?'

Ethan was thinking about the Asian lady at the hospital. Dr Lee. Her concerns about the neurotoxin.

'Maybe. If you're the government.'

'*Our* government?' Yeung looked sceptical.

'*A* government. I know we're ruled by a bunch of corrupt, self-absorbed assholes, but I don't think they're in the business of drowning babies. Not yet anyhow.'

'You thinking of calling in the Feds?'

'No. This is thin, Raymond. Like a fucking skeleton. They'd

laugh us out the building. We gotta know more about this than we do – a lot more.' He ran a hand along his hairline, thinking. 'Put this out to CPIC, see if anything like this has happened before.'

'And Interpol?'

Ethan shot Raymond a surprised glance. The sergeant looked at his desk, embarrassed.

'Maybe it's overkill,' he amended. 'It's just—'

'No, you're right. CPIC is national. If this is a foreign government maybe they've done something similar abroad. Let's do it. But Raymond?'

'Yeah?'

'Do it on the down-low. If it turns out the bitch wife did it, we're going to look all kinds of stupid. We'll never live it down.'

'*You'll* never live it down,' Raymond said smiling. 'Me?' A mock German accent. 'I vas only obeying orders.'

'If I go down, you fuck, I'm taking you with me.'

'Understood,' Raymond said grinning. 'Down-low it is.' He tapped the top of his computer. 'Also, before I got distracted by Interpol and shit, I was about to tell you. The cameras weren't a complete bust. Almost, but not quite.'

Ethan threw a sharp glance in the sergeant's direction.

'How so?'

Raymond started playing with the feed from the door cam across the street.

'So, I got to thinking. Our guy didn't walk all the way to the Almeida Building, jamming security cams on the go. He had to drive there. And with the size of gear he had, it'd have to be a van or a small truck.' Raymond paused for a moment, making small adjustments to the picture. 'On Tuesday morning this camera goes on the fritz at ten twenty-nine, yeah? Well, five minutes before that, this white box van passes in front of the Okoros' building northbound,\see?'

Ethan nodded. The van in question was, so far as he could tell, completely nondescript. Seen sideways on, it had no distinguishing markings whatsoever.

'And then, seven minutes *after* the cam goes on the fritz at twelve thirty-seven, here's a white box van heading south. Maybe it's a coincidence, but my money's on it being the same van. And if it's the same van, it belongs to our guy.'

Ethan pursed his lips.

'There have got to be thousands of white box vans in Chicago.'

'Agreed.' Raymond allowed himself a smug smile. 'But a truck coming up Sheridan either came up Sheridan the whole way, or would have joined it from Lake Shore Drive—'

'Du Sable Drive,' Ethan corrected sourly.

'Whatever. And come back the same way. And guess what building at Sheridan and *Du Sable* has security cams covering the whole intersection?' Raymond paused, waiting for the penny to drop.

'The Greek Orthodox church.' Ethan could feel the smile spreading across his face. 'You get the feeds?'

'We did. Every which way.' Raymond threw a couple of frozen images onto his computer screen. 'Given the time stamps, this here's our van. The pictures are a bunch of crap but the nerds'll clean it up.' Fingers beat a triumphant tattoo on the desk. 'We're never going to get a complete plate given the angle but there's enough there for a partial. I'm sure of it.'

Twenty

'Ms Okoro?'

Ethan fought hard to keep the surprise from showing on his face. There was Jennifer Freeman Okoro, just as the desk sergeant had said, sitting primly in the precinct's reception. Dressed entirely in black, she looked much better than when he'd last seen her, even if the darkness of her attire made her look paler than she should have been.

'There's a coffee shop down the block,' he said. 'It's a helluva lot nicer than hanging around here, and I was about to take my lunch break.'

'Okay.'

Seated out of the sun by a plate-glass window and with a plastic cup of coffee for each of them, Ethan waited for Jennifer Okoro to say whatever she had come to say. Refusing to meet his eye, she was staring out at the traffic, both hands clasping her coffee. Her nails, Ethan noted, had been freshly painted. He took a sip from his drink. And almost spat it out.

It tasted of rotten eggs.

They'd warned him about this. He just hadn't expected it to happen so soon. Grateful that Jennifer was paying him no attention, he forced himself to swallow. He set the cup down at arm's length. A young couple passed by outside, smiling and laughing and heedless of the heat.

Jennifer shifted in her seat.

'This has happened before,' she said at last.

'What's happened before, Ms Okoro?'

'A drowning. In my husband's family.'

Jennifer Okoro was looking him in the eye now, her face strangely expressionless.

'My brother-in-law drowned at home. And his mother.' The voice was flat, devoid of intonation. 'My niece, too.'

'By accident?'

Jennifer shook her head.

'Six months ago, now. In Lagos, Nigeria.' Her tongue flashed nervously between her lips. 'They lived in an apartment complex with a pool. The police said they must have been drowned there and taken upstairs to delay discovery. It worked, too. My sister-in-law was out of town, so it was almost a week before they were found.'

'What about the father – your father-in-law? Didn't he come looking for his wife?'

Another shake of the head.

'My father-in-law's dead – of natural causes. Years ago, before Amadi and I got together.'

'Uh-huh. Did they find out who did it?'

'No. There were no witnesses. No one saw or heard anything. Amadi was very bitter. Said the police were incompetent. Or they were covering something up.'

'Did he suspect someone?'

Jennifer hesitated.

'No one specific. Zulu – my brother-in-law – was a

businessman. In a country like Nigeria business can be . . . dangerous. Amadi reckoned he'd crossed the wrong people, people with enough clout to buy off the police. People who'd killed him.'

'And you think the same people might have come for your husband?'

'Yes.'

'But why? If this was about business, I mean. I thought your husband was a med student?'

'He is . . . was. He had nothing to do with the business. But Zulu and his daughter were found drowned in their apartment. And now Amadi and Ben . . . Amadi and Ben . . .'

The mask she'd been wearing broke and shattered. Ethan, in an attempt to give her privacy, stared out through the plate-glass window. But he could still see the woman's reflection, her shoulders heaving to the irregular rhythm of grief.

Twenty-One

Monday the 7th: 1.07 p.m. CDT

'Did you believe her?' Raymond Yeung asked.

Ethan put his feet up on the desk.

'I believe her about her brother-in-law drowning. She's gotta know we're going to run that down with the Nigerian authorities.'

'And it gives us a reason to go to Interpol without making *you* look like a complete douche.' Raymond grinned wickedly.

Ethan grinned back.

'Like I said, sergeant, I go down, you go down. Thank the spouse for getting us both out from under.'

'Uh-huh. If you believe her about the drowning, what *don't* you believe?'

'Everything else.' The grin vanished from his face as quickly as it had arrived. 'The way the wife tells it, the MO is virtually identical. Which means either there's some sort of weird African vendetta going on – a vendetta where the kids are fair game but the wives aren't – or the wife simply copied the way her brother-in-law died in order to put us off the scent.'

'Including injecting herself with some weird-ass neurotoxin?'

'Yeah . . . though that's a problem.'

'Why? Our druggie friends inject themselves with all sorts of shit all day every day.'

'Sure, she could inject herself if she was determined enough. But this is, like you said, a "weird-ass neurotoxin". Which leaves us with this as your goddamn Final Jeopardy.'

Suddenly uncomfortable, Ethan took his feet off the desk and stood up.

'If it's as weird ass as they say, where the fuck did she get it?'

Twenty-Two

Tuesday the 8th: 9.58 a.m. BST

Abidemi was paying too much attention to the heavens. The grey clouds and drizzly rain she had thought permanent here had given way to a startlingly blue sky and bright sunshine. Although that wasn't what she was looking at.

What she was looking at was the moon. She knew about it from The Story, of course. And the files. But to see it for real was something else. It was huge, and pearlescent, and bright enough to be visible by day. Flawlessly round, it was so large and close that she could make out mountains, and craters, and vast, dark grey plains.

It looked uninhabited.

Max Kwan, the lecturer in maritime history, was where he was meant to be. He was standing awkwardly by the Cary Grant statue in Millennium Square. He seemed entirely uninterested in the sky, staring down at his shoes instead. They shuffled nervously atop the smooth, slightly slippery stones the *oyinbo*s had used for paving.

'Good morning, doc. You got news for me?'

'Yes. But maybe not the kind you're looking for.' He nodded at someone or something over Abi's shoulder.

If she hadn't been so focused on the sky, she'd have noticed them earlier. Two men in jeans and rumpled jackets, one *oyinbo*, one normal, standing off to one side and pretending to examine the portly bronze figure of a person called William Penn. They walked over at a brisk pace, every step they took redolent of some kind of authority.

'This her?' the normal one asked Kwan. He wasn't as tall as Lloyd, the man whose wrist she'd crushed at Harlequin Taxis. And he lacked Lloyd's magnificent mane, preferring to keep his hair close cropped to his scalp. But there was a hardness about him that was easily a match for the other man.

'Yes,' Kwan responded, his entire face a portrait of aggrievement. 'She broke into my house, drugged my family, and threatened me.'

'Police,' the normal one said to her. 'I'm Detective Sergeant Yarborough, this is DC Jenner. You're under arrest for—'

Abi ran. The *oyinbo* officer, Jenner, tried to block her route but it was a simple matter to knock him to the ground. She hurtled across the square, Yarborough's pursuing footsteps fading away as she left him behind. All that remained was the jagged static of radio waves pounding inside her head. Yarborough or Jenner calling for help, she guessed. Long strides took her past a decorative metal sphere and into the streets beyond.

Suddenly, there were radio waves up ahead. A garishly coloured automobile was coming up the road towards her. She didn't need to read the bright *oyinbo* script in which it was covered to know that it said POLICE. The car screeched to a halt. A pair of doors flew open, and the occupants jumped out, both of them dressed in identical dark uniforms and body armour.

'Oi! You! Stop where you are!' Both officers produced menacing looking sticks. Blocked her path.

The sting of combat chemicals lanced through her wrist. The world slowed to a crawl.

The officers, a man and a woman, were clearly trained. She could tell by the way they held themselves, the way they were swinging the sticks to incapacitate her.

But the sticks were barely moving now. She bent herself past them, an elbow smashing into the woman's face, a hard-edged jab to the man's windpipe. They fell towards the ground slow as gossamer, a lake of red oozing from the woman's nose as she did so.

Abi was gone before they hit the pavement.

Twenty-Three

Tuesday the 8th: 9.30 a.m. CDT

'Are you sure?' Ethan asked the operator, not quite believing what she'd told him.

'That's what the man says, lieutenant. You want me to put him through or not?'

'Fuck it. Go ahead.'

The hissing coming through the earpiece of his desk phone had more to do with distance than the shitty quality of the equipment.

'Chicago PD, Detective Lieutenant Krol speaking.'

'Good afternoon, detective.' The voice at the other end spoke quickly, with the distinctive sing-song lilt that Ethan associated with Africa. 'My name is Inspector Christopher Danjuma of the Nigeria Police Force. I would like to talk with you about one of my cases.' A warm chuckle made its way across the Atlantic. 'It is driving my brain to great madness, and I am thinking that maybe you can be of assistance to me.'

Between the accent and the hissing on the line, the man was difficult to understand. Ethan found himself frowning with concentration. Raymond Yeung, sitting across the way at his workstation, looked at him curiously.

'How'd you find me, inspector? Interpol?'

'Google.' The same warm chuckle. Despite himself, Ethan couldn't help but smile in response. 'I have an unsolved case, very mysterious, very difficult to comprehend. So every day I search the internet with my computer to seek a similar case and I find this case of yours yesterday. This is the reason why I am calling you this afternoon.'

Ethan, whose workday had barely begun, envied the other man his approaching evening.

'Are you talking about the Okoro murders? Amadi and Benedict?'

'Precisely.'

Ethan's mind wandered to the coffee shop down the block. Jennifer Freeman Okoro breaking down in tears, skin pale and washed out against dark clothing.

'Would this have something to do with the death of . . .' He struggled to remember the name. 'Zulu Okoro?'

'It would,' Danjuma said, sounding delighted. 'You are moving quickly with your investigations, I see. Yes. Yes. This is the case concerning which I wish to talk to you. The assassinations of Chizulukeme Okoro, his mother, Erinma, and his daughter, Ndidi.'

'Chi . . . Chi . . .'

'Zulu will work, detective. It is an Igbo name and, if I were you, it is no doubt a little bit of a tongue twister.'

'Eri . . . mah and . . . Deedee?'

'Close enough.' That warm chuckle again.

Ethan pressed down on a jolt of annoyance. He didn't like being the cause of the Nigerian's amusement but there wasn't much he could do about it.

'And you said they were assassinated?'

'Yes.'

'So, you think this is political?'

There was a long pause at the other end.

'I have no reason to think in this way. Why do you ask this?'

'You said they were assassinated.'

Another long pause.

'People are assassinated every day. By the criminal element. It seldom has very much to do with politics.'

'My bad, inspector. I misunderstood you. You were telling me about your case?'

'Yes. Mr Okoro and daughter were discovered assassinated in their flat in Ikoyi—'

'I thought Mr Okoro died in Lagos?'

'Ikoyi is in Lagos. It is a very upscale neighbourhood, like your Manhattan. The Okoros lived in a very superb, very exclusive complex, with gates and security guards on an upper floor. And yet they were all drowned. We told all individuals that they had been drowned in the swimming pool of the complex and taken up the stairs after the assassinations.' An uncomfortable pause. 'This story, it was a lie, lieutenant. We were embarrassed at not being able to understand what had happened in this case. And so we wanted to avoid panic and recriminations.'

I'll bet.

'So, what's the true story?'

'Nothing we can explain. Unless you believe in *juju*, which I do not. We think the Okoros were killed in their flat. No one saw them at the pool that day and the pool is full of fresh water. The Okoros drowned to their deaths in—'

'Seawater?'

'Precisely.' Though he was thousands of miles distant, Ethan fancied he could feel the inspector leaning forward in his chair.

'You have the same case as we have here in Nigeria, perhaps? A drowning at sea on dry land?'

Ethan's gaze flitted around the room, unable to settle.

'It's too similar to be coincidental, I'm thinking. Does the Okoro family have enemies?'

'They are big people, very wealthy. All wealthy families have enemies. But no one who would kill a little girl. If one is striking at a family like this, with violence, you kill the man only.'

'Was the family in any particular line of business?'

'Not really. They own a lot of property, much of it abroad. Also, some oil companies, mostly in Imo and Rivers States. And many stocks and shares. Other things, too. They are old money – for Nigeria, in any event. They deny it now, obviously, but all the rumours say the Okoros made their money from the colonialists. By trading with the British. But we could find nothing in their business interests to explain such a dastardly crime as this.'

'What about the wife?'

'She was visiting with her relatives in Imo State at the time of the assassinations. We found no evidence of any involvement by her. We could discover no attempt to hire an assassin and, even if she hated her husband – and no persons say this was the case – she would have to be very deranged to kill her only child. Also, and this I examined before I am calling you, she has never been to America. If my assassin is your assassin. It cannot be the wife.'

'Did you have any suspects?'

'No. It is very . . . shameful.'

'If I told you that we're looking for a tall Black man, well over six foot tall, with scars on both cheeks, would that point you in the right direction?'

'And does this man of yours have a name?'

'He signed himself in as *A. Bello*.'

Loud, if tinny, laughter erupted from Ethan's earpiece.

'Truly this assassin you are looking for has a sense of humour! Ahmadu Bello is a very famous man. He was the first prime minister of Nigeria. You cannot go anywhere is this country without crashing into the name of the great Ahmadu Bello.' More laughter. 'I do not believe Ahmadu Bello is the assassin's real name.'

'You think?'

'But perhaps we can agree that our assassin is from Nigeria. Only a Nigerian would find this such a great source of amusement.'

'Makes sense,' Ethan agreed. 'He said he worked for a company called Super Eagles Plumbing.'

More laughter.

'The Super Eagles is the nickname of—'

'The Nigerian men's soccer team. Yes, I know. The company does not exist.'

'Unlike our assassin's sense of humour.'

Ethan found himself smiling again.

'Is the description of A. Bello any use to you . . . to us?'

'I am sorry to say, no. A man like that? In Nigeria? He could be anybody.'

Twenty-Four

Tuesday the 8th: 2.50 p.m. BST

The amulet on her wrist had exacted a price. Powered by combat chemistry, Abi had easily outrun her pursuers. Unsure of the tenacity of the local police, she had run too fast for too long. The effort had left her weak, shaking, and ravenously hungry. Barely able to do more than walk, she had slipped into an *oyinbo* establishment that served breakfast, and forced a variety of disgusting, tasteless nutrients into her stomach. Some hours later, though, she'd happened upon an Indian restaurant in the process of opening its doors. After a thorough sampling of its wares, she had emerged into bright sunshine feeling much more like herself.

Now she was walking amid a steady trickle of young people along a quiet street labelled WOODLAND ROAD. Most of the buildings, heavy-set but with a certain primitive dignity, claimed to be associated in some way with the University of Bristol. She stepped quickly behind a chattering, unkempt couple who had turned off the pavement at a sign labelled HUMANITIES BUILDING. Careful not to intrude on either their conversation or field of vision, she waited for one of them to swipe a small polymer card over the door scanner and slipped inside behind them.

The building had a distinctive smell that she couldn't quite place: an undefined melange of old wood, new polymers, vaporous chemicals, and people. Her boots squeaked on the polished floor. The corridors were busy with what looked like a shift change: young people coming out of a variety of rooms, forcing their way past other young people trying to get in.

She had to ask a couple of times for directions, but she got where she needed to go in short order. She knocked on the door. A dutiful, respectful rap. Like a student in need of assistance.

'Come in.'

It was clear from his expression that Max Kwan wished he could take the words back. Abi watched the blood drain from his face.

'Hiya, doc. Good to see ya.'

'You! G . . . get out. Right now. Before I call the police.'

Abi pretended not to hear him.

'Nice place you got here, doc. These are . . . books, I guess?' She reached out to touch one, a stonelike block of paper and card. There were hundreds of them stacked vertically – mostly vertically – against every available wall. The book was warm to the touch, and comforting. She caressed it for longer than she intended, enjoying the sensation.

'You have no right . . .' The man's voice was trembling. And why shouldn't it? He was trapped behind a book-cluttered desk with no way out. The room, not big to begin with, and further constricted by the packed bookshelves, only had space enough for a small expanse of carpet and a couple of well-worn, straight-backed chairs. Abi took one, clasped her hands in her lap, and stared in what she hoped was a good-natured fashion at her host. He looked different from the other *oyinbo*s, she realized, but she couldn't quite put her finger on why.

Maybe it was the hair.

He glanced surreptitiously at the phone on his desk.

'I ain't here to hurt you, doc. Unless you're truly reckoning on calling the filth.'

Kwan's head snapped back in distaste. But he made no attempt to reach for the phone.

'What do you want?' he asked sullenly.

'What I asked you for before. Information.'

'Yes, well, I don't have it. After what you did to me and my family, I called the police instead. Go and ask someone else. Leave me alone.'

Abi allowed herself a small smile.

'Now, see here, doc. I come a long way and gone to a lot of trouble to find you. And I ain't minded to go looking for no one else, capeesh? And I'm guessing, you being a man of learning and curious that way, that you couldn't resist having a looksee. Am I right?'

'No.' But he wouldn't look her in the eye.

'Well, that's just a darn shame. I'm gonna have to barricade that there door and keep you here till you get me what I'm looking for.'

Kwan licked his lips. A quick, nervous gesture.

'If you do that, my wife will know something's wrong. She'll call the police.'

Abi's smile vanished.

'I had to hurt a couple of police officers this morning, thanks to you. Did you know that? Not bad, mind you, but bad enough. I don't want to hurt any more that come my way.' She made a great play of examining her fingernails. 'But I will. And then I might have to hurt *you*, which would be a real shame.' She heard a sharp intake of breath but didn't look up. 'You're a brave man, doc. Calling the police like that. But they can't help you. And I know, after this morning, that you ain't so stupid as to think they can.' She met his gaze now: honest, and open, and direct. 'So why don't you quit fooling around and tell me what you know? I'll be gone before you know it.'

Kwan held her stare for a long, long time.

Blinked.

'All right, all right. You win. I did take a quick look. Just at the digitized records. The ship you're interested in, the *Esperance*, does in fact exist. Or *did*, rather. She was laid down—'

'What does that mean?'

'She was *built* in a French shipyard: Bayonne, to be precise, in 1781. Though she wasn't called *Esperance*, then.' He rummaged on his desk for a moment, retrieving a large, well-worn notepad. 'She was christened *Thérèse Séraphique* and sold to a shipping syndicate headed up by a Monsieur Étienne Roux, a trader based in Nantes. He went bankrupt after she was captured by the British off the Florida coast in January 1783. She was then sold at a prize court in New York to the Wolfe Shipping Company, who renamed her *Esperance*. Wolfe then owned her for more than twenty years. Until she was recaptured by the French in December 1805 in the Indian Ocean.' He glanced up briefly from his notes. 'Not that they had her for long, mind you. Not long enough to rename her at any rate. She was sunk by the Royal Navy off the coast of what was then Ceylon in July 1806.' Kwan sat back and tossed the notepad onto his desk. 'And that's pretty much it. Not an atypical history for a vessel of that era.'

Abi filed away what she'd been told. Then played it back.

'The Wolfe Shipping Company. Who were they?'

'I can't help with that. There are no easily accessible records about them. At least, not here. The owners might have been American, as the ship was sold in New York. Or maybe British and then American. Or American and then British. Who knows? The American Revolution was coming to an end at that time, so the situation over there would have been ... fluid.' Kwan allowed himself a small smile at the thought, before becoming more serious. 'But whoever owned her, she was mostly based right here. Out of Bristol.'

Well, Abidemi thought, *he's right about that, at least.*

'And the captain? Who was the captain?'

'There were a number of ship's masters. The first was—'

'I'm only interested in 1791. Who was the captain then?'

Kwan consulted his notepad.

'Theodore Bradock, of Greenock, Scotland. He was ship's master from 1785 till 1794.'

'What else do we know about him?'

'Nothing.' She must have let the disappointment show on her face, because something compelled him to add: 'Look, miss. These are shipping records we're talking about, here. You're not going to get a detailed biography of the crew. That's not what shipping records are for.'

'I guess not.' She rose languidly from the chair, made to leave, and then stopped. She turned back, dropping her hands into her backpack. Kwan watched her warily.

'You know, doc, that was a pretty reckless thing you did this morning: calling the filth.'

'You broke into my home. Attacked my wife and my son.' Kwan's voice was shaky but defiant. 'You can't do stuff like that and get away with it.'

'Actually, doc. I can. What you did was dumb. And people got hurt because of it.' She continued to rummage in the backpack.

'You're gonna have to pay for that. There must be . . .' She struggled to find the right word and failed. '. . . *Gbese*.'

'Bay . . .?'

The hands in the backpack found what they were looking for. Mouth tight with disapproval, Abi stepped rapidly towards the *oyinbo*. Kwan's eyes widened in fear.

She tossed three passports onto the desk.

'There's a business in this here city called Harlequin Taxis. Run by a lowlife. Name of Dean Slim. He's . . .' She reached back to her conversation with Hollie. '. . . *trafficking* women. I found these passports in his office. There's at least one more. From Liberia.' She placed her hands on the desk and leaned over, staring into the *oyinbo*'s eyes. 'You call up your cop buddies and you tell 'em, okay? About the trafficking. Do that and *gbese* is satisfied. Don't do it, and you'll answer to me. Got it?'

'Um . . . yes. I can do that.' Kwan stared down at the passports. His jaw firmed. 'I *will* do that.'

Abi removed her hands from the desk and stood up. She favoured him with a small smile.

'Well, doc. Thanks for your help. I'll be on my way, now.'

Air puffed out of Kwan's mouth in an explosive sigh.

'That's it?'

'Of course that's it,' Abi said, glancing down at him in surprise. 'What else would it be?'

'I thought you were going to kill me.'

Abi gave the man a long, slow, look.

'You ain't on my list.'

She slipped out of his office and followed a gaggle of students towards the exit, her boots squeaking on the polished floor.

Twenty-Five

Ethan's cell phone was ringing out. The caller ID said—
The letters on the caller ID made no sense at all. They were just letters. An H. And that was an L. He could tell they were real words but . . .

RHODE ISLAND. The caller ID was from Rhode Island. Spam. He hit DECLINE, heart thumping against his ribs.

'Is this thing any good?' he asked.

Raymond Yeung shrugged his shoulders.

'It's the best our witnesses could come up with. Who knows?'

The face staring up at him from the paper was long, and thin, and Black. The sketch showed a crescent-shaped scar sitting at the high point of each cheek, the eyes above them flat and menacing, like a shark's, the hair close-cropped to the point of baldness.

'Where'd the top of his head come from?' Ethan asked. 'I thought the guy was wearing a baseball cap.'

'From Jennifer Okoro. Nearly all of this is from her, to be honest. The doorman was basically useless.'

'Let me guess. "They all look alike."?'

'Yeah, pretty much.'

'We got a version with a hat?'

'Here. Look.'

'Great. Let's not put it out to the media just yet, in case it's crap. I'm not sure Ms Okoro was in her right mind when she saw this guy. Keep it in-house for now.'

'Okay.'

His cell phone rang again. Same Rhode Island number. The spammer's computer system must be glitching today. He declined it with a snort of annoyance.

'In other news,' Raymond announced, 'the nerds got a partial on our perp's van. Illinois plate. Not as good as I'd hoped but it's something.'

'How many possibles are we looking at?'

'They're working on that now. My guess is, once we've eliminated anything that can't be a box van, you're still going to be looking at a couple of hundred.'

'Yeah, right. Try—'

His cell phone rang again. Rhode Island. Again.

'Fuck this.' He shut the thing off. Took a breath. 'Okay, look. When we get the list of possibles, start with anyone or any company that sounds African.'

'African?'

'Yeah. Anything with too many vowels that isn't Italian. Come to think of it, unless you're *certain* it's Italian, run them down too. *A. Bello* doesn't sound African at all. Until you know what the *A* stands for.'

'You don't think it's a long shot?'

'Of course it's a long shot. But our guy has a sense of humour. An African sense of humour. *Super Eagles*? *A. Bello*? There's got to be at least a chance that if that van is registered in anything other than his real name, there's an African connection somewhere. And dollars to doughnuts, if he's used his *real* name, it's going to be at least as African as Oko . . . *Fuck*!'

The phone was ringing again. It took a second or two to realize it was the landline.

'Chicago PD. Lieutenant Krol speaking.'

'You're a hard man to get ahold of, lieutenant. Detective Nicole Gutierrez, City of Providence PD.' The voice at the other end of the line was brisk and businesslike. There was only the faintest hint of an Hispanic accent.

'Providence, Rhode Island?'

'The very same.'

'Sorry, detective. I thought you were spam.'

'I've been called worse.'

Ethan laughed at that.

'How can I help you?'

'I'm just off of CPIC, and I think you can help me with a case of mine. I want to know everything you know about drowning at sea. On dry land.'

Twenty-Six

*A*bi's bedroom had no lock, so she'd wedged the mattress against the door to guard against Hollie, or anyone else for that matter, barging in uninvited. It wouldn't do to have the *oyinbos* see her with her right eye hanging out. The moist orb was hanging on her cheek, the squishy string of her augmented optic nerve, the delicate pathway between eyeball and brain, the only thing stopping it from rolling onto the floor.

The amulet was doing its best. But even with a healthy dose of drugs, her eye socket felt itchy and uncomfortable. Of course, the absence of an eye was not the only source of discomfort. The silver disc parked across the empty socket and pushing microscopic filaments into her cerebellum was a much bigger part of the problem.

She gave a little huff of pain as the *opolo abe* continued with its work. Her right eye was shut down because its angle of vision was making her nauseous. Her left eye, however, was open, the tiny, *oyinbo* bedroom a blurred backdrop to the stream of readouts scrolling across her retina.

The scrolling stopped. Polygonal, unchanging script flashed insistently.

'Like I'd just take you at your word,' she muttered. But she knew the little machine was right. The cacophony of signals she'd had to filter out on arrival were streamlined now, coherent. The *oyinbos*' ill-disciplined use of electromagnetic wavelengths had been demodulated into something she could work with.

She reached out with the augmented parts of her brain.

Across the room, the cluster of laptops and mobile phones that Hollie Rogers called the *Apollo Cagey* flickered into life.

She had . . . what had Hollie called it? Oh . . . yes.

She had Wi-Fi.

She sat patiently while the *opolo abe* disentangled itself from the inside of her head and sterilized the eye socket. Once it was done, she replaced her eye, returned the *opolo abe* to her backpack, and tidied the room.

'What have you been doing in here?' Hollie asked, sometime later, when she put her head around the door. 'Your room smells like disinfectant.'

'Brain surgery, babe. You know how it is.'

'Ha ha.' Hollie stepped into the room. Peered over Abi's shoulder.

Abi, sitting in front of the *opolo keji*, was staring at websites that made no sense.

'What are you looking at?'

'Nothing I can use. So far this whole deal has been nothing but a trip for biscuits.'

Hollie giggled.

'You really do talk funny.'

'So you've said.'

'Maybe I can help. What are you trying to find?'

Once again, Abi hesitated, unwilling to get the *oyinbo* woman involved. Just as before, however, she needed the help.

'I'm looking for a . . . a finder of ancestors.' She waved a frustrated hand at the screens in front her. 'But all I'm getting are crumbs and hucksters.'

Hollie examined the *opolo keji* with a bemused expression.

'"Madame Bovan, genuine psychic. Ten minutes for just five dollars." Oh my god. "Speak to your departed loved ones . . ."!' Hollie dissolved into giggles. '*This* . . . this . . . is not the sort of thing I'd have you down for. You want to . . . to . . . speak to the *dead*?' The giggles were overlaid now with snorts of derision.

'No, I do not want to speak to the dead,' Abi snapped. 'Speaking to the dead is not possible. At least not . . . here. I want to know who the dead were is all.'

'Any dead in particular, or are you not . . . *particular*?' Hollie's disturbing blue eyes sparkled with mischief.

'The guy I'm looking for went by the name Theodore Bradock. He lived in the Year of Our Lord 1791.'

'Why? I mean, why are you looking? What's Theodore Bradock to you?'

Everything.

'I'm looking for his kids. And his kids' kids. And his—'

'Oh . . . *oh*!' The disturbing eyes widened in understanding. 'You're not looking for ancestors. You're looking for *descendants*.'

'I am?'

'Yeah, you are. And what you need is a frigging genealogist. Someone who traces family trees and shit like that.'

Without a finger being raised or a word spoken, the displays on the *opolo keji* went through a profound shift. A new website appeared, offering the very services Abi was looking for.

'Like this?'

'Not quite.' Hollie grinned wickedly. 'Asheville, North Carolina is too long a bus ride for us. Find someone closer.'

Twenty-Seven

'It says on your website that you're a qualified genealogist.'
Abi tried not to sound sceptical.

'That's right,' Angela Cleland replied breezily. 'I'm a genealogist and I'm fully certified. Please sit. Sit. No formality here.'
She removed a pile of folders from a slightly dusty sofa to make
room for Abi and Hollie. Unsure what to do with them, she
balanced the folders atop a pile of books that had already been
wedged into the windowsill behind her desk. The folders tee-
tered dangerously, silhouetted against the rain-sodden daylight
on the other side of the glass.

Apparently satisfied, Angela sat down at her desk. Only her
head was visible above various piles of paper.

'Now then, what can I do for the two of you?'

Abi could feel herself frowning. Max Kwan's office had been
cluttered, but this was mess on an entirely different level. The
genealogist's office was even smaller than the lecturer's and was
quite clearly part of her home, a small, unimpressive rock-cube
that Hollie had described as 'a semi'.

'This is one crummy joint,' she muttered to Hollie as she sat down. 'Maybe we should make tracks and try someplace else.' The sharp tang of dust flicked at her nostrils.

'The reviews are good,' Hollie whispered back. 'Give the woman a chance, eh?'

Abi sighed.

'I'm trying to track down the . . . *descendants* of a guy who lived a coupla hundred years ago. Went by the name of Theodore Bradock.'

'I see. Do you know anything else about him?'

'Like what?'

'Like when he was born, what parish, that kind of thing?'

'No. I thought that was your job.'

Angela favoured her with a tired smile.

'Do you know when he was alive?'

'The Year of Our Lord 1791.'

The genealogist raised an eyebrow at that.

'Any idea how old he was then?'

'Nope.'

'Or where he was living?'

'Here, I guess. Bristol. He was a ship's captain.'

'Well, that's something. You wouldn't happen to know the name of the ship, would you?'

'*Esperance*. She was based in Bristol and owned by the Wolfe Shipping Company.'

'Anything else you can tell me? Something about the shipping company, perhaps?'

''Fraid not, lady. That's pretty much it.'

Angela Cleland pursed her lips, leaching them of colour.

'It's not much to go on, I'm afraid. The ties to Bristol are useful. And if he was a ship's captain, he'd probably be at least thirty years old.' She stared vacantly into the middle distance.

'I have a few ideas,' she said, after a moment or two. 'We might be able to get somewhere. But no promises, you understand. If you're still interested my rate is twenty-five pounds an hour.'

'That's quite expensive,' Hollie said. 'Maybe—'

'Twenty-five it is,' Abi cut in, not in the mood to dicker. 'How long before you can tell me what I need to know?'

'Oh, gosh. That's tricky in a case like this. Several weeks at a minimum. Probably several months. We can't do anything really until we can tie Theodore Bradock to both the *Esperance* and some birth or death records. That alone could take months. It's a little bit like looking for a needle in a haystack.'

'Months is too long. Weeks too, maybe. We gotta move quicker.'

'We can't move quicker. Not unless you have a magic wand.'

A slow smile spread across Abi's face.

'I can do better than a magic wand, lady. Come home with me. You can work with the *opolo keji*.'

'The Apollo what?'

'It's like a mini supercomputer,' Hollie said excitedly. 'Totally next level. It can go places you didn't even know existed.'

'And this . . . mini supercomputer . . . is going to help me look up records from the eighteenth century?' Angela's face was a mask of disbelief.

'If you can tell it what to look for, the *opolo keji* will find it,' Abi said. 'Anything – ' she scanned her memories for the word ' – anything *digitized*, that is. I'd do it myself but I ain't got the skills of no genealogist like you.'

'And where will I find this mini supercomputer?'

Abi was vaguely aware of Hollie's hand fluttering at her wrist, but she didn't understand why.

'Knowle West,' she said firmly.

The genealogist's face became suddenly stiff. Hollie sighed.

'I'm sorry,' Angela said, icily polite. 'But I don't think going to your home is appropriate.'

Abi put her hand inside her jacket and withdrew a large wad of slick, multi-coloured *oyinbo* currency. With careful deliberation she spread a wide fan of notes atop one of the piles of paper that littered the genealogist's desk.

'That's five hundred bucks—'

'Quid,' Hollie whispered.

'Five hundred quid: half a G on the nail. Work with me on the *opolo keji* and I'll double it. On top of your hourly rate.'

Hollie took one look at the genealogist's face and burst out laughing.

'Knowle West ain't half so scary now, is it?'

Twenty-Eight

Wednesday the 9th: 9.00 a.m. EDT

Ethan hated the East Coast. It was cramped, and dirty, and full of roads that went nowhere. Even the GPS had trouble making sense of it.

He tried to blame his sour mood on the fact that he'd driven through the night to get here. But there was more to it than that. He'd spent an hour parked on some middle-of-nowhere road in eastern Ohio, unable to drive because of a blinding headache. Literally blinding. With no warning, jagged white shards had shot across his vision, a pulsing accompaniment to the stabbing pain at the back of his eyes. He'd barely gotten off the inter-state alive. The attack had faded after a few minutes but he'd remained parked, hands shaking on the steering wheel, screwing up the courage to get moving again.

Maybe he should have flown. It was quicker. Safer for sure. But then he'd still be in Chicago, waiting for the fucking bean counters to process the paperwork, or – distinct possibility – tell him to go take a hike. This way, assuming he didn't kill himself first, he could move shit forward.

Grit scratched at the underside of his eyelids. He turned left where the GPS told him to.

The street was wide by East Coast standards, lined with old, full-leaved trees. Basking in the early morning sun, they cast long shadows across mowed lawns and manicured shrubbery. Well-maintained wooden houses rose up behind them. They would have been suburban if they hadn't been jammed so close together. It was as if some giant had taken Oak Park in its hands and squeezed. The thought brought a brief smile to his lips.

Of course, Oak Park didn't have hills. The road was climbing steeply and curved for no apparent reason. It was only when he topped the summit that he saw the white bulk of a police cruiser. He pulled up in front of a handsome home with expensive cedar siding and steep gables, its dark, shingled roof splashed with moss.

A slim, trouser-suited woman came up to him as he got out of the car.

'Detective Lieutenant Nicole Gutierrez. Lieutenant Krol, I presume?'

'Sure am.' He shook the proffered hand. She had a firm, confident grip. The eyes that stared up at him were brown and good-humoured.

'Let me show you around. We finished processing the scene yesterday, so it's just you, me, and a uni to hold back the gawkers. House is empty.'

'You have many of them? Gawkers, I mean.'

'Monday and yesterday, sure. Today, not so much. But it's early and this is College Hill. These are not the sort of folks who make a fast start to the day.' She looked around, lips quirking. 'There'll be a curtain twitching somewhere, though.'

The uniform, who was standing at the front door, opened it to let them in. The first thing Ethan noticed was the reek of seawater. He wrinkled his nose.

'Hard to miss, isn't it?' Gutierrez said.

Ethan just nodded, looking around. The house was old and slightly battered looking on the inside. Not battered because it was run down. Battered because it was lived in. There were terracotta tiles on the floor, a few of which were cracked, and oak panelling on the hallway walls, some of which were scratched. The prints that hung down from an old-fashioned picture rail looked expensive.

'You said there were three vics?'

'Yes.' Gutierrez's professional tone acquired a distinct edge. 'A mother and two kids. Sonia Vielfrass Hollander, aged forty-two, married. She was a history professor at Brown: Pre-Colombian America or something like that. Two kids: Edward, sixteen, and Olivia, fourteen. All found in the living room; all drowned.'

'What about the husband?'

'James Hollander. Asshole banker. He called it in Monday morning, claiming his wife and kids had been killed on Sunday, but he won't talk without his lawyer. What I just told you came from the nine-one-one tape. We're going to interview him this afternoon. I'd arrest him right now if I could figure out how he did it.'

'You think he's good for it?'

Gutierrez sucked on her teeth in frustration.

'Honestly? No. Unless he has some connection to Chicago or your vics. Plus, your suspect is Black. This guy's about as Caucasian as they come. If he had any less colour, he'd be see-through.'

Ethan smiled wryly.

'Any sign of a struggle?'

'Not really.' The Providence detective opened the door to the living room. Like the hallway panelling it was oak and looked heavy.

The room beyond was what Ethan had heard referred to as 'shabby chic'. Nothing matched, and everything looked slightly worn, but it was all expensive, from the salt-stained Persian rug on the hardwood floor, to the antique European furniture in multiple styles, to the modern but deliberately retro chandelier. Everything seemed to be in its assigned, studiously asymmetrical place.

Except for a pile of books stacked neatly on the floor.

'What's that about?' he asked.

'We think our perp cleared a bookshelf to make space for something.' Gutierrez pointed to a horizontal void in a tall bookshelf. 'He drilled a hole into the wall behind for some reason. But also there, and there, and there.'

There were holes in all four walls.

'Our guy did the same thing in Chicago. It sure looked like he must have bolted something in, but we've no idea what, or why.'

'Our working theory is cameras.'

'Really?'

'Yes. Whoever did this was here a long time. He's careful, and meticulous. He puts the books on the floor, but in a tidy stack. He disturbs almost nothing. This – all this – was planned, maybe for months. If he's a planner and he took his time, there's a good chance he's a sadist. And if he's a sadist, maybe he recorded it for posterity. From multiple angles.' Gutierrez must have mistaken the look he was giving her for scepticism, because she added apologetically, 'It's pretty thin, I know, but it's the best we could come up with.'

'Which is way more than we did. We came up with fuck all. Except maybe that our perp has a thing for mindless drilling.'

The Rhode Island officer chuckled. Unbent a little.

'We think he drowned them in the bath – either the one across the hallway, or the one upstairs. They're both big enough. But—'

'No sign of a struggle in either bathroom and no water slopped between the bathroom and where you found the bodies,' Ethan cut in. He pushed a scuffed toecap into the carpeting, watched a small residue of water well up around the sole. 'I'm guessing the water you found here drained out of the vics' clothes?'

'Right. On all counts.' Gutierrez grimaced. 'It's a stumper.'

Ethan was staring at the ceiling.

'You get anything back from the medical examiner?' he asked.

'Not yet. Later today, maybe.'

'I'll bet you Cubs tickets to doughnuts that you're going to find plaster under at least one of your vics' fingernails.'

'Well, I'll be . . .' Gutierrez murmured. 'We did *not* catch that.' Following Ethan's gaze, she pulled out her phone and pointed the camera above her head.

The ceiling was marked with the same parallel gouges he'd seen in the Okoros' apartment. More of them, in fact, but harder to see because the ceiling itself was in shadow.

Ethan grabbed a wooden chair and placed it under the chandelier. He gave the chair a slightly distrustful look. It was a beautiful antique piece, with faded velvet upholstery, a carved, curving back, and legs to match. He wasn't at all sure it could take his weight. With a muttered imprecation he stepped up.

The chair creaked but refused to give way. His head was inches from the bottom of the ornate glass. He reached out and tapped it. A mournful, crystal chime floated across the room.

'You see something?'

'Yeah. I think so.' Ethan glanced down at the carpet, gauging the distance. 'You may want to get your forensic guys back here. There's water in the chandelier. I'm going to take a wild guess and say it's seawater.'

'You have got to be kidding me.'

'I wish I was.' He stepped gingerly back to the floor.

Gutierrez's gaze went from Ethan to the chandelier and back. 'This is just fucking weird.'

The uni from outside stuck his head around the door.

'Lieutenant?'

'Yes?' Both Ethan and Gutierrez answered at the same time. Ethan stepped back with an apologetic wave of the hand.

'I got a guy outside says he might have seen something. I asked a few preliminaries, and we missed him on the first canvass because he was out of town. But he lives across the street, and he was here on Sunday.'

Ethan and Gutierrez exchanged a look.

'Bring him in,' she ordered.

Emmanuel Ratcliffe was just a kid, really. Tall and gawky looking, with ripped jeans, a faded tee shirt promoting a band Ethan had never heard of, and expensive Converse sneakers. Unkempt, floppy hair kept falling across his eyes.

'You're a student at Brown?' Gutierrez was asking.

'Yes.'

'And how'd you know to come over and talk to my officer?'

'My housemates told me Prof Hollander had been murdered. Said the police had been around to talk to them but they hadn't seen anything.'

Gutierrez produced a notebook.

'Did you know the professor?'

'Sure. I mean, not well, but she's faculty, so we'd see her around campus and such. And she was always friendly if she met us on the street. One of my housemates took a class with her last year. She was cool.'

The boy looked sad.

'You weren't at home when my officers came around?'

'No. My girlfriend has an internship out of town for the summer. In Boston. I was visiting her.'

'Why not visit on the weekend?'

'She was working. We arranged to meet up Monday and Tuesday.'

'And when did you get back?'

'About thirty minutes ago.'

'And when did you leave to go visit her?'

'First thing Monday morning. Maybe seven a.m.'

'Okay, good.' Gutierrez flashed him an encouraging smile. 'So. What do you have to tell me?'

'Yeah, well, I live across the street like I said, and my room looks over this way. It's in the attic, so I kinda get a bird's eye view of what goes on over here.'

'And was something going on?'

'Just the usual, at first. Pretty much every Sunday the whole family packs up and heads out somewhere. Last Sunday was no different. They piled into their van and drove off.'

'What time was that do you think?'

'Same as always. About nine thirty.'

'Then what happened?'

'About ten o'clock, this van pulls up in their driveway, and this dude gets out of the cab and starts wheeling out this big-ass crate from the back of the van. And I'm thinking, "man you are so S.O.L. You just missed these guys and now you're gonna have to reload the freaking crate and come back tomorrow." That thing looked *heavy*. I felt sorry for the guy.'

'And is that what happened? Did he reload the crate?'

'Uh, no. He drags that thing up the front steps and parks it on the porch. And now I'm thinking this dude is *strong*. He stands at the front door for a couple of minutes, waiting for them to answer the doorbell, I guess. And all the while I'm waiting for him to give it up and manhandle that sucker back off the porch.'

'I'm guessing that didn't happen?'

'Exactamundo. The front door opened.'

Ethan found himself opening his mouth to ask the question but forced it shut again just in time.

'Did he open it, or did someone open it for him?'

The boy frowned.

'I'm not sure. I *think* someone opened it, though I didn't see anyone. But I'm pretty sure the dude was standing by the crate when it opened, so I don't see how he could have done it himself.'

'Is it possible the crate was blocking your view of the door?'

'Maybe. Yeah, sure. It was a big-ass crate like I said, maybe four-foot, five-foot tall, so it could totally have blocked the view.'

'And what did this man look like?'

'African-American dude. Real tall. Over six foot, easy. Thin, like a basketball player, you know. But freaking *strong*.'

The boy's eyes glittered with admiration. Ethan wanted to throttle him. This was a man who'd murdered *children*, for god's sake, and all the kid could do was talk about how strong the creep was.

'And after the door opened, the man went inside?'

'Yes.'

'With the crate?'

'Totally.'

'Did you see anyone help him bring the crate inside, a glimpse of a hand, something like that?'

'Uh-uh.' The boy shook his head. 'Dude just wheeled it in.'

'And how long was he inside for?'

The boy hesitated.

'I'm not sure. I didn't see him leave. He was there for at least a couple of hours though. I remember going to the kitchen to make a sandwich about twelve thirty and the van was still there. But after that, I kinda lost track of it.'

'Okay. No worries. What about the professor and her family? Did you see them come home?'

'No. Sorry.' The boy shook his head.

'Not a problem. You've been very helpful.' Gutierrez turned to Ethan. 'Any questions, lieutenant?'

'Just a few.' He fished his phone out of his pocket and brought up the police sketch of A. Bello. 'Did the guy look anything like this?'

The kid frowned.

'Maybe? I was like, too far away to see his face that well. But the shape of it seems right.'

'Okay. This van the man arrived in. Can you describe it?'

'Not really. It was a van, man. They all look alike.'

Ethan gave the kid a friendly smile.

'Well, was it all of a piece, like a Ford Transit or a giant minivan, or was it a box truck: you know, like those U-Hauls you see on the road? You're a student, I bet you know what a U-Haul looks like, right?'

The boy grinned.

'Sure. It was like a U-Haul. Almost exactly.'

'And what colour was it?'

'No colour, really. It was white all over.'

'Any writing?'

The kid screwed up his face, trying to remember.

'I don't think so.'

Ethan nodded.

'That's all I got. Thank you, Emmanuel, you've been—'

'Wait, wait!' The boy was practically jumping up and down with excitement. 'There was something else. It's just come back to me. The plates. I remember thinking that you don't see many of those around here. Kind of exotic, you know? I don't remember the number, for sure, but I definitely remember the plates. The plates were from Illinois. LAND OF LINCOLN, yeah?'

Twenty-Nine

Wednesday the 9th: 2.54 p.m. EDT

Ethan, sitting in the passenger seat of Gutierrez's immaculate vehicle, gave a low whistle.

'So, I guess this is how the one per cent live.'

'I guess.' Gutierrez snorted in amusement. 'Old money. There's a lot of that in Rhode Island.'

The driveway to Hope House was long and designedly impressive: cobbled, well maintained, and lined with tall trees. They perfectly framed the three storeys of tan, neo-classical stone that was their destination. Blue sky provided a picturesque backdrop to the entire edifice. The sky itself was wide and clear, the way sky is when it sits atop an open body of water. Ethan didn't have to see the ocean to know it was there, or to guess that the rear of the house would overlook it.

The driveway terminated in a wide circle that allowed Gutierrez to park at the foot of porticoed stone steps. They were worn with use and climbed gently towards a pair of massive wooden doors. Except for the modern gaze of security cameras, it was like stepping into the past.

A short, Hispanic woman that Ethan took to be the housekeeper escorted them across a marbled hallway and into a drawing room at the back of the house. The room was drowned in light. It poured in through the high windows, so bright that everything else appeared in silhouette. Beyond the windows, a sloping lawn terminated abruptly at a sharp drop that gave way to a wide expanse of water. There was a steeply rising headland on the far side, dotted with modern, crowded-together buildings. None was as impressive as the one he was standing in.

The view, and the backlit nature of the room, distracted him momentarily from its occupants.

'These are the detectives,' the housekeeper announced.

A tall, stately looking woman with grey hair, a simple black dress and pearls rose to meet them. From the state of her eyes, she'd only recently stopped crying. A much younger man, mid-forties and haughty, stepped up beside her. Before they could introduce themselves, however, another man stepped in front of them: grey suit, grey hair, bland tie. He extended a firm hand.

'David Tern,' he announced, his smile wide and oleaginous. 'I'm representing Mr Hollander in this matter. Ms Vielfrass,' he added, indicating the woman in pearls, 'has very kindly allowed us to use this room for the interview. It's rather nicer than the police station, I think.'

Ethan refused to smile back. So did Gutierrez.

'Can I arrange for tea? Coffee?' Ms Vielfrass asked.

'No thank you, ma'am,' Gutierrez replied.

'Then I'll leave you to it.' Ms Vielfrass glided out of the room. The housekeeper followed.

The lawyer and his client sat down in high-backed armchairs that must have been at least a hundred years old, a modern glass coffee table pressing against their shins. The only feasible option for the detectives was a deep leather sofa. The two of them sat together – perched, really – uncomfortable in the opulence.

Gutierrez pulled out her notebook.

'Thank you for agreeing to speak with us, Mr Hollander. We appreciate the cooperation. And we are so very sorry for your loss.'

'Before we get started,' Tern said, staring at Ethan, 'perhaps you can explain why there's a Chicago police officer in the room. You're a little outside your jurisdiction, detective.'

'He's helping us with our inquiries,' Gutierrez said, before Ethan could answer. 'There are . . . similarities with a Chicago case. Detective Krol is very interested in what your client has to say.'

'You're not suggesting that Mr Hollander has anything to do with a killing in Chicago, I hope.'

'No, sir. Let me make this clear, Mr Tern. Your client is not the target of our investigations at this time. We just want to hear what he has to say.'

A faint smile quirked at James Hollander's lips. The lips were thin, in keeping with the pale, narrow face and washed-out blue eyes. His suit, like the lawyer's, was grey. Even the cut was identical. Unlike the lawyer, he wore no tie.

Tern favoured the detectives with a small nod.

'Thank you for the assurance, detective. In that case, I'll try and keep out of your way.' He sat back in his armchair, relaxed but watchful.

Gutierrez redirected her attention to Hollander.

'Can you tell me where you went Sunday morning?'

Hollander's pale eyes blinked with what might have been surprise.

'Is that really relevant?' he asked impatiently. He glanced over at his lawyer.

'We need to build a timeline of events, sir. Helps us put everything in context.'

The lawyer signalled his agreement.

'Oh very well. If you must. We come here every Sunday to spend the day with Dottie — my mother-in-law. You met her just now. This is her house. Been in her family for generations.'

And I bet you can't wait to move in.

'What time did you leave your house?'

'About nine thirty, quarter till ten.'

'You drove, I imagine?'

'Of course.'

'In what vehicle?'

'A Dodge Chrysler minivan.'

'And who was in the vehicle?'

'My family. Sonia and the kids.'

'When you left, did you leave anyone at home? Housekeeper, guest, anyone like that?'

'No.'

'Were you expecting anyone at the house that day? A friend, or maybe a plumber, anyone like that?'

'No.'

'Does anyone outside your immediate family have a key to your house?'

'No.'

'Okay. What time did you and your family get home?'

'About six.'

'When you got home, before you entered the house, did you notice anything unusual?'

'No.'

'Did you see any kind of parked van, a box van, like . . . like a U-Haul?'

Ethan smiled at that.

'Not that I remember.'

'Okay. Who entered the house first?'

'Sonia: she had the key. Then the kids. I stayed behind to clean out the van.'

'And how long did that take?'

'Cleaning out the van? Two or three minutes. Olivia always manages – managed – to make a mess.' Grief twisted at the man's face for the briefest of moment's. For the first time, Ethan felt a stab of sympathy for him. Asshole banker or not, lawyered up or not, the man was grieving.

'When you entered the house, what happened next?'

'I walked into the hallway, and I was heading for the pantry when I saw Sonia's legs sticking out through the living-room door. I thought she'd fallen and hurt herself, so I rushed over to help and then I saw . . .'

He turned away. The lawyer reached over and patted his knee. Gutierrez waited.

'Sorry . . . sorry. I . . . uh . . . I saw my kids. They were collapsed on the back stairs. They were all . . . my wife, my kids, they . . . they were lying there dead.'

Ethan and Gutierrez exchanged a look. Sooner or later someone would have to tell James Hollander that his family had died a lot less quickly than he thought.

But not today.

'And then what happened?' Gutierrez's voice was soft, and feminine, and full of sympathy.

'Whoever did this must have snuck up behind me. They stuck me in the neck with a needle. The next thing I remember, I woke up on my bed and it was Monday morning.' A grimace.

'I thought maybe I'd had some nightmare. I called out and rushed down the stairs. But it was true.' Hollander's voice dropped to a hoarse whisper. 'It was all true.'

'When you went down the stairs, were your wife and kids where you last saw them?'

'No. They'd been moved into the middle of the living room and drenched in water. Seawater. The place smelled like the beach at low tide. I tried to wake them up, but they were cold. God, they were cold! That's when I called nine one one.'

Holland bit his bottom lip, turning it white.

'Any questions, Detective Krol?'

'If you don't mind my asking, James – can I call you James?'

'I prefer Jim.'

'Jim. Thank you. If you don't mind me asking, what do you do for a living? I mean, I understand you work at a bank, but I don't know what that means.'

Hollander managed a faint smile.

'I'm an investment banker. I introduce people who need money for their business to people who want to lend money to businesses. And we take a cut off the top.'

'Do any of these businesses have connections to Africa?'

The banker frowned then, thinking.

'Maybe. Some of our clients are in the energy business. Oil, power generation, renewables. Some of their projects are in Africa.'

'Have you ever been there?'

'Africa?' A short, dismissive laugh. 'No.'

'What about your wife?'

'A couple of times, I think, several years ago. She travelled a lot before we married and settled down. She's mentioned it a couple of times.'

'Where did she go?'

'Ghana, maybe? South Africa? I don't recall. I wasn't that interested to be honest. No skiing.'

Ethan made sure to smile politely.

'Could it have been Nigeria?'

'Maybe. But I really don't remember. It could have been Timbuktu – is that in Africa?' Ethan shrugged. 'Well, anyway, it could have been Timbuktu for all I know. I'd just be guessing.'

'That's okay. Does the name Okoro mean anything to you?'

'No.'

'How about Bello? As in Bello Plumbing.'

'No.'

'Do you ever visit Chicago?'

'Very rarely. I was there on business . . . five, six years ago, I think.'

'And did that business have any connection to Africa?'

'To Africa? In *Chicago*? Absolutely not. I don't remember the details, but it had something to do with pharmaceuticals. Bond financing for R and D, something like that.'

'Fair enough. One last thing. When you went into the house after cleaning out your minivan, you told Lieutenant Gutierrez you were headed to the pantry?'

'Yes.'

'Why? The pantry's not usually the place for car trash, or stuff your kids had left behind. Why go there?'

'I . . . I'm not sure.' Hollander's pale eyes flickered upwards as he struggled to remember. 'Oh, wait. I was looking for a can of Raid.'

'Raid?'

'The hallway was alive with bugs. Needed taking care of.'

'Huh.' He glanced at Gutierrez before returning his attention to Hollander. 'Thanks, Jim. That was very helpful. Do you think your mother-in-law would mind giving us a few minutes of her time?'

Thirty

*D*ottie Vielfrass agreed to meet them in the summer house, which turned out to be a cedar shed on steroids. It was maybe a hundred yards from the main home, with furniture, and power, and plate-glass windows overlooking the sea. It sat between a steep drop to the water and a crushed limestone track that ran parallel to the shore at the back of the house. The track, Ethan guessed, would have been the old rear entrance for servants and tradesmen.

Unlike the main house, which reeked of antiquity, the summer house was minimalist modern, the seating light wood with finely patterned upholstery. There was even a computer station and a large, ultra-modern TV. Sea whispered ceaselessly through the wooden walls, breathing salt into the air.

Ethan sat down when he and Gutierrez were invited to do so, feeling far more relaxed than in the Brahmin opulence of the drawing room.

'How can I help you, officers?'

Gutierrez allowed Ethan to take the lead.

'We were hoping you could help us out with some background, ma'am.'

'Call me Dottie, please.'

'Thank you, Dottie. And once again, we are so very sorry for your loss. Jim mentioned that he thought Sonia had visited Africa when she was younger. Is that true?'

Dottie smiled in remembrance.

'Yes, a couple of times. She was very adventurous. Quite the world traveller, in fact. At least until she got married and Teddy came along.'

'Do you remember where she went?'

'A safari in East Africa was one trip. She hiked Mount Kilimanjaro. She wanted to see it before the snow disappeared from the top. And the other trip was a tour of West Africa. She went to Liberia, and Sierra Leone, and . . . Ghana, I think.'

'Did she spend any time in Nigeria?'

'No. That wasn't one of the countries she was interested in visiting.'

'Any idea why that would be the case?'

Dottie's eyes took on a hooded look.

'I couldn't say.'

'You sure?'

'I'm not in the habit of repeating myself, detective.'

'Does the name Okoro mean anything to you?'

'I'm afraid not.'

'How about Bello? Or Bello Plumbing?'

'No. Does this have something to do with Sonia's death?'

'Possibly. Apart from Sonia, do you have any other children?'

'There's my son, Charles.' Dottie's face assumed an expression of distaste. 'He *insists* on being called Chuck. Thinks he's some kind of filmmaker, though he has absolutely *no* talent for it. He'd throw his entire inheritance away on one stupid project after another if I let him. As it is . . .' She sighed. 'Anyway, he's my only other child. My *only* child, now, I suppose.'

She looked away, staring over the ocean.

'Does Charles have any children?' Ethan prompted, after a moment or two. He was careful to keep his voice gentle.

'Yes. Sebastian and Claire. Lovely kids. They mostly live with Brenna, his ex-wife. I hate to say it, but it's better that way. Particularly now that he's living with that . . . that *woman*.'

'And who would that be?'

'Charlene something or other. God alone knows what gutter he found her in. Charlene isn't even her real name. It's something Chinese. Charlene is just what she goes by.'

'Do Charles and . . . *Charlene* live locally?'

'Yes. In Fox Point. Suffering for his art in the condo I pay for.' Dottie let loose a derisive snort.

'What about Brenna?'

'She lives close by. She's good about letting Charles see the children. Makes it easier.'

Ethan glanced over at Gutierrez to see if she had any follow-up. The Rhode Island detective shook her head. They rose to leave.

'Well, thank you for your time, Dottie. We'll see ourselves out.'

Neither officer said anything as they rounded the vast flank of the main house and headed for the car. It was only when she was unlocking it that Gutierrez gave voice to what was troubling her.

'You think the son is in danger?' she asked.

Ethan nodded.

'I do,' he said. 'There's a pattern to this – a connection – that we just can't see yet. But whatever it is, it involves families. Both

Okoro siblings ended up getting murdered, one after the other. And now we have a dead vic with a still-living brother. You ask me, I wouldn't want to be Chuck Vielfrass right now. No matter how big his inheritance.'

'And the mother? There was a mother killed in Nigeria, right?'

'Yeah. Mother, son, granddaughter. The complete fucking trifecta.'

Gutierrez looked over at the house, her expression turning wry.

'I guess she's pretty safe up here. She has *staff*, for chrissakes. I doubt this place is ever empty, so our guy's not going to be able to sneak in like he did in College Hill.'

Ethan followed Gutierrez's gaze. The house was massive, like a fortress. Security cameras. An alarm system. The big double doors looked impenetrable.

Still.

'You sure you want to take the chance?'

Gutierrez gave him a rueful shake of the head.

'I'll get the unis to keep an eye on the front drive, in case that van of yours shows up. And I'll arrange some protection for Chuck.'

She slid into the driver's seat, started up the engine.

'Let's hit the road, Chicago. Things to do, people to see.'

Thirty-One

Wednesday the 9th: 9.07 p.m. BST

'Your computer system is amazing!' Angela Cleland was saying. 'I've never seen anything like it – ever. You could make an absolute fortune with this! And you made it yourself?'

'Yes,' Abi replied absently. She was staring out of her bedroom window, looking at the long narrow strip of gravel, cracked paving stones and weeds that comprised Hollie's back garden. Only now was it finally starting to get dark. There was a kind of twilight here that seemed to go on forever. The *oyinbo* sun, when not obscured by clouds, rolled across the sky too slowly, like a ball coated in syrup.

Not like home at all. She ignored the brief, aching knot in her chest.

Hollie and Angela were staring at her strangely.

'Er . . . sorry?'

'I said: "Are you a computer scientist?"' Angela asked.

'Nah. But I'm good at k-balling. Building things, I mean. My old man taught me.'

The knot again. Sharper. Less brief.

'Yes, well, even if you're not a computer scientist, you should get this thing patented or something. You could be a tech billionaire, easy.' The genealogist rubbed a pale hand across the makeshift manual interface. 'It's so fast!'

Abi bit on her tongue and nodded. Truth was, it had been painfully slow. She had avoided using either voice or mental commands to operate the *opolo keji* directly. Instead, having reconfigured the keyboard to display scrawny *oyinbo* lettering, she'd allowed the genealogist to treat it like the computer she thought it was and tap in searches with slow fingers. She'd had no choice, because only Angela Cleland knew what she was looking for. All Abi could do was try and figure out what the woman was up to and supplement the primitive keystrokes with instructions from her augments. And then, when the *opolo keji* came back from a sweep of the world's various data systems, she'd slowed down the output so that the genealogist could read it.

Not only slow. Exhausting. She swallowed back a yawn.

'Did you find what we were looking for?' Abi asked.

'Did I ever!' Angela's eyes gleamed in the fading light. 'We know that Theodore Bradock was born in Greenock, Scotland, on the twenty-eighth of September 1748. He spent most of his life at sea but still managed to marry twice. His first wife, Elizabeth Blythe, died in Bristol of smallpox in 1775. They had one child, Duncan, who died at the age of nine. Theodore didn't marry again until 1797. He was nearly fifty, so quite old for an eighteenth-century male. It looks like he'd given up the sea by then because his profession is listed as merchant. And he's moved back to Greenock, getting wed to a Margaret Ross, who was barely nineteen by the look of it. They had four children, three of whom survived to adulthood: Robert—'

'Sorry, lady, but we gotta cut to the chase. This Theodore guy: he got any direct descendants?'

The genealogist frowned.

'We've had this conversation, Abidemi. What you're looking for isn't as simple as a direct descendant. The man was alive well over two hundred years ago. He could have hundreds of thousands of direct descendants for all I know.' With a long-suffering sigh she opened a large, beige notebook and tapped on the pages. 'You gave me fifty-seven rules of descent. *Fifty-seven*. I know because I wrote them all down. That's an incredibly narrow subset. I don't know what you'd call the result but "direct descendant" doesn't even begin to do it justice.'

There was a very precise word for what Abi was looking for. But it was a *masu amfana* one. She couldn't pronounce it without using a voice simulator. And *that*, she was fairly sure, would freak them out.

'Sorry, lady. I know it's a lot of rules, but I also know you did a great job with 'em. Our guy, Theodore. He got any of the descendants I'm looking for?'

'Yes,' Angela said, visibly mollified. 'Just the one. Kirsty Forbes, née Robertson, though it looks like she's divorced. No kids. She's descended from Captain Bradock through her deceased mother. Looks like she's mostly lived in and around Edinburgh.'

'Where's that?'

Angela gave her one of those strange *oyinbo* looks she was starting to get used to.

'Scotland. It's the capital city. Pretend capital, anyway.'

Abi consulted her files, augments linking with neurons and downloading data. There was almost nothing about Scotland.

'So, the country north of here, yes?'

'Yes,' Angela and Hollie said together. They were trying hard not to smile.

'And you got an address for this gal?'

The genealogist looked suddenly uncomfortable.

'Not exactly.'

'What's that supposed to mean?'

'Well, she moves around a lot and—'

'The *opolo keji* is designed to find people, Angela. If there's a – what do you call it? – a *digitized* trail, the *opolo keji* would have followed it – or tried to follow it – without special instruction from you. So, where is she?'

Angela ran nervous hands through her hair.

'Until last week, she was . . . an inmate at Stirling Prison.'

'A prison?' Abi was pretty sure her jaw had dropped open, if only for a moment.

'According to your Apollo Cagey, anyway. Looks like Kirsty Forbes is a druggie and a thief. She's got an extensive criminal record. Probably steals to feed her habit.' Angela tapped one of the *opolo keji*'s screens. 'It says here that she's serving a twelve-month sentence for theft and possession. Or rather, she *was*. They discharged her a few days ago. No forwarding address.'

Thirty-Two

The Ocean View Motel did not have a view of the ocean. Not that it would have mattered. Ethan wouldn't have thought to look out the window. He took slow paces up and down his room, trying – and failing – to fit together the pieces of a multi-state, multi-*country* puzzle. The carpet tiles were hard and unyielding beneath his feet.

Gutierrez had left him at the motel hours ago. She had rushed off to arrange the tracking down of Chuck Vielfrass and to sort out protection for both him and his mother. She'd promised to call when Chuck was ready for interview but so far he'd heard nothing. He worried that she was screwing him over but rejected the idea. Gutierrez seemed like good people. And witnesses could be hard to find, or hard to sit down with, and there was nothing he could do about it anyway, so he resolved to wait till morning. He'd gotten ahold of Chinese takeout and a couple of beers instead.

It was almost certain there was a family connection between the Okoro murders in Chicago and Africa. That was too much of a coincidence to be otherwise. But he couldn't see any connection between an African businessman in Africa, an African med student in Chicago, and a white college professor in Providence,

Rhode Island. It was possible, of course, that the husband was either lying about, or simply unaware of, a connection between his business affairs and Nigeria. But that would link *him* with the Okoros, and the husband was very much alive. It was the woman who was dead. And their kids. A. Bello, or whatever his real name was, was careful. And a planner. And his plans had gone off as intended. He had chosen *not* to kill the husband. Which meant neither the husband nor his bank's business, in Africa or otherwise, was behind any of it.

The little biracial baby stared up at him from a hardwood floor and a puddle of ocean. He pushed the image out of his mind. Sat down on the edge of the bed. Tried to relax.

But now, all he could see was a night-black road in rural Ohio. His car tilted on the grass shoulder, hands pale and shaking on the steering wheel.

He grabbed his phone. Punched up a number. A familiar voice answered after a couple of rings.

'Hey, Dad. How's it going?' Cara asked.

'Okay. You?'

'Okay.'

A long pause.

'Dad, did you call for a reason, or do you just want to listen to me breathe down the phone?'

'I just wanted to see how you are.'

'Well, like I said, I'm fine.' Another pause. 'Are you okay? *Really*, I mean?'

'I'm good. I just . . .' He could hear murmuring coming down the phone. A quiet male voice. Devin. Asking what was going on probably. 'It's nothing, sweetie. I gotta go. Speak later.'

'Dad—'

He hung up.

Thirty-Three

Thursday the 10th: 5.03 a.m. EDT

The ringing of his cell phone ripped apart some vaporous, unremembered dream, the sound of it unwanted and insistent. Ethan reached out to retrieve it with eyes still closed but it wasn't where he expected it to be.

Because he wasn't at home. He was in a shitty motel room in Providence, Rhode Island.

He opened his eyes. Grabbed the phone from the nightstand. 'Hello?' His voice was croaky with sleep.

'This is Gutierrez. Get your ass over to Hope House, stat. I'll meet you there. Unis have just called for backup.'

Words guaranteed to banish any thoughts of slumber. Ethan sat up in bed.

'What's happened?'

'The unit we put at the bottom of the drive failed to check in. Turns out he's unconscious in his cruiser and there's a white box van at the front entrance.'

She hung up on him without waiting for a response.

Ethan didn't need GPS to tell him he was arriving at his destination. The road ahead was full of the swirling blue of police beacons racing the same way. In these last minutes of darkness, they threw everything around them into swooping, unnatural shadow. He pulled to the side of the road just short of the driveway to Hope House. A couple more police cruisers pulled up behind him.

He found Gutierrez talking in hurried whispers to an opposite number in uniform. She broke off when she saw him approach.

'Good,' she said. 'You're here. No time to be fancy. We're just going to charge right in and scare him into stopping whatever he's doing. The van's still there. Unis will lead the way. We'll follow in behind.'

He joined her in her spotless vehicle. Words crackled out of the radio.

'Here we go,' she said.

A cacophony of sirens exploded into the night. Five cruisers raced up the long, cobbled driveway, Gutierrez on their tail. Hope House loomed ahead, deep black against a less black sky.

'He's on the move,' a voice said over the radio.

Sure enough, the van was lurching into motion, moving across the front of the house onto rough ground and making to turn around the corner of the building.

Gutierrez grabbed the handset to her radio.

'All units, all units, be aware that there's a track at the back of the building leading off the grounds.'

'Ten-four,' crackled back at her. The cruisers raced off in pursuit, bouncing over grass and flower beds. Plants and dirt sprayed from their tyres, stark in the headlights. Gutierrez pulled up at the porticoed front steps.

'What are you doing?' Ethan asked. 'Our perp's gone.'

'Unis can deal with him. We need to render assistance.'

She raced up the steps, Ethan close behind. His shoes made an unexpected splashing sound. He looked down in surprise.

Then shock.

Water was pouring out from under the front doors and cascading down the steps. The tang of seawater hit his nostrils.

Gutierrez pulled on the front door. She was almost knocked to the ground as it slammed open under the pressure of water that had built up behind it. The water gushed past them – *through* them – in a foaming torrent. Ethan's shoe lost its grip, forcing him down onto one knee that banged hard against the stone. Cursing, he regained his footing and followed the Providence detective inside.

The marbled hallway was awash with water, all of it headed to the front door. A piece of seaweed curled around his ankle. A small streak of silver that could only be a fish zipped between his legs.

'Jesus fucking Christ.' Gutierrez came to a sudden halt.

The water in the hallway was coming from the same drawing room that Gutierrez and Ethan had sat in the previous day. The drowned body of Dottie Vielfrass lay in the open doorway, jammed there by the foaming current. Silk pyjamas, eggshell blue and drenched, clung indecently to her body. A loose arm waved back and forth in the flow. A mocking imitation of life.

The water drained away, leaving only puddles, and soaked furnishings, and the rank smell of a beach at low tide.

Thirty-Four

Thursday the 10th: 7.56 a.m. EDT

'What do you mean, you lost him?' Gutierrez demanded. 'He was in a *box van*, for chrissakes!'

Hope House's ornate front doors were wide open, allowing a melancholy, early morning light to illuminate the hallway. The uniform lieutenant, a good six inches taller than his plainclothes counterpart, shrugged apologetically.

'I don't know what to tell you, Nicole. We had a . . . glitch.'

'A what?'

'Glitch.' The uniform squirmed with embarrassment. 'We followed him down that goat track of a back lane until he hit the public road. He turned right, we didn't. Our lead cruiser just . . . just died at the intersection. Electrics, computers, some shit like that. The whole system went tits up. Thing is, none of the rest of us could get past. By the time we got the intersection cleared the fucker was long gone. No sign of him anywhere.' The lieutenant's expression hardened. 'We'll find him though. My guys are leaving no goddamned stone unturned.'

Gutierrez opened and closed her mouth several times before settling for, 'Did you get the plates at least?'

'It was *dark*, Nicole. So, no.'

'Jesus fucking . . .'

Ethan tuned out, taking another look at his surroundings. Even though he was standing right in the middle of it, it all felt slightly unreal, as if he were watching on video. Hope House looked more like the aftermath of a disaster movie than a crime scene. The water had torn fixtures and fittings from their appointed places, dumping them willy-nilly in the hallway. Expensive wallpaper was already curling off the underlying plaster, and a couple of small fish, which had to be dead by now, had ceased flopping uselessly against an overturned side table.

Everything stank of seawater.

A click-clacking of metal and plastic drew his attention to the set of broad, curving stairs that led up to the second floor. EMTs were manoeuvring a stretcher down the steps towards a waiting ambulance.

The housekeeper. He'd discovered her unbreathing but somehow not dead in a third-floor bedroom. She'd been tucked neatly in bed. An older Hispanic man, in a similar state of unconsciousness, was seated – if seated was the right word for it – in a nearby armchair. Attempts to revive them had failed but they didn't seem to be getting any worse.

Gutierrez stalked from the hallway to the drawing room, temper barely in check. Ethan followed her, stepping over Dottie Vielfrass's untouched body as he did so. He scratched idly at the back of his hand. The latex gloves he'd borrowed from Gutierrez were a different make than he was used to. They felt weird against his skin.

'Fucking unis,' she muttered. 'They had one job. One lousy fucking job, and they fucking well fucked it up.'

'They're unis. Fucking up *is* their job.'

He was happy to see a smile, brief and bitter though it was.

'Does this make *any* sense to you?' he asked.

'No.' A plastic-shrouded foot kicked at a cable on the floor. 'What the hell *is* this?'

'Something to do with that, presumably,' Ethan said, pointing at a nearby wall. 'It sure ain't a camera.'

'It might be. It could be anything.'

The object of Ethan's attention was the remains of a black box, charred and melted and twisted, but still anchored to the oak panelling by a metal bolt. The cable that Gutierrez had kicked in irritation fed into it.

Identically ruined boxes clung like limpets to the remaining walls, each with its attendant cable. The cables themselves snaked across the floor to the middle of the room but didn't quite meet.

Weren't long enough to meet. They ended at a ragged circle of charred floor.

'There was something else here,' Ethan said. 'Something these wires must have plugged into.'

'Sure, but what? None of this . . . *none* of this makes any sense.' Gutierrez's voice trembled. Frustration maybe.

Or fear.

'Agreed.' Ethan said. He took a deep breath, trying to still his own racing thoughts. 'None of this makes sense. But it *happened*. We saw it. Some of it, anyway.' Ethan stared up at the room's high ceiling. Then walked across to Dottie Vielfrass's prone body and squatted down. Briny liquid was seeping out of her pyjamas. A couple of her nails were broken. The water had failed to wash away the blood beneath them. He stood up again. 'We can be pretty damn sure of at least a couple of things.' He ticked them off on his fingers. 'One: until we got here, this room was full of seawater. And two: Dottie Vielfrass was high enough to scratch the ceiling before she died.'

'You're saying she *floated* up there?'

'I'm not saying it makes sense. Except it kinda does.'

'This is insane. This isn't a bathtub you're talking about here. That would take hundreds – maybe thousands – of gallons of seawater.'

'And what do you think was pouring out of here when we came in?'

'I know, I know. I just don't *believe* it. I *can't* believe it.' Gutierrez put a hand to her forehead. Rubbed her temples. 'I gotta get out of here. I need some fucking air.'

Ethan followed her outside. He said nothing while they removed their shoe covers on the still damp front steps. Said nothing as her morose gaze picked out the churned-up earth in the flower beds, the aftermath of the failed pursuit of Bello. Said nothing as she strode off in the same direction as the tyre tracks. Dirt from the gardens clung to their shoes. He continued to say nothing as he tailed her along the side of the house, her rapid steps making him struggle to keep up.

It was Gutierrez who broke the silence, her voice calmer than before.

'Maybe we shouldn't worry too much about the how,' she said. 'It's too fucking hard. Let's think about the why. Or at least let's work on the connection between the Okoros and the Vielfrasses. There has to be one.'

Something that had been brewing at the back of his mind bubbled to life. Ethan stopped dead.

'I know what it is,' he said.

'You do?' Gutierrez turned to face him, her face alive with curiosity.

'Not the connection exactly, but the pattern. This isn't about families. It's about bloodlines.'

'I'm not following.'

'This thing started in Nigeria. So far as we know, anyway. And in Nigeria, our perp killed Zulu Okoro, his mother, and his daughter. He didn't kill the spouse. Same in Chicago. Father and son are killed, but not the spouse. And—'

'It's the same here,' Gutierrez broke in, comprehension dawning. 'Dottie Vielfrass, her daughter, and grandkids. The son-in-law was left alone because he was never a target. There's no blood relationship.'

Ethan started walking again, following the tyre tracks. The remains of a rose bush lay scattered atop the grass, wicked thorns broken and bent against their stems

'Whatever this is,' Ethan said, 'our perp has a beef with the Okoros and the Vielfrasses specifically. Relatives by marriage need not apply.'

'Chuck Vielfrass is going to be next.' Gutierrez's voice was equal parts anxiety and excitement. 'We can set up an op. Wait for him to go after Chuck, and – bam!' She pounded a manicured fist into the palm of her hand.

'Where are we with him?' Ethan asked.

'We're trying to move Chuck and his girlfriend to a safe house. But they're kinda resisting.' She gave him a wry grin. 'Probably worried we'll wander into his condo and find his stash – he's just the type. Unis are keeping an eye on them in the meantime. We can speak to them later today.'

'And what about his kids?'

'The kids are with their mother. She's agreed to move out of town and stay with her mom for a while.' She gave him an appraising look. 'As a matter of fact, we could use your help with that. The mom's mom is from your neck of the woods. We need to hurry them along, stat. No need to give our guy *two* targets.'

Thirty-Five

Thursday the 10th: 9.28 a.m. BST

Beyond the train's slightly grimy windows the sun was shining out of a clear sky. Bright daylight lit the landscape into a deep, verdant green that the *oyinbos* had chopped into a patchwork of stone-walled fields. Hollie had identified the white, fluffy quadrupeds contained within them as sheep. Rolling along on twin ribbons of metal, the vehicle generated a pleasant rumble that smoothed the edges off Abi's sense of frustration.

'Is something up with your phone?' Hollie enquired.

'No,' Abi replied. 'Why are you asking?' The object of Hollie's attention lay on the flimsy, fold-down table in front of them. A bump in the rails made it bounce towards the edge.

''Cause you're looking at it like you want to do it harm, that's why. If you looked at me that way, I'd be running for my life.'

'Sorry, doll.' Abi flashed her a quick smile. 'This here's my thinking face.'

'Well try not to think so hard, eh?'

Abi tried to do as Hollie suggested. If Hollie had noticed, so might others and she didn't want to draw attention to herself. But it was difficult. In order to stay in contact with the *opolo keji* in Bristol, she had to link her augments to the phone and use the phone's connections to the various *oyinbo* networks. But even upgraded, the phone's bandwidth was pitiful. Everything was taking far longer than it should.

Aha.

The *opolo keji* had been running loose in a computer system belonging to the Avon and Somerset Police. Finally, after many dead ends and a few dropped connections, it had found what she was looking for. A statement from a Dr Maximilian Kwan concerning allegations of human trafficking. She nodded, satisfied. *Gbese* had been paid.

When she looked up, Hollie was staring at her expectantly.

'Sorry, doll. Did you say something?'

'I asked what you were thinking about. Something weird, I bet, to have a thinking face like *that*.'

'Nothing, really.' Abi tried to laugh it off. 'Boring visitor stuff.' Seeing that Hollie wasn't buying it, she added: 'On the subject of which, have you got your passport?'

'Yes.' A small hiss of good-natured exasperation. 'But like I told you before, you don't need a passport to go to Scotland.'

'It's a separate country.' The files were clear about that.

Hollie gave her a look.

'Kinda . . . yeah. It's a country, sort of. But it's not separate. Not yet anyway. You don't need a passport to go there.'

Abi shook her head. She knew more about travel than the *oyinbo*s. There were no gates here. Almost no gates. And without gates . . .

'Even so, babe, you never know when it'll come in useful.'

Hollie snorted, her attention turning towards her own phone. The country on the other side of the windows grew steadily wilder and more hilly. Clouds built up on the horizon, the streaky shadows beneath them hinting at rain. Abi and the *opolo keji* continued their silent battle with *oyinbo* technology.

'Can I look at it again?' Hollie asked suddenly.

'At what?'

'You know what. The box.'

Abi found herself smiling indulgently.

'Why? You've seen it a hundred times already.'

'I know. But it's just so gorgeous.' The blue eyes were wide and pleading. It suddenly struck Abi that if you looked at them the right way, Hollie's eyes could be . . . not so disturbing.

'Okay, babe. But you're gonna have to break yourself of the habit. This don't belong to us.'

She pulled down her backpack from the train's overhead shelf and reached inside.

'There you go.'

The box she'd placed on the table in front of them was small enough to fit in the palm of her hand. It was dark, and wooden, with intricately carved leaves, and strange looking animals, and raised polygonal characters. Every edge was inlaid with small, red jewels that burned from within.

'Wow. Just . . . wow.' Hollie picked it up. The black gloss of her nail polish glinted as she turned it over and over, examining it from every angle. Abi tried not to wince as she gave it a shake.

'Does it open? It looks like it should open.'

'Good luck with that.'

'What you're doing is really nice, you know that? Coming all the way from Africa to give this to a complete stranger. Honestly? If it was me, I'd just keep it.'

'It's not mine, babe. Or yours. It belongs to Kirsty Forbes. It's her inheritance, she being a particular descendant of Theodore Bradock and all.' She hoped Hollie hadn't noticed the way her knuckles tightened on the table. She forced out a grin, instead. 'Besides, you're getting a free trip to Edinburgh out of it. That oughta be enough.'

'I'm not complaining. And thank you by the way. Except for sailboat deliveries, I haven't been out of Bristol in, like, forever.'

'You're welcome.'

Still holding the box, Hollie stared out of the window a moment. There were streaks of rain on the glass now, the landscape beyond a frozen ocean of yellow grasses, its tussocky waves misted by weather.

'Do you think we'll find her?' Hollie asked. 'We still don't have an address.'

'You can count on it.'

Data was flowing out of the *opolo keji*, squeezing itself through the phone, and landing on her augments. Neurons fired in response, arranging themselves into the appropriate sequences.

The grin that spread across her face was far more genuine than its predecessor. She pretended to consult her phone.

'We just got ourselves a whole bunch of leads.'

Thirty-Six

'*W*ow,' Hollie said. 'This place is amazing.'

Even Abi had to concede that the woman had a point. Downtown Edinburgh – or the city centre, whatever – was built of the same chunks of rock that the *oyinbos* used for almost everything, but the end result here was distinctly different. Overlooked by a looming, ancient fortress, the streets were terraced in grey and tan three- and four-storey buildings. They seemed to have a more harmonious shape than in Bristol, their relationship to each other giving the impression of a city created by a serene, single mind.

The only disappointment was the sky. The clouds were grey enough, and thick enough, and seemed to be pressing low to the ground, but there was no rain. Despite the dry pavement beneath her feet, Abi tilted her head up, hoping to feel a few drops, at least. None were to be had.

As they knocked at one fruitless address after another, however, the attractions of the city began to pale. And as they headed west, the usual *oyinbo* sensibilities began to reassert themselves. Handsome buildings were supplanted by shabby imitations and then vanished altogether, replaced by the usual rock-cubes. Nor were the rock-cubes the only dwellings to sadden the soul. They were interspersed with larger, even uglier constructions that Hollie referred to as blocks of flats.

It was to one of these that the *opolo keji* led them next.

'Okay, doll, this is the place.'

'You said that last time.'

'And this time, I'll be right. Maybe.'

Hollie smiled wryly at that. She put down the holdall that comprised her luggage and rubbed the back of her calf through black leggings. The *oyinbo* woman hadn't said anything but maybe they'd done too much walking. Abi had been hoping to walk in the rain. But walking in hope of rain wasn't going to make it happen.

And it was taking too long. Perhaps it was time to think about taxis.

Unlike most *oyinbo* doors, the one to the block of flats was mostly glass, framed by chipped, blue-painted wood. Abi opened it, crossed a small, cramped lobby and started climbing the steps. Her boots squeaked a little on the tiled polymer.

'What if he's not in?' Hollie asked, her breathing heavy as she tried to keep up.

'The *opolo keji* says he works shifts. He'll be in.'

At the second landing, faced by two unnumbered doors, she hesitated. She frowned a little with the effort of scanning, her eyes awash in the soft glows of infra-red.

One of the flats was warmer than the other.

'This one.' She rapped on the door. Waited. Rapped again. Turned up her hearing.

Someone was shuffling about inside.

'Who is it?' said a croaky, sleep-addled voice.

'We're friends of Kirsty Forbes,' Abi answered.

'Then you can fuck off.'

'We can't, it's important.'

The door swung open. A short, heavily freckled *oyinbo* with dishevelled hair stared out at them. He was wearing the same sort of loudly striped two-piece suit that Max Kwan slept in.

'What do you want?'

Abi was too busy staring at the freckles to reply.

'Um . . . are you Graham Forbes?' Hollie asked.

'Aye. And who are you?'

'I'm Hollie. This is my friend, Abi. We're looking for Kirsty.'

'Well, you're no going to find her here, are you? That druggie besom's no got anything to do with me. No anymore.'

'But you're her ex-husband, yeah? You'll know where she is.'

'And why should I tell you that?' The man's eyes narrowed suspiciously. 'I'm no in the habit of chatting away on my doorstep to a couple of sassenachs I've no seen before.'

Hollie gazed helplessly at Abi.

'Look, pal,' Abi said. 'Your ex is in a heap of trouble. It's important we find her. Real important.'

The man looked at her curiously.

'Where are you from, hen?' Interest in Abi's origins seemed to have drained the anger from him. Abi rewarded him with a smile.

'Nigeria.'

'You don't talk like a Nigerian. No exactly, anyway.'

'So I've been told.'

'And what kind of trouble is Kirsty in? Drug trouble?'

Abi nodded.

'We're trying to get her out of it,' Hollie said.

'Fat chance.' The man's laugh was bitter.

'You got that right,' Abi said. 'Unless you tell us where to find her.'

'She's in Stirling. The jail, no the toon. So she'll be in less trouble than usual. I wouldnae worry about her just the now. She got twelve months.'

'Sorry, man. The gal's done her time. She got let out of the big house last week. That's why we can't find her.'

'But she's no tried to hit me up for cash.' The surprise on the man's face was genuine. He turned reflective. 'Perhaps she's just no desperate enough.'

'If she's out of the hoosegow, where'd your lady make tracks to?'

'The wha—?'

'Prison,' Hollie interrupted. 'If she didn't come to see you, where would Kirsty go when she got out?

Forbes's expression darkened considerably.

'She'll have fallen in with that daft eejit, Jimmy MacRae.'

Thirty-Seven

Thursday the 10th: 4.07 p.m. BST

'*A*re ye sure ye want tae get oot here, hen? It's no the safest place, ken.'

This was the second time Abi had been compared to *oyinbo* poultry. Enough to be sure it wasn't intended as an insult. It took her longer than she would have liked to disentangle what the taxi driver was trying to say, though the concern in his voice was obvious.

'I'm sure, pal, but thanks anyway.'

She stepped out onto the damp pavement. Hollie followed reluctantly, hands clutched tightly around her holdall. She looked longingly at the automobile as it moved slowly away. Then, with a sigh, turned to examine her surroundings.

'Not the nicest place I've ever seen,' Hollie said.

At long last, the hoped-for rain had started to fall. Though it wasn't falling so much as floating down in a light mist. It was almost as if they were standing within the clouds themselves, a phenomenon Abi found so entrancing that Hollie had to repeat herself before she responded.

'I guess not, doll, but the *opolo keji* says this here's where we need to be.' She hesitated a moment, practising the strange name in her head before saying it out loud, worrying about the harsh, choppy consonants *oyinbos* loved so much. 'Bannockburn Court.'

With the exception of a small, fenced park at one end of the street, everything around them was grey or black. There were the usual rock-cubes that the *oyinbos* called home, two storeys tall and crowded together. These ones were covered in a rain-stained grey stucco beneath steep, grimily tiled roofs. The roofs must once have been red but now looked almost as grey as everything else. At the top of the black asphalt street, with its equally asphalt pavements, there stood a very large, very grey block of flats, maybe twelve storeys tall. Although, to be fair to the flats, they weren't *entirely* grey. The shorter sides of the rectangular structure were decorated in a drab brown.

Why did the *oyinbos* build such things? She'd seen the city's handsome downtown. They could obviously do better. And to judge by the reactions of both Hollie and the taxi driver, even the *oyinbos* found the scene in front of her deeply unpleasant.

The disquiet in Hollie's voice had been so pronounced Abi felt the need to double-check their surroundings. A few *oyinbo* children were playing on the park's grassy expanse, kicking both a ball and each other with great enthusiasm. They presented no imminent danger. On the other side of the road, a young *oyinbo* woman with alarming orange hair was pushing a wheeled contraption containing an infant. Only the child's head was visible, swathed in a brightly coloured hat and sheltered beneath the vehicle's lowered awning. The rest of it was covered in polymer sheeting to keep out the rain. Scans indicated no concealed weaponry.

An automobile, sleek and out of place, drove slowly past. A young male *oyinbo* with a scarred cheek stared at them through the window. Abi stiffened. The man was armed. A projectile weapon of some sort. Stored in a small compartment in front of the passenger seat. Abi probed further and let out a small gasp of surprise. Coherent signals brushed across her augments.

'Drug dealer would be my guess,' Hollie said, following her gaze. 'Only reason you'd ever see a car like that round here.'

'But it . . . talks,' Abi said, stumbling to find the right words. 'That there automobile has computers. They can talk to the *oyin* . . . to your networks.'

'A car like that? Sure. I've read about those. It has an autopilot and everything. It can practically drive itself, so I've heard.' Hollie let out a sigh. 'Lucky bastard.'

The car rolled away, its driver intent on other matters. Abi thought about interfering with the computers so it would stop and she could have a closer look. She resisted the temptation.

'We should get going.' She set off in the direction of the flats.

Bannockburn Court's lobby was dark and smelled faintly of urine. Ugly looking messages and inexplicable symbols, none of which appeared to be part of the original design, had been daubed on the walls. Hollie pressed a button so as to summon a transportation device she referred to as a lift. She pressed it repeatedly, her blue eyes darting nervously from one corner of the lobby to another. When the doors to the mechanism finally slid open, she stepped hurriedly inside.

Abi hesitated. The lift smelled even worse than the lobby. It was probably her imagination, but it felt as if her amulet was tingling, alert to the possibility it might have to dose her with prophylactics.

'You getting in or what?'

Abi sighed, turned down her sense of smell, and stepped across the threshold. The lift rattled and wheezed as it dragged them upwards. Abi tried not to breathe. After what felt like an eternity, the doors slid open and the two of them stepped into a narrow corridor. Grey light seeped in from windows at both ends.

Doors with multiple locks lined the walls.

'What was the number again?' Hollie asked.

'Four oh nine.'

Abi must have missed some visual cue because Hollie knew immediately to turn left. She rapped on one of the doors.

'Someone's inside,' Abi said. 'I can hear the . . . what did you call it? The telly.'

'Really?' Hollie looked surprised. 'Then you're probably right about someone being in. They must be watching it. It's on way too low to deter burglars.'

Before Abi had a chance to ask Hollie what a burglar was, there was a clicking of locks and the door cracked open.

'You the polis?'

A large eye, blue, like Hollie's but more washed out, stared at them through the gap. The voice that accompanied it was male and querulous.

'Do we look like the police?' Hollie said.

The man, taking in Hollie's all-black ensemble, with its heavily frilled skirt, black leggings, and lace-up boots, opened the door a little farther. He gave both women an appreciative leer.

'So, what can I do for yous?'

'We're looking for Kirsty Forbes. Does she live here?'

'Who's asking?'

'I'm Hollie, this is Abi. We're friends of hers.'

'Kirsty doesnae have friends.' He made to shut the door. Abi placed her booted foot across the threshold, preventing it from closing.

'Move it, hen. If ye want tae keep it attached tae yer leg.'

'Make me.'

The man was laughably small. Barely a threat. He smiled wryly and gave a small nod.

'Okay then, have it your way.'

He opened the door and stepped back, inviting her in with an exaggerated bow.

'Thanks, mister.'

'Abi. Don't—'

Abi stepped forward.

Her nose exploded in pain. She reeled backwards, hands flying to her face.

The little *oyinbo* had been unbelievably quick. Just a little stutter step and his head had snapped forward in a movement that was as brutal as it was efficient.

'That'll teach ye, ye little . . .'

But the words were already slowing down, becoming harder and harder to understand. Her wrist felt like the amulet was sawing at it with a blunt knife. And then she could feel nothing. The *oyinbo* was moving as if through molasses, his arm reaching out to close the door.

She grabbed the outstretched limb. Pulled on it so hard that he flew into the corridor and slammed head first into the wall opposite. He drifted to the floor as slowly as the misting rain outside, an ungainly heap on worn-through carpet tiles.

Abi gripped the door frame to steady herself as the amulet brought her back down. A wave of numbing cold passed through her, making her shiver. Sensation returned to her face. A dull, throbbing pain that the meds were working to wipe away. She put a hand up to her nose.

Hollie was staring at her open mouthed, her expression some-where between fascination and horror.

'Are you okay? Is he . . . you know? Is he . . . dead?'

Abi gave herself a couple more breaths before she let go of the door frame.

'I'm fine, babe. Nothing hurt but my pride.' She pressed on her nose again. 'Guy played me for a sucker.' She scanned the slumped body in the corridor – Jimmy MacRae's, she pre-sumed – before heaving it onto her shoulder. 'Our buddy here ain't dead, though it'd serve the son-of-a-gun right if he was.' Angling slightly to accommodate her load, she stepped through the doorway to the flat. 'Now then. Let's see if the lady of the house is at home.'

The door led to a tiny hallway. There was a small bathroom to the left and, to the right, a grubby bedroom. The bedroom was little more than a rumpled mattress on the floor jammed against a damp wall, the wall itself decorated with pictures of unclothed females. Both rooms were empty.

There was a closed door at the far end, presumably leading into the rest of the living space. The sound of a television on the other side was loud enough for even Hollie to hear.

Abi, however, could hear something else. She rushed for the door handle. Pulled it open.

The television seemed to be almost the same size as the room. So big, in fact, that it took Abi more than a moment to drag her attention towards the chamber's sole occupant.

Kirsty Forbes was sprawled face up and unconscious on a stained couch, its grey, ribbed material worn nearly bare. A small bottle of pills had spilled their contents onto an orange carpet.

The *oyinbo* was choking on her own vomit. Liquid bubbled

from her lips, but her chest wasn't strong enough to expel it. She
was breathing it in. Drowning.

'Oh my god,' Hollie said.

Abi dropped her load onto the floor. Jimmy MacRae groaned
a little but lay still. As still as the woman on the couch.

Abi regarded her coldly, face rigid with contempt. There'd
be no need to kill this one. She was too busy doing it to herself.

'Jesus, Abi! Don't just stand there. Give me a hand.'

Hollie was trying to turn the woman onto her stomach but
she wasn't strong enough.

'Abs!'

Abi stepped across and lent her weight to the effort. Kirsty's
body was so loose, it flowed around her arms like water, heavy
and difficult to move. The two of them managed to turn her
onto her stomach, head hanging off the edge of the sofa. Gravity
pulled the bile out of the woman's mouth and nose. She coughed
and sputtered, expelling more liquid.

Started to breathe again.

'How is she?' Abi asked. It seemed an appropriate thing to say.

'Fucked if I know.' Hollie peered worriedly at the woman's
prostrate body. She failed to see a small, spider-like mechanism
drop onto the floor from Abi's backpack and scuttle towards the
unconscious *oyinbo* male. 'We should call an ambulance.'

'I may have something that can help.'

Abi took off her backpack and reached inside.

'What's that, then?'

'Think of it as a . . . a stethoscope.'

'Funny looking stethoscope.'

'In Nigeria we have many such things.'

It was a med-kit, similar to the amulet on Abi's wrist, but
more specialized. The ivory-like material of which it was made

was covered in a variety of symbols, some abstract, some less so. She slipped it over the woman's wrist. Hollie gasped as it changed shape to hug the skin.

Readouts started to scroll across Abi's vision.

'Gal's gone and poisoned herself with . . . ah . . . I don't have the words. *Opium*. But worse.'

'It's fentanyl,' Hollie said, picking up the bottle of pills from the floor. 'She's OD'd.' Hollie's blue eyes fixed on her curiously. 'Your "stethoscope" tell you that?' She looked pointedly at the med-kit, as passive looking and inactive as jewellery. 'How?'

Abi hesitated. Explaining the cybernetics in her head would not be a good idea. The *oyinbo* might be gullible but there were limits. She did a quick bit of coding instead.

'It says so here.'

She pulled the mobile phone from her pocket. Neat formations of polygonal characters moved from right to left across the screen, a few of them flashing ominously.

'You got eyes in your pocket, or what?'

'I ain't digging you, babe.'

'How can you read a phone when it's in your pockets?'

Uh-oh.

'I can't, doll. I took it out and looked at it.'

'But—'

'You really think I have eyes in my pockets?'

'No. But—'

'This gal is going to be A-okay.'

'Really?'

'Yes. Sure as eggs is eggs.'

The med-kit was dosing the *oyinbo* with drugs and nanobots. They were stabilizing her metabolism, rearranging her neural feedback systems, breaking down the poisons.

A shame, really.

Kirsty Forbes opened her eyes. They were, thankfully, normal. Abi had had enough of blue irises for one day. The woman's gaze skittered about in a confused manner, before fixing on the prostrate form of Jimmy MacRae. The *alantakun* would have drugged him by now. Abi wondered if the bitemark was visible.

'What's happening? Who the hell are you? What have you done to my—'

'Easy, lady, easy.' Abi knelt on the carpet beside the sofa. Tried not to think about how filthy it was. Tried to be reassuring instead. 'You've had a bad time of it is all. You'll come around soon enough.' She pointed a careless thumb over her shoulder. 'As for your man here, he'll be fine. Drinks too much would be my guess.'

The med-kit released its grip on Kirsty's wrist, making a sucking sound as it did so.

'And what the fuck is *that*?' The woman's voice climbed in alarm. She rushed to get the device off her arm, as if repelled by the noise it had made. It rolled onto the floor where Abi quickly retrieved it. If the med-kit got it into its head that the carpet was a patient, they'd be here till the sun went nova.

Kirsty tried to get up from the couch, but it was too much effort. Weak hands fluttered at her temples.

'Lay back, lady. Lay back. That's it. Try to relax.' A thought, disgusting but plausible, popped into her head. 'Would you like a cup of tea?'

Kirsty nodded, the taut expression on her face easing a little.

'Milk. Two sugars. Not too strong.'

'I'll get it,' Hollie said. Without asking for directions, she disappeared through the room's only other door. There was a sound of banging cupboards.

With exaggerated care, Kirsty raised herself to a sitting position. She slumped against the back of the sofa, breath escaping her lips in a soft sigh.

'Who are you?' she repeated. 'The Social?'

'If you like.' Abi wasn't looking at her. She was peering into her backpack.

'Look, I'm sorry, it won't happen again. Don't call the polis, okay? It's just the pills were there, and Jimmy said they wouldn't . . . what's that?'

There was a dark wooden box in the palm of Abi's hand, intricately carved. Inlaid with small, red jewels that seemed to burn from within.

'*Gbese* must be paid,' Abi said, her voice cold.

'What did you say? A bay-see?'

An unseen signal flowed through Abi's hand. The box opened.

Kirsty would have screamed, but Abi clamped a hand across her mouth and nose.

'I *said*: "*gbese* must be paid."'

It looked like a centipede, the thing that was emerging from the box, *oyinbo*-pale and translucent, with endless pairs of multi-jointed legs that splayed almost as wide as the body was long.

Abi placed the box on the arm of the sofa.

Kirsty managed to make a noise this time but the sound was weak, still muffled by Abi's hand. She tried to thrash her way clear of Abi's grip but lacked the strength.

The centipede was in no particular hurry, its motions sinuous, the legs moving in an inevitable wave, one after the other, front to back, back to front, front to back. It climbed onto the back of the sofa. The legs continued to move. Front to back, back to front. The centipede rippled over the upholstery.

Toward Kirsty's head.

'Somewhere on this world of yours,' Abi said, her voice quiet as a whisper, 'there is a man. He also thinks that *gbese* should be paid. He is coming to kill you. He wants your death to be hard, because the *gbese* he feels is very great. I'm here to make you ready for him. And like it or not, lady, you're gonna be.'

Frail though she was, even Abi had trouble holding the woman down as the centipede reached her hair. Front to back. Back to front. It crawled across her scalp, down across her forehead. Her left eye. The quivering cheek. Back to front. Front to back.

Abi took her hand away from Kirsty's mouth. She opened it. The beginning of the scream she had been so desperate to get out.

The centipede scuttled inside.

The *oyinbo*'s eyes bulged wide. Abi stepped back. Watched expressionless as the woman grabbed at her throat, made choking noises. Her legs kicked frantically against the filthy carpet.

And stopped. She fell to one side, barely breathing.

Abi propped her up.

'Here you go . . . Oh. She fallen asleep?' Hollie was standing in the kitchen doorway, a chipped mug of tea in one hand.

'Looks like it.' Abi closed the inlaid wooden box. Placed it on the arm of the sofa. 'Lady's got her inheritance. Let's blow this joint.'

Thirty-Eight

Thursday the 10th: 12.02 p.m. EDT

'*I* can't believe this. You really think someone's out to get me? Jesus. *Jee-zus!*'

Guy hasn't mentioned his mother. Not once. Or his kids. Fucking asshole.

Ethan kept his expression professionally sympathetic. Chuck Vielfrass paced from one end of his condo's living room to the other. The man loved black, apparently. Black sneakers, black jeans, black jacket over a black, collarless tee shirt: merch from some long-ago film festival. The only thing on him that wasn't black was a diamond ear stud.

Fucking pretentious asshole.

He averted his gaze. Except for where they were interrupted by glass sliding doors that led onto a balcony, the condo's walls were covered with framed posters for documentaries no one had ever heard of. PRODUCED BY CHUCK VIELFRASS. No relief there, then. The living room's leather and steel sofa, though, was a different matter. Vielfrass's live-in girlfriend, Charlene Zhao, was perched on one end of it, done up to the nines with only a hint of make-up, and looking altogether too classy for her jag-off of a partner.

Of course, the jag-off had money. Even more so now that the mother was dead. But she looked genuinely worried for him all the same. Luminous brown eyes followed his back-and-forth perambulations.

'Have you ever heard of a Nigerian family called the Okoros?' Gutierrez was asking.

'No. Never.'

'Have you got any connection to Nigeria? Ever been there, for instance?'

'No.'

'Can you think of any connection either your sister or your mother would have had to Nigeria? Any connection that might have gotten them in trouble.'

'Sonia went there once when she was younger. But that was years ago.'

'To Nigeria? Not Ghana or some other country?'

Vielfrass made an exasperated sound.

'It was Africa, okay? That's all I know. Some voyage of self-discovery, getting to know herself better. She did stuff like that before she sold out.' He stopped pacing long enough to straighten one of the posters. Catching his reflection in the glass, he peered closer to examine it, running a hand through lightly gelled hair. 'Look, I know my mother and sister are dead, but what about the living? What are you going to do to protect me from this guy?'

'We want to move you to a safe house. That way we can—'

'I already told you no. No safe house. I need to stay here.'

'Chuck, honey. Maybe—'

'I said no.'

Charlene subsided without pressing the issue.

'Sir,' Ethan ventured. 'I really think you should take Lieutenant Gutierrez's advice.'

'And that's the official view of the Chicago PD, is it? You're a thousand miles outside your jurisdiction, detective.'

'And tomorrow, I will still be outside my jurisdiction. You, however, may very well be dead.'

Charlene's hands flew to her mouth.

'My work is here. My *art*. Why don't you guys get that? I have things I need to work on. *Important* things. I can't just up and leave. I've a meeting in LA next week, with producers. I don't expect you to understand but these are big, important people. Serious, I mean *serious* money, and everything has to be perfect. Has to be. This is the one, babe,' he said, turning to Charlene. 'I know it.'

'Sure, hon.' Charlene's words – and her tone – were supportive. But her expression, to Ethan's mind at any rate, indicated that she'd heard it all before.

Chuck, hearing only the words, turned to face Gutierrez.

'We're staying.'

'You understand,' she asked pointedly, 'that you're volunteering to be bait?'

Charlene's breath hitched.

'I get it,' Chuck said. 'But if I stay, the police will protect me?'

Gutierrez nodded. Reluctantly. A strange excitement gleamed in the man's eyes.

'I'm going to be at the heart of a police operation to catch a killer. And when you catch him, it'll be right here, in this room.'

'If he gets to this room, sir, we'll have failed.' Gutierrez walked to the glass sliding doors that led to the balcony. It was adorned with two metal chairs, a table, and a potted palm of some kind. She opened the doors and stepped through, leaning over the balcony railing. She was checking out the terrain, Ethan realized. The Vielfrass condo was at the rear of the building, invisible from the street. The Rhode Island detective wouldn't want to be caught flat-footed.

'There's no way in at the back? No service entrance for trash collection or anything like that?'

'There isn't even parking. Just a few spots at the front, which is nowhere near enough for everyone who lives here.' A petulant frown flashed across the man's face. 'And trash is at the side, right next to the parking spaces. The only way in or out is through the lobby. You can take the main entrance to the front, or the side entrance if you want to go straight to the cans, but there's nothing at the back.'

Gutierrez nodded, apparently satisfied.

'Good. If we park on the opposite side of the street and a little ways down, we can cover both entrances at once. If our man comes for you – and we're pretty sure he will – we'll catch him the moment he commits.'

'What about Claire and Sebastian?' Charlene asked. 'We have them every other weekend. We're due to pick them up tomorrow.'

'Not this time, I'm afraid. They'll have to stay with their mother. We've already made the arrangements. The kids are going to visit their maternal grandmother in Chicago, where Detective Krol's colleagues can keep an eye on them.' Gutierrez looked pointedly at Chuck. 'Like I keep saying, it's not safe.'

'How unsafe can it be, really? I mean, you said yourself, there's basically only one way in.' That gleam in the eye again. Ethan imagined Chuck with a mic in his hand, cameras rolling. 'So, lieutenant, how are you going to protect me?'

Gutierrez made no attempt to stifle a sigh.

'We'll have at least one vehicle parked outside the building at all times. If you need to leave the building for any reason, let us know and we'll arrange for someone to escort you. There'll be an officer posted in the corridor outside. We'll also have a squad of officers on standby, ready to react the moment this guy shows his face. He *will* make a play for you, and we'll be ready. But I'm not going to lie, sir. I'd be a hell of a lot happier if you were as far away from here as humanly possible.'

'No need, lieutenant, no need.' Chuck stopped pacing. He sat down on a steel and leather chair that matched the sofa, crossing thin, black-clad legs. 'That sounds more than satisfactory. In fact, I'm gonna call my guy Nick and have him bring over his gear. We'll record the whole thing. Make a production out of it.' Chuck's smiled broadly, showing perfectly manicured teeth. 'Must-watch TV.'

Ethan stared pointedly at his shoes.

Thirty-Nine

Thursday the 10th: 4.57 p.m. EDT

'*I*'m fine, lieutenant. Really. What I need is a cigarette.'

Officer John Fredericks did not look fine. But Ethan had to concede it might have more to do with circumstances than anything else. The City of Providence officer was sitting in a wheelchair wearing nothing more than a hospital gown. The cramped office at the Roger Williams Medical Center, which Gutierrez had commandeered for the duration, was illuminated by a bare strip of fluorescent lighting. It accentuated the ashen pallor of the man's skin, and he was badly in need of a shave. Short, powerful fingers beat out a fidgety tattoo.

'Why don't you tell us what happened?' Gutierrez began, her voice gentle.

'Darned if I know. I was sitting in my cruiser and keeping an eye on Hope House. Everything was normal and then – bam! I'm waking up in a hospital ward with a splitting headache.'

'You sure everything was normal? Did anything – and I mean anything, no matter how trivial – seem off to you?'

Fredericks looked thoughtful for a moment.

'Honestly, Lou. I can't think of anything. It was a nice night, quiet, not a lot of traffic. I had the windows down to take in the air, you know. The insects got a bit buzzy, so I was going to roll up the window and that's pretty much the last thing I remember.'

'Okay, John. You remember anything else, let us know.'

'So, Ms Beltran. Tell us what happened.'

'I don't know nothing about it,' the housekeeper said, agitated and teary. 'I cleaned up in the kitchen like I always do around nine o'clock, asked Mrs Vielfrass if she wanted anything else done, which she said no to, and I went to bed. I have a little apartment on the third floor. Next thing I know, I'm waking up here, and Mrs Vielfrass . . .'

She dissolved into sobs.

'Don't worry, Mr Alejo, you're not in any sort of trouble. We're just trying to piece together what happened.'

'Uh . . . okay.'

'Let's start with who you are. We found you in Ms Beltran's bedroom. Are you some sort of relative?'

'What? Uh . . . no. No. I work for Mrs Vielfrass.' He rubbed at his eyes, as if trying to get them to work better. 'I didn't go to Maria's rooms. At least . . . at least I don't remember going there.'

'Okay. Let's put a pin in that for a while. What was your job at Hope House?'

'Officially, I was Mrs Vielfrass's driver. But mostly I did odd jobs about the place.'

'And you lived in the house, like Ms Beltran?'

'Yeah. I have a couple of rooms in . . . the attic, I guess you'd call it. It's tucked away in the roof. Real private. I'm divorced and my kids are all growed up, so it suits me. And I think Mrs Vielfrass liked having a man about the place after her husband passed.'

'Okay. Let's talk about last night, the early hours of this morning. Did anything unusual happen?'

'Like what?'

Ethan, whose attention had been wandering, pricked up his ears. Even for a grown-ass man in a hospital gown, Dottie Vielfrass's driver looked uncomfortable.

'Anything at all, Mr Alejo. You tell me.'

'I ain't got nothing to say.'

'But—'

'I'm telling you, *señorita*, nothing. I didn't see nothing, I didn't do nothing, and I didn't kill nobody. Can I go now?'

'Lieutenant?' Ethan asked. 'Mind if I have a word?' He reached for his phone.

'Go ahead.'

Ethan handed his phone to the driver.

'Mr Alejo, have you ever seen this man before?' The phone glowed with the sketch CPD had gotten from Jennifer Okoro.

The blood drained from Alejo's face. His hands started to shake. Ethan retrieved his phone before the man could drop it.

'Look, Mr Alejo. We know you have a story to tell. And we know it involves this man. And that this man is, er, *unusual*. Lieutenant Gutierrez and I, we're willing to listen to whatever you have to say. We aren't here to judge.'

'I didn't think anyone would believe me,' Alejo muttered. 'It was like, unreal, man. Un. Real.'

'That's okay. Let's take it from the top. Just tell us what happened.' Ethan allowed himself a small smile. 'I don't normally say this, sir, because I'm a homicide detective, but the way this case is going, anything you say, I'm pretty much gonna believe you.'

Alejo nodded. He made a wiping movement across his mouth, cleaning it off.

'Okay. So. Yeah . . . Around ten, ten thirty last night, I'm doing what I always do, which is go around the house making sure the doors and windows is locked. Then I set the alarm as usual, and check in on Mrs Vielfrass, see if she needs anything—'

'And where was Mrs Vielfrass when you did this?'

'Still in the drawing room, reading.' A sad little grin. 'That room's full of encyclopedias and history books and everything, but she never read any of them. She loved romance books. She'd buy like three or four a week. She'd send me down to the library every month to give 'em away.'

'Was she dressed for bed, anything like that?'

'No. Mrs Vielfrass didn't usually go to bed till around midnight, one a.m. She was a night person.

'So, I asks her if there's anything she needs and she says, "My youth," waving the book at me, and I head on up to bed. Then, maybe around two o'clock, I hear a car in the driveway. I figure it's the police doing their thing, okay. And I start to go back to sleep. But then I think, maybe I can hear voices. I'm not sure 'cause of where I am in the house. Anyway, I keep a baseball bat in my room in case we have intruders, so I pick that up and head downstairs. The door to Mrs Vielfrass's bedroom is wide open and the light is on, so I take a look inside. She ain't there, but the sheets is all thrown back and there's pillows scattered on the floor, so now I'm getting worried. Then I hear shouting, and then screaming from downstairs and it's definitely Mrs Vielfrass . . . Man, she sounded so scared. So, I'm running down the stairs two at a time but when I get to the main hall everything is quiet again. I'm looking and looking but I don't see nothing, except there's a light coming from under the drawing-room door, so I open it and . . .'

'And what, Mr Alejo?'

'Look, you've got to believe me, okay? Otherwise, it means I've gone loco. Please.'

'Just tell us what you saw.'

'I open the door and . . .' Alejo pointed a wavering finger at Ethan's phone. 'I see *that* guy. He's standing with his back to me, and he's surrounded by cables and boxes and stuff that he's pulled out of a big metal crate. He must have wheeled that sucker in on a trolley, 'cause there's a trolley that ain't ours propped against the wall. And Mrs Vielfrass is on the floor, man. And she's like *chained*. The metal's so heavy, I don't think she could even lift it.

'So, I take the bat and charge at the guy and I'm going to swing it at his head and Mrs Vielfrass starts screaming, "Run, Luis! Run!" but I've got the drop on him so why should I run. I got this, okay. And then I swing the bat and . . .'

Alejo stopped again. Ran both hands over his face. When he dropped them, the eyes that stared out at Ethan were wide and pleading.

'It's like he just . . . *disappeared*, man. I swear, the bat was, like, an inch from his skull and I'm going to get him but good and then he's just . . . gone. The next thing I know, the guy's *behind* me and he takes one hand and rips the bat away like it was nothing. *Madre de dios*, the man was strong, and he's staring at me but it's like he doesn't even see me, like I'm nothing to him. And I know he's going to kill me and not think twice about it, so I run, man. Faster than I ever ran in my life. And I make it out the door back into the hallway and . . . and . . .'

Alejo's face was a mask of puzzlement and confusion. Tears sparkled at the corners of his eyes.

'And then I wake up here. I swear to God, I don't remember anything else. And I did *not* go upstairs to see Maria.'

'The man in the room, did he have any water with him? A lot of water? Like in a tank?'

'Water? No, man. The only thing he had with him was the big-ass crate.'

'Do you believe him?' Gutierrez asked later, after the driver had left.

'I don't know what to believe. But I don't think the guy was lying. Whatever really happened in there, *he* believes it.'

'Then I guess we only know one thing for sure.'

'And what's that?'

'That your witness, Jennifer Okoro, got it right. That shitty sketch of yours is accurate. You should get it out to the media.'

Forty

'The Scots,' Hollie announced, as she threw a square of pressed meat into the frying pan, 'are not quite right.'

'Hmmm?' Abi wasn't really listening. Spread out in front of her on the large, wooden . . . *dining* table, Hollie had called it, were an array of tools and a disembowelled mobile phone. With the magnification in her right eye turned up to maximum, she probed gently at the innards. There was a quiet hiss followed by the smell of burned metal.

'I mean, look at this.' Hollie held up another square of pressed meat, examining it with a critical eye. 'I ordered sausages online and when I went to pick them up, they gave me *this* instead. I mean, what the fuck?'

'What's wrong with it?' Abi picked another point on the mobile and pressed down. Another hiss. More burned metal.

'What's wrong is it's not a sausage, that's what.'

'How can you tell?' Abi looked up now, mildly curious.

'I mean look at it. Does that look like a sausage to you?'

'I'm sorry, doll. I ain't never seen a sausage.'

'They don't have sausages in Nigeria?'

'Nope.'

'Figures. You sure you don't want one?' Hollie peered into the frying pan. 'Whatever they are, they smell pretty good.'

'No thanks.' Abi hoped the heave in her stomach had escaped Hollie's notice. 'Eggs, beans, and toast will do me just fine.' Tasteless, but fine. She leaned back from the table and scanned the mobile phone with her augments. The link to the *opolo keji* was still not great, but it was better. Given the limitations of the *oyinbo* networks, it would be foolish to hope for anything more. 'You still liking our cave?'

Hollie frowned briefly, trying to make sense of what Abi had said. But then she beamed.

'Of course. This place is wonderful. Right in the middle of town with a view of the castle?' She waved an enthusiastic hand in the direction of the nearest window. 'What's not to like?' The frown returned. 'I know you have a ton of money now, but are you sure you can afford this? I saw what you paid on the internet, and this is primo expensive.'

'Don't worry about the cost, babe. Your friend Dean Slim is paying. He was very generous.' Abi suspected her smile had a feral edge to it. Buying things online required a credit/debit card, and she only had cash. But once Hollie had explained what a credit/debit card was, it hadn't taken much effort for the *opolo keji* to crack the man's financials wide open.

The rock-cube they found themselves in was divided into flats, and the two of them were comfortably ensconced on the topmost floor. The accommodations were still eye-wateringly primitive but far better than she had experienced so far. She thought about Hollie's damp house in Bristol, and the filthy home Kirsty Forbes lived in. Her brows, she could tell, were knitting together.

'Why is this pad so much nicer than yours, or Kirsty Forbes's?'

Hollie shrugged.

'It just is.'

'But why?'

'Some people have more money than others. If you have money, you can have a nice life. And if you don't . . .' Hollie shrugged again.

'And why do some people have more money than others?'

'They just do.' Hollie's face had a complicated, mostly angry expression that Abi couldn't read. 'And don't go telling me it's any different in Nigeria because that would be bullshit.'

'Then I won't.' Realizing she was on dangerous ground, she thought it best to change the subject. 'Let's see what's on the telly, heh?' A large black rectangle hanging above the kitchen counter sprang to life. Someone was sitting at a desk, mouthing silent words above a red-backed logo. Abi struggled a moment before the lettering made sense. CNN INTERNATIONAL.

'How'd you do that?' Hollie asked, startled.

Idiot. Oyinbos *don't have augments.*

'I didn't do nothing, babe. It just switched itself on. Goofy, huh?'

'Creepy, more li— hey!'

'Sorry, sorry.' In her rush to get to the remote, Abi had almost knocked Hollie off her feet. The symbols on the little buttons were much easier to read than *oyinbo* letters. She turned up the volume.

'. . . are looking for a person of interest in a series of homicides in the city of Chicago, and Providence, Rhode Island . . .'

Abi had to force herself to listen to the woman's words. It was as if her ears had been deafened by the handmade drawing on the right side of the screen. Primitively sketched, it lacked the accuracy of an AI's rendition, but there was something about it that an AI couldn't quite capture. A sense of . . . essence. Hairs prickled on the back of her neck. She could almost feel him in the room with her.

'. . . possibly going by the name of Ahmadu Bello, anyone with information about this man is asked to contact law enforcement in either Chicago or Providence as a matter of urgency. Authorities stress that members of the public should not, on any account, approach him directly as he is believed to be armed and extremely dangerous.'

'Hollie?'

'Uh-huh?'

'Where is Providence, Rhode Island?'

Forty-One

'Hey, Pumpkin. What's up?' His unused voice sounded like scrunched gravel.

'Oh, I'm sorry, Dad. Did I wake you?'

'No.' It wasn't quite a lie. His eyes were open, at least. Pointless thoughts had raced NASCAR-like around the inside of his skull for most of the night, depriving him of rest. Sleep had finally come for him around four a.m., only to be driven away by shards of sunlight slicing through the thin curtains of his motel room. 'You okay? Is anything wrong?'

'I'm fine,' Cara said. 'But I'm worried about you. You sounded weird the other night, that's all, so I thought I'd give you a call to, you know, check up on you. Was there something you wanted to talk about?'

As if on cue, his head started to ache. Like someone was pinching his eyeballs from the back. Perhaps it was time he—

'Nope.'

'Dad, c'mon. You call me at ten o'clock in the evening sounding stressed out, say next to nothing and then hang up. That's not normal, even for you.'

'I'm changing up my game.'

A hiss of exasperation. Like her mother.

'Why won't you *talk* to me? I know there's something wrong. I know it. This is why you and Mom broke up, you get that, right? Because you kept all your shit to yourself and wouldn't let anyone in.'

'We broke up because your mother's a f—'

'Don't!'

'Yeah, well. You don't know the half of it.'

'Because you don't *talk* about it! What is going on with you, lately?'

He couldn't even begin to answer that one. His stilled tongue let the silence stretch and stretch.

'This is about Devin, isn't it?'

'What? No. No, it's not.'

'Then why won't you come to the wedding?'

Because I won't live long enough to make it.

'I never said I wouldn't come to the wedding.'

'So you're coming then?'

'It's complicated.'

'It so isn't. I'm your daughter. You're my dad. You walk me down the aisle wearing a tuxedo and a big stupid smile. Simple.'

There were tears on his cheeks. He brushed them angrily away.

'There's nothing simple about a white girl marrying a Black guy. You're signing up for a world of hurt.'

'Oh my god. Because Black people are so . . . So *what*, Dad? Why don't you go ahead and just say it out loud?'

'Different. He's different from you and you're different from him. Opposites attract is a myth. Opposites collide. Opposites don't understand each other. You marry this guy, you're gonna end up miserable.'

'We love each o—'

'It isn't enough! If it was, your mom and I would still be together.'

His cell phone emitted an insistent beep.

'I'm sorry, hon, I gotta go. Work.'

'Dad, wait. Don't—'

'You awake yet?' Raymond Yeung asked.

'No. You've reached my fucking voicemail.'

'Very funny. Anyway, good news. The picture we released to the media last night looks like it's gotten us a lead.' Ethan fancied he could hear Raymond riffling through his notes. 'I'm just off a call with a Professor John MacPherson at Northwestern. Early riser. The prof is adamant that he's met our guy. But get this. Two *years* ago. Came to see him looking for advice.'

'On what?'

'History.'

'Huh.'

'You wanna talk to him?'

'I'm still in Rhode Island. Waiting for some pretentious, self-important, trust-fund-baby piece of shit to lure our man in. Go see this history guy on his home turf. Put him at ease. See what you can shake loose.'

'Well, here's the thing. He's out by you at some kinda conference. Brandeis.'

'Brandeis?'

'It's a school, lieutenant: edge of Boston. You should be able to walk there, seeing it's the East Coast and everything's right next door to everything else. Am I right?'

Forty-Two

'Step this way please, miss.'

'But—'

'This way, if you would.'

Hollie watched curiously from the far side of the security gate as the airfield official ushered Abi politely but firmly to one side. He waved a black wand over her that screamed incessantly, before calling over a female associate. The associate patted her down so closely that the amulet on her wrist started to tingle.

'Can you take the bracelet off, please?' the woman asked.

'No can do, lady. It's attached to my skin.'

The woman blinked.

'Attached, you say?'

'Sure did. See?' She held her arm up for the woman's inspection.

Slowly, as if unable to resist, the officer reached out and gingerly touched the amulet, trying to turn it.

Abi winced.

'Sorry, madam.' The officer shot her an apologetic smile and retreated towards a small group of airfield staff, none of whom, interestingly, were *oyinbos*. The group huddled around a display screen.

Abi winced again as she turned up her hearing. The ambient noise at the airfield was very high. It made listening in uncomfortable.

'I've never seen anything like it,' a grey-haired man said. The most senior, probably. 'It's like her whole body is wired.'

'You think she's maybe a human bomb?' asked another, younger man. The expression on the senior's face deterred him from saying anything else.

'She's not carrying anything dodgy,' said the woman who'd patted Abi down. 'But get this. That bracelet on her wrist? It's *attached* to her. It won't come off.'

'Anything else odd about it?' the senior asked.

'Nope. Except I'm pretty sure it's made of pure ivory.'

'Which makes sense. Piece is probably older than she is. She's clearly African, after all. I don't think we can detain her under the Ivory Act.' The senior nodded, more to himself than anyone else. He pointed at the monitor. 'Most likely it's the result of surgery. She must have been banged up pretty bad.'

He detached himself from the group and approached her.

'Sorry to detain you, madam. Just a couple of questions if I may. Have you ever had surgery?'

'Sure have.' Abi made sure to look suitably pained. 'I was banged up pretty bad.'

'And did you have surgical implants?'

'Why yes, sir. I did. I sometimes think they're the only things holding me together.'

'I see. Well, for future reference, please tell us before you enter the scanners. It'll save you a lot of delay going forward.'

'Thank you, officer. I'll be sure to do that.'

'What was all that about?' Hollie asked, when Abi finally joined her. 'They gave you a right going over.'

'I have surgical implants. Should have warned 'em ahead of time, they said.'

'Bummer. Well, never mind.' She glanced up at a departures board and tugged lightly on Abi's wrist. 'We've still got a couple of hours before boarding. Let's go hit the duty free.'

Forty-Three

The quaint wooden sign was almost drowned out by the wall to which it was attached, an anarchic collection of multi-coloured stones separated by slapdash swathes of mortar. It was sandwiched between a steeply pitched red gable above and an arched doorway below. CHOLMONDELEY'S, it said. The whole thing looked vaguely medieval. Like something left over from a Renaissance fair.

'How the fuck do you even *say* that?' Ethan muttered. He stepped aside as a pair of students came out of the building, too busy talking to even notice him.

'We don't need to say it,' Gutierrez said. 'We just need to go in.' She followed her own advice and stepped into the coffee shop ahead of him.

Cholmondeley's interior was in stark contrast to its outward appearance, with bright yellow walls, modern leather furnishings, and a highly polished parquet floor. Light flooded in through a series of large windows, luminescent and airy. A complicated collection of stage lights hung from the ceiling.

The place was practically empty, so it was easy to pick out John MacPherson, the Northwestern professor. Contrary to the image in Ethan's head, he was a trim, African-American man in a neatly tailored corduroy jacket. He was nursing a cup of coffee and sitting next to one of the windows. Smooth skin gleamed in the sunlight. He waved at them in greeting. Smiling brightly, he looked like an older version of Devin.

Remembering Cara's early morning phone call, he tamped down on a stab of irritation.

'Welcome to Chum's,' MacPherson said.

'Chum's?' Gutierrez asked.

'That's what the students call it, apparently. I'm told, despite the spelling, that the full name of this place is pronounced "Chumley's". Waste of letters, if you ask me.'

'Thank you for agreeing to meet with us,' Ethan said. Too abruptly, he knew. He sat down across the table and slid over his phone. A. Bello's picture glowed faintly, the screen washed pale by the summer sun. 'I understand from my sergeant that you can tell us something about this guy? That you met him a couple of years ago?'

MacPherson nodded, suddenly businesslike in response to Ethan's blunt demeanour.

'Closer to three, now that I come to think of it. He'd found my name on the school website and wanted to consult with me.'

Ethan pulled out his notebook.

'And this man, when he came to see you, did he give you a name?'

'Of course. He was called Yemi something.' The professor looked faintly embarrassed. 'I don't remember his last name. We tried to dig it out for you but I'm in a temporary office this summer – building work – so everything's a mess right now, including my records. It'll be sitting in a box somewhere. As soon as we find it, I'll let you know.'

'We?'

'My assistant, Anne, and I. She keeps me organized. I have a receipt from him but it's on paper.' Mistaking Ethan's expression for criticism, he felt compelled to add. 'He insisted on paying me in cash for my time, so I wrote him a receipt by hand: otherwise there'd be an electronic record and it'd be easier to track down.'

'Okay.'

'I can tell you it was a Yoruba name, though. From Nigeria. I do remember that much.'

Ethan's pen skipped lightly across his notebook.

'Thank you. And if you and, er, Anne, could make finding this receipt a priority, we'd really appreciate it. Was Yemi local, do you know? Did he live in Chicago?'

'I think so, though he sounded like he was American by choice. He had a pretty pronounced accent.'

'African?'

'Yes. But not quite.' MacPherson was frowning now. He pinched thumb and forefinger together, as if struggling to find precisely the right words. 'I guess he sounded like a guy who'd lived here quite a long time, or who'd learned English from an American. There was definitely a hint of that in the way he was speaking. But there was more to it. Some of the words he used were really odd.' The frown deepened. 'It was like someone with a Nigerian accent imitating John Wayne. Or maybe Al Capone.' An apologetic shake of the head. 'It's hard to explain. But it was . . . an acquired taste.'

Gutierrez chuckled. Even Ethan found his lips twitching upwards.

'When he paid in cash and you made out the receipt, did he give you an address?'

'No. He was kinda cagey about his background, where he

lived, stuff like that. It's one of the reasons I remember him. It's also one of the reasons I insisted on a receipt in the first place, so it was all above board.'

'Okay. Let's talk a bit about why he came to see you. Was there anything specific that he wanted to talk about?'

'Hmm. Yes. He had a lot of questions about the late eighteenth century. It's why he came to see me, I guess. I specialize in Early Modern Britain and the Mid-Atlantic Triangle. He was particularly interested in maritime trade. Which ports were involved, which ships, how they got built, who paid for them, that sort of thing. I got the impression he'd already done quite a lot of research and just needed to be pointed in the right direction.'

'Research?'

'Yeah. He didn't actually say, but I got the impression he was working on some kind of book.'

'Did he ask you questions related to the modern day?'

'Oh no. His interest was purely historical.'

'Uh-huh. You said he needed pointing in the right direction. What direction did you point him in?'

'Quite a number, to be honest. I don't remember the details. Well . . . I do recall that he wanted advice on how to research a sea merchant from that particular era. It was the most granular thing he asked me, which is why I remember it. Everything else we talked about was big picture. I was able to suggest some lines of enquiry for him, but I don't know if anything came of it. I never saw him again. I forget the merchant's name . . . No . . . Wait. It's on the tip of my tongue. Nathaniel Wolfe. Owned a ship called the *Esperance*.'

Forty-Four

Friday the 11th: 5.07 p.m. EDT

For a tiny state, Ethan thought, Rhode Island sure had big traffic. He was sitting in the immaculate passenger seat of Gutierrez's car as they edged south, stop-go style, on I-95. The stone and small glass of Providence's downtown remained stubbornly out of reach.

Ethan's cell phone rang, a familiar number glowing on the screen.

'Hey, Raymond. How's it going?'

'No new murders today, so kinda good, I guess. You were looking for me earlier?'

'Yep. Wanted to see how you were getting on with the licence plate on that box van.'

'Slowly. I had no idea there were so many Africans here. But we're running 'em down one by one. Another day maybe.'

'No decent prospects I'm guessing.'

A dry chuckle on the other end of the line.

'Right, 'cause if we'd found the guy, I'd have fucking well kept it to myself and not told you.'

'Fair enough,' Ethan said, laughing in return. 'So let me lighten your labours. Your history professor had a name for us.

First name, anyway. "Yemi": Young, Edward, Mary, Ida. Can't be too many of them around.'

'Assuming it's not an alias.'

'Fair point. But worth a look. Also, call up Northwestern and get ahold of MacPherson's assistant. He says the guy paid him for a consultation almost three years back and that he kept a receipt with our guy's full name on it. She might be able to dig it up for us before he gets back to town.'

'Assuming it's a she, of course.'

'It is. Goes by the name of Anne. And when the fuck did you get woke, sergeant?'

'This morning, when my alarm went off.'

Ethan hung up with a smile on his face. Noticed that Gutierrez was frowning at him.

'Hey,' he said, 'I didn't mean anything by the woke crack. It was just a joke.'

'What? No. I was just thinking, that's all.' She slapped the wheel in irritation. 'Not much else to do in traffic like this.' The car crept forward, the view through the windshield obscured by the lumbering stern of an SUV.

'And has your thinking produced anything useful?'

'Not really. I'm wondering what being a cold-blooded serial killer has to do with a love of history.'

'I was thinking the same thing. You know the answer I came up with?'

'What?'

'Nothing.'

Gutierrez gave a short bark of laughter.

'I'm serious,' Ethan said, smiling nonetheless. 'When they're not murdering people, serial killers have lives. Ordinary lives, often. This guy, so far as we know, didn't start killing people till six months ago, in Nigeria. He waltzed into Northwestern at least two years earlier. Talking to a college professor doesn't turn you into a serial killer.'

'Unless you're paying the tuition.'

Now it was Ethan's turn to laugh. The SUV in front of them changed lanes, making for a much better view.

'Our guy Yemi, whatever else he is, is no fool, yeah? For all we know he may be super fucking bright.'

'Okay. So?'

'Well, super fucking bright people do super fucking bright things, don't they? Maybe the good professor has it right. Maybe, when he's not busy killing people, our super fucking bright perp writes books.'

'Huh.'

Ethan couldn't tell if Gutierrez was responding to what he'd said or to the sight of the exit ramp. She swung the wheel, plunging them into the bowels of the city.

Forty-Five

Friday the 11th: 5.54 p.m. EDT

While Gutierrez slipped through the Friday rush-hour traffic, Ethan and his phone consulted Amazon and a number of other book sites, each one kookier than the last. Yemi, while not a common author name, still accounted for a significant number of books, ranging from ethnic cooking, through Christian-themed romances, to serious politics. None of the books touched on history, though, and when he could lay his hands on an author photo, none of the pictures matched what he was looking for, either. He sat back with a sigh just as Gutierrez pulled to the kerb, only to start with surprise when he looked out the window.

'What are we doing here?' he asked.

'I just want to have another crack at this guy.' Gutierrez slid smoothly out of her seat and headed briskly towards the lobby of Chuck Vielfrass's condo building. She waved to the uniform sitting in the police cruiser across the street. When she got off the elevator at Vielfrass's floor, she exchanged a quick word with the uni sitting in the hallway, too. This, Ethan thought, was a woman who liked to be liked.

And who could pull in a lot of favours as a result. Like two unis to guard an asshole wannabe film producer.

When Charlene Zhao quietly let them in, the wannabe film producer was in his element, his living room rigged with cameras and movie lights. Someone had set up a boom mike so that it hung just beneath the ceiling. Vielfrass himself was sitting on the sofa, ostentatiously leafing through what looked like an old-fashioned photo album. He was talking in hushed, scripted tones towards an expensive-looking lens.

'When tragedy strikes,' he said, 'it changes you. Strips you down to the essentials. Makes you confront who you really are. When I look at these photos now, I don't see the old Chuck Vielfrass. I see—'

'Sir, do you mind if we have a quick word?'

'Fuck!' Vielfrass reached under a sofa cushion for a hidden remote and started stabbing buttons. The movie lights died away, leaving the room looking suddenly gloomy. 'Can you not see I'm working here? Charlie, why'd you let these people in, huh? They've gone and ruined a perfectly good take.'

'I'm so sorry, sir,' Gutierrez said, before Charlene could answer. 'We thought it was just a rehearsal, didn't we, Ethan?' Gutierrez's expression was studiedly guileless. Ethan fought to hold back a smirk. He wasn't sure that he'd succeeded.

'Did I *look* like I was "just" rehearsing?'

'Well . . . yes.'

Ethan looked away. Caught a ghost of a smile on Charlene's lips.

'Jesus fucking . . . Okay, okay. You're here now. Why don't you sit down on the sofa with me while your Chicago friend stays out of shot. We can record the interview. Gotta be good for something, right?'

'Sir, I don't think—'

'Look, *you* came to see *me*.' He pointed at the cameras. 'You want me to talk? This is the price of admission.'

With a small sigh, Gutierrez pulled out her notebook and sat down, the abandoned photo album forming a barrier between herself and Vielfrass. Vielfrass pushed the buttons on his remote and shoved it back behind the sofa cushion. The lights came up. Gutierrez stiffened, forced herself to relax again.

'Sir—'

'Please, call me Chuck.' An oily smile.

'Chuck. Where does your money come from?'

The smile vanished.

'I'm a film producer. I make documentaries. It's what I do.'

'I understand, sir . . . sorry. *Chuck*. But what do you live on? Your mother made it very clear to us that you relied on the family money. There's a trust fund?'

'That's not . . . completely true.'

'You're saying there's no trust fund?'

'No. Just that it's not my only source of income.'

'Okay. I just want to talk about the trust fund. Understand?'

Chuck nodded.

'If the trust fund is family money. Where did the money come from?'

'From the family, obviously.'

'And how did your family make its money?'

Vielfrass ran a distracted hand through his hair.

'Geez, lieutenant, I don't really know. It's *old* money. Now it's all stocks and bonds, that sort of thing. But back in the day it was textiles. Did you know Rhode Island is the birthplace of the US textile industry? We stole the technology from the British around the time of the Revolutionary War. Anyway, my ancestors were heavily involved in that, and then it was railroads, and god knows what else. But nowadays the family's investments are "diversified" as James likes to say.' A brief loathing surfaced on his features. 'I don't think I can tell you much else.'

'And these diversified assets. Is it possible you have family investments in Chicago? In Africa?'

Chuck shrugged.

'It's possible, I guess. You'd have to ask James. He's the guy who cares about money.'

'I thought you'd never been to Africa,' Gutierrez said, peering at the photo album. She reached out a finger and tapped a page. 'But this says "Elmina Castle, Ghana".'

'It's a family album. These pictures,' he stabbed rapidly at the open pages, 'are mine. That one is Mom's and these two, including the African one, are Sonia's. Like I told you before, Sonia was into travelling before she settled down. Including Ghana, it looks like.'

'You see, sir – Chuck – the thing is, while I can't get into the details, we are very comfortable that there's a connection between the murder of your sister, niece and nephew, and Nigeria. Can you think of anything, anything at all, that pulls those things together?'

'No. I already told you . . . Well . . . let's see.' He picked up the photo album and started leafing through it. 'This is from the year of her African tour. Has to be. Right, here's one: Sierra Leone.' The pages whispered as he turned them. 'Sierra Leone . . . Sierra Leone . . . Sierra Leone . . . Liberia . . . Liberia . . . Ghana . . . Ghana . . . and Ghana. That's it. No Nigeria anywhere.'

Gutierrez folded up her notebook. Glanced at Ethan.

'Chuck, do you mind if I ask you a couple of questions?'

Vielfrass glanced between the two detectives and shrugged.

'Go ahead.'

'Making movies is expensive, isn't it?' He gestured vaguely around the room. 'All this equipment, technicians, the whole shebang, am I right?'

'More than you know, lieutenant. More than you know.' Chuck favoured him with a world-weary smile.

'Your mother led us to believe that you couldn't get enough money out of your trust fund to fund your projects. Is that right?'

Vielfrass's smile vanished.

'Did Mom really tell you that, or was it James? James, I'll bet. Arrogant fucking bastard.'

'Is it true? About the money?'

'Yeah. It's tied up in a bunch of deeds and stuff. Mom would have let me have access to it, but that f— James nixed the whole plan. Cost me the project that would have made my name.'

Ethan, remembering Dottie's strong views on the subject, doubted that Chuck Vielfrass was telling the truth. He let it pass, however.

'So where'd you get the money? You borrowed it, yes?'

'Obviously.'

'From who?'

Chuck shifted uneasily on the sofa.

'From . . . film people. Investors. It's very normal.'

'And did these investors make their money back?'

A small smile played on Chuck Vielfrass's lips.

'Contrary to what you might have heard, people don't invest in the film industry to make money, lieutenant. Well, not on any individual project. Sure, if a project comes up big, great. But it's the *journey* that counts. The joy of sharing a vision, bringing it to fruition, seeing it up there on the big screen. It's a creative high.'

'Uh-huh. And did any of these investors complain about not getting their money back?'

'A few, I guess.'

'And were any of these folks capable of using violence?'

'What? No!' Chuck looked pale. Ethan just stared at him. A thin tongue flickered over the man's lips.

'Look, some of my investors have . . . interesting backgrounds. But they've never threatened me, or my family. They're in it for the rush, like I said. And if a couple of them insist on getting paid back, I find a way. Always. It's not worth the risk. I don't want to wake up with a horse's head in my bed.'

Ethan had to smile at that.

'Have any Nigerians invested in your films?'

'No.'

'You're sure?'

'I'm sure. I know all my investors personally. This is a very face-to-face business.'

Ethan exchanged a glance with Gutierrez.

'Okay, Chuck. Thank you for your time. But if you think of any connection that will help us, let us know.' He raised an eyebrow. 'Your life may depend on it.'

Forty-Six

'Wow,' Hollie said. 'I mean, just . . . wow. It's like the movies, isn't it? Just like the movies. I—'

Whatever she'd been about to say was interrupted by a violent blast of sound. Some kind of proximity warning, Abi guessed. Hollie slammed on the brakes. Another vehicle flashed by, the sound travelling with it.

'Shit! Sorry about that. This driving on the wrong side of the road is going to take a bit of getting used to.'

Abi, whose eyes were occupied by the stream of data flowing out of her augments, gazed blindly in Hollie's direction.

'Why are we driving on the wrong side of the road? That doesn't sound good.'

Hollie giggled.

'No worries. We're on the right side of the road. Now anyway. It's just that in England it would be wrong.'

'Really?'

'Sure. Everything is backwards.' She patted the steering wheel of their rental. 'This is a left-hand-drive car. Like in a lot of foreign countries. Thank god it's an automatic, I don't think I could change gears with my right hand.'

Compared to its driver, the automobile Abi had hired for them was huge. Hollie was perched on the front of the seat, peering over the steering wheel into an industrial night. Lights, and wire fencing, and the half-shapes of buildings slipped by as she cautiously followed the directions given by the vehicle's onboard navigation system. Hollie drove in her bare feet, Abi noticed. Of the sky there was no sign. It lay black and unseen beyond the cloaking glare of neon.

'This is what we want: I-95 South, yeah?'

Abi nodded absently, her attention once more on the data stream. Hollie swung the wheel, moving the vehicle onto a different route. Concrete thrummed beneath the tyres.

'Look, Abs. The road signs are green. Green! Like I said, it's just like the movies. And did you hear all those American accents in the terminal? Like, really, really cool.' She gave a dramatic flip of the head, sending her purple-tipped hair into a swirling dance. 'Who knows? Maybe I'll be discovered by some famous Hollywood director.'

Fuelled by airfield coffee and excitement, Hollie didn't seem to notice that it was the early hours of her body's morning. Abi, on the other hand, was very aware that her circadian rhythms were badly out of step. Even with several hours of artificially induced sleep and some dosing from her amulet, she felt creaky and slow. A faint headache thumped half-heartedly behind her eyes. She consulted her files.

'Hollywood's on the other side of the country, doll. Some guy comes up to you with a story like that, sawbucks to doughnuts he's a grifter.'

'A girl can dream, can't she?'

The road they were on was extremely wide, with markings clearly set out in such a way as to allow multiple vehicles to travel in parallel. A thought that made Abi a little nervous. Fortunately, there was not much in the way of traffic. She glanced over at Hollie, still hunched over the wheel but looking a little more relaxed.

'You figured out where we're going once we get to Providence?' Hollie asked.

'Almost.' The stream of information flitting across her retinas was beginning to slow down. She pretended to consult her phone.

'Can we stay in a motel? They have motels here. Proper ones. It's where yanks go when they want to keep a low profile. Like us.'

'Sure.' Abidemi wished she could access the *oyinbo*, Angela. The people she was interested in were hard to track down without the genealogist's assistance. Yemi was further ahead of her than she'd hoped. On the other hand, she was now in a position to reverse engineer his work.

Most recently, he'd killed a Providence woman, Dorothy Vielfrass, as well as her daughter and the daughter's children. But the *opolo keji* was hinting that there were others. A son by the name of Charles Vielfrass, for instance. He seemed real enough. There was an address in Providence. A good target if she could beat Yemi to the punch. But the *opolo keji* was less sure about whether this Charles Vielfrass had children. If he did, they didn't live in the same compound, which made no sense. And if there was a mother, the *opolo keji* was unsure as to who she was and where she might be found. There were a number of potential mates associated with Vielfrass. Two in Providence, three in Los Angeles, and maybe an additional one in Chicago, although that might be the same as one of the Providence possibles.

Another possibility occurred to her.

'Hollie?'

'Yes.'

'If a guy makes whoopee with another guy, can they have kids?'

Hollie seemed to find the question funny.

'I don't think that's how sex works, Abs.'

'With assistance, I mean. Do you have birthing vats here?'

The automobile swerved unnervingly as Hollie turned to look at her.

'Birthing *what*?'

'Never mind. If I'm a guy and my mate is another guy, is there any way for the two of us to have kids?'

Hollie's eyes returned to the road. The route ahead was shrouded in night, lit here and there by splashes of light from lonely vehicles. Patches of deeper black on either side hinted at an unseen landscape sweeping past the windows.

'Sure. You could adopt. Or maybe get a surrogate mother.'

'A surrogate—?'

'Mother. A woman to give birth for you. It's pretty hard though – at least it is at home. I think Americans do it quite a lot.'

'Got it. Thanks, doll.' Abi allowed herself a small sigh of relief. Limiting the parameters to biological births meant less work for the AI. 'How does Xanadu Motel sound? You can park right outside the door to your room.'

Forty-Seven

Saturday the 12th: 1.19 a.m. EDT

The room was comfortable enough, and reasonably clean by *oyinbo* standards, with two large beds and an attached bathroom, but Abidemi could not understand Hollie's excitement about it. Perhaps sleeping at ground level was some kind of treat for her.

A stark, artificial light forced its way through the chamber's thin curtains, casting the place in faint gloom. Without resorting to infrared or any other type of scan, it was possible to see Hollie's blanketed outline on the neighbouring bed. She was sleeping soundly. For the first time since they'd met, Abi envied her. She envied the backward simplicity of Hollie's life, her joy at the completion of an overlong, lumbering journey in a flying metal tube, the wonder of being in a place that was strange, even to her.

The fact that when she went back home nothing would have changed.

Lying in her own bed and staring at the ceiling, Abi touched both hands softly to the *ila* on each cheek, feeling the small, scarred depressions she'd had since childhood. She tried to remember the feathery touch of Ayo and Kehinde kissing them, the feel of their hot tears mixing with her own, the regretful but insistent tug of the *masu amfana* as it pulled them away. But she couldn't. Not really. It was just another entry in the files.

Supplanted by cold rain and an endless ocean of grass.

The amulet was insisting she get some sleep but she resisted. The mechanism could put her under but it couldn't make her sleep well. She would wake up, as she had on the bumpy, cramped *oyinbo* airplane, groggy and disoriented. She overrode it. She allowed her mind to wander, images of *oyinbos* and home chasing each other through her thoughts while she waited for her eyelids to grow heavy on their own.

They almost did, too. Just as she felt herself dropping off, an odd, out-of-place sensation pulsed through her augments. Thinking that spillover from the endless *oyinbo* transmissions was making it through her filters, she started to adjust the settings.

And stopped.

The frequencies and phasing were all wrong. Too complex to be *oyinbo*, too harmonious. Too non-binary.

'*Oluwa o!*' She threw off the blankets. Swung bare feet onto scratchy carpet tiles.

'What?' Hollie shifted on her bed.

'Go back to sleep, doll. I gotta check something out.'

She threw on her clothes, glad of their night-matching blackness, fumbled around for her phone and key card and headed out the door. It was warmer here than in Bristol or Edinburgh, her black leather jacket serving no function other than decoration. She drew the comforting air into her lungs, consulted the new map the *opolo keji* had placed in the files, and started to run. A score of long strides took her past the curtilage of the motel and out onto the road. It was long and straight and slightly uphill.

She settled into an urgent, pounding rhythm, augments and amulet combining to push her to speeds few *oyinbo*s could hope to match. The pulsing sensation grew stronger.

As if in response, the road got hillier, started to twist and turn. She was dealing with intersections now, lefts and rights as the *opolo keji* directed. The buildings, previously spread out, began to huddle together and press close to the street. They were cuboid in the *oyinbo* fashion but not always rock. Some of them were wooden. Gardens were few and far between: just dull oblongs of grass or concrete for the most part. She was glad it was night.

A brief burst of garbly static, painfully familiar, caused her to slow down and duck into a doorway. Sure enough, a moment or two later, the low, humped shape of an automobile rolled quietly into the street. It slid past Abi without slowing, stark and white, its sole occupant either unseeing or uninterested in her. The word PROVIDENCE was splashed across its side in hard-to-read *oyinbo* script and then, towards its front, in much smaller letters, POLICE.

Abi stiffened in surprise. Though not because it was a police vehicle. After the radio burst, so similar to the ones in Bristol, she'd expected that. It was the car itself. Like the Edinburgh drug dealer's, it was packed with primitive AI. Given the right input, it could drive itself. Or the opposite. Easy enough to reach out across the *oyinbo* networks and . . .

The vehicle turned a corner and vanished from sight, the staticky interference fading with it.

Abi ran on. She reached a street where the *oyinbo*s were still very much awake, eating and drinking and shouting above the music in garishly lit buildings. There were so many of them, she thought, briefly awestruck. And this was just one city among, what? Tens of thousands? Millions?

She slowed to a walk so as not to attract attention, turned right at the next intersection, and came to a halt.

There.

The building was squat and blocky, four storeys tall and sub-divided into separate dwellings. A block of flats, but significantly better maintained than the ones Abi had seen so far. This one was constructed with neatly dressed rock, large windows, and open-air terraces. There was no damp in the walls, no sign of decay. She once again found herself struggling with how *oyinbo*s could bear to live in such wildly different circumstances. She pushed the thought out of her head. It was no concern of hers.

And *gbese* must be paid.

There was a police vehicle parked across from the entrance. This one lacked the obvious markings of the one she'd encountered earlier, but it was packed with the same communications equipment and had the same primitive AI. Scans revealed two occupants, one male, one female. The man was drinking something hot from a cup. Tea, no doubt, or even worse, coffee. She remembered Hollie downing the stuff at the Boston airfield as if it were some sort of medicine. The reek of it had compelled Abi to strengthen her filters.

That the police were here, waiting, couldn't be a coincidence. *Cleverer than I give them credit for, these* oyinbos. *Be careful.*

But the pulsing in her head was strong and getting stronger. She was already behind. She didn't have time to be careful. And besides, no one here was looking for her.

Yet.

She removed her leather jacket and slung it over her shoulder, imagining that she was heading back to her rock-cube after a night out around the corner. She walked towards the block of flats at an unhurried pace, scanning the occupants of the police vehicle as she did so. They were both watching her, but neither seemed unduly interested.

She reached the large glass doors that marked the entrance to the building and gave one of the handles a nonchalant pull. A woman returning to her rock-cube.

The door remained stubbornly shut. She pulled at it again, harder this time.

Nothing.

It was locked, she realized belatedly. A hurried scan revealed an electronically controlled deadbolt tied to a card reader, not unlike the one in her motel room. But not like, either. The key card in her pocket wouldn't work here. Conscious of the police gaze drilling into her back, she pulled it out anyway, as if she'd absent-mindedly forgotten the need for it.

Her mind raced far ahead of her body. The door was glass, the deadbolt metal. If she pulled hard enough the lock would break. But so would the door. And even if by some miracle it didn't shatter, the noise of the breaking lock would certainly attract the interest of her watchers. Alternatively, a good running jump would allow her to grab on to the lowest of the open-air terraces and climb from there. But that, too, had obvious drawbacks. Praying to whatever nameless *orisha* held sway here, she scanned the reader, hoping for a way in.

The *orisha* was kind. The reader was connected to a small, underpowered network, almost certainly confined to the building. She made a great show of presenting the motel key card while her implants used the phone to activate the necessary ones and zeroes.

The deadbolt gave way with a satisfying click. She stepped through, a hiss of quiet relief sliding through her lips. The need for role-playing over, she put the leather jacket back on. For what was coming, she would require both hands.

She needed no assistance from the *opolo keji* to help her with directions now. The pulsing energy she'd followed so assiduously was thudding into her from somewhere above. Not trusting possible interference from the inside of a metal box, Abi eschewed the silvery doors of the building's lift and took the steps, up and up and up until there were no more stairs, just a simple wooden door.

She stepped through into a typical *oyinbo* passageway, doors to the various dwellings on either side. Even with the filters turned up full, the pulses in her augments were so loud it was hard to hear herself think.

It took her a moment to register that there was a body slumped in the corridor.

A few quick strides and she was at the woman's side. A police officer of some sort, judging by the uniform, normal looking, with hair close-cropped to her ebony scalp. A faint hiss of static emanated from the device on her chest. She wasn't breathing but Abi didn't need a scan to know the woman was still alive. She allowed herself a small twinge of sympathy before reaching for the door the police officer had once guarded.

'Police! Stop right there, hands above your head, nice and easy.'

The burning heat of combat chemicals flooded her system. The world slowed as she turned.

The man and woman from the car must have followed her in. They stood side by side in the corridor, blocking her way back to the stairwell, weapons drawn. Not sticks these, like in Bristol, but projectile weapons, their round muzzles housed in an incongruously square design. Boosted or not, there was no way to close the gap before one or other of them got a shot off. In the confined space of the corridor they could hardly miss.

She slammed through a door instead. Not the one being guarded. The one opposite.

Hinges and deadlocks bent and gave way. Wood cracked and splintered. Bone, too, her collarbone and scapula shattering under forces they were never designed to withstand. The chemicals lied about the pain, downplayed it. The lancing, unbearable agony would come later.

For now, though, the unhinged door was flying into the living room beyond. Blue carpet. Pale wood furniture. Abstract paintings on the walls. She followed the door inside as the twin blasts of projectile weapons exploded in the hallway. A bullet plucked at her undamaged shoulder, grazing the skin.

The door seemed to float to the floor, an oblong leaf drifting in the wind. There were voices now, slowed beyond articulation to the primal emotions beneath. Surprise and anger from the corridor, alarm and fear from the violated dwelling. Abi adjusted her footing and pressed herself to the wall next to the torn-open entrance, out of sight from the man and woman whose slowed-down steps were beginning to crash along the passageway outside.

Clump . . . clump.

A door – another door – was opening into the living room. From a sleeping chamber, probably.

Clump . . . clump.

A face appeared at the bedroom door. A man, his skin comfortingly dark. And handsome. At least, when his face wasn't twisted out of shape by terror.

Clump.

The male pursuer reached the main entrance and stepped

inside, his weapon pointed unwaveringly at the owner of the dwelling. His finger squeezed on the firing contact.

The pursuer's focus on the wrong target made it almost too easy. Abi, remembering to use her undamaged arm and in the policeman's blind spot, jammed a hard fist into his temple.

Flame and smoke erupted from the muzzle of the man's weapon as he collapsed towards the ground. Abi was dimly aware of the projectile tearing through a painting, gouts of glass and wood and pieces of artificial rock spewing across the room. She scooped up the unconscious *oyinbo* before he could hit the floor and carried him on her good shoulder into the hallway, cannoning into the man's female partner. She dropped his dead weight on top of her, forcing her to the ground. The woman was prostrate on her back, but not helpless. She'd maintained a firm grip on her weapon.

Abi kicked her in the head before she could use it.

In the distance she could hear the keening wail of police sirens. Judging by the changes in pitch, they were all headed her way. She started towards the once-guarded apartment but changed her mind. Yemi had beaten her to it. He would either have succeeded or not. With the commotion outside he would be long gone. Indulging her curiosity would only cost time, time she didn't have. The chemicals would wear off soon, leaving her incapacitated and in agony. She needed to be away from here before more police arrived.

She headed back to the stairwell at a brisk trot, the throbbing in her shoulder growing more pronounced with every step.

Forty-Eight

Saturday the 12th: 2.26 a.m. EDT

'*A*re you all right?'

No.

Strong, uniformed arms were hauling Ethan to his feet. It was all he could do to stop himself from bursting into tears.

I could have killed that guy.

He'd seen the man standing there, wide-eyed and naked apart from his pyjama bottoms But he hadn't *understood*. The woman had been Black, and sleek, and powerful. And fast. Crazy fast. One moment she was there, the next there'd been the shattering sound of a door coming off its hinges and she was gone. He'd entered the condo expecting to confront her. Knowing, from the sheer violence of her evasion, that she could kill him without breaking a sweat.

And he'd seen the man, not her. But his brain refused to see the difference until it was too late. He'd pulled the trigger, aiming squarely for centre mass, just as what felt like a ball-peen hammer had smashed into the side of his head. He'd felt his grip slackening on the butt of his service weapon, sensed rather than seen the bullet go into the wall. Death avoided by inches. And then: lights out.

'I'll live,' he grunted. His vision was blurry. Concussion probably. But he could see well enough. The unknown Black woman had stoved the door in with such force that it was lying in the middle of the living room, a giant coffee table without legs, incongruous against the cornflower blue of the carpet. The condo owner, his tall, mocha body now wrapped in a dressing gown, was standing on the balcony, talking in animated, angry tones with a uniform sergeant. The sliding glass doors that separated it from the living room were closed, so he couldn't hear what was being said. But it was easy enough to guess.

Your racist cop buddy over there almost blew my head off.

Something unpleasant shifted in the pit of his stomach. He thought about Cara, and Devin, and how he'd shot at a man and not a woman. He wasn't racist. He wasn't. But . . .

He thrust a pair of shaking hands into his pocket.

'You okay?' Gutierrez asked.

'I should be asking you that. You look like shit.'

She did, too. Her olive skin was unnaturally pale, a giant bruise already beginning to spread across the left side of her face. She rubbed her hand against her jaw, as if surprised it wasn't broken.

'Thanks for that. Way to build up a girl's confidence.' The hand moved to the bruise, making her wince. 'The bitch got me good. Goddamn it she was fast! I've never seen anything like it.' She favoured him with a wry look. 'You were right about her, though. She's definitely connected.'

Ethan managed a grin.

'You owe me ten bucks,' he said. 'No one who lives here would have taken that long to get through the door. Like I was saying, she must have faked out the lock somehow.'

'How, though?'

'No clue. We'll figure it out when we catch her.'

'And there was me thinking you were an old, racist white guy.'

That twisting in his stomach again.

'How's the uni in the corridor?' he asked, desperate to think about something else. 'Is she—?'

'Not dead, thank god. Though, god knows, she looks it. She's barely breathing.'

'Neurotoxin. Has to be. Same as Chicago. Probably the same as your man James.'

Gutierrez was frowning.

'You know, Ethan, catching this woman might take a SWAT team. She has serious skills. Serious. Bypasses an electronically locked entryway, subdues a uniformed officer with neurotoxin, incapacitates two armed detectives who were *shooting* at her, for fuck's sake. Blows through a deadbolted door like it's nothing. You think she's military?'

'Has to be. Maybe special ops. Wherever that woman did her service, it wasn't kitchen patrol.'

Gutierrez was looking at the hole in the wall, the shattered picture.

'You got a shot off before she dropped you, yeah? Please tell me you got a piece of her.'

'I missed. Almost killed a civilian.' He clamped his mouth shut against a torrent of confession.

Gutierrez's eyes skipped to the balcony. Oceans of anger beating against a cliff face of polite, professional scepticism. She dismissed it with a small shrug.

'"Almost" is the operative word. Worry about it later. Let's go see what our friend Chuck has to say. Maybe all this nonsense will have loosened up something useful. Guy had a narrow escape after all.'

'I'm surprised he isn't out here already,' Ethan said, smiling. 'Filming his look-at-me-aren't-I-great documentary.'

The smile faded.

'Why isn't he out here already?'

Gutierrez was three steps ahead of him, leading the way out of the condo and across the hallway, banging on Chuck Vielfrass's closed, locked and undamaged door. She pounded on the finely grained wood, her small fist producing a booming noise that echoed down the corridor.

'Mr Vielfrass? It's the police. Open up, please.' More pounding. 'Mr Vielfrass? Chuck? We need to know you're okay. Open the door. Hello? Hello? Mr Vielfrass . . .'

Neither Ethan nor Gutierrez was stupid enough to barge the door down. That was for the movies. The exploits of the escaped Black woman notwithstanding, the door would remain intact and one or both of them would come away with a broken shoulder. It took a minute or two, but the uniforms rustled up a ram, a dense metal tube with easy-to-grip handles, its matte black surface pitted and scarred from frequent use. The operator, a Black officer with arms almost as thick as Ethan's legs, and with a pair of industrial goggles protecting his eyes, swung the device with brutal efficiency. With a crack like a shotgun, the door burst open, shards of door frame exploding across the threshold.

Ethan rushed in behind two other uniforms and caromed into the back of them as they skidded to an abrupt halt.

'What the . . .' he began. And then stopped. One sentence was replaced by another.

'Holy Mother of God.'

Forty-Nine

*A*bidemi had to stop. She was collapsed in a small alleyway, hidden from sight by a large metal receptacle for domestic refuse. The reek of decaying organic matter overcame her filters and forced its way into her nostrils, making her gag. Traitorous limbs had turned to rubber, unable to support her weight or obey her commands, spasming and cramping. Tsunamis of agony radiated from her shattered shoulder, the pain too great to be tamped down by the amulet, not without putting her under anyway. Blood pounded in her head with so much force it blurred her vision. She lay curled up in a ball. Filthy, gravelly ground pressed against her.

I can't stay here, she thought. *Too close. Too close. Got to keep moving.*

But she couldn't.

She had run until her body had given way, the sound of sirens some distance behind her. The *oyinbo*s would be confused for a while, tending to their injured, trying to make sense of what had happened. But then they would come looking for her. It was all too easy to imagine the low, white hump of a police vehicle turning into the alley, its wheels crunching on the uneven roadway. If they had the technology, probing sensors would have no trouble picking up the fevered heat of her body against a background of rock, gravel and garbage.

Her stomach heaved. A small trickle of bile dripped from her mouth, adding to the sum of filth and unpleasantness in which she lay.

She felt better though. Dragged herself into a sitting position.

Oyinbo police didn't have sensors. Just eyes. And miserable unmodified ones at that. She was safe enough for the moment. She just needed to gather her strength.

And stop the amulet from putting her under.

She forced herself to wait longer than she thought necessary before struggling to her feet. A sensible precaution, given the wave of dizziness that followed. She took a deep breath. Composed herself. The slow-moving *oyinbo* sun would not be up for some time yet. There would be few people about. All she had to do was walk back to the motel and look uninjured. A wry smile twisted her lips.

Easier said than done.

But she did it anyway, internal diagnostics scrolling across the inside of her eyelids. There was a lot of damage. A lot. The amulet needed help. And not just from the med kit.

She tensed as she walked into the courtyard of the Xanadu Motel. On the far side, beyond the scattering of parked vehicles, a shadow was coming out of one of the rooms

Another resident. Or maybe not. A visitor, perhaps. Scans of the room the man had left showed another occupant, female and apparently asleep. The man paid Abi no attention, padding instead to a nearby vehicle and starting it up. Bright lights washed across her as she found the door to her room. She reached into a pocket for a key card and swore softly. It must have fallen out while she was flopping about in the alley.

She tapped gently on the door. It was clear from the heat signature beyond that Hollie, like the other female, was fast asleep. She knocked harder. The blurry form in the scans finally stirred. A light came on. The door creaked as it opened, matching Hollie's yawn.

'Jesus, Abs. Do they not have key cards in Nigeria?'

'Sorry, doll. I must have dropped it.' She stumbled past Hollie, and sat gingerly on her bed, the sheets cold and rumpled from her previous attempt at sleep. She tried to shrug out of her leather jacket, but the pain was too much.

'Are you okay?' Hollie asked.

'I'm f—'

'You are definitely *not* fine.' Hollie sat down beside her, her face a mask of concern. 'Here. Let me help with that.' Gently, she peeled the jacket from Abi's shoulders. Gentle or not, the motion made Abi gasp. 'Holy fuck! What the hell happened to you?' The room's unforgiving light kept no secrets. Abi's right shoulder was clearly broken, horribly and asymmetrically misshapen compared with her left, the outline of her snapped collarbone clearly visible. The smooth blackness of her skin was scraped raw and bloody, except where it was mottled with huge, irregularly shaped bruises. Ugly, purple-black islands in an ebony sea.

'I ran into a door. Gave it a helluva beating.' The room seemed to be spinning. Abi wasn't sure she could hold the amulet off for much longer. She reached out. Grabbed Hollie by the hand. 'I need a favour.'

'What you need, Abs, is a hospital.' Hollie's face frowned in sudden worry. 'I think you have to pay for them here. I hope to Christ they take credit cards.'

Abi's grip tightened.

'No hospitals, doll. But I do need you to find me some stuff. I need a lot of calcium and a lot, a *lot* of protein. Do you think you can do that for me?'

'I guess so. They have twenty-four-hour shops here. I've seen 'em in the movies. I'll google it. How about milk? Milk has calcium.'

Abi would have shaken her head if it didn't hurt so much.

'Not enough. I need *ofún* . . . ah . . .' She struggled to find the right word. 'Chalk. I need chalk. Or eggshells.'

Hollie made a face.

'You're going to eat eggshells?'

'A lot of eggshells. At least forty.'

'Jesus Chr— okay. And eggs have protein. That's two birds with one stone.'

'Not enough. I need a mix of proteins. Like in the body.'

'I could buy some steaks.'

Abi's stomach heaved in revulsion. She forced it into submission. After all, what choice did she have, really?

Hollie was giving her a shrewd look.

'If you won't eat meat, I could maybe get those protein shakes bodybuilders use. Would that work?'

Abi's grateful smile was all the answer Hollie needed. She threw on some clothes and headed for the door, car keys in hand. She threw a worried glance over her shoulder.

'Eating isn't going to fix a broken bone, Abs. Sooner or later, we're going to have to take you to the hospital.'

'We'll see, doll. Eat first, doctor later.'

Even after she'd closed it behind her, Hollie's scepticism seemed to burn through the door. Abi regretted not asking for help with her boots. She made a half-hearted attempt to do it on her own but gave up after unknotting the laces. More or less one-handed, she wrestled the med-kit out of her backpack and slipped it over her free wrist. With a sigh and a grimace, she lay back on the bed, closed her eyes, and let the machines have their way.

Fifty

Ethan, and everyone else in the room, stood transfixed in horror, gazing at the spectacle in front of them. He was seeing it, but –

'I don't believe it,' Gutierrez said, her voice little more than a whisper. 'This has got to be some kind of trick. Hasn't it?' She turned to Ethan as if seeking reassurance.

Ethan was unable to provide it. He lacked even the most basic of words. He kept staring. It felt like an eternity before his brain began to unfreeze itself.

Chuck Vielfrass was dead. Drowned like the others, his lungs full of the sea.

The only difference being that the sea was still here.

The deceased's living room, with its steel-and-leather furniture, ego-stroking posters, and camera equipment, was dominated by a giant tank of what had to be seawater. The tank was hovering – Jesus fucking Christ, *hovering* – maybe a couple of feet above the floor and ran to within an inch or two of the ceiling. Chuck Vielfrass's corpse, naked apart from a pair of black, silk boxer shorts, floated upright inside it. It looked like a bizarre imitation of a stadium wave, bare feet almost touching the bottom, arms raised towards the surface. A couple of his fingernails were broken. Doubtless from scratching at the ceiling, trying to hold himself above the water while his strength gave out.

A warm breeze blew in through the open door to the balcony, earthly and normal, evincing a rattle from the undrawn, vertical blinds.

Someone, either Yemi, or the escaped woman, or the two of them together, had dumped Chuck Vielfrass in a floating tank of ocean and let him drown.

Ethan's mind jumped to the Caribbean Reef exhibit at the Shedd Aquarium. His idle thoughts about what would happen if someone fell into that beautiful, wet world, trapped on the wrong side of the glass.

Which is when it hit him. *Tank* was the wrong word for whatever it was he was looking at. There was no glass. This wasn't a floating tank of water, it was a floating *cube* of water, held in place by nothing other than air.

He found himself stumbling forward, hand outstretched.

'Don't,' Gutierrez said.

She was too late. His hand made contact with the water.

Or tried to. His hand was on the water. He could see it. But he couldn't feel it. There was something solid in the way, something so thin as to be invisible. He pushed. Nothing happened, except perhaps for a faint tingling in the palm of his hand. He stepped back, pulled a pen from his pocket and tossed it at the cube.

It bounced, landing with a *clickety-clack* on the hardwood floor. Bone dry.

A couple of the uniforms had taken out their phones. Were taking pictures.

'Quit that,' Gutierrez snapped. 'Try and be professional, for fuck's sake.'

She looked around the room.

'Where is she?' she muttered. Pulling a pair of latex gloves from her pocket, she strode past the water cube, refusing to look at its strangeness. Without waiting to put them on, she put the wadded-up gloves between her hand and the bedroom door handle, opening it up.

'Better clear the area,' Ethan said to the nearest uniform. 'This is a crime scene now.' He followed Gutierrez into the bedroom.

Charlene Zhao was stretched out on the bed as if laid in a coffin. She lay atop the covers flat on her back, hands clasped together on her stomach. She was wearing one of her boyfriend's pretentious black tee shirts, the fit long enough to reach the middle of her thighs. Ethan was oddly relieved she looked halfway decent. He wouldn't have cared so much if she were dead, but he was pretty sure, like James before her, and Jennifer before him, that she was simply unconscious.

Gutierrez laid two fingers on the woman's neck. She kept them there for an unusually long time.

'There's a heartbeat,' she announced. 'But slow.' She pulled out her phone and called for an ambulance.

Ethan, meanwhile, took a deep breath and forced himself to examine the scene, to not recoil from its sheer impossibility.

A few of the things he'd initially taken for camera equipment were nothing of the sort, he realized. Beneath the cube, masked by the sheer volume of water, there was a round, transparent disc maybe two feet across and a couple of inches deep. And on each wall, some of Chuck Vielfrass's posters had been taken down, allowing either Yemi or the woman to attach four see-through cubes, twelve inches to a side. An open trunk, scuffed and grey and parked neatly in one corner, was half full of power tools, a couple of lengths of chain, and various colours of duct tape. Cables, ordinary hardware store cables, snaked from the cubes on the wall to the disc on the floor and from the disc on the floor to a power outlet. Where the cables ran into the disc and cubes though, they seemed to blur away to nothing. Ethan rubbed his eyes. There was no doubt about it. Try as he might, he couldn't see the connection. Nor, he suddenly realized, could he see the floor beneath the disc or the wall behind the cubes. Contrary to his initial impression, they weren't transparent at all. It was more like he was looking *into* something, 3D TV screens of –

Water.

His breath caught as a fish, fleeting and silvery, flashed through one of the cubes. It was gone before he could properly register what he'd seen. Before he could *believe* what he'd seen.

'How'd he get in?'

Maybe if Ethan hadn't been so spooked already, he wouldn't have jumped at the sound of Gutierrez's voice. He waited for his heart to slow a little before replying.

'What makes you think it was him?' he asked. 'Why not her?'

'Because she walked in through the lobby entrance. You said yourself that she didn't belong. She wasn't familiar with the door. She wasn't expecting to be held up. It was her first time here, I'd say. And this . . .' Her voice weakened to nothing in the face of strangeness. She licked her lips. 'This,' she continued, 'took time. A lot of time. If it had been her, she would already have been here. Hours ago. For us to see her she would have to have gone out for some reason and then come back. She would have been familiar with the set-up. The door wouldn't have been a surprise. You ask me, she was joining him. Maybe to help him finish the job, tidy up, whatever. But he, Yemi, A.

Bello, whoever the fuck he is, he was already here. So. How did he get in?'

'Not through the lobby. We've been sitting outside since we left the apartment. There's no way he could have gotten in without us seeing him.'

'What if he was invisible?' Gutierrez blushed furiously under Ethan's shocked stare. 'I mean, I know . . . I *know*, okay? It's insane. *I'm* insane. But *look* at this shit, man. If he can do this, what else can he do?'

Ethan's mouth was suddenly dry. It took him a moment or two to get out the words.

'Okay, this whole thing is insane, I get it. But he wasn't invisible in Chicago. We have him entering and leaving the Okoro's apartment. Twice. People *saw* him. And your college student, what's his name?'

'Emmanuel Ratcliffe.'

'Emmanuel Ratcliffe saw him in Providence. And we saw the woman. No invisibility cloak there.' He allowed himself a low whistle. 'She's built like a fucking Amazon. Hard to miss, if you know what I mean. If she had some kind of magic invisibility cloak, she'd have used it.'

'Why? She didn't know we were here. She'd no reason to hide. We noticed her – you noticed her – breaking in, but no one else would have. There was no one around to see. Why would she bother?'

'Fair enough. But that applies to Yemi, too. No one knows we're here, least of all him. He'd have come in the same way he did before: through the front door, fully visible, wheeling a crate.' He pointed to the open grey trunk. '*That* crate.'

'Except he didn't,' Gutierrez said flatly.

'Except he didn't. Yeah.' The sigh that escaped Ethan's lips was like a suddenly deflating tyre. He stepped out on the balcony for a breath of fresh air. Found himself fixating on the wrought-iron railings. 'Nicole, come look at this.'

Gutierrez joined him on the balcony. There was no need for him to explain.

'A pulley?' she muttered. 'A fucking pulley?'

The contraption looked eerily like a scaffold. The sort you hang people from. A pole of square-tubed metal, painted black like the balcony railings, and attached to a three-legged stand at the bottom. At the top, bolted pieces of metalwork projected a couple of feet over the balcony's edge. The frame housed a robust-looking hoist mechanism, operated by a rotating handle, maybe halfway up the pole. Braided metal wire gleamed brightly in the light streaming from the condo's living room. It ran up the frame from the handle, out over the balcony and terminated in something that looked like a heavy-duty clothes hanger.

'You could hoist a helluva a lot with this thing,' Ethan said.

'But why? And how'd he get it up here in the first place?'

Ethan stared at his shoes a moment.

'I have an idea, but you're not gonna like it.'

'Try me.'

'I think he climbed up here.'

'No. No way.'

'Wait. Hear me out. That . . . woman, like you said: she had skills. Serious, military-type skills. What if our pal here's the same? Remember Dottie's driver, Alejo? How scared he was when we showed him Yemi's picture? He told us he swung a baseball bat at the guy, and he moved so fast it was like he disappeared? Sound familiar?'

Slowly, reluctantly, Gutierrez started to nod.

'Do you think a guy like that, a military guy, would have any trouble scaling the back of this building with a grappling hook and a rope?' Ethan asked. 'Fuck, all he'd have to do is reach the second-floor balcony. Easy enough to reach the next one up from there. I've had perps back in Chicago who could do that – did do that – without breaking a sweat.'

'So . . . what? You think he climbed up here with bits of pulley on his back, bolted it together, pulled up his crate of whatever-the-fuck-that-shit-in-there-is, and then drowned our wannabe movie mogul?'

'Yeah. Pretty much.'

'But why? I'll give you that Yemi, if he's anything like his sister-in-arms, could do everything you say he did but, like you said, it's not his MO. This guy walks in through the front door. He did it in Chicago and he did it here: certainly at Sonia's and probably at Dottie's. There's no reason why he'd change it up now.' She looked suddenly downcast. 'Except that he did, I guess.'

'I think maybe he knew we were here,' Ethan said slowly. 'It's the only thing that makes sense. Maybe he figured we were onto him because of what happened at Dottie's, or because his sketch has been all over the news, or maybe he was casing the joint already and saw us arrive. Either which way, he knew enough not to come in through the lobby.'

'So why didn't his gal pal?'

'Who knows?' Ethan replied with a shrug. 'We had no idea she existed. Maybe she thought she could get away with it.' He allowed himself a self-satisfied smile. 'She almost did.'

'Smug asshole.' Gutierrez was only pretending to be annoyed.

'On the plus side, both Yemi and the woman had to leave in a hurry.' Ethan directed his gaze from the balcony to the living room, at the impossible strangeness of what was waiting for them. 'Maybe they left us some leads.' He stepped gingerly back inside. 'How long before your forensics guys get here?'

Gutierrez grimaced.

'Knowing them, not for a while. They hate the early a.m.'

'Lieutenant?' One of the unis was at the door, careful not to step across the threshold.

'What is it, Lee?'

'Found this across the hall.' The officer was holding a white, featureless piece of plastic in an evidence bag. 'Looks like a hotel key card. Owner says it isn't his and he doesn't know how it got there.'

'Thanks.' Gutierrez took ahold of it. 'Not very classy, is it? No logo, no name, not even an address. But it might be something.' She returned it to the officer. 'Canvass the local hotels – the cheap ones. Maybe we'll catch a break.'

'Yes, ma'am.'

Ethan watched the man depart, envying him the prospect of actual police work instead of . . . this.

The EMTs made it before forensics. Unnerved by the floating cube of ocean and its dead body, they fumbled the transfer of Charlene Zhao from bed to stretcher, and then banged the stretcher into the door frame on the way out.

'I guess it's not something they see every day,' Gutierrez observed drily.

Ethan grunted absent-mindedly, his attention taken by the banged-up grey crate Yemi had hoisted up on his pulley. So far as he could tell, there was nothing unusual about it. Certainly nothing that screamed military or black ops. It was metal and scuffed and unremarkable. The contents, duct tape and chains and some power tools, wouldn't have looked out of place in a pickup truck commercial. There was nothing to explain the nightmare scene behind him.

Something tickled his nose.

'Do you smell burning?' Gutierrez asked.

There was a flickering at the edge of Ethan's vision. Lifting his gaze from the crate, he saw that the wall-mounted cube nearest him, the one that had ever so briefly contained a fish, was dotted with imperfections. Freckles of red and blue and deep, deep violet stained the surface, winking in and out of existence, seemingly at random. But as he watched the freckles grew more numerous, turning into blotches that took longer and longer to disappear, darkening towards black as they did so.

Wisps of smoke were curling up from some of the power cables, the acrid stench of burnt plastic started to sting at his eyes.

He ran for the front door, grabbing Gutierrez by the arm as he did so. She yelped in surprise as he dragged her along with him, wrenching the door open with his free hand.

'What the—?'

Ethan's grip tightened, almost dragging Gutierrez off her feet. He barrelled down the corridor. 'Get out!' he yelled to the various uniforms milling about. 'Get the fuck out now!'

He reached the door at the far end of the corridor and slammed it open, followed by Gutierrez and the heavy footfalls of other officers, their boots echoing in the concrete hollows of the stairwell as they hurtled down. Ethan got as far as the second floor before a dull roaring reached his ears.

Seconds later, foaming water was rushing past them down the steps, threatening to sweep them off their feet, filling their noses with the salted tang of ocean. A police sergeant slipped, landing heavily on his tailbone and bouncing downwards with grunts of pain. Ethan gripped the banister, steadying himself against the torrent until it weakened to a lethargic dripping. At the bottom of the stairs though, the water had formed a foaming, unquiet pool, maybe a foot or two deep, dammed by the fire door that slowed its access to the lobby beyond. Ethan half expected to see Chuck's body floating face down in the middle of it. The corpse, however, would be somewhere above them, swept into the corridor, or pushed against the balcony railings, or just dumped in some ignominious corner of his living room, overlooked by pointless, vainglorious posters.

'You okay, Dino?' Gutierrez asked the sergeant.

'Nothing hurt but my pride, lieutenant.' Ethan, watching the sergeant get slowly to his feet, doubted that the man was telling the truth.

'Your forensics guys are going to wish they'd gotten out of bed sooner,' he said to Gutierrez. 'They ain't gonna to find shit now.'

Fifty-One

Saturday the 12th: 4.38 a.m. EDT

'That is *disgusting*,' Hollie said.

But not disgusting enough, Abi thought wryly, to stop the little *oyinbo* woman from staring at her. Hollie's intriguingly coloured eyes watched in round wonder as she pulled the last of the large white eggs from its box and popped it in her mouth. Abi chewed with exaggerated slowness. She took pleasure in the way Hollie winced as the shell cracked and crunched between her teeth, the gravelly rattle softened only by the gelatinous flow of raw egg across her tongue. She swallowed, smacked her lips for the sheer hell of it, and washed the remains down with several mouthfuls of protein shake. The shake, unlike the egg, was almost too revolting for words.

'Don't you feel sick?' Hollie asked. Empty egg boxes and drained bottles of protein shake had long since overflowed the motel room's trash can.

'A little,' Abi admitted, although not for the reason Hollie thought. The amulet and med-kit, now they had enough raw material to work with, were working feverishly to repair her. She gritted her teeth against waves of nausea as armies of nano-bots began to realign her broken bones. Prickly infusions of drugs were kicking her body's healing mechanisms into over-drive, causing heat and itching in places too deep to scratch. She could feel beads of sweat blossoming on her forehead. 'I think I'll lie down for a minute.'

'We should get you to a doctor.'

Abi bit back a jolt of irritation.

'I heard you the first time, doll.' It had to be the fiftieth time Hollie had raised the ghoulish prospect of *oyinbo* medicine.

'Really? Because if you had, we'd be headed to the hospital right now.' She grabbed Abi's weakened hand. Squeezed gently. 'You don't look good, Abs. We should find one before something bad happens.' Hollie's lips formed a worried smile. 'If it's the wait you're worried about, I doubt A and E will be busy right now. It's nearly five in the morning. Plenty of time to be dealing with last night's drunks.'

Abi's irritation distilled itself into guilt. The woman was trying to help. *Cared* enough to help. And she didn't know any better.

'I'll be all right, I swear. A couple of days' rest and I'll be good as new.'

'Because of the healing power of eggs?'

'Because of the healing power of eggs.' Abi's eyelids were suddenly too heavy to keep open. The darkness was warm and comforting. Like Hollie's voice. Like her hand on hers.

'Abi?'

'Yes, babe?'

'Where are you from?'

'Nigeria.'

'No. Where are you from, really? Your passport is Liberian.'

'Liberia, then.'

'And the name in it isn't yours.'

'It could be.'

'Is it, though?'

'No.'

'So, where are you from?' There was a hint of fear in Hollie's voice, but she didn't let go of her hand. 'The things you do. The things you know how to do. No one can do that. *No one*. Not here, not anywhere.' The voice was trembling now, the grip on her hand still strong. 'Are you an . . . alien? Are you, like, only pretending to be human? Is that why you don't want to go to the hospital, because they'll figure out what you are?'

Abi was too sleepy to laugh but she could feel a soft smile tugging at her lips.

'I'm as human as you are, babe. Believe me. I just . . .' The words were as heavy as her eyelids, too difficult to move off her tongue. '. . . don't like doctors.'

She gave into sleep then, with Hollie's soft hand in hers, dreaming of Ayo and Kehinde, of rolling brown hills with their dust devils and ramrod-straight stands of yellow-leaved sosume, of geysers of gleaming water shooting from the rocky earth.

And of Yemi. She was chasing him through the house, laughing, his running shape refracted and distorted by translucent walls, misted moisture cooling her against the heat. But he'd reached the gate first, and now he was behind her, and it was she who was running from him, and the house had gone with its curves and spires and gleaming walls, and she was surrounded by rock-cubes and shadows and crowds of foul-smelling *oyinbos* who were slowing her down. And now Hollie was taking her by the hand with her beautiful blue eyes and leading her to the motel, where she entered the room and locked the door, but something was creeping about outside waiting to be let in, slithering and sliding and dripping venom that made the ground hiss and steam.

Abi was groggy with drugs and healing and fatigue. Otherwise, she might have realized more quickly that it wasn't a dream, not entirely. Something *was* outside. There were heat signatures on the other side of the door. And next to the window.

Grey dawn light was slipping through a crack in the curtains. She tried to prop herself up on her good elbow, but it was hard to move, every muscle leaden, weighted down by drugs.

'Hollie,' she rasped. 'Hol—'

The glass in the window shattered with a piercing crack. Abi sensed rather than saw something flying into the room, flashing through the curtains like they were nothing: black, and cylindrical, and spinning end over end.

BOOM!

The room exploded in light and noise and smoke. Abi's filters were overwhelmed. She couldn't see or hear and her stomach was threatening to revolt.

The door was open, somehow. Figures, bulky and armoured, poured across the threshold, pinning her to the bed and rebreaking delicately knitted bone. A voice, high and shrill, screamed in Abi's ear. It took her a moment to realize it was her.

She was rolled roughly onto her front, arms pinned behind her back and restrained with cold and painful metal. The barrel of a projectile weapon pressed against her skull.

'You're under arrest for the murder of Dorothy and Charles Vielfrass,' said a female voice, slightly out of breath. 'You have the right to remain silent . . .' The words faded away, displaced by Hollie's wrenching, terrified sobs from the other side of the room.

Fifty-Two

'Patience Robertson? From Liberia?'

Ethan sat quietly beside Gutierrez as she riffled through the green passport, comparing the picture with the woman sitting on the other side of the interrogation room's table.

'That's what it says,' the woman said. Even sitting down, with her right arm in a sling and the left chained to the table, she radiated a feline power. Skin so black as to be almost blue; smoothly and impossibly perfect except for two small, matching scars on the top of each cheek. Lips curved in a lazy half-smile that sometimes parted to reveal the gleaming teeth behind.

A mountain lion at rest. It was hard to equate her with the dishevelled, disoriented creature they had dragged out of the motel. Except for the most hardened criminals, time in the cells usually softened people up, put them on the defensive. Instead, this one looked more relaxed, as if her time in holding had only made her stronger.

An uneasy feeling stirred in Ethan's stomach. Enough so that he wondered if the damaged arm should be restrained. If they should have tried harder to remove the ivory bracelets. If the pair of armed uniforms at the back of the interview room would be sufficient protection.

He would have been happier with an actual mountain lion.

Gutierrez pushed a small pouch onto the table.

'These yours?'

'Yes.'

'Care to tell me what you're doing with hundreds of thousands of dollars' worth of diamonds?'

'Girl's gotta eat.'

'Where'd you get 'em?'

'From home. They're personal property. Easier to haul around than cash.'

'Did you declare them at customs?'

The woman looked genuinely puzzled.

'When you arrived in this country, did you inform an official that you had these?'

'Thought didn't rightly occur. Them being mine and all.'

'Money laundering is a serious offence, you know that.'

'Money what?' The woman's perplexed expression deepened. 'Cleaning money is a crime?'

'This isn't a joking matter, Ms Robertson.' Gutierrez pushed a rectangle of white plastic into the middle of the table.

'Do you recognize this?'

'Should I?'

'It's your motel room key. It's covered in your fingerprints.'

'If you say so.'

'We found it in the condo across the hall from Chuck Vielfrass's. What were you doing there?'

'Trying not to get whacked by you and your buddy.'

Ethan remembered the uncanny speed with which she'd

moved. The gunshot crack of the door exploding off its hinges. The actual gunshots that had somehow missed.

'Funny. What were you doing in the building?'

'I was attracted to it.' A slow smile. 'Say, this place of yours has real good Wi-Fi. You know that?'

Gutierrez ignored the aside. She opened a file and pushed three photographs across the table. The woman's smile faded away, replaced by something more guardedly neutral.

'Sonia Vielfrass Hollander. Drowned at home. Her children, Edward and Olivia. Drowned with her. Why?'

'Ask the person who drowned them.'

'I'm asking you.'

'I ain't got nothing to say on that particular subject.'

'Did you drown them?'

'No.'

'Do you know who did?'

The faintest of hesitations.

'A guy that ain't me.'

'Tell me how you know this guy,' Gutierrez asked, producing the artist's sketch of Yemi.

'What makes you think I know him?'

'Stop wasting my time, Patience. We know you know him. We want to know how you know him.'

'I gotta disagree with you there, detective. When it comes to wasting time, it's you who's wasting mine. I'd say Patience is being real patient with *you*.' That smile again. 'You don't know nothing about nothing. If you did, you wouldn't be giving me the third degree.' The woman examined her surroundings with what appeared to be genuine curiosity. 'Say, shouldn't you be blinding me with a light or something? This is a lot tamer than I was expecting.' Large brown eyes, bottomless in their darkness, flicked to the uniforms at the back of the room before settling on Ethan. 'I'd have thought your gentlemen friends would be smacking me in the kisser about now. But maybe they aren't up to it.'

Ethan was surprised to find that his fists were clenched.

'I'm out of my jurisdiction,' he said tightly. Gutierrez shot him a look. Pushed another photograph across the table.

'Dorothy Vielfrass, Sonia's mother. Also drowned at home. Tell me why you killed her.'

A hiss of exasperation escaped the woman's lips.

'Just how many people do you think I've killed?'

'Answer the question.'

'Your question is stupid. Here's a better one. Where was Patience when these drownings took place, heh? Answer? Not here. Followed by this. If Patience wasn't here, who is responsible and where are they now?'

'Okay. Where were you in the early hours of Thursday morning, when Dorothy Vielfrass was killed?'

'I told you already. Not here.'

The woman stirred impatiently in her seat. Stretched herself out. Her strange, feline power seemed to fill the room. Ethan felt small in her presence. Insignificant. For a brief, ludicrous moment, he even thought the chain holding her to the table was about to snap.

'This is the worst third degree I ever seen. No more questions. Take me back to my cell. I ain't got nothing more to say to you.'

Fifty-Three

'*I* think . . . I think I need a lawyer.'

The accent was British, matching the passport. And frightened: in keeping with the woman's wide eyes and trembling lips; in contrast to her fuck-you Goth clothing. The small, cuffed hands on the table were beating a nervous tattoo, black nail polish gleaming under the fluorescents.

'You can have a phone call if you like,' Gutierrez said. 'But it's the weekend. It'll be hours before anyone gets here.' She looked regretful – and sympathetic. 'Maybe we can sort this out without waiting. Maybe even get you out of here.' When the woman looked doubtful, she added: 'Look, let's ask a few questions and see where we get to. You feel too uncomfortable, just say so and we'll stop. No pressure. You can have a lawyer any time you like. I promise. Sound like a plan?'

'I . . . guess so.'

'Great. How long have you known . . . aw, gee . . . I'm blanking on the name. Wait. Wait. It'll come to me.' Gutierrez gave the girl a shamefaced smile. 'Gosh, I'd forget my own name if I hadn't had it so long. Sorry. How long have you known . . . er—?'

'Abs?'

'Yes. Abs. That's not her full name, though.'

'No. It's Abidemi. Abidemi Eniola.'

'And how are you spelling that?'

'Honestly? No idea.' The woman let loose a nervous giggle. 'It's Nigerian.'

Ethan fought the urge to lean forward, to let his interest show.

'No worries. We've got it somewhere, I'm sure. And how long have you known, ah, Abs?'

'Just a few days, though it feels like forever.'

Ethan hoped he'd managed to keep the surprise off his face.

'How'd you meet?'

'She bumped into me in town. Literally. She knocked me over and I was a real bitch to her about it, but she was really nice and we kind of got to talking. We've been getting on like a house on fire ever since.'

'And which town is that? Where she knocked you over?'

'Bristol.'

'Bristol . . . England?'

'Well, yeah.'

'And do you remember *when* she knocked you over? The date, I mean.'

'Oh, let's see. Like I said, I feel like it's been ages, but it really hasn't. It'd be . . . er . . . It was a week ago. Exactly. Saturday the fifth.'

Ethan could feel his stomach clenching.

'So, last Saturday, you and Abidemi were in Bristol, England?'

'Totes.'

'And that was the first time you met her?'

'Yes.'

'And so you decide to travel to the States with a complete stranger?'

'Yeah, no. We went to Scotland first.'

'Scotland?'

'Yeah. Edinburgh. Abs needed to see someone. She came over from Africa to return some stuff. You know, heirlooms.'

'Heirlooms? Like the tomato?'

The woman laughed. High and nervous.

'No. Like inheritances. Abs delivered this beautiful wooden box to a lady called Kirsty Forbes.'

'And what can you tell me about Kirsty?'

'Not much. Thirty-something, divorced, hard life. Lived with some thug called Jimmy MacRae.' An expression dangerously close to awe flitted across the woman's face. 'Abs beat the shit out of him.'

'Do you have an address for these people?'

The woman squinted. Stared at the ceiling for a moment.

'Four oh nine Bannockburn Court.'

'Okay. And when did you come to the States?'

'We got here last night.'

Ethan and Gutierrez exchanged a look.

'*Last* night?'

'Yeah.'

'And Abidemi didn't come ahead or anything like that?'

'No. I've been with her every day for the past week. I'm kind of like a tour guide. She's super, *super* intelligent. But she's not always across how stuff works. I don't think she could have got here without me and, like I said, we didn't get here till last night.'

Fifty-Four

'Well . . . shit,' Ethan found himself saying. 'You're sure?'

'Hundred per cent,' Gutierrez replied. 'What Goth Gal had to say checks out. They landed at Logan last night, picked up a rental, drove straight down here and checked in. Unless we're missing something, there's no way she had anything to do with . . . the thing that happened to Chuck. And there's no record of Patience Robertson entering the country prior to last night.'

'Could have used a different passport. Patience isn't the only name she goes by.'

'True. But it's not looking likely. Unless our Brit friend is the coolest customer since the ice man instead of some kid way out of her depth, neither of them were here for the attack on Sonia's house. Which means it's pretty unlikely either of them had anything to do with your vics in Chicago. Plus, let's face it, Abidemi, Patience, whatever, is unmistakably female.' Gutierrez's expression took on a slightly envious cast. 'That woman could win Miss Universe without breaking a sweat. The perp's male. We may not know much, but we know *that*.'

'But she's connected. Has to be. She didn't fly across the

fucking Atlantic and turn up at Chuck's place at random. With a bag of diamonds and a ton of special ops stuff we can't even figure out in that backpack of hers? No. This is not a coincidence.'

'No,' Gutierrez agreed slowly. 'It's not. But whatever the connection is – and there's got to be one – it doesn't make her our killer. Maybe a bagman of some kind? The diamonds could be payment for Yemi, something like that.'

Ethan pursed his lips thoughtfully. As top-of-the-head theories went, it wasn't terrible.

'So, what now?' he asked.

'They can cool their asses until Monday. We'll charge 'em with immigration offences and money laundering; plus felony assault, and breaking and entering for our Nigerian friend. They're both foreign, which makes them flight risks, so the bail hearing on Monday will not go well for them. We can keep them locked up for quite a while, I'm thinking.'

'Makes sense,' Ethan said, nodding. 'But I gotta get back to Chicago.'

'Why?' Gutierrez didn't bother to hide her surprise.

'Perp's still out there.' In his mind's eye he was looking at a dead baby, damp with seawater, its eyes filmed over in unseeing ocean blue. 'Chuck's ex is in Chicago, with the kids. And whatever protection my people have going on back home, it ain't enough. Not by a long shot. Feel free to tag along.'

He could practically see the gears whirring inside her head. Figuring out who she could stick with the bail hearing. Her lips moved into a grim smile.

'I just might. But I'm flying. If you think I'm travelling to fly-over country in that beater car of yours, you are sadly mistaken.'

Fifty-Five

*W*i-Fi reception in the cells was not good, and wherever they'd stored her mobile, it was a good deal farther than her augments could easily handle.

That, however, was the least of Abi's worries. The med-kit, quiescent during her interrogation, was once more in full effect. She lay stretched out on a lumpy, uncomfortable bunk, malodorous with the stink of previous occupants. Although her skin crawled with the filth of it, she lacked the strength to escape. She gritted her teeth instead, sweat dotting her forehead as the med-kit went about its business. The machine was maxed out, its AI unmoved by the endless waves of nausea rampaging through her body.

Her stomach heaved yet again, forcing a trickle of bile from her lips. She smeared the taste of it against the back of her hand and stared angrily at the ceiling.

The real problem, worse than either poor reception or nanobot induced agony, was easy to say and difficult to fix: she had no idea what she was doing. She closed her eyes, letting the flow of stolen data glide across her retinas. Even with a barely working mobile, the police network was easy enough to infiltrate. But their information, stored remotely on something bizarrely referred to as a cloud, was almost impenetrable. Ludicrous-looking standardized documents identified only by numbers, filing systems that defied both rhyme and reason, endless catalogues of artefacts to be used in evidence but lumped into meaningless, chaotic categories.

A minefield of bizarre idiosyncrasies, resistant to analysis.

Eventually, though, she found what she was looking for.

The Vielfrass files.

The *oyinbo* police had been surprisingly thorough. And they were more technically proficient than she would have thought possible. Little wonder they'd been waiting for her at Charles Vielfrass's place.

She corrected herself. It wasn't her they'd been waiting for. They'd been waiting for Yemi. Yemi, of course, would have made them easily enough, just as she had, and improvised. She was quietly surprised at the equipment he'd used. But then again, he must have been here for quite a while by now. More than enough time to settle in, to retrace every single step of The Story. To adapt.

To do things with style. He'd always had a thing about that.

She sucked at her teeth in annoyance. She had a lot of catching up to do.

The Vielfrass mother was dead, and both children. The grandchildren, though, were still alive and hiding out in . . . Chicago, Illinois. Local police were keeping an eye on them.

Police. Her mind flashed back to the sharp bang of a stun grenade, the rush of armoured bodies, the cold click of metal around her wrists.

She would not underestimate them again.

Chicago, then.

Which, in turn, was a question of paperwork. She found it. Rewrote it. Rewrote it again. And again. She stared up at the ceiling and sighed.

She had all the documents: of that she was sure. But the words, placed side by side and row by row in scraggly *oyinbo* script, were a gamble, the *opolo keji*'s reworking of patterns that had gone before. A fake incantation, uttered with neither passion nor understanding.

She wished Hollie were here.

The *oyinbo* sun moved with its accustomed and unnatural slowness but, even so, the shadows on the floor had covered a significant distance before she finally let go. There was nothing more she could do.

It either worked, or it didn't.

She gave an experimental shrug of her right shoulder. Pleasantly surprised by the absence of pain, she sat up, her back against the cell-block wall. She fixed her eyes on the heavy metal of the cell door.

And waited.

There was a sound of approaching footsteps. A rattle and clanking of keys.

The door swung open.

'Patience Robertson?' The police officer was older, his expression one of placid good nature, no doubt used to dealing with the occupants of cells like this one. He was reading a clipboard held loosely in one hand.

'That's me.'

'Time to go.' He looked at her curiously. 'It's your lucky day, Patience. Our detective friends don't usually change their minds as quick as this. Must have found a better lead, I guess.' He chuckled quietly, his outstretched arm an invitation to cross the threshold. Abi accepted it. Resisted the temptation to break into a run.

Hollie was waiting in the police station's reception area.

'I don't understand,' she said. 'They're just letting us out?'

'They sure are.' Abi was going through the contents of her backpack, making sure everything was there. Looking up and seeing Hollie's disbelieving expression, she felt compelled to add, 'Say, doll, did you do anything wrong before the filth dragged us in here?'

Hollie shook her head.

'Yeah, well neither did I. This was all just a big ol' misunderstanding. They mistook us for someone else, I guess.' She pushed through the station's heavy revolving door and into the parking lot beyond. Summer heat wrapped around her like a welcoming blanket. Automobiles, free and uncaring, roared along a nearby road. She looked up into the blue sky with its faint hint of evening and breathed deep. There was, alas, no sign of rain.

She glanced down at her companion: small and frail, and only vaguely aware of the danger to which Abidemi Eniola had exposed her. Hollie was staring sightlessly across the parking lot, her face a mask of uncertainty.

'Do you want to go home?' Abi asked. 'We can head back to the airfield and I'll buy you a ticket.'

Hollie's mouth opened and closed a couple of times before she answered.

'No,' she said slowly. 'Home is boring compared to this. And the weather's shit. And when will I get another chance to see America?' A wry grin. 'I want to see this thing of yours through to the end.' To Abi's surprise, Hollie grabbed her by the forearm, fixing her with an earnest, almost pleading stare. 'But you've got to tell me what's really going on, okay?'

'Sure, babe. Not now, though. Not here.' Knowing full well that Hollie's increased curiosity was a problem deferred rather than solved, Abi made a point of glancing back at the brooding presence of the police station. 'We should make tracks lickety-split.'

She favoured Hollie with a sudden, reckless grin, inexplicably glad the woman was staying.

'You and I? We got things to do, places to be.'

Fifty-Six

Sunday the 13th: 8.00 a.m. CDT

'I don't like this,' Ethan muttered. Exhausted from an overnight drive and only a couple of hours sleep, the words came out more harshly than he intended. 'There are too many approaches and way too much cover.'

Raymond Yeung shrugged.

'It is what it is, lieutenant. What do you want me to do, ask the good citizens of Aldrin Street to level the neighbourhood and start again?'

Ethan, conscious that Nicole Gutierrez was looking at them with an amused smile, glared past Yeung's shoulder at the object of his irritation.

Unlike the rest of Chicago's Lincoln Park neighbourhood, where some of the inhabitants made more in a week than he and Raymond pulled down in a year, Aldrin Street was not lined from end to end with heavily fortified mega-mansions. The layout was irritatingly atypical. Running from north to south, the obscure, one-block road dead-ended to the north at a small park. To the south, it opened onto the wide expanse of North Avenue, directly opposite a jarringly out of place fifteen-storey luxury hotel. To the west it was bounded by the low, rambling buildings of Newton Science Academy, and to the east by a rats' nest of town houses known as the Lincoln Trails Estates. It was the 'Trails' part of the name that was causing Ethan the most concern: shrub-lined paths that wandered randomly between tight clusters of two- and three-storey homes. The paths occasionally widened out into landscaped courtyards or came to an abrupt stop at the little cobbled lanes that provided vehicular access. It was a surveillance nightmare.

And Chuck Vielfrass's ex-mother-in-law lived right in the middle of it.

'We gotta get 'em out of there,' Ethan muttered. The low morning sun would be hanging over Lake Michigan somewhere, still hidden by buildings and trees, but it was threatening to be a hot one.

'To where?' Raymond challenged. 'There's no budget for a safe house, you know that. And look, we've got unmarked vehicles at both ends of the road, a SWAT team camped out in the school—'

'The school?' Gutierrez interrupted. 'How?'

'It's summer vacation. We were able to pull some strings with CPS – that's Chicago Public Schools, lieutenant.' Raymond looked more than pleased with himself. 'Plus, we've got a drone in the air – high up, so our guy can't hear it. There's no way this asshole's getting within a hundred yards of that house without us seeing him.'

Ethan and Gutierrez exchanged a look. Ethan had not yet explained – had so far lacked the balls to explain – the drowned corpse floating in a floating body of water in the middle of Chuck Vielfrass's condo. All he'd told Raymond during the long ride home was that Chuck had drowned like the others, and that Providence PD had a couple of suspected accomplices in the slammer. He couldn't bring himself to put words to his memories. The further he got from Rhode Island, the less real the whole thing seemed: to the point where he could almost imagine that he'd imagined it.

Except that the look in Gutierrez's eyes told him otherwise. That Yemi and his Amazonian girlfriend were trained military with access to a lot of weird black-ops shit. That if Yemi were half as fast, half as well trained as the woman, Chicago's finest were seriously outmatched.

'What about east of the Trails?' he asked. 'Have we got the alley covered?'

Raymond shot him a pitying look.

'There isn't an alley. The school kind of fucks up the grid. There's wooden fencing all along the east side of the complex. The fence runs along the backyards of the row houses on Locust, which is the next street over. They're row houses, so there's no way to get to the Trails from Locust. Unless you can fly, I guess. In which case, we got bigger problems.' The sergeant gave Ethan an earnest stare. 'It's really not as bad as you think. The Trails look sketchy because they're, you know, trails. But you can't get to them unless you walk up or down the street or cross over through the school. Those approaches are covered. And we have an eye in the sky. We're good here.'

Ethan hesitated, objections dying half-formed on the tip of his tongue. Eventually, he gave a slow nod.

'You've done great, Raymond.' He forced a smile and clapped the sergeant on the shoulder. 'Now, let's go see these folks.'

Brenna Clayton – the Vielfrass was silent now – made good coffee. Ethan took a grateful sip. And wondered how the woman sitting across from him had ever gotten herself involved with a pretentious asshole like her ex-husband.

Despite their protests, Brenna had insisted the three detectives settle upon a large sectional. It was the living room's major piece of furniture. She herself sat rigidly on a wooden chair snatched from under a dining table. Ringlets of mousey brown hair, with a faint trace of grey, cascaded onto the shoulders of an oversized DePaul tee shirt which, in turn, hung loosely over faded denim shorts. Bare feet ended in toes with slightly chipped nail polish, same as with her fingers, which wrapped themselves too tightly around a Cubs coffee mug. Nothing about her screamed Hollywood wannabe.

Of course, kids might have changed her. He could hear their excited chatter from somewhere beneath him, children and grandmother hiding out in an unseen basement while Brenna Clayton and the detectives talked murder.

'You don't think I'm safe here?' she asked.

'We think you'll be safer elsewhere,' Ethan said. 'The man we're looking for is very capable, very resourceful. Very . . . persistent. We've captured his accomplices but the man himself is still at large. If he knows your mother lives here – and he might – we'd rather you all went away for a few days. To someplace random, where he won't know to look. We'll keep watch here, and if he comes, we'll collar him. But I'd breathe a lot easier if you and your family weren't around when we did.'

'Detective Gutierrez told me we'd be safe here in Chicago, and now you're telling I'm not?'

Ethan could feel Gutierrez stiffening beside him on the sectional.

'We know a lot more than we did when she spoke to you, ma'am. And Lieutenant Gutierrez wasn't wrong at the time, it's just that the situation has changed. Thanks to her, you and your kids are still with us. But your ex-husband . . .'

His voice trailed off, stilled by the tears pooling in Brenna Clayton's eyes.

'He was a prick,' she sniffled. 'A pompous, preening, unfaithful prick. But he's the kids' dad and they love him, you know?' She stared out the window, where the sun daubed light and strong shadow on the spreading leaves of a Japanese maple. 'I haven't told them. I . . . I don't know how. Jesus! How do you tell your children that their father is dead?' She broke into a small sob, quickly stifled.

'I can do it if you like,' Gutierrez said. 'Get it over with for you.'

Brenna shot her a wan smile.

'Thanks, but no. They should hear it from me.' She paused, her face complicated, as a scream of laughter floated up from the basement. 'But not just yet. Tomorrow, maybe.' She took a deep breath. 'And tomorrow we'll head out somewhere nice. Somewhere away from here like you want.'

'It's the right decision, Brenna.' There was a vibration from somewhere in Gutierrez's pantsuit. She pulled out her phone and glanced at it. 'Excuse me while I take this.' She headed out of the house, phone pressed against her ear.

'Could you not leave today?' Ethan asked. 'I don't want to be a jerk about this but it's kind of urgent.'

Brenna shot him a look halfway between exasperated and amused.

'Have you ever tried moving a cranky mother and two kids at short notice to a literally random place you've never heard of? On a Sunday? There's no way.'

'Okay. But in that case, do you mind if we put someone inside the house with you? Just for tonight.'

Brenna took a sip of her coffee and nodded.

'Mom won't like it, but I'll make her see sense.' Her face suddenly brightened. 'At least I know where to take everyone. They'll love it there. We're going to—'

'Stop,' Ethan said firmly. 'We literally don't want to know.'

The front door of the Clayton house opened onto a small courtyard. When Ethan and Raymond took their leave, they found Gutierrez swearing into her cell phone. It continued unabated for at least half a minute before she noticed the Chicago detectives staring at her.

'Speak later,' she snapped, and hung up.

'Trouble in Paradise?' Ethan asked smiling.

'You could say that.' Gutierrez swore again, long and loud. 'Our Black Amazon and her limey Goth sidekick? Fucking gone. *Gone.* They just . . . they just . . . walked out of the goddamn fucking station like they owned the place. FUCK!'

'Wait. What? How is that even possible?'

'Oh, you're going to love this. The uniformed fuckwits I have to work with every day are saying I signed the goddamn releases.'

Fifty-Seven

Sunday the 13th: 9.07 a.m. CDT

'How can you tell they're police?' Hollie asked. 'They could be anybody.'

'You just gotta know what you're looking for, doll.'

The Valkyrie Hotel on Chicago's North Avenue was, as the *opolo keji* had suggested, the perfect place to observe Aldrin Street. Abi had used the journey from Providence to reserve the penthouse suite. The garishly opulent, north-facing rooms opened out onto a broad, marble-slabbed terrace. It afforded a view along Aldrin Street's entire length, the right-hand side of which comprised clusters of flat-roofed rock-cubes, one of which, Number 1631, housed the children of Chuck Vielfrass. The reason they weren't already knocking on the door was the subject of their present conversation.

'See that automobile?' she said, pointing to a low-slung vehicle near the junction with North Avenue.

'Yes.'

'It's got an exact twin at the other end of the street, same colour, the works. They're secret police cars.'

Hollie smiled at that.

'I think you mean "unmarked police cars". Could be coincidence. The fact they look the same, I mean.'

Not if you can hear the transmissions.

'Sure. But look at the school.' Abi was pointing to the other side of the street now. 'Those are actual cop cars with markings, and they're tucked away out of sight. We can only see them because we're way up here. What are the cops doing in a school, heh? Particularly when the school is otherwise empty. I'm telling you, the filth is up to something.'

Her ears twitched at the buzz of whining machinery. The police had a small, remotely piloted aircraft somewhere overhead. She was about to mention this to Hollie when it occurred to her that the woman might not be able to hear it.

Hollie's sapphire eyes were scanning the ground. Eventually she nodded.

'I suppose you're right. But what's that got to do with us? Whatever they're up to doesn't matter. It's not as if we're wanted criminals, right?' There was a pause. '*Right*, Abs?'

Hollie's eyes were looking at her intently. Abi couldn't properly recall why she'd ever found them ugly.

'We're in the clear, doll. Definitely. But after yesterday, I'm in no mood to run the risk of being felt up by the cops on another misunderstanding. We'll deliver the kids' inheritance when the boys in blue are out of the way.'

Or after dark, when you're fast asleep.

'Sounds good. Oh, I've been meaning to ask. How's your arm?'

Abi gave her right arm an exuberant swing. The machines had done their work.

'Feels great. Good as new.'

'So tell me why *I* shouldn't call the police.' The brittle edge to Hollie's voice made Abi turn quickly around. Too quickly, maybe. Hollie flinched, looking scared. The *oyinbo* backed off the terrace, seemingly half-torn between making a run for it or standing up for herself.

She chose the latter, gripping the edge of the suite's sliding glass doors for support.

'Where are you from, really?' When Abi made to bat the question away, Hollie cut her off. 'You've put this off long enough. First you said you had to heal, and then you were too busy on the plane, and then you were tired. But none of those things are true anymore and I want to know. Right now, Abi. And don't give me shit about Nigeria 'cause I won't believe you.'

'You're free to believe whatever you like, doll. Ain't no one stopping you.'

'I mean it, Abs. If you don't tell me what's going on, I'm going to call the cops.'

'I wouldn't do that if I were you.'

'Or what? You'll do me in? Is that it?'

The words, the expression on her face, were like a knife to the stomach. Worse.

'No, doll. Never. Never. Not in a million years.' The words came out ragged and disjointed. Abi took a moment to harden herself. 'But if you call the cops, I'll be gone before they get here. And when they do get here, they're going to drag you down the precinct.'

'Why? They let us go.'

'They let us go because their paperwork got all screwy. I doubt that'll happen again. If those fine folks down there figure out who you are,' she gestured over the terrace railing to the ground below, 'you'll be back in a cell in no time.'

Abi tried to ignore the sinking feeling as she watched the

blood drain from Hollie's face. *I'm not here for her,* she told herself. But the words, lacking the weight of conviction, floated pointlessly against the inside of her skull.

'What did you *do*?' Hollie asked. Moisture glistened at the corner of her eyes.

'Nothing terrible. And not what they accused me of, that's for sure. I did have business with that Vielfrass guy, same as with the Forbes gal in Edinburgh, but he done gone and got himself whacked. Ain't nothing I could do about that. Problem is, the cops want to pin it on me. On the both of us.'

Hollie reeled backwards into the suite's living area and collapsed into a plush, florally upholstered armchair. Hands flew to her temples and stayed there. Her black fingernail polish, Abi noticed, had become chipped.

'I don't believe this. This is a nightmare. A fucking nightmare. Do you have any idea what they do to people accused of murder in this country? This isn't Britain, in case you hadn't noticed. We could *die* here.'

Abi chuckled.

'It's not funny, Abs. I'm serious.'

'I know it, babe. But it ain't gonna happen. Not if you stick with me, anyways. I'll see you home in one piece.'

I hope.

'How?' Fear and trust battled for control of Hollie's face.

'I got plans. But step one is you not calling the police.' She larded each syllable with as much confidence as she could muster.

Trust gained a slight edge.

'And what's step two?'

'Shopping.'

No matter how down you are or how hard life is, everything looks better after a good shop.

'You what?'

'Shopping. Can't be doing anything with the Vielfrass kids right now, not when the street is crawling with filth. And I've been working the Wi-Fi. This here city has a lot to offer the likes of you and me.' Abi flashed her biggest, brightest grin. A plea for forgiveness. 'Whaddya know about the Magnificent Mile?'

Fifty-Eight

Sunday the 13th: 1.14 p.m. CDT

Raymond Yeung had set up shop in the Newton Science Academy gym. The only condition imposed by Chicago Public Schools had been that they cover the hardwood floor of the basketball court with heavy canvas tarp.

A sensible precaution, given the force with which a pacing Nicole Gutierrez was slamming into it with her heels.

'Somehow, *somehow* these two managed to hack the police computer system. Remember how Abidemi made that crack about our having great Wi-Fi? Looks like she wasn't kidding.'

'How?' Raymond asked, before Ethan could do the same.

'Best guess? Someone hacked in from the outside. Probably Yemi.'

'Makes sense,' Raymond said. 'We know he can mess with security cameras, why not computers?'

'Wait. It gets worse. They drove back to Logan, dropped the rental cool as you please and that's it: trail's gone cold. For now, at least.'

'What does that mean?' Ethan asked.

'It means it's Sunday and things take time,' Gutierrez said, sighing. 'Assuming they caught a flight, we're not going to get passenger manifests or credit card hits for a couple of days probably. I'm going to make a few calls, see if I can pull in some favours on the credit cards. But in the meantime—'

'They could be fucking anywhere,' Ethan finished.

'Could they, though?' Raymond said. 'There's only two places that make sense. They've either caught a flight home to England, in which case there's nothing much to do right now. Or, if they *didn't* make a run for it, if they're carrying on as usual, we already know where they're going. Only place that makes sense.'

Ethan and Raymond exchanged a look.

'I'll call the Cap,' Ethan said. 'We're gonna need more bodies.'

'Bad choice of words, lieutenant.'

Any retort Ethan might have made was forestalled by the ringing of Yeung's cell phone.

'Hello?'

Ethan watched as a slow, increasingly predatory smile spread across the sergeant's face. He hung up.

'What are you looking so fucking pleased about?'

'Remember the partial on the A. Bello box van? Well, we finally got a hit. South Side address. Seventy-three hundred block of Borman. The guy's name is Yemi all right. Yemi fucking *Eniola.*'

'Same as our Amazon,' said Gutierrez. She slapped a small fist into the palm of her hand. 'There's our connection. And now she and her sidekick are headed here when they should be locked up at home. Jesus *fuck!*'

'Hey, Nicole, this isn't all bad, not by a long shot,' Ethan said. 'We can grab them all at once, red-handed. Five'll get you ten, our gals didn't make a run for England and they're all three of them on Borman right now getting tooled up. Whatever happened in Chuck Vielfrass's condo, we know it didn't go according to plan, otherwise Yemi'd never have left all that special ops stuff behind. Guy left in a hurry. Twice, now. He'll be needing more gear, which, seeing as he lives there, will be stashed on Borman. If we move fast, we can wrap this thing up tonight.'

The expression on Gutierrez's face brought him up short.

'What?' he asked.

'You know there'll be two of them, right?'

'Three. You're forgetting the Brit.'

Despite herself, Gutierrez snorted with derision.

'Look,' Ethan went on. 'We're not going to get caught out like that again. We know what we're dealing with now. Ex-military. But the woman is hurt. Your doc said she'd broken her shoulder in, what? Three places? She won't give us half as much trouble as she did yesterday. Plus, we'll go in hot and heavy with our SWAT buddies and as many extra uniforms as I can squeeze out of my commanders, which, given the circumstances, will be a lot. Fuckers won't know what hit 'em, okay?'

'From the guy who was worried about not having enough resources to protect the Claytons against just one perp, this is a complete one eighty,' Gutierrez said pointedly. 'What gives?'

'We're not playing defence, is what gives. We know where they are and there's no way they're sneaking past us. We're going in, hardcore. It's a hell of a lot easier than sitting on our asses and waiting for them to figure out how to fuck us over.'

Gutierrez nodded.

'How long to get a warrant?'

Ethan glanced over at Raymond.

'An hour or two, max,' the sergeant said. 'What do you reckon, ready to go by six? It'll take time to get the extra uniforms and we've still got to cover our bases back here.'

Ethan shook his head.

'We'll wait till it gets dark. I know Borman. There's not a lot of cover down there. Don't want to be seen till we're right at the door.'

'You sure that's wise, boss? We could miss 'em.'

Ethan shook his head.

'Our guy's MO is to go in after midnight. He's not going to be hanging around up here for very long. Neighbourhood like this, they see him loitering in that box van and they'll call us in a heartbeat. It's too risky. If I were him, I wouldn't leave the house before eleven at the earliest. Later probably.'

'He walked into Sonia Hollander's house in broad daylight,' Gutierrez reminded him.

'Here, too,' Raymond said. 'Guy signed in at the desk and everything like a regular guy.'

'Sure, but that was when the homes he was trying to get into were empty and he didn't know we were onto him. He slipped past police protection at Dorothy's and at Chuck's in the early hours of the morning. Do you really think he's going to walk past a police cordon that's on the lookout for him in the middle of the afternoon?'

With wry smiles, the others both nodded.

'Great. Tonight it is. One way or another, those creeps are coming out of Borman in custody. There's only one question.'

'Which is what?' Gutierrez asked.

'Whether they come out dead or alive.'

Fifty-Nine

'Take a picture.' Hollie thrust her mobile into Abi's hands. Over the course of the day, Abi had become well acquainted with the image-gathering function on the woman's phone. Freshly showered, dressed in all-new, all-black clothing, and with jewelled eyes aglow in a face made even paler than usual by a coating of unnecessary white powder, Hollie stood rigidly at attention, holding one of the hotel's forks in her right hand. Freshly polished nails gleamed dark against the silver metal.

Abi pressed the camera button. White light flashed briefly across the room, throwing their suite's soft furnishings into hard-edged relief.

'Thanks, Abs.' Hollie took the phone back, examined the picture and then flipped it around to show Abi. 'Isn't it great? I'm going to call it American Goth.'

'Why?'

'Because of the painting, the one we saw at the Art Institute. You know, the pitchfork? I'm a Goth, in America, wearing American stuff, holding a fork. Get it?'

'Now I do. Very clever.' Abi feared her face was giving lie to the words.

'I guess it's not a . . . *Nigerian* thing,' Hollie said, sighing. Abi noted the sceptical emphasis but took comfort in the fact that it hadn't dented her good humour. It had taken Hollie a while to process the shock of the morning's conversation, and she'd been unnaturally quiet when they'd headed out to Michigan Avenue. But a day of shopping, and manicures and sightseeing, coupled with the fact that no one had tried to arrest them, had eventually restored her to normal.

Almost normal. Leaning over the rail of an ọkọ ojú omi (the *oyinbo* word for water-going vehicle had managed to elude her), she'd been staring enraptured at the jaw-dropping expanse of Lake Michigan, at the sheer volume of water lying naked in the sun, when she'd caught Hollie giving her a long, thoughtful stare. The woman had looked quickly away. But there'd been more of them throughout the rest of the day, whenever Hollie thought she wasn't paying attention.

Still, she was here, and cheerful, and hadn't called the police.

Abi was shocked at how happy she was about that.

She stepped onto the terrace, a gentle breeze taking the edge off the day's waning heat. The *oyinbo* sun was continuing its slow, syrupy descent towards the horizon, rock-cube shadows stretching lazy and long across the pavement below.

In an hour or two it would be dark. Time to think about how to get to the Vielfrass children before Yemi. Her hands tightened on the terrace railing.

If he wasn't here already, he would be soon.

Hollie stepped beside her, leaning out to look straight down at the roofs of the automobiles rushing along North Avenue, revelling in how high they were above the ground. With a sigh she straightened up again and turned to face the weakening sun, eyes closed as she bathed in its radiation.

'It's beautiful here, isn't it, Abs?'

It's a hideous, polluted jumble of boring cubes, and things that want to be cubes, with people jammed together so tight they can hardly move. And it smells.

But then again, there's the lake. And maybe the river. And maybe . . .

'Sure is, doll.'

'I wish I could stay here forever.'

'Then why don't you?'

'It's not that simple. Anyway, I'd miss home, I think. And my friends. And . . .' She paused, squinting into the distance. 'That's interesting.'

'What is?'

Hollie pointed, arm pale against the black sleeve of her tee shirt.

'Down in the school playground. See? All the police cars are gone.'

A prickle of excitement raised hairs on the back of Abi's neck.

'So they are.'

The unmarked vehicles were still at either end of Aldrin Street, and there was still an aircraft overhead, the high pitch of its motor buzzy in her augments, but that was it.

Abidemi Eniola found herself grinning from ear to ear.

This is going to be so much easier than I thought.

Sixty

Sunday the 13th: 9.45 p.m. CDT

*T*HUMP! THUMP! THUMP!
'Police! We're coming in!'
CRACK!

Even for Ethan, who knew it was coming, the knock and announcement came almost too quick to process. A ram-wielding SWAT officer, looking more military than police in his green combat gear, smashed the neatly painted front door off its hinges. Two large policemen, armed, armoured, and crouching behind ballistic shields, rushed the front hallway of 7307 South Borman, followed by a phalanx of fast-moving team members. They vanished from sight, pouring over the well-maintained front porch and into the depths of the three-storey building. Through the battered-down doorway Ethan could hear boots thumping on stairways, harshly shouted orders, and increasingly distant renditions of one word.

'Clear.'
'Clear.'
'Clear.'
'Clear.'
What the fuck?

Ethan, leaning on the open door of a police cruiser, half-expected to hear the car's radio crackle to life, announcing that the fugitives had burst out of the garage at the back of the property and into the rear alley, only to be apprehended by the officers who lay in wait there.

Nothing.

The SWAT lieutenant reappeared on the front porch, his helmet tucked under one arm in the hot night air. The man waved him over. Ethan went to meet him, conscious of the mix of curious and resentful stares directed at them from the neighbours, listening to the footfalls of Raymond Yeung and Nicole Gutierrez a handful of steps behind him.

'Nobody's home,' the lieutenant said. 'From the feel of the place, no one's been here for days. Whoever lives here is tidy as fuck but there's mouldy bread in the kitchen and expired milk in the refrigerator.'

'Maybe he's just sloppy with groceries,' Raymond said.

'Maybe.' The lieutenant stood to one side of the front door as some of his officers trooped out. They gathered in the front yard to await further orders. One of them lit up a cigarette. The others exchanged low, whispered words, their postures relaxed by anticlimax. 'Like I said, it's a well-kept home. Neat, clean, not a lot of personal effects. Three bedrooms upstairs, one empty, one made up, and another one with a sleeping mat on the floor.' The lieutenant turned and led the way inside. 'Third floor's basically just an empty loft space, nothing there but cabling for the satellite dishes.'

Ethan grunted at that. The only oddity 7307 had presented to outside inspection had been a half-dozen satellite dishes of various shapes and sizes clustered on the roof.

'The cables go anywhere?' he asked.

'See, that's the odd thing. The cables disappear through the floor and into the walls, like you'd expect, but there's only one TV and cable box in the place. Tuned to the Animal Channel, if you can believe that. There are no Wi-Fi routers, or anything else you might expect to be hooked up to a dish. Nothing. Far as I can tell, all the rest of them are still in the walls.'

'The cables check in,' Raymond mused. 'They don't check out.'

Ethan found his lips quirking with amusement.

'And the garage?' he asked.

'No vehicle. It's easily big enough for a box van, though, even with all the shelving. There's a bunch of electrical gear in there. And a charging station.'

'The van's electric?'

'Looks like. Hybrid, maybe.'

'And gone.' Ethan hadn't meant to say the words out loud. Something knotted in his stomach. 'Raymond?'

'Yes, lieutenant?'

'Call the precinct, see if you can get some extra uniforms over to Aldrin.' He looked at his watch. 'If he sticks to his MO, we've still got time to get back there, but a few more bodies wouldn't do any harm.'

'On it.' Raymond's head disappeared into his cell phone.

'It's possible we're ahead of the game,' Gutierrez said.

'What makes you think that?'

'We're assuming he got the jump on us in Providence, split, and headed here ahead of us, right?'

'Sure.'

'But what if he didn't? We know he left the Vielfrass condo in a hurry, but we don't know he left Providence. He hacked into our systems, remember. That's how our Amazon and the Goth girl got sprung. Abidemi is injured, we know that. What if the three of them met up, went to Logan to lay a false trail, and are making their way here *by truck*? They're clever, one of them is hurt, and they'll want to keep a low profile. They may not be moving quickly at all. And there's a real good chance they've stayed off of the interstate. Even if Yemi can mess with cameras like you say, why take the chance at the toll booths? Or with the state troopers? They may still be on the road.'

'Makes sense.' The knot in Ethan's stomach eased, if only a little. 'What about the basement?' he asked the SWAT lieutenant.

'Your guy looks like he's pretty handy. Couple of work-benches, sawhorses, power tools, spools of wire, that kind of stuff. It's like a commercial for Home Depot down there.' The lieutenant ventured a wry grin. 'I'm glad my wife isn't here to see it. It'd give her way too many ideas for my honey-do list.'

Ethan and Raymond chuckled at that.

'Let's start with the basement,' Ethan suggested.

The lieutenant led them to the back of the house and into what must have been a spotless kitchen before his people had trampled through it. Gleaming steel appliances distorted their reflections as they walked past. The lieutenant turned a corner into what was either a large nook or a very short corridor with a door at the end of it.

Gutierrez gave a low whistle.

'That's kind of cool,' she said, pointing.

The door and its surrounding wall had been painted over to form a mural. An eerie desert scene, where a low sun cast long shadows across rolling, red-brown hills and strangely shaped trees, all of which guided the eye to a distant, curving building of sparkling glass, every surface a slightly different colour from its neighbour, a slightly different shape.

Ethan rubbed his eyes.

'Is it me or is that building moving?'

'I'm not sure. It's . . . like rippling water, don't you think? Or not,' Gutierrez said.

'You're imagining things,' said Raymond. 'At least, I think so. It's a trick of the light.' He reached out a hand to touch it. As he did so, everything seemed to settle down, become static.

'Neat trick,' Gutierrez breathed.

'We're not here for the fucking art,' Ethan groused, annoyed at himself for getting sucked in. 'This the door to the basement?' he asked the SWAT lieutenant.

'Sure is.'

The stairs down were steep, but well-lit and modern in an industrial chic kind of way. They ended in a stark, open space with a polished concrete floor and whitewashed brick walls. Like the SWAT lieutenant had said, it was clearly a workshop of sorts. Shelves of tools and small crates of electrical equipment lined the walls, some of it identical to what they'd found at the Vielfrass condo. A large flashlight, yellow and boxy and businesslike, nestled between two cans of paint thinner and what looked like a carton of emergency rations. In one corner there was a neatly folded pile of drop cloths, paint spatter clearly visible on the topmost one. A couple of fire extinguishers, shocking in their bright red, nestled between gaps in the shelving. Two spotless workbenches and a sawhorse sat in the middle of the floor, waiting for someone to use them. A powerful winch, its support mechanism running from floor to ceiling and bolted at both ends, spoke to someone well used to handling heavy equipment.

Raymond nodded approvingly.

'Guy knows his stuff.'

'Guy's a fucking murderer,' Ethan snapped. Something about

the basement was putting him on edge. Despite its neatness, its well-maintained equipment, its sense of, well, *order*, something felt wrong. Out of balance.

He turned slowly around, trying to get his bearings. The stairs, supported by a frame so minimal that the steps seemed to float in the air, came down into the middle of the room. If you came down the stairs and looked to your left, the far wall contained two high-up windows and a heavy-looking door. Ethan didn't need to push it open to know what he'd find there: a below-ground, concrete stairwell and a steep set of steps leading up to the backyard. At the rear of said yard, there'd be a stand-alone garage that gave vehicular access to the alley beyond. Almost every house in the neighbourhood had the same set-up.

The side walls, whitewashed and windowless, were mostly lined with shelving. The wall at the front of the house, to the right of the stairs as you came down them, was completely bare.

'Something's off,' Gutierrez said.

He found her synchronicity of thought startling.

'How do you mean?'

'I don't know. It's just . . . off.'

'Hey, Lou!'

The voice rushed down at them from the top of the stairs.

'What is it, Falco?' the SWAT lieutenant asked.

'Captain wants a sitrep.'

'Tell him we found fuck all.'

'I told him already. He wants to hear it from you.'

With a sigh, the lieutenant climbed the stairs. Ethan could hear the two men talking, the lieutenant annoyed, the other quietly amused, accompanied by the booted thump of feet on the ceiling above him. Still talking, they stomped across the kitchen, between Ethan and the back of the house. Then turned and walked above Ethan's head in the direction of the destroyed front door. The footsteps crossed the ceiling to the top of the front wall. Passed it. Kept on going. Faded away as they reached the front porch.

The three detectives looked at each other.

'Well, fuck me,' Raymond said.

'I knew something was off,' Gutierrez said. 'This basement's too small for the house. The front wall's false. Gotta be. There's something behind it. Something worth hiding.' She pressed her hands against the wall, feeling from one side of the room to the other. 'And somewhere, there has to be a door.'

The two men joined her, probing for cracks, the hint of a hinge. Anything. The wall was cool and glassy smooth under Ethan's fingers. Featureless. Try as they might, they couldn't find a way in.

'Fuck this,' Ethan said at last. And then to Raymond: 'Go see if our SWAT pals have a sledgehammer or something. Guys like that gotta know a thing or two about breaking down walls.'

'On it.'

SWAT teams being what they were, Yeung returned with not one but two sledgehammers and a handful of curious, uniformed onlookers. Taking one of the sledgehammers from his sergeant, Ethan hefted it in his hands before swinging as hard he could. The hammer's heavy, rust-brown head swung through the air faster than the eye could follow. It struck the wall with a sound like a church bell, almost twisting out of Ethan's hands.

'You need to work out more,' Raymond said drily.

'Fuck you.'

The wall was entirely unscathed. Not even the whitewash was chipped.

Raymond grinned and swung, his movement more fluid,

the blow significantly harder than the one Ethan had landed. Ethan resisted the urge to clap his hands to his ears as the basement echoed with the sound of contact. Gutierrez retreated towards the outside door, hands firmly pressed against her head.

Not a mark.

Frowning, Raymond handed his sledgehammer to the nearest SWAT officer, a giant of a man who seemed purpose-built for the breaking down of barriers. A second SWAT guy plucked the other one from Ethan's unresisting hands. The two officers swung with a will, raining down blow after blow, the room booming like a Sunday morning cathedral. Deafened by the noise, Ethan imagined he could see sparks.

'Stop!' he yelled. His voice sounded fuzzy and far away in his ringing ears. 'Stop, dammit!'

The SWAT guys did as they were told, panting heavily, sweat gleaming on their foreheads.

'That can't be right,' one of them said. 'Can't be.'

The undamaged wall stood in mute mockery of their efforts.

Not believing his eyes, Ethan ran his hand across the wall's smooth surface. He stopped almost immediately.

'Feel this,' he said to the detectives. 'Tell me if you can feel, actually *feel* the individual bricks.'

Raymond, he could see, was resisting the urge to laugh in his face, eyes twinkling with undelivered humour. Gutierrez, on the other hand, looked thoughtful. Both did as they were told.

The twinkle in Raymond's eyes vanished.

'I can't,' he said at last. 'I mean, I *thought* I could. But now I really think about it, it's just . . . smooth. He leaned in close. This is fucking weird. I can see my finger touching the brick, the whitewash. But what it feels like is—'

'Glass,' Gutierrez finished for him. The colour had drained from her face.

He remembered Chuck Vielfrass's apartment. The cube of water in its invisible tank. The cables snaking out from the walls.

Ethan turned to the giant SWAT officer.

'You,' he said. 'Go back to your truck, fetch a pair of bolt cutters or whatever you guys use to cut the power and—'

'Cut the power. Sure thing, Lou.'

The officer clattered up the stairs. 'Hey, Sparkie,' the detectives heard him yelling once he reached the top. 'Time to go do your thing.'

One of the remaining SWAT officers turned on a flashlight. Five minutes later, accompanied by the clunking of unseen breakers, the power went out.

'Jesus, Mary, and Joseph,' Ethan muttered. Hushed whispers broke out behind him.

The recalcitrant wall had vanished. Every whitewashed brick of it. The blue-tinged beam of the flashlight bounced unsteadily into the space beyond. Other flashlights joined it. Jagged shadows jumped and warped against the walls.

It was like looking into another world.

If the other world was a Frankenstein version of IKEA. And Africa. Wherever Ethan looked, his gaze lit upon African memorabilia: carvings, shields, tribal masks; a startling, beaten-bronze statue of a lance-wielding Black man on a horse. Every chair, every desk, every lamp, every bookshelf, looked like it had been ordered from a Scandinavian furniture catalogue. Everything was designed with clean lines, and light wood, and slightly quirky dimensions. But while the chairs and lamps looked perfectly normal, the desks and bookshelves had been . . . well, *fused* was the word that sprang to Ethan's mind. Fused with a bewildering array of electronics. Neatly bundled cables emerged organically from the walls and floor, and sank smoothly into the wooden furniture with no sign of a drill hole. The furniture itself was melded with keyboards, and computer screens, and pieces of laptop, and cell phones assembled into ziggurats of gutted and repurposed technology. It was impossible to tell where the wood ended and the technology began. Ethan half expected the desks to get up and walk, like a phalanx of killer robots. Something that looked like the tall and hollow rectangle of an airport metal detector, carefully encased in what looked like jewel-encrusted wood, stood slightly apart in the corner next to a stripped-down, seventy-two-inch TV.

The three detectives stood on the edge of where the wall had been, all reluctant to step across, all looking to someone else to be the first to go.

Ethan took a deep breath and walked forward. His shoulders tensed, expecting . . . something.

Nothing happened.

'Good thing the guy didn't think to buy a backup generator,' Raymond quipped.

'It's Chicago, not the fucking boonies,' Ethan said, smiling.

He peered closely at the nearest of the Frankenstein desks, hoping to come across something he could understand. Something that made sense. But the screens were dark, the equipment dead. There was nothing to learn.

'You think these were lit up before SWAT cut the power?' Raymond asked.

'No idea,' Ethan said, shrugging. Then, with a mischievous smile, 'Shall we get 'em to turn it back on, see what happens?'

'Let's not.'

Ethan's smile widened into a grin.

'Come look at this,' Gutierrez said. She'd been peering at the equipment on Yemi's shelves. And now she was holding an ancient, leather-bound book, the cover a light calfskin brown and flaking with decay. Ethan could understand why she'd picked it up. It must have looked out of place beside the freakish piles of Rube Goldberg technology cramming the shelving from end to end. He took the proffered volume from her gingerly, fearful it would break apart in his hands. He needn't have worried. Despite the odour of dusty decay that filled his nostrils, it felt reassuringly solid. The cover was far thicker than you'd find on a modern book and gave slightly when he pressed it with his fingers. There was a small rectangle of darker material, slightly torn, towards the top of the book's spine. It was embossed with fading gold letters.

JOURNAL OF A VOYAGE

Ethan opened it up. Looked at the first page. The handwriting on the aged, sepia paper was ornate and spidery, the ink faded to a brown that was barely darker than that of the page itself.

> Being an Account of the Voyage of the Vessel
> Esperance, lately of Bristol, England, Commencing
> this 4th Day of February, 1791
> Theodore H. Bradock, Master

'Must be part of his historical research,' Ethan said. 'Any sign of a manuscript?'

'What manuscript?'

'The book he was working on when he went to see Professor MacPherson.'

'The prof didn't—'

Whatever Gutierrez was about to say was interrupted by the ringing of her cell phone.

'Hello?'

She listened in silence for a while, glancing over at Ethan from time to time, the tinny sound of whomever she was speaking with too indistinct for others to hear.

'Tell the Nerd thanks from me, okay? I owe him one. And I will totally sign off on his overtime. Leave the warrant with me, I'll make sure it gets done.' Her face had acquired a grim smile. 'Later.'

'What was that about?' Ethan asked.

'We just caught ourselves a break. I pulled in a favour from a guy who pulled in a favour from a guy at the credit card company. On a *Sunday*, so be sure to be goddamned impressed when I'm done. Abidemi Eniola bought two one-way tickets out of Logan to Chicago O'Hare, arriving last night. Spent a shit-ton of money today *shopping* if you can believe that. But guess where they're staying.'

'Gotta be some cheap-ass motel on the edge of town,' Ethan said, thinking of the basic accommodation they'd been arrested in. 'By the airport, maybe. There sure aren't cheap-ass motels *in* town.'

'Not even close,' Gutierrez replied, grinning. 'They're staying at the Valkyrie. On North Avenue.'

'Jesus fucking Christ!'

'I guess you could say he's impressed,' Raymond chuckled.

'*I* sure am,' said a voice.

Ethan whirled around, reaching for his gun.

There was a man: tall and thin and blacker than asphalt, standing in a corner of the basement, looking for all the world like he'd just stepped out of the bejewelled metal detector behind him. He stood unblinking in the glare of a SWAT officer's flashlight. His eyes, for the briefest of moments, glittered like a cat's.

There was a *click-click-click* of released safeties.

All Ethan could think about was a middle-aged Black man in pyjamas; a brain that refused to constrain his trigger finger; the horrific consequences of being on target. His stomach rippled at the thought.

'GUNS DOWN!' Ethan roared. 'Unless you want to be on CNN in the worst possible way.'

'How the—?' Gutierrez began.

'You set off a number of alarms when you barged in here,' Yemi Eniola said, mildly. 'I had to park my truck—'

'Stay right where you are,' Ethan said. His own service weapon, gripped in two hands that ought to be shaking but weren't, was pointed at the man's chest. 'Face down on the ground! Now!' Ethan didn't take his eyes off the target – he was too afraid – but behind him he could hear the shuffling of booted feet. The SWAT guns might be pointed downwards but their owners remained tripwire tense.

Slowly, deliberately, Yemi raised his arms above his head. Lowered himself to his knees.

'Now then, I'd sure appreciate it if you fine folks wouldn't go putting holes in me. I ain't resisting. Just playing nice like you asked.'

He stretched his long body onto the floor, facedown. Three SWAT officers swarmed him, pinning him to the ground with painful ferocity, wrenching his arms behind his back.

'Yemi Eniola,' Ethan intoned, 'I'm arresting you for the murder of Amadi Okoro and Benedict Okoro. You have the right to remain silent. Anything you say can and will be used against you in a court of law. You have the right to talk to a lawyer and have him or her present with you while you are being questioned. If you cannot afford to hire a lawyer one will be appointed to represent you before any questioning if you wish. You can decide at any time to exercise these rights and not answer any questions or make any statements. Do you understand each of these rights I have explained to you?'

'Sure, detective, whatever you say.' Yemi's voice was muffled by the press of bodies.

'Lieutenant,' Raymond said.

'What?'

'Look.'

It took a moment to figure out what the sergeant wanted him to look at.

The basement's technology, once dark in the apparent absence of power, was now glowing a faint, baleful red. The gleam of it reached into every corner of the room, too weak to illuminate, just strong enough to make the whole space look like it was wreathed in faint tendrils of mist.

The sudden whine of a mosquito zipped past his ear.

There was a shattering crash of a flashlight. A SWAT officer on the far side of the basement collapsed to the ground.

Ethan advanced on Yemi, his finger tight against the trigger guard of his pistol.

'You son of a—'

'I didn't touch him,' Yemi said. He sounded as if he was having trouble breathing under the weight of the three SWAT officers. Ethan didn't much care. 'I'm right here under your nose, detective. You can see it ain't me.'

'Get him out of here – and do it fast,' Ethan growled. There were goosebumps prickling on the back of his neck. His ears hummed with the buzzing of insects. Ethan briefly wondered if someone had accidentally disturbed a wasps' nest.

The SWAT guys dragged Yemi to his feet. He towered above them, thin and rangy, but somehow his burly, flack-jacketed guards appeared frail and insubstantial in comparison. The coal black of his skin soaked up both the instruments' red glow and the lurching white of police flashlights, making it difficult to read his expression. Ethan, however, sensed he was trying not to smile. He tightened his grip on his weapon.

Just give me an excuse, you bastard. We'll see who's grinning then.

Nicole Gutierrez collapsed. Then Raymond Yeung. The SWAT officers rushed Yemi towards the stairs.

There was a buzzing above Ethan's head. A swarm of mosquitoes.

Of . . . something.

Suddenly it made sense. Jennifer Okoro had said she'd been bitten. And so she had, but not in the way she'd thought. James Hollander had headed to his pantry for a can of Raid. The Providence police officer had tried to close his car window because the insects had gotten buzzy.

Ethan ducked down low and ran. Holstering his gun, he dragged a red fire extinguisher from the wall and pulled the pin. Icy white powder filled the air with a cold whoosh as Ethan spun around, directing the extinguisher towards the ceiling. There was a metallic *tick-tick-tick* of things hitting the floor, as if someone had poured out a giant box of needles.

'Clever *oyinbo*,' Yemi said.

The voice was right by Ethan's ear. He whirled around, swinging hard with the fire extinguisher. Metal collided with flesh.

And bounced. Ethan found himself looking up at Yemi's dark

eyes. They were expressionless. Uncaring. Like the shark at the Caribbean Reef.

Yemi grabbed his wrist. Except it didn't feel like that. It felt like someone had smashed his arm with one of the SWAT team's sledgehammers.

He screamed as the extinguisher went skittering across the floor, bouncing to rest against the unmoving boot of a downed SWAT officer. They lay in a crumpled heap at the bottom of the steps.

Ethan Krol was the last man standing.

Another sledgehammer slammed into the back of his knees, taking his legs out from under him. He collapsed onto the cold concrete floor, his shoulder taking most of the impact. He rolled over, desperate to get up, to escape.

Something landed on his neck, light and feathery. He felt it jabbing uselessly against his skin. One of Yemi's fake mosquitoes, crippled by the blast from the fire extinguisher but still trying to do its job.

He swatted hard, felt a savage satisfaction as it crunched beneath his palm. He struggled to his knees, then his feet, intent on reaching the door that led out to the backyard.

Yemi stood to one side, watching him curiously. Ethan had no time to be puzzled by his good fortune. He sprinted for the door.

Tried to sprint. All he could manage was a stutter step.

The world went black before he hit the floor.

Sixty-One

Sunday the 13th: 10.55 p.m. CDT

'I'm coming, too,' Hollie announced, arms folded stubbornly against her chest. Behind her, muted pictures from something called a sports roundup were scrolling across the hotel suite's TV.

'No can do, doll.' Abi pointed at her backpack, waiting to be plucked from the corner of a large sofa. 'All I'm doing is delivering a couple of heirlooms, same as I did in Edinburgh. I won't be gone more than – ' she hesitated momentarily, struggling to convert to the *oyinbo* measurements – 'half an hour, an hour, tops. Piece of cake. I'll be back before you know it.'

'If it's a piece of cake, then I should come, just like in Edinburgh.'

Abi sighed softly.

'There weren't no cops in Edinburgh. I'm one hundred per cent certain the cops down there are guarding the family I gotta spend time with.'

'Why?'

'Who knows? Point is, they ain't just gonna let me waltz in there and visit, and I ain't got the time to come back another day. You don't want to be arrested again, do ya?'

'Do you think you'll get arrested?'

'Heck, no.'

'Then I should come. You can't stop me, you know.'

That's what you think.

And Hollie would never trust her again.

'Okay, okay, you can come. But if it all goes south, don't come complaining to me, got it?'

'Great, let's go.' Hollie practically skipped towards the door.

'Hold your horses, babe,' Abi said laughing. She moved in the opposite direction, stepping out onto the terrace. The night air was still warm. Automobiles, headlamps throwing white puddles of light on the road ahead of them, still rumbled along North Avenue. The secret – no, *unmarked* – police cars still sat at either end of Aldrin. And a faint glow from the school indicated that at least one of the rooms there was still occupied.

'What are we doing out here, Abs? We going to fly down?' Hollie giggled.

'Shush,' Abi said, raising a hand. She leant over the terrace railing, listening intently. 'Somewhere up there is an aircraft.' Abi's voice was low, little more than a whisper. 'It don't have a pilot. Someone, probably in the school over there, is using radio signals to control it from the ground.'

'Like a drone, you mean?'

'No. This is not a "mindless worker" or a "cog in the machine". It *is* the machine, remotely operated and designed for surveillance.'

Hollie burst out laughing.

'That's also a drone, doofus. The word has more than one meaning.'

Abi tried to minimize the frown she could feel spreading across her face.

'I see,' she said slowly. 'So, anything remotely controlled and designed for surveillance is—'

'A drone, exactly.'

'A good word.' Good enough, *advanced* enough to describe her *alantakun*. She'd known her language files would be out of date – how could they not be – but the extent of the deficit was daunting.

'So, this, ah, *drone* has been circling that housing complex all day, probably waiting for someone – us, I guess – to come visit. At which point the filth will get outta their cars and try and arrest us.'

'But I thought you said we wouldn't get arrested?'

'I said "try", babe. *Try.* I also said you shouldn't come. Honestly, this'd be a helluva lot easier if you stayed.'

'No.' Abi could sense the firm tilt of Hollie's chin without looking. She bit back a smile.

'Okay. But here's the thing.' She pulled out her mobile for Hollie's benefit, pretended to press the keys. 'If the drones can't see us, they can't tell the cops we're out there. It'd be easy enough to blind 'em, see, but blinding ain't enough here: just blinding 'em would tip them off that something was wrong. The real trick,' she jabbed at the mobile while her augments did the work, 'is to replace the live camera feed with a fake one so no one realizes anything is wrong.'

She flashed a broad grin.

'Done. Time to go.'

When they emerged from the hotel lobby onto North Avenue, Abi refused to lead them across the road and up Aldrin. She turned right instead, heading east to the next intersection. A battered green sign affixed to a lamp post identified the name of the cross street as LOCUST.

Heading north on Locust, Abi found herself confronted with an elongated rock-cube, its length subdivided into dwellings in much the same manner as Hollie's terraced housing back in Knowle West. In that puzzling *oyinbo* way, though, these seemed much nicer. Lights glowed out of a succession of small, square windows.

Abi paused in front of a house that showed no lights at all and scanned it in a variety of wavelengths. She sighed quietly and moved on: three doors down to the next lightless dwelling.

'This looks like it'll do okay.'

'And what is it that we're doing?'

'You'll see.' She summoned the *alantakun*.

Hollie screamed. Abi swung around and clapped her hands over the woman's mouth. The eyes above Abi's firm grip were wide and frightened.

'You gotta be quiet for me, doll. Okay? Can you do that?'

Hollie nodded. Abi let her hand fall away.

'What's wrong?'

'There were . . . *spiders* crawling all over your backpack.'

'Like these?' Abi couldn't resist a grin as she revealed her other hand, where the three *alantakun* had now gathered.

Hollie stepped back with a gasp, one hand flying to her mouth.

'Oh, god. I think I'm going to be sick. That's disgusting.'

Abi let the *alantakun* fall to the pavement. They landed with a faint, metallic sound, skittering off in the direction of the dark-windowed rock-cube.

'They're machines, babe. They're gonna help me see what's inside the house. Like your, ah, *drone*, heh? Excepting they don't fly.'

'Let me guess. You brought them from *Nigeria*.'

'Sure did.'

'Uh-huh. And what are they doing now?'

'Sliding under the door.'

'How do you know that?'

'I can see through their cameras.'

'Without a screen?'

Abi cursed herself. The damned mobile was still sitting in her pocket. She should think of something: maybe hide behind her poor language skills.

'I have a small screen in my eye.' She avoided Hollie's gaze, taking off her backpack and rummaging through it until she found what she was looking for. A small, ornately decorated box. It burned hot in her hand.

'And this . . . eye screen of yours. Also from Nigeria?'

'You got it.'

Hollie sighed.

'The house is empty, doll, let's go.'

'So now we're just going to break into someone's house?'

'Nope.' Abi opened the box. Showed the contents to Hollie. 'We have keys.'

Abi unlocked the front door and led the way to the back of the dwelling, grateful that it was too dark for Hollie to see the *alantakun* climbing up her legs and crawling into her backpack. The two women exited through sliding glass doors and into a small back garden. At the far end, a tall wooden fence separated the garden from the housing complex beyond. Abi leapt at the fence, her foot making contact about halfway up and propelling her over the top. She landed gracefully on the far side with barely a sound.

As she started to step away, she heard a furious scrabbling behind her. Hollie's reddened face appeared over the top of the fence, the rest of her reluctant to follow. The head disappeared followed by a crashing sound, softly whispered swear words, and more scrabbling.

An even redder face appeared at the top of the fence. This time, though, the body followed. Hollie's brand-new, flouncy black skirt made for a difficult transition from one side of the fence to the other, but she made it. Abi caught her as she dropped down, softening an otherwise clumsy landing.

'Maybe trousers next time, heh? Make things easy on—'

A staticky hiss washed against Abi's implants.

'What is it?' Hollie whispered. She seemed unnerved by Abi's sudden stillness.

'Wait here.'

Abi crept softly away from the fence, making barely a sound as she gained the paved surface of a path. She hesitated, unsure as to direction when the signal was distorted by so many rock-cubes packed tightly together. Getting her bearings at last, she headed north, eyes scanning the night in infrared.

The path took a hard left. She stopped before the turn. Her breathing slowed to almost nothing.

The police officer came around the corner, his radio emitting an audible crackle. The man's eyes widened in surprise.

And closed as he slumped unconscious from a blow to the head.

Abi bent over the policeman's slumped form, dragging him off the path and into some bushes.

Which is why she didn't see the second officer. All she heard was the metallic sound of a projectile weapon being readied to fire.

The amulet doused her with combat chemicals and the world slowed to a crawl. She turned to find the downed officer's partner, a short, *oyinbo* woman, her arm outstretched, finger on the firing contact of a black, blocky projectile weapon.

Abi stepped across the space between them. The woman might barely be moving, but she wasn't still. The grip on the contact was tightening towards a point of no return. If it fired, there would be no time to dodge and she might very well be dead on this filthy, backward world, *gbese* still unpaid. Even if it somehow missed, the noise of the discharge would arouse every *oyinbo* in the neighbourhood. They would flood the street. Call more police. The task would become impossible.

Fear of failure added urgency to her stride. She grabbed the woman's wrist. There was a creaking of bones, the crushing of tendons, a piercing, elongated scream. The projectile weapon fell unfired from the officer's crippled hand. Abi, in a swift, practised movement, took the woman's legs from under her and knocked her unconscious before she hit the ground.

Damage, however, had been done. A scream might not be as loud as a gunshot, but it was still loud. Dizzied by combat chemicals, Abi picked the downed woman up and tossed her into the bushes beside her partner. Red mist blurred the edges of her vision as she hurtled towards her destination, worried that the chemicals coursing through her body might have altered her sense of direction.

They had not. 1631 Aldrin was exactly where it was supposed to be.

There was time now for neither *alantakun* nor keys. She kicked the door in.

She could hear screams from the rock-cube's interior. A *third* officer, not an *oyinbo* this time, but tall and handsome, appeared in the tiny, cramped hallway on the other side of the entrance.

Abi had plenty of time for regret as she landed a blow to his throat and finished him off.

The screams were coming from above, where the *oyinbo*s liked to sleep. She climbed the stairs up from the hallway four at a time.

There was a woman at the top of the steps. The mother, Abi decided.

'I don't want to hurt you,' she said. Tried to say. 'I'm not here for you.' The chemicals made it difficult to talk. It was hard to slow down enough to form the lumpy *oyinbo* words. She stopped. Gave the lumps time to reach the woman's brain.

Perhaps she'd failed to make herself understood. Perhaps the woman was too desperate, too protective of her children, to give way. She simply stood there terrified. Pale, cracked hands bunched into pitifully small fists.

Abi climbed the last step. She let the woman hit her once, twice, three times as she forced the *oyinbo* back across the narrow upper hallway.

'I don't want to hurt you,' she said again.

The woman tried a fourth strike, the movement as syrupy slow as the *oyinbo* sun.

Abi didn't let it land. She reached out to the woman's thin, pink-splotched neck and squeezed.

'I don't want to hurt you.'

It was no good. The woman writhed and struggled until the light faded from her eyes. Abi let her drop, looking around for her true targets.

The Vielfrass children.

The rock-cube had fallen eerily silent. Abi stood on the upper hallway, the *oyinbo* woman crumpled at her feet, listening.

Nothing. Even the outside seemed quiet. No neighbours

coming to examine the broken front door, no shouts of alarm over the fallen police officers.

She turned up her hearing.

Still nothing. A bird chirped in the darkness, air chuffing under a night beat of wings.

A whimper. Quickly stifled.

Abi followed the sound. Came to a door. A scan revealed the heat of three bodies on the other side, a female and two juveniles, huddled together among the ceramic fixtures and fittings of a bathroom.

All that stood between her and her quarry was a flimsy bolt.

But she still couldn't talk. Couldn't make herself understood. It would be easier if they could be made to follow orders. Cleaner.

She needed the drugs out of her system.

The amulet started the purge. Short though the interval had been, she'd been dosed too long to escape without consequences. She leaned against the bathroom door, shivering with cold and nausea. Her vision blurred, the red mist moving in from the edges and tinging everything. She would be weak and wobbly for a while, she knew: until she'd eaten. But she didn't need much strength to take on an *oyinbo* lady and two kids.

She just needed to be understood.

'Come on out, whoever you are.' Words in her own language. But not hers.

She staggered to the top of the stairs and looked down.

Yemi Eniola's feral smile faltered at the sight of her.

'You,' he said. 'The *masu amfana* sent . . . you?' He was dressed from helmeted head to foot in an olive-coloured uniform. The word POLICE was stencilled across the front of the clunky armour encasing his torso. It was like no police uniform

Abi had yet seen but she had no doubt it was authentic. Behind him the front door had been closed, as much as it could be, anyway. To one side, partly obscured by the stairs' banister, was a large metal crate, still on its trolley. Equipment presumably. He must have wheeled it up the street. Which meant that the occupants of the unmarked police cars had been in no position to stop him.

'They sent me,' Abi said. 'As you can see. Or have your eyes grown feeble with age? You are too late.'

The smile brightened again.

'It is you who are too late. One more act and *gbese* will have been paid. A perfect ending to all this.' The smile tightened, no longer reaching his eyes. 'Give me the children.'

'Make me.' She could barely stand.

'Always challenging. Good to see. But, if I were you, I would consider my position more carefully.'

'And if I were you, I would talk less and act more. Or has age wearied your muscles as well as your eyes?'

'One should not mock age when one's own head is filled with sand. I think you have grown too close to the *oyinbos*. One of them, anyway.'

Abi's augments caught the barest flicker of a signal. The latches on the crate made a faint hissing sound as they unlocked. The lid swung open.

Hollie Rogers's unconscious body tumbled onto the floor, the muffled *thud* as it did so masking Abi's gasp of shock.

'The box is for the children. I have measured it very carefully. But, as you can see, I filled it on the way here.' Yemi's tone hardened. 'I want only the children. It is *gbese*. Your skinless friend here is no part of that. But oppose me in this and the woman will never wake.' Yemi reached for the small of his back and pulled out a long, wicked-looking knife. The blade's jagged edge glittered faintly in the pale light of the hallway.

Abi shrugged.

'Do as you wish with the *oyinbo*. She is no concern of mine.'

Yemi laughed at that.

'You underestimate the interest the Chicago police have taken in you. They can track your credit card spending. You did not know that, I think. And they know – and I know – that you and your friend are staying together in a very expensive hotel. And that you spent the day, ah, *shopping.*' Yemi prodded Hollie's unconscious form with the toe of his boot, his gaze as disinterested as if she were a pile of stones. 'You would not do such things if she meant nothing to you.'

'And still you are mistaken.'

'Really? Well, I have been wrong before.'

He plunged the knife into Hollie's heart. Pulled it out, the jagged blade coated with blood.

Abi didn't properly understand that the keening in her ears was the sound of her own screaming. She was hurling herself from the top of the stairs, aiming boots first for Yemi's head. But she was slow and weakened, and Yemi twisted out of the way, leaving one of Abi's feet to collide with the top of the empty crate while the other scrabbled at nothing, sending her into an ungainly spin that ended with her crashing against the closed front door.

Sparks of pain flared across her vision, air fled from her lungs. She spun around, trying to spring to her feet, but could only manage to make it to her hands and knees. She gasped and coughed, dripping red-stained spittle on the floor.

Yemi looked down at her, his expression one of unmitigated disappointment.

And that, somehow, was the worst thing of all.

The bloodstained knife he'd been holding in his hand flickered and disappeared.

'A cheap trick, child. Fit only for primitives. And you, apparently.'

The boot that slammed into her temple put an end to the geyser of humiliation that had been welling up inside her.

Sixty-Two

Sunday the 13th: 11.34 p.m. CDT

Abi lurched awake to the sound of still distant sirens. She sat for a moment with her back against the front door, legs splayed out in front of her.

Nothing seemed to be badly damaged. The amulet was already dealing with the thumping headache brought about by Yemi's violence, her ill-fated leap down the stairs hadn't broken anything and, most importantly of all, the debilitating after-effects of the combat chemicals had mostly played themselves out. She was shaky and still a bit weak but, all things considered, in pretty good shape.

The thought evinced a bitter laugh. Physically, maybe. Everything else had gone sideways. Hollie was slumped on the floor beside her, still unconscious, her body pressed against the police officer she'd incapacitated earlier. Yemi had taken no chances with that one, she noticed. He was every bit as drugged up as the woman.

Abi shrugged off her backpack and rummaged inside. She pulled out the med-kit and slipped the ivory-looking bracelet over Hollie's lifeless wrist. It vibrated slightly, as if irritated by the simplicity of the task ahead of it.

Abi got to her feet and went in search of the kitchen. Half-a-dozen cookies and a carton of orange juice later, the last of the shakiness disappeared. She took a deep, steadying breath, stepped past Hollie's slumped body, and climbed the stairs one more time. The woman she had strangled still lay in the upper hallway. Her chest, too, was unnaturally still.

The man was nothing if not thorough. She left the woman to her drugged torpor and strode towards the bathroom.

The once-bolted door had been kicked off its hinges and lay aslant against the bathtub. The home's other female, older than the one in the upper hallway, her skin wrinkled, the knuckles on her hands swollen and red from some *oyinbo* affliction, had been stuffed unconscious into the small space between the toilet bowl and the sink.

The children, as expected, were gone.

Abi sucked at her teeth in displeasure. What had she thought to find here? The children, hidden behind a shower curtain safe and sound? Some clue as to Yemi's whereabouts? She was wasting time. The sirens were getting closer.

She descended the stairs to find Hollie on her hands and knees, struggling to get up.

'What happened? I was—'

'Not now, doll.' Abi extended an arm and hauled her to her feet. Hollie's unsteady legs were barely able to keep her upright. Abi pulled her in close, turned her so that she could gaze down onto the pale face with its bright, sapphire eyes. 'We need to get out of here before the filth arrive. Do you think you can walk?'

After a moment's hesitation, Hollie nodded.

'Good. Let's split.'

'Where are we going?'

Which was a far more difficult question than Abi was prepared to admit out loud. Yemi was gone, the children packed in his crate like cargo. She had no idea where.

But someone else might.

'Not far.'

They stepped out into the night. Abi half-expected to be confronted by a crowd of hostile *oyinbo*s but there was no one. She could tell that the neighbouring rock-cubes were no longer asleep. Even in the visual spectrum, it was easy enough to see the silhouettes of people standing at their various windows, peering around heavily drawn drapes, or using cautious fingers to pry apart the closed slat of a blind.

Grateful though she was for the lack of interference, Abi couldn't quite smother the small flame of contempt that flickered in her chest.

With neighbours like these, who needs enemies?

They made it to Aldrin and hurried north. The med-kit continued to do its job. Hollie's stride strengthened with every step. By the time they reached the end of the street, she was strong enough to dig in her heels and stop Abi's progress altogether.

'Abs, what are you doing?' Hollie pointed diagonally across the road. 'We're going to walk right past that unmarked police car. We could get nicked.'

'We're not walking past, babe,' Abi chuckled. 'We're walking *to*.'

She stepped into the road, leading both of them to the object of Hollie's concern. It was a silver-coloured automobile, unremarkable except for the occasional burst of police-frequency static that leaked from its coms system.

The driver's side window had been wound down. Abi had no trouble imagining Yemi, dressed in his police uniform, sauntering over with a big smile on his face and tapping on the glass.

Sure enough, the vehicle's sole occupant was slumped forward, head pressed against the steering wheel.

Abi dragged him out and tossed him onto the rear seat.

'C'mon,' she said to Hollie. 'I need you to drive this thing.'

Abi settled into the passenger seat and consulted her maps. By the time Hollie had adjusted the driver's seat so she could reach the pedals, and coaxed the automobile's wheezy, rattly propulsion system into life, she knew exactly where she wanted to go. Following Abi's directions, Hollie drove them north through a small park and then east until they reached the low, shadowed buildings of a school, not so different from the one on Aldrin. This one, though, called itself a 'Language Academy', as if science and language were different things. Hollie drove slowly onto the school grounds, coming to rest in the middle of an open plain of black asphalt. Light from the street barely made it here, swallowed up by distance and the soft rustle of trees. To *oyinbo* eyes they were practically invisible. Hollie turned off the headlights, making the darkness complete.

'Can I have that back, doll?' Abi asked, pointing to the med-kit on Hollie's wrist. 'I don't think you'll be needing it now.'

Bursts of communication flitted from Abi's augments. Hollie looked startled as the med-kit, once so snug against her skin, suddenly hung loose.

Having recovered the bracelet, Abi pulled the unconscious police officer out of the car, propped him against the side of the vehicle, and slipped the med-kit over the man's wrist. It was some time before his eyes fluttered open. In normal light they would have come across as a weird shade of green. Abi was grateful to be looking at them in a non-visible spectrum.

Seeing Abi leaning over him in the darkness, the officer tried to scramble away. But he was far too weak. Using about as much force as Hollie would have been able to muster, Abi pinned him back against the side of the car.

'Say now, that ain't no way to treat someone who's just trying to be friendly.'

'Fuck you.' The words were slurred but vehement.

'Don't you want to get the egg that did this to ya?'

The eyes blinked then. Tried a little harder to focus.

'You did this to me.'

'The hell I did. That was a guy, remember?' She gestured at herself and Hollie, who was watching the proceedings with unabashed curiosity. 'We're just a couple of gals trying to do you a favour.'

'Then let me go.' He tried to raise himself from the car. Abi pushed him back down with a lot more force than necessary.

A *lot* more. The man's eyes flickered with fear.

'You can be on your way just as soon as you tell me what I need to know.'

'Which is what, exactly?'

'Where can I find Detective Ethan Krol?'

'Go fuck yourself.'

Abi sighed.

'This is going to hurt you a lot more than it hurts me.'

Sixty-Three

Monday the 14th: 1.07 a.m. CDT

Ethan couldn't decide which was worse, the pain shooting through his wrist or the banging in his head. He ground his teeth together to stop from groaning out loud and allowed his eyes to flutter open. It was dark and summer hot, rough concrete pressing against his cheek. He held his body still, in case Yemi was close by, watching.

He was no longer in the basement, that much he could tell. But still indoors. A place with no windows, though a little light – street light, he thought – was leaking in from somewhere. He could make out a brick wall a few feet in front of his face, partly obscured by a bicycle. The sweet smell of motor oil wafted into his nose.

I'm in a garage. Yemi's probably.

He strained his ears for signs that he wasn't alone. A quietly drawn breath, the soft scrape of a chair, the rustle of clothing.

Nothing.

Trying not to put any weight on his swollen right wrist, he twisted himself into a sitting position, took in the rest of his surroundings.

And screamed. Short and sharp and brought to an end by jamming a fist into his mouth.

The floor of the garage was covered in bodies. Neatly laid out and face down.

He staggered to his feet. The whole SWAT team was here. Yeung and Gutierrez were here, too, side by side, heads almost touching the garage's roller door, their skin pallid and sweaty in the light creeping past the door's uneven edges.

Dead people don't sweat.

He forced himself to calm down. To think.

Yemi and his partner were vicious, ruthless killers. But there was a twisted logic to their killing. They killed men, women and children without compunction. But there were always survivors. A spouse, the staff at Dorothy Vielfrass's grand New England mansion . . . himself. Twice now. He'd been beaten unconscious in Rhode Island, and drugged unconscious on the South Side. That he continued to draw breath was the result of a deliberate choice. He remembered the smooth, predatory grace with which Yemi and the woman moved. Then tried and failed to suppress the frisson of fear clenching his stomach. Whatever else they were, they were ex-military, black-ops types. With access to all sorts of hi-tech equipment.

They had *targets*. Killing him would have been easy and they hadn't. That he was still alive meant he wasn't on the list.

Wincing with pain, he scrambled over to Gutierrez. Placed two fingers of his good left hand against her neck. Waited.

Waited some more.

There.

A pulse. Strong. Easy to detect.

But more than a minute in coming. Ethan was no doctor, but he was in no doubt she'd been dosed with neurotoxin. Nicole

Gutierrez, Raymond Yeung, the whole SWAT team would be out well into the next day, maybe longer.

So why was he, middle-aged, slightly overweight, not-in-great-shape Ethan Krol up and about when the super-fit SWAT team was not?

He remembered the crunching of the fake mosquito against his neck. The way he'd been able to stagger towards the basement door before collapsing. Yemi's curious stare.

A grim smile spread across his face. He'd been able to crush it to bits before it could give him a full dose. Or maybe it was no longer capable of delivering one. Either way, he was awake.

Screw you, Yemi.

Picking his way through the unconscious officers, he made his way to the back of the garage, to the wall opposite the roller door. Sure enough, there was a door here, too. A normal, household one. He pushed it open and stepped into the backyard of 7307 South Borman.

The air was cooler here, but only because there was a slight breeze blowing. Glancing up, it was possible to make out a few stars bright enough to overcome the looming glare of street lights. In front of him, the house loomed dark and forbidding. There was no outward sign of life.

Which didn't mean Yemi wasn't in there. He must have been hiding the whole time they'd been searching the building, waiting for the right moment. Behind another magic wall, maybe. One they'd not even thought to look for.

Or maybe he'd just crept in unnoticed, black-ops style.

The throbbing in his head continued to build, stabbing at his temples, sending jagged lines of lightning white across his vision. Ethan collapsed to his knees, clutching his head in an agony that had nothing to do with Yemi and his neurotoxins. He waited it out, this overture of mortality, with his head bowed, his breathing somewhere between a gasp and a whimper.

The moment passed.

Using his right hand as little as possible, he rummaged through his pockets looking for his phone. His wallet, and badge and flashlight were still there, as was his service weapon. But the phone was gone.

Bastard.

With a great deal of difficulty, he drew his gun. Transferred it to his left hand. The grip was clumsy and didn't inspire much in the way of confidence, but it was better than nothing.

He crept towards the back of the house, reaching the steep steps that led down into the shadowed darkness of the stairwell.

He followed them down, step by ginger step. The faint outline of the back door to the basement loomed out at him. His right wrist lanced with pain as he turned the handle. The door opened, smooth and silent on its hinges. Ethan crept in, weapon raised.

There was no one there. The basement glowed a soft, eerie red that came and went with the pulsing of the equipment. Ethan reached out to the light switch by the door and flicked it. Nothing happened. Wherever the power for Yemi's gear was coming from, it wasn't from the outside. SWAT hadn't fucked up when they'd cut the electricity. Something else was going on here.

His eyes swept through the gloom, looking around. There was no sign of the struggle that had taken place here, no hint of disorder. Even the fire extinguisher he'd used had been put back in its place. Apart from the red lights flashing instead of glowing, everything seemed to be as he remembered it.

Almost everything. The ancient logbook with its flaking,

brown leather cover was nowhere to be seen. Ethan grunted at the oddity. Moved on.

Stopped.

The ceiling above his head was creaking with footsteps. Someone – more than one – was crossing the kitchen floor. Quite possibly heading for the basement.

Heart pounding in his throat, Ethan aimed his gun at where the inside stairs vanished into the basement ceiling. The moment Yemi appeared he would pull the trigger. There would be no time for hesitation.

Except there were at least two of them up there. If it was Yemi and the woman, the one he didn't shoot would overpower him. He was under no illusions about that. Even without a useless right wrist, his chances would have been well under fifty-fifty. With only his left hand to shoot with, he was well and truly fucked.

Say he killed one with his first shot, what then? He doubted he'd be left to live after that. And as for the guys in the garage, who was to say they wouldn't be offed, too? Yemi and his partner had killed a fucking *baby*, for chrissakes. They wouldn't be above slaughtering a bunch of unconscious officers to send a message: you kill one of us, we kill twenty of you.

Or was he just a frightened, middle-aged man making excuses for himself?

Yemi and Abidemi Eniola were about to come down those steps.

And he was fucking terrified.

Ethan found himself chewing his lower lip. Something he hadn't done since third grade.

The footsteps reached the basement door.

He glanced around, his eyes lighting upon a dark, rectangular shape in the corner of the room. Yemi's stack of drop cloths, their spatters of paint barely visible in the strobing gloom. He grabbed the top one, sat with his back to the wall and pulled it over himself, gun pointed forward.

The door to the basement opened. He could hear footsteps coming down the stairs.

And voices.

Female voices.

'How do we know he isn't down there?' Even though the words were spoken in a whisper, there was no mistaking the British accent. The Amazon's little sidekick, Hollie Rogers.

'I can read his machines, doll. And they're telling me he's already gone.' The footsteps on the stairs came to a halt. 'See the red lights? The way they're going on and off?'

'Yeah.'

'They're telling us we don't have a lot of time. Yemi ain't planning on coming back here, ever. This stuff of his is going to melt away, and soon. Might take the whole house with it, too. It's a gosh-darned shame. Some of this, heck, *all* of it, is k-balling genius.' Abidemi's voice seemed sadder than the statement seemed to warrant.

'And what about Detective Krol?'

Ethan's finger tightened on the trigger.

'We don't need him no more.' The footsteps started down the stairs again. 'I'd been hoping to get ahold of him and pump him for information. Turns out this here place is exactly where we needed to get to.'

'So torturing that policeman turned out just fine then.'

A sigh. 'I didn't "torture" him. He was stubborn is all.'

'You broke his ribs.'

'I broke *a* rib. Which I fixed, thanking you kindly.'

'With your med-kit?'

'Yep.'

'From Nigeria?'

'Just so, doll. Just so.'

Ethan couldn't tell whether she was taking the Brit's stinging sarcasm in stride, or if she was simply unaware of it.

Nigeria, though. The Okoros were Nigerian. So far as he could tell from what Inspector Danjuma had told him, Nigeria was also where the first of these insane murders had taken place. No way was that a coincidence.

The tenor of the footsteps changed. To the scratchy sound of shoes meeting concrete.

'The med-kit from "Nigeria" that you also used to knock him unconscious,' the Brit was saying. 'Again.'

'I was just putting him back the way I found him.' Another sigh. 'Look, we couldn't have him getting on that radio of his and telling the filth we were coming. And when he comes around, he won't even know his rib was busted in the first place. Good as new.'

'Just because—'

'Say, doll, can we give this a rest? I found the guy unconscious, I left him the same way. I broke a rib – by accident – and I fixed it. We got what we needed and now we ain't anywhere as far behind the grind as we used to be. You wanna get ahold of these kids or not?'

Silence. The footsteps headed towards Yemi's still pulsing equipment.

'Well?'

'Yes, I want to find them. And I know you had to do what you did. Time isn't on our side. I get that. But it was hard to watch, you know?'

Slowly, carefully, Ethan shifted beneath the drop cloth until one eye was able to peep around the edge. Abidemi, the Brit girl tiny beside her, was staring at the jewel-encrusted airport metal detector in the corner of the room. The Black woman's presence seemed to fill the space, making everything around her, himself included, small and insignificant. She showed no sign of the injury she'd sustained in Providence. There was no sling, and she seemed to be holding her right shoulder without pain.

She was unarmed. With her back to him. She couldn't dodge a bullet she wasn't expecting.

His left hand jerked tighter on the trigger of his gun as he lined up the shot. With Abidemi down, his one good arm would be more than enough to deal with Hollie Rogers.

Unless he missed, of course. The gun felt leaden and clumsy in his hand.

'What is that?' Hollie asked.

'It's a . . . gate.' Ethan was surprised by the note of awe in Abidemi's voice. 'How the heck could he? In this place?' A short bark of a laugh bounced off the ceiling. 'That man can make anything he wants.'

'It doesn't look like a gate. It looks like a metal detector. You know, like the ones at the airport.'

'I'm guessing it was once. Not now, mind you. This . . . *this* took a heck of a lot of work. He must have been here for years.' Abidemi paused, opening a number of containers on a nearby worktop and peering inside. 'We got the math wrong,' she added, talking to herself more than her companion. 'We got the math wrong real bad.'

'Maths? What maths?'

'Don't you pay that no mind, babe. Not right now.' Abidemi was unscrewing the top of a mason jar. She raised its broad mouth to her nose and sniffed. 'Gotcha.' Apparently satisfied, she reached in and pulled something out. In the pulsing red gloom it was impossible for Ethan to make out what it was. She pressed it into her companion's palm. 'Here, take this.'

'What? *Ew!* No way am I putting *that* in my mouth.'

'Forget what it looks like. It tastes like mom's apple pie. I swear.'

'This is some creepy fucking pie.'

'But it tastes *so* good. Trust me.'

In the darkness, Hollie put her hand to her mouth.

And screamed. Like a blur, the Black woman was at Hollie's side, overpowering her. Her hand clasped over Hollie's mouth, the firm grip preventing her from spitting out whatever she'd put in there. Hollie was spasming against Abidemi's body. Suffocating.

The woman was being murdered right in front of his eyes.

Detective Ethan Krol pulled the trigger on his service weapon.

Sixty-Four

The room exploded in white light and the roar of discharge. Blind and deaf from the blast of his weapon, Ethan lurched awkwardly to his feet, the drop cloth scratching against his skin as it fell away. Red blotches danced in front of his face, shifting and sliding. Ethan stabbed his gun at all of them in case one was Abidemi.

Nothing happened. No one erupted from the lava-lamp chaos to crush his one good wrist.

Or break his neck.

Something like normal vision started to return. And hearing. Though all he could hear — feel, really — was his heart pounding in his chest. He staggered forward, looking to the floor where the two dead women lay wrapped in each other's arms.

Except they weren't there.

He whirled around, gasping, expecting Abidemi to be bearing down on him.

Nothing. Just the basement, fading in and out in an oscillation of red light.

Shielding his damaged wrist, he got down on his knees where the women should have been and patted the floor with his left hand, expecting to feel what the darkness wouldn't allow him to see: the warm damp of blood.

Nothing. Just the dusty scrape of grit against his palm.

The various red lights on Yemi's gadgets were pulsing faster now, the light strong enough to cast the faintest of shadows. Moved by a vague memory, Ethan stood up and scanned the various shelves and workbenches, the neatly stored tools and pieces of equipment.

He'd seen one, he was certain of it. Almost certain.

There.

Up on a high shelf, stacked between two cans of paint thinner and a box of emergency rations, was a flashlight. Large and industrial yellow, with a suitcase-like handle and a lens the size of a headlamp. Ethan retrieved it and switched it on.

He squinted against the sudden glare, objects leaping into view, harsh-edged in the brightness, their shadows jerking with every twitch of the lamp. He directed the fake daylight in the direction of the floor. Let out a small sigh.

He hadn't missed. Not entirely anyway. There *was* blood on the floor. Just a few drops, easily missed in the dark. They led not to the stairs or the door to the backyard, the room's only exits, but to the weirdly decorated airport metal detector. The thing Abidemi had described as a gate.

An unpleasant sensation wriggled to life in his stomach.

The blood trail stopped at the metal detector.

This is bullshit. You are losing your fucking mind.

Ethan winced at the thought. It was too close to the truth. He rubbed at a sudden aching behind his left eye. His brain fucking with him.

Abidemi had access to a lot of tech. A lot. Maybe Area 51 stuff. And she'd called it a gate.

Gates went somewhere. And the blood didn't lie. She hadn't gone up the stairs or into the backyard. She'd come here. To a gate. And vanished.

His heart was pounding so hard, he could no longer hear anything else. He stared at the metal detector, tall and impassive, telling him nothing. Ethan took a last, deep breath, and stepped through.

And found himself facing the wall of the basement. Nothing, absolutely nothing had happened. Except that he felt like a complete idiot. He allowed himself the luxury of an embarrassed laugh, pressed his head against the cool brickwork of the basement wall and let the relief flood through him. What the fuck had he been thinking? *Gates?* Jesus.

He strode to the door that exited into the backyard and opened it. There was no blood on either side of the threshold, or on the steep steps up to the garden. An examination of the interior stairs to the kitchen yielded similar results.

The feeling of relief faded. The thing in his stomach uncoiled again. He thought about walking away, banging on a neighbour's door, calling for help. He got halfway up the steps to the kitchen before he stopped. He sat down on the stairs instead, trying to think his way through.

Certain things were true. The two women had been in the basement. He had fired his gun. He had hit someone. He was the only one left.

Certain things were probably true. There had been no time, between him firing his weapon and lurching out from behind the drop cloth, for the women to have reached either the back door or the interior stairs without him noticing, even allowing for the blinding and deafening effect of the gunshot. Also, despite his diagnosis, his brain still worked: he was not prone to hallucinations or flights of fancy. He was a detective lieutenant in the Chicago PD for fuck's sake.

Which meant that one thing *might* be true. Two women had vanished into thin air. Literally.

He sat, for several minutes it felt like, staring at the basement floor, seeing only the grain of the concrete in the blue-white glare of the flashlight, the faint imperfections of the surface. He could feel the coolness of the steps beneath him, the pressure of the treads against his pants and shoes.

Things that were fucking real.

But he couldn't stay that way forever. Slowly, reluctantly, his mind began to turn again, wrestling with the impossibility of his own logic. He descended the steps and began to pace up and down. All alone with only an insane collection of thoughts for company.

Strangely, it was the fact he was alone that finally moved him to action. If he *was* mad, there was no one around to see it. Which meant that once this particular excursion to Crazy Town ended, he could go back to being normal and no one would ever know.

He walked up to the airport metal detector.

The women had somehow managed to disappear. The blood trail led to the metal detector. And stopped. That had to mean *something*. Didn't it? The Black woman had murdered the white one and carried her somewhere.

But why, though? He'd shot her. Abidemi was injured. The blood on the floor said so. And she must be seriously injured or he'd be dead already. Why, having been shot, would she carry away the victim's body but leave a witness behind? Murderers don't hide bodies for fun – at least, not usually. They hide bodies to conceal what they've done. And you can't conceal something when the person who saw you do it is still alive. Abidemi was injured. Carrying Hollie would have been hard, even for her. There had to be a reason for that.

Which meant that Hollie Rogers was still alive. Had to be. That was the only way she would matter enough for Abidemi to carry off. She'd have been dumped on the basement floor otherwise.

So not a murder then.

But if not murder, what? Not a kidnapping, for sure. The two women had come down the basement stairs bickering but thick as thieves. If Hollie Rogers was to be believed, they'd known each other for little more than a week, yet he could see for himself that the two of them had become close.

His mind skipped back to the interrogations, the admiring tones Hollie Rogers had used to describe Abidemi's assault of some Scottish lowlife. Hollie Rogers would follow Abidemi Eniola pretty much anywhere. There'd be no need for Abidemi to kidnap her.

But for Hollie to follow, Abidemi, who could have swatted her like a fly, must want to lead. Why? What did Abidemi Eniola, with her almost superhuman strength and black-ops skills, see in her?

She's super, super *intelligent,* Hollie had told them. *But she's not always across how stuff works.*

So. There were things Abidemi *couldn't* do that Hollie Rogers could. The two of them were a team. One complementing the other.

Opposites attract.

The words popped into his mind unbidden, bringing back the nasty little row with Cara. Stupid. Stupid of him to feel so sorry for himself and his non-existent future that he let the conversation get out of hand.

And what if he was wrong? What if Cara and Devin weren't some 2.0 version of him and Dianne? What if they were more like Hollie and Abidemi, using their differences to get shit done – even if it was bad shit – rather than kill each other?

His right wrist throbbed, making him gasp in pain.

The world was changing, and not for the fucking better. Black-ops mercenaries. CEOs and billionaires grinding people to dust and making everything harder: more rushed, more complicated, more insecure. Maybe people who saw that world a little differently – one in colour, the other in infrared – would be better equipped to deal with the crap that was headed their way. Maybe . . .

His nose twitched, bringing him back to the here and now, and the acrid aroma of burning plastic. He swung the beam of his torch across the basement. Thin wisps of smoke, blue and dusty in the searchlight, were coiling up from some of Yemi's equipment, the flashing red lights pulsing faster, more urgently.

This stuff of his is going to melt away, and soon, Abidemi had said. *Might take the whole house with it, too.*

He didn't have a lot of time. One way or another, he had to get out of here.

If he wasn't mad – if – Abidemi and Hollie Rogers had stepped through some kind of magical 'gate' and disappeared. But when he'd tried to do the same nothing had happened.

What had they done different? He played back everything the two women had done since coming down the steps into the basement. Which was basically nothing but chatter. Except, of course, for that one thing.

With the smell of smoke noticeably stronger, Ethan went to the workbench where Abidemi had been riffling through containers. He picked up the mason jar that she'd left with the top off and peered inside.

And jerked back in alarm, almost dropping it.

It was full of centipedes. Ugly, dried out, very dead centipedes. A distinct smell reached his nose, easily detectable over the rising levels of smoke: an ungodly mix of vinegar and rotten eggs.

It took him three attempts to put his hand in the jar. Five before he was able to pick up one of the spiky, multi-legged husks between finger and thumb. It was squishier than he expected, which didn't help in the slightest.

It tasted like candy, Abidemi had said. Given Hollie's reaction, he was pretty fucking certain that was a lie. He was less certain about whether or not it would kill him.

But then again, he was a dead man walking anyway. He closed his eyes, opened his mouth and popped the centipede in.

Where it promptly came alive and started wriggling on his tongue.

He spat it out. And kept spitting long after it hit the floor, wriggling aimlessly before he stamped it into oblivion.

His eyes were starting to water from the smoke. Some of the red was no longer coming from the read-outs on Yemi's equipment. Some of it was the components inside glowing red hot.

He was out of time.

Trying not to think, he plunged his hand back in the mason jar, retrieved another centipede, stuck it in his mouth and swallowed.

Tried to swallow. The centipede was wriggling in the opposite direction, away from his throat. Towards the back of his nose. He tried not to gag.

Which became a lot easier to do when he felt the stabbing

pain behind his eyes. Everything turned red, as if his eyeballs were filling with blood. He would have screamed if he'd been able to open his mouth, but something was holding it shut. He couldn't breathe.

He couldn't fucking breathe.

The world got redder. Tilted sideways. He collapsed to the floor, smashing his knees on the unyielding concrete. He could feel heat now against his back, the pop and crackle of something bursting into flames.

And then, suddenly, he could open his mouth. He dragged in a desperate lungful of air, coughing and spluttering against the smoke that rushed in with it.

He clambered to his feet. The basement's two workbenches were fully alight now, flames licking at a ceiling already hidden behind a layer of black, roiling smoke. The way to the stairs was blocked by fire. It was either the door to the backyard or –

The metal detector was starting to burn. The outside of it anyway.

But the inside . . . the inside was glowing and rippling with a strange, golden light, as if a pool of water was reflecting the flames behind him. Except that this light was too soothing, too fluid to have anything to do with the blazing monster at his back. He lurched towards the calm, golden luminescence and staggered through.

Sixty-Five

'Jesus fuck,' Hollie was saying. 'Jesus fuck.' Followed by, 'You're hurt.'

'It's nothing,' Abi said, through gritted teeth. Had they not been clamped together they would have been chattering with the cold. 'We gotta get moving. We ain't got a lot of time.' She pressed a hand to the right side of her ribcage, where the bullet from nowhere had splintered bone on its way in and out of her body. The amulet wanted to put her under while it repaired the damage, but she wouldn't let it. She started to breathe easier, though, as the painkillers did their work.

Hugging her leather jacket close to her body, she started down the hill towards the city below, the steep grade and tussocky grasses threatening to turn an ankle as she headed for the comparative safety of an asphalted path. An older *oyinbo* man, well wrapped against the chilly air, was walking with a small, carnivorous quadruped yoked loosely to one arm. A weak sun shone ghostly white through ragged tendrils of cloud. The weight of her boots squeezed water out of the damp ground. A wonder.

If only there was more time to appreciate it.

'That's it?' Hollie asked, querulously. She was stepping lightly across the ground, unfazed – and unimpressed – by the terrain. She jabbed a finger at the slate grey city stretched out far below. 'You think I don't know where we are? This is *Edinburgh*, for fuck's sake! A minute ago we were in Chicago and you've been fucking shot, but all you've got to say is "we gotta get moving"? Come *on*!' The black grit of the asphalted path crunched underfoot as they reached it. She grabbed at Abi's forearm, bringing her to a stop. 'We've got to talk about this.'

Abi watched the *oyinbo* man and his strange companion drop away, disappearing behind a precipitous curve in the hillside. She should shake Hollie off and keep moving. The woman was slowing her down.

And yet.

'Okay, doll, what do you want to know?'

'What planet you're from, for starters.'

Abi found herself smiling at the directness of it.

'It's called Ibi Aabo.'

A small gasp, quickly stifled. Hollie opened her mouth two or three times before the words finally came out.

'Is that some kind of rubber suit you've got on? To make you look like one of us?'

Abi started to head downhill again, slower than before.

'I don't look anything like you, Hollie. You are a very small person. And you have no skin.'

Abi wasn't sure whether the sound that shot out of Hollie's mouth was amusement or anger.

'I mean, to make you look human.'

'I told you before, doll. I'm as human as you are.'

'Humans don't have little TV screens inside their eyes, Abs.'

'Sure they do. At least, they do where I come from. It's perfectly normal. I have a lot of small machines and tiny creatures inside me. They let me do some things. That's why you had to swallow the *ogorun*. It breaks down into machines that let you see the gate and let the gate see you. Otherwise, it wouldn't be able to grab ahold of you and bring you here.'

'That was fucking awful, by the way. I thought I was going to die.'

'I'm truly sorry about that, babe. I didn't have time to explain. We needed to get out of there in a hurry.'

'So we wouldn't get shot?'

'So we wouldn't get burned alive. And so we could get through the gate before it destroyed itself. Getting shot was my own damn fault.' Abi sucked at her teeth. 'I didn't think there was anyone there but us. It was that policeman. Detective Krol. He must have been hiding in the corner instead of being stacked up in the garage with his buddies. I didn't think to scan the room, and with you and I talking so much I maybe didn't listen as good, either. Stupid. *Stupid*. Your cops are cleverer than I thought, and very stubborn. I keep underestimating them.' Her hand flitted briefly to her damaged ribcage. 'Gotta stop doing that.'

'Where did you park your spaceship? Is it in Bristol?'

Abi's laughter pealed across the hillside.

'I don't have a spaceship, doll. That's not how I got there.'

'How then?'

'Same way we got here. By gate.'

'So: what? You just step through a gate and, *poof*, you're on another planet?'

Something knotted in Abi's chest. She took a breath before replying. 'Pretty much.'

'And why are you here?'

'To find Yemi. We have business to conduct.'

'Yemi's in Edinburgh?' Hollie's voice was suddenly high and strained.

'Looks like. Yemi went through it before we did and he can't alter the settings from the other side. *This* gate –' she pointed to the shimmering golden circle at the top of the hill – 'can be reset remotely. But Yemi's . . .' Her voice trembled and trailed off. She had to compose herself before continuing. 'Yemi's good, but he's not *that* good, and he had to k-ball his gate from whatever he could lay his hands on. If the gate sent us here it's because Yemi got here first.'

'And we have to find him?' Hollie's tone made it clear that she would like the answer to her question to be 'no'.

Abi patted her gently on the shoulder.

'Yeah, babe. We really do.'

Hollie swallowed. Nodded.

'And how do we do that? You got a magic tracker or something?'

'Nope. Well, not yet. Soon, maybe. But if he's brought us to Edinburgh, I'm pretty sure we know where he's headed.' She glanced down at her boots, at the miracle of water oozing out from under the soles.

She started moving again, Hollie crunching along the asphalt path beside her. They descended past the slate-grey rooftops to the streets of the city below.

Sixty-Six

Monday the 14th: 6.42 a.m. BST

'Fuck!'

Ethan found himself stumbling across a wet expanse of brown, striated rock, eyes squinting against blinding daylight. Damp cold slithered through his clothes, raising his skin into shocked goosebumps: a biting contrast to the inferno he'd somehow left behind.

Because, wherever he was, it was definitely not the South Side of Chicago.

Ahead of him the rock quickly gave way to mud and tufted grass, which then plunged dizzyingly downwards. He was standing on the flat top of a steep hillside. A high, windswept island rising above a sea of grey, slated rooftops. And beyond the rooftops, half hidden in haze, something that might be the real, actual sea. Behind him was a bizarre collection of random buildings: some domes; some pillared ruins, if ruins could be well maintained: a round, gazebo of blackened granite behind a low, wrought-iron fence. Between him and the buildings, though, was a circle of rippling, glowing gold. Without doubt the other side of the 'gate' he'd just stepped through. It was just floating there, untrammelled by any type of frame or mechanism. It looked alive.

Alien.

A voice in his ear startled him.

He whirled around to find a middle-aged lady standing beside him, stout walking stick in one hand. Even though she was looking in the direction of the gate, nothing in her expression indicated that she could see it.

'Excuse me?' he said. It took him several embarrassing seconds to tune into the accent.

'It's a gey fine morning now that the rain's stopped.'

'Er . . . sure is.' He was trying not to shiver.

'You're American.'

'Guilty.'

'Aye well, this is the best time to see the city. While it's still quiet, before aw the stooshie gets going. How lang are ye here fer?'

Ethan couldn't help but laugh.

'I really don't know, ma'am. I just arrived.' He tried to look like an enthusiastic tourist. 'I'm trying to say the name of the city like you guys do, but I'm not having much luck.'

The woman grinned at him.

'Well it's no Edin-burg, okay. It's Edin-bruh.' She rolled the 'r' like a Spanish speaker.

Ethan could feel his eyes blinking far too rapidly.

'Edin-boro . . . Scotland?'

'Better than burg, anyhow,' the woman chuckled. She made to move off. 'Enjoy your visit.'

'I will, thank you.' He watched her head off, her firmly planted walking stick allowing for strong, rapid steps. She walked through the gate like it wasn't there.

Ethan turned downhill, half-walking, half-falling towards the city below.

Edinburgh. Edinburgh, Scotland. A freezing hellscape three thousand miles from home and he'd gotten here in a single step. Jesus. Fucking. Christ.

He picked up a path that made the going easier. People were heading the other way, dog walkers, joggers. Some freak of nature on a mountain bike. All blissfully unaware of how the man they were passing had arrived.

Edinburgh.

Abidemi and Hollie had flown into Logan from Edinburgh. The Goth girl had admitted to being here. Abidemi had gone to see someone, she'd said. Had needed to give that someone something important. And now she was back.

He tried to retrieve his notebook from his inside jacket pocket but his right hand hurt too much and his left wouldn't reach. He had to take the damn thing off in order to get what he wanted.

If he'd been cold before, he was freezing now. He ignored it, flipping through the notebook's worn pages with dogged determination. His face broke into something more grimace than smile when he found what he was looking for.

He needed to pay a visit to 409 Bannockburn Court. The address of a woman called Kirsty Forbes.

Sixty-Seven

'This does not look good,' Hollie said.

The block of flats was every bit as dispiriting as Abi remembered: the dark lobby with writing daubed on the walls, the reeking lift, the narrow passageway lined with heavily locked doors.

Not that the door to 409 Bannockburn Court was locked. It had been forced open, the jamb disfigured by gashes of bright, honey-coloured wood where the deadbolts had been torn from their housings.

'It's not all bad,' Abi murmured, distracted by her need to interact with the *opolo keji*. The AI was not telling her what she wanted to know. She squatted down on the floor and picked something up. It glittered an iridescent brown in her hand.

Hollie looked at it and grimaced.

'Is that a cockroach . . . or something else?' she asked.

Abi smiled approvingly. The woman was learning.

'Something else. This is a . . . a *drone*, yes? To see inside and open doors. But it failed. Its programming got wiped and Yemi had to kick the door in, which would have been very noisy. He wouldn't have wanted to attract the attention of the filth.'

Hollie raised an eyebrow.

'I don't think they call the police round here.'

Abi, remembering how Brenna Clayton's neighbours had heard everything and done nothing, suspected Hollie was right. The whole planet was wall-to-wall people but you couldn't count on any of them for help.

She let loose a small sigh and stepped across the threshold into the hallway beyond.

There was blood on the closed door to the left. The one Abi remembered as leading to the bathroom. A still-wet smear around the handle. To the right, the open bedroom door revealed signs of a struggle. Sheets had been torn off the bed-less mattress, the floor littered with torn pictures of unclothed women that had recently been hanging on the walls. A wooden-handled knife, blade broken, lay uselessly in one corner.

Abi squatted down, examining the sheets more closely.

They were covered in mosquitoes. Dozens of them.

She stood up again. Scanned the dwelling more thoroughly. Of Kirsty Forbes there was no sign.

Which was not to say that the place was empty. Abi stepped across to the bathroom door and tapped gently.

'Are you coming out of there on your own or am I going to have to kick the door down?'

Silence. Abi was conscious of Hollie's wide-eyed stare burning against her cheek.

'I'm gonna count to three. One. Two. Thr—'

Metal scraped against metal on the other side of the door. It opened the merest crack. Just enough to reveal the large, washed-out blue eye she remembered from before.

'Leave me alone,' Jimmy MacRae croaked. 'I dinnae want more trouble.'

'Too late for that.' Abi pushed on the door without ceremony, forcing the little *oyinbo* to scramble away to the far wall, the small of his back jammed against a stained sink. Water dripped loudly from the faucet.

The man was a shadow of his former self. He'd always been small, even by *oyinbo* standards, but now he was shrivelled down to almost nothing. His nose was a smashed wreck, dried blood staining the front of a pale tee shirt and baggy, striped sleeping-trousers. The blood he'd smeared on the door handle was streaked across the patterned polymer of the shower curtain and the curved edges of the bath beneath. His chest rose and fell in short, panicky breaths, the same panic that forced his blue eyes into jerky little movements, fixed on every detail of Abi's face, seeking for the slightest sign that she was about to do him harm.

Further harm.

'I see you've met my friend, Yemi.' Abi's dry amusement raised a faint echo from the bathroom tiles. Her head ached with the effort of linking to the *opolo keji*. Still no luck. 'Where's Kirsty?'

'He . . . he took her. He burst intae the house and dragged her out. I tried to stop him,' MacRae made a stabbing motion with his right hand, 'but I didnae ken how strong he was. And *fast*. And then he . . . did this, and took her.'

'And then what?' Hollie spat. 'You ran away and hid in the bathroom?'

'Aye, hen. That's exactly what I did. And so would yous if yous had a brain mair use than a chocolate teapot.'

Abi took a step towards him. When he flinched, she stopped moving. She bent forward instead, hands on her knees, until she was at eye level with him. She hoped the smile she was forcing onto her face was appropriately kind.

'Okay, Jimmy. I want you to think real hard about what I'm going to ask you. Understand?'

The man nodded, suddenly eager to please.

'After Yemi came into the house, where was he when you first saw him?'

'In the bedroom.'

'And what did he look like?'

'Like six and a half feet of black fucking death.'

Hollie snorted with laughter. MacRae glared at her.

'I mean did he look angry or sad? Was he in pain?'

MacRae's washed-out eyes widened a little.

'Aye, he was. He was hawding his heid like it was bursting. That's when I grabbed my knife and had a go at him, but he was too fucking quick. The guy grabbed it off a me, smashed it against the wall and broke my fucking nose. Knocked me aff my feet.'

'And where was Kirsty when all this was happening?'

'Curled up in the corner screaming her heid aff.'

'And after he knocked you off your feet, what happened next?'

'He went tae grab . . . no. *No*. The room was hoaching wi' midgies. Big yins. Buzzing around like flying chainsaws. And then they . . .'

'Died?' Abi prompted.

'Aye. They stopped flying and fell tae the floor. Aw at once.'

'What did Yemi do then?'

'He was . . . staggering about like, still hawding his heid. Then he makes a grab for Kirsty and the moment he touches her he starts screaming like he's in fucking agony, but he doesnae let go. And I get up and jump the guy, 'cause he's like crippled or something, but he bats me away like I'm nothing and says if I'm still in the room when he turns around, I'm a deid man.'

'Is that when you ran and hid in the bathroom?'

'Aye.' MacRae's expression was a roiling mix of defiant and sheepish. 'I could hear Kirsty screaming for me tae help her, but then he must've belted her one 'cause it aw went quiet and I could hear him dragging her out the house.'

'So, if he'd already made tracks, why are you still hiding in the john?'

'I wasnae sure he'd really gone. And I didnae much fancy being deid.'

'How long have you been in here?'

'Fifteen, twenty minutes?'

'We just missed him,' Hollie said. She didn't bother trying to sound disappointed.

'He's got to be close,' Abi muttered. 'Got to be. I just . . . *aha*!' The *opolo keji*, hampered by the pitiful bandwidth available to it, had finally found what she was looking for. 'I know where he is,' she announced.

'How?' Hollie asked.

Abi ushered Hollie into the living room. It was smellier and tattier than she remembered. She closed the door. Jimmy MacRae's primitive *oyinbo* hearing might not be up to much but she wasn't prepared to take chances.

'You remember when we came here before, I said I had a gift for Kirsty Forbes?'

'You said it was an heirloom.'

'So maybe I lied a little bit.'

'No shit, Sherlock.' Hollie favoured her with a wry smile.

Abi, having no idea what a sherlock was, filed it away for later. She pointed across the living room to the kitchen.

'When you were in there making tea, I put something inside Kirsty Forbes. Something like the *ogorun* you needed to get through the gate. But bigger and more powerful.'

'And what does this big o . . . o . . . creepy crawly do?'

Abi frowned, trying to wrestle the *oyinbos*' lumpy, tongue-bruising language into something that would make sense.

'It makes a . . . a protective field. The machines inside her send out . . . poisonous messages that make it difficult for Yemi's machines to work. He had to kick in the door because the drone he tried to open it with broke down. His little flying machines, the ones that look like mosquitoes, which he uses to inject people with sleeping draughts, crashed to the ground before they could attack anyone. The machines inside Yemi's body, and he has many millions of them, don't work properly when he's close to her. That's why he was distracted and in so much pain.'

'Not enough to stop him taking her, though.'

Abi frowned.

'You're right about that. He should have been stopped dead in his tracks. But it's still slowing him down. And makes it so he doesn't notice things.'

'Like what?'

Abi allowed a slow smile to spread across her face.

'Like machines sliding through his skin. When he laid hands on her, machines on her skin jumped onto his. These machines are real small, see? His own machines are so busy dealing with the poisonous messages, they can't detect the intrusion and his amulet doesn't know to get rid of them. Once inside, they build more machines – not too many, otherwise he'd notice – and those machines . . . talk to the *opolo keji*, real quiet, like, so he can't hear them.'

'Your magic tracker!' Hollie exclaimed. She was almost hopping up and down with excitement. 'That's what you've been doing, isn't it? You've never been interested in the descendants of some dead sea captain, or that family in Chicago. That was

Yemi.' The sapphire-blue eyes narrowed shrewdly. 'It's *him* you've been looking for. If he found them after you got to them first, he'd be like totes tagged, yeah?'

Abi nodded, impressed.

'Not just tagged: incapacitated. The guy was meant to be down for the count. And then all I had to do was wait for the *opolo keji* to tell me where he was.' She shook her head ruefully. 'It was meant to be easy, babe. I'd stop by, pick up his unconscious ass, and take him home to face justice. As it is . . . well, we can still track him.'

Hollie looked suddenly worried.

'But Kirsty Forbes, those American kids. He's going to kill them, isn't he?'

'Not if we get to him first.' Data from the *opolo keji*, faint but distinct, was flowing through her augments. She headed to the closed living-room door. Opened it. 'Let's dangle, we gotta get going.'

'No one's going anywhere.'

The cop, Ethan Krol, was standing in the hallway, his pale *oyinbo* face blanched paler with pain, a projectile weapon held clumsily in the wrong hand.

But at that distance, he couldn't miss.

Sixty-Eight

Monday the 14th: 7.17 a.m. BST

'Over there,' Ethan said. 'With the other two, but not in front of them, understand? You block my view for even a second and I'm going to start shooting.' He could hear the quaver in his voice. Fatigue and way too much adrenaline. Blood was pounding through his ears.

The guy who'd been lurking in the bathroom, hunched over and broken nosed, shuffled across to stand beside the doorway to the living room. The tall, Black Amazon and her Brit sidekick stood unmoving in the threshold. A still life, framed by the chipped paint of the door frame.

'I'm no wi' them,' the man whined.

'I don't care.' Ethan didn't spare him a second glance. He had eyes only for the Amazon. She was watching him back, eyes almost as dark as her skin. Warily, he realized. There was no trace of the amusement he'd been treated to in the past.

She would kill him this time. If she got the chance.

'Get on your knees,' he ordered.

'No.' The word was flat and hard and hurled at him so quickly it seemed to arrive before he'd finished speaking.

'I'm not kidding around, ma'am. On your knees. Now.'

'I will not kneel. Not to you, nor any one of your kind.' The anger, deep and boiling, seemed to heat the air around her. Powerful muscles rippled along her jawline.

She was going to kill him. Right now.

He pulled the—

'Chill, Abs. Chill.' The Brit had laid a soft, fluttering hand on Abidemi's elbow. 'You're scaring him. And the man has a gun, like in the movies.'

Ethan had a sudden image of how he must look to the Goth girl, with his gun and his accent and his holster showing underneath his jacket. A man out of place. Not quite real. As if he'd actually stepped off the silver screen.

Or rather, through a rippling gold one.

His finger eased off the trigger.

The girl, sheltering behind Abidemi's powerful arm, shot him a quick, placating smile.

'He's already shot you once, Abs. You really want him to do it again?'

The fury seemed to leach out of the Amazon's body. But it still danced on the edges of her voice.

'I will not kneel.'

'Okay, that's cool, that's cool. No problem. No problem at all. Why don't we take a few steps back, like super, *super* slow, and sit on the settee? It's hard to start a fight if you're sat on a sofa.'

The words were directed at Abidemi, but the large blue eyes were looking at Ethan, pleading.

He gave her a curt nod. The two women backed into the living room, reversing themselves towards a well-worn grey couch.

'What about me?' the man asked. He was still pressed against the wall next to the doorway.

'You, too.' Ethan jerked his head in the direction of the living room. 'Take a seat.'

The three of them jammed onto the too-small sofa looked faintly ridiculous, like the cast of a 1980s sitcom with only one camera angle. He relaxed a little, still standing but leaning back against the wall opposite them for support. Immediate danger over, the throbbing pain from his right wrist was able to reach his brain. He fought to keep the grimace off his face. His gun remained pointed at Abidemi.

'Either of you have a cell phone?'

For a moment, the three of them looked at him blankly. But then the Goth's blue eyes flickered with understanding.

'You mean a mobile?'

'Yeah, whatever.'

'I have one.'

'Good. Take it out, put it on speakerphone and call the police.'

'We don't have time for the police,' Abidemi said. Even seated, she seemed to fill the room with a coiled energy. A cat, before the claws come out.

I'm a lieutenant in the Chicago PD, he told himself firmly. *I'm not a fucking mouse.*

'I *am* the police, lady. Just not here. You two are going inside where you belong.'

'You want those kidnapped kids to die?'

'You tell me where they are, and I'll make sure the judge cuts you a break at sentencing.'

Peals of genuine laughter bounced off the low, nicotine-stained ceiling.

'Sure,' Abidemi said. 'Why not?' Her laser-bright smile faded just a little, the dark eyes becoming slightly vacant. It was almost as if she was listening to someone whispering in her ear. Except, of course, that no one was. 'Assuming they're with him, they're heading into downtown Edinburgh. Given the speed of travel, I'd say they're in a vehicle of some sort. And if I had to guess, I'd say they were headed to some place called – ' her eyelids flickered with unnatural speed – 'Calton Hill.' Her gaze became focused again. Dark, dark eyes bored into his own. 'And once they get there, they're going to be somewhere else lickety-split. Like the other side of the planet. After which, well . . .' She let the words trail off with a shrug of the shoulders.

'You expect me to believe that you know where these kids are by just . . . *sitting* there? Come on! Enough of the hocus-pocus already. I know you and Yemi are in this together. Cut the bullshit and tell me where they're going.'

Abidemi had stopped smiling.

'Yemi and I are *not* in this together. I'm here to stop him, not help him, see? And thanks to a couple of things that went down before you got here, I now know exactly where he is at all times. At least, until he figures out what's happened. Yemi, in case you hadn't noticed, is no fool.'

'Why should I believe a—'

'I'm from another world.'

Ethan wasn't the only one in the room who gasped. The man with the busted nose did so, too. But the man with the busted nose was sitting down. Ethan's knees buckled from under him. He had to lean hard against the wall behind him to stay upright.

'No.' Even in his own ears his voice was hoarse and vaporous. 'You're a merc. Ex-special forces. Black ops—'

'For fuck's sake,' Hollie exploded. 'Are all yanks this stupid or is it just you? Did "black ops" fucking fly you here? In a plane? No, they did not. You stepped through some crazy-weird inter-dimensional portal thingamajig, same as we did. After eating some disgusting bug thing. No one on Planet Earth can do that. No one.'

Ethan was having trouble keeping the room in focus. It seemed to be spinning.

'Top secret tech,' he mumbled. 'Who knows what the government is hiding from us?' The words made him cringe inside. Like he was some fucked-up conspiracy theorist in a tinfoil hat.

'Yeah, right. *Whose* government? Yours? Mine? Nigeria's? And even if they had it, do you actually think they'd hand out stuff like that to a . . . a what? A *merc*? A private citizen? So he could go round murdering people? I don't know what you're smoking, sunshine, but I'd sure as hell like some of it. Sounds like a trip.'

'We didn't kill anyone,' Abidemi said, her voice surprisingly gentle. 'You know we didn't. We weren't even there, remember? We were here, in Britain.'

'Except it would only take you half a second to—'

'Step through a "crazy-weird inter-dimensional portal thing-amajig" built by aliens?'

Ethan's knees, even aided by the wall behind him, could no longer keep him upright. He collapsed to the floor, knees under his chin, fatigue and terror and bewilderment washing over him like a tsunami.

But he still managed to point his gun in the right direction.

'I'm a police officer. I don't . . . I can't . . .'

Careful not to get up and moving with exaggerated slowness, Abidemi leaned forward on the sofa, elbows on her knees, strong, shapely hands steepled under her chin.

'We don't have police where I come from, lieutenant, but I'm as close to one as you're going to get. As one . . . officer of the law to another, help me catch this guy instead of getting in my way.'

Some tiny spark of normality flickered in Ethan's brain. He chased it down, grabbed it close.

'And if we get him, he faces justice? *American* justice?'

Abidemi smiled like a mother with a wayward child.

'Your American justice can't hold him, Ethan. He'll screw with your networks and escape, the same way Hollie and I walked out of that police station in Rhode Island. Yemi has to come with me. But if we hurry, *really* hurry, you could still save those kids – and the gal who lives here – from a real bad end.'

'Let's pretend for one second that I believe all this, that I'm not lying on the floor of a South Side basement, overcome by smoke and hallucinating. That this really is Edinburgh, Scotland, and that you're a real fucking alien. Why hasn't your alien buddy Yemi whacked them already? Everyone else he's killed, he's killed in their home. Why not these three?'

Abidemi pondered a moment before answering.

'Yemi is a . . . showman. He likes to take his time. To make a point. When he came for the kids in Chicago, he'd have known the place was crawling with cops. He'd opt to take them from right under your nose to somewhere else. Somewhere he'd have room to work.'

'Like here?'

'Maybe.' She turned to the man with the busted nose. 'Jimmy, when Yemi arrived here did he have boxes, bags, any kind of gear?'

The man, Jimmy, shook his head.

'Not here, then. My guess is that he's known about Kirsty Forbes – the gal who lives here – for a long time. Years, maybe. He was saving her for last which, knowing Yemi, means something special. Now, instead of one *oyin* . . . victim, he's gonna have fun with three.' Her eyes became momentarily unfocused.

'He's reached Calton Hill. Another few of your minutes, he's gonna reach the gate and he'll be gone.'

'But you can follow him?'

'Sure. Until he figures out what I've done, we can track him. But once he goes through the gate, there ain't no guarantee it's going to stay on Calton Hill. If it moves, I don't have the equipment to find it. We'd have to get on an airplane.'

'How can a gate move?' Hollie asked.

For the first time since he'd met her, the Amazon looked nonplussed.

'Hmmm. It's like . . . Well . . . Shoot. I don't guess any of you guys are down with physics?'

Ethan, and Hollie, and Jimmy shook their heads.

'Okay . . . okay. Let me think. So . . . imagine you're holding a piece of rubber hose that's maybe as long as my arm. And you're holding it at one end, see? The other end is going to flop around a bit. Now if you're strong enough and you've got the need, you can hold your end of the hose just so, so that the end you ain't holding is exactly where you want it to be. But if you aren't strong enough, or you don't care, the other end'll drift, within limits, all over the place. The gate on Calton Hill is the loose end of the hose. In truth, the hose exists in many times and many places, some ends fixed, some not. But we don't need to worry about that right now. Once Yemi gets to where he's going, he could either set the loose end adrift, or he could direct it to someplace else. Whichever, it'll take a little time for anything he does at the fixed end of the hose to mess with the loose end. But he's either going to move the loose end to someplace else he's interested in or he's going to shut off the machines that keep the loose end on Calton Hill. And once it moves, we're gonna have to fly to get where we're going.' She directed a wry smile in Ethan's direction. 'I'm guessing you don't have your passport?'

Ethan smiled wryly in return.

'Lady, I don't *own* a passport.'

'Then we need to get going.' She paused, looking at him. 'Can I get up now?'

Ethan nodded. He started to get up himself but made the mistake of trying to put weight on his right hand. He fell back against the wall, a hiss of pain sliding through gritted teeth.

'I can help you with that, if you'll let me.' The Amazon took a step towards him.

Ethan's grip tightened on his gun.

'All due respect, I don't want you coming anywhere near me.'

Amusement returned to Abidemi's features, followed by something altogether more businesslike.

'Whatever Yemi has done to your arm, I can fix it. Maybe not in time for when we meet him but at least enough that it won't hurt if you need to shoot that gat of yours with the correct hand. Which you really need to do.' One hand landed briefly on her side. ''Cause your aim with the other one is lousy.'

Ethan smiled despite himself.

'Okay.' The smile dissipated. 'But any funny business and I'm pulling this trigger anyway.'

'Deal.'

Abidemi slipped off one of her two ivory bracelets and held it out to him. He tried to keep the shock off his face. In Providence, she'd claimed the bracelets were impossible to remove without surgery. And no one had been able to pull them off.

'Put it on.'

He took it, surprised by its heft. Then peered at it critically.

'It's too small.'

'Try anyway.'

Squeezing his fingers as tight as his badly swollen wrist would allow, he made a half-hearted stab at sliding the thing on.

The bracelet changed suddenly in his grip, as if alive. For a brief moment it felt warm and soft, sliding easily over his hand. But the moment passed too soon for his brain to fully process what was happening. It was an ivory bracelet again, fitted snugly against distended purpling flesh.

It should have hurt like fuck but he felt . . . nothing. Except maybe a quick wave of dizziness that passed almost as soon as it arrived. The Amazon, he noticed, was looking at him curiously. He stood up.

'I'm fine,' he said. 'Let's go.'

'What about me?' Jimmy asked. Unlike the others, he was still on the sofa, making no attempt to move. The blood around his nose looked like a giant ink stain.

'Stay right where you are,' Hollie suggested coldly, 'and watch the telly. It's not like you're much good for anything else.'

She closed the living room door behind her before he had a chance to reply.

Sixty-Nine

Their driver deposited them at the bottom of the hill – Calton Hill – that she and Hollie had descended earlier that morning. The journey back had taken significantly longer than she'd expected, the roads jammed with *oyinbo* automobiles, the intersections alive with dense swarms of obstructive people who'd all decided to get up at the same time and go someplace.

Yemi, of course, had stepped through the gate sometime before. It had taken the *opolo keji* quite a while to reacquire him and, even now, Abi wasn't quite sure where he was. Well, she knew where he was on the planet, and that alone was enough to drape every racing thought with a soft pall of foreboding, but not exactly where he was on the ground. The signal was strangely scattered, hard to pin down. She wondered briefly if Yemi had discovered the tracking nanobots and interfered with them but discounted the idea. If Yemi had found them, he'd have purged them from his system and there'd be no signal at all. Something else was at play.

She resisted the urge to run to the top of the hill, settling instead for a brisk walk. But even so, the *oyinbos* were struggling to keep up, the air crashing in and out of their lo-tech lungs in ragged gasps.

Thick, grey clouds were massing overhead, smothering the sun. Abi looked up hopefully. A single drop of water splashed against her face. Then another. And another. Behind her, the policeman uttered a soft string of swear words. She stopped for a moment, allowing the man and Hollie to catch up, allowing the rain to run across the contours of her face, into her mouth. Water fell across her tongue. Raw, untreated, laced with the faint aftertaste of pollutants.

Incredible.

'We should get a move on,' the policeman said. 'Before we get soaked.'

'You don't want to get soaked?'

'Fuck no. Do you?'

Abi chose not to answer, resumed her steady progress uphill.

The clouds seemed to have fallen from the sky, wreathing the top of the climb in a thick, damp fog. Thick enough that Abi adjusted her eyesight to look through it. She could only imagine how the *oyinbos* were coping, visually impaired as they must surely be. But then again, she thought, they must be used to it.

The gate, she was relieved to see, was still there, round and rippling and golden. Already, though, it was starting to drift. Compared with her filed memories, it had moved maybe a hand's width to the left. Over the next few hours the rate of drift would accelerate. By nightfall it might be on the other side of the world. Or off of it entirely.

She waited for the others to catch up. She could tell by their expressions, Hollie's rapt, Ethan's wary, that they could still see it. A confirmation that the gate would be able to pick them up and carry them along with her.

'Ready?' she asked.

'Ready,' Hollie said. The policeman just nodded, his thin *oyinbo* lips pressed into an even thinner line.

'Okay, then. Let's split.' She stepped through.

And found herself flailing in mid-air, hot and humid, her feet scrabbling for purchase on the non-existent ground.

She was falling.

A motion arrested by the sudden shock of water smashing against her body. She plunged beneath the surface, the salt of it filling her mouth and nose, closing over her in a roiling chaos of bubbles and distorted sound.

A panic-stricken thrashing of limbs brought her briefly to the surface, long enough to see she was in some kind of tank, the sides rising sheer and smooth above her, offering no purchase, no means of escape.

And then, despite her thrashing and screaming and calling out to whatever *orisha* presided over this hellish place, she sank below the surface.

Abidemi Eniola came from a world with little rain and almost no surface water.

She had never learned to swim.

Seventy

Monday the 14th: 3.04 a.m. EST

'Help! Somebody help!' The words were spluttered through stinging seawater that once again found its way into Ethan's mouth, robbing them of force.

One moment he'd been standing on a freezing Scottish hillside, fog clammy against his skin, the next falling through warm, soupy air into a giant water tank, Hollie Rogers bellyflopping beside him. Of the Amazon there was no sign.

He should never have trusted the bitch.

He'd dumped his jacket to lessen the weight threatening to suck him below and made his way to the side of the tank. A circular construct of shining stainless steel, its walls rose too high to offer any hope of escape. But if you placed your hands against them, there was just enough friction to hold your head above water with the odd kick from below.

Not for much longer, though. He was overweight and out of condition and weakening by the minute. He looked up for some sign of rescue and found none. Just the uncaring glare of fluorescents beneath a distant, corrugated iron roof.

'How are you doing?' he asked Hollie. He tried very hard not to gasp.

'Okay.' And in truth, the Goth girl sounded better than he did. Her black skirt had ballooned around her like a lace jelly-fish, giving her the illusion of buoyancy, and she seemed able to tread water without holding to the wall. Her movements – those he could see, at any rate – were slow and economical and well-practised.

And then she vanished below the surface, the waters rippling an oily, impenetrable black where her head had been.

'Hollie!' He was stuck to the side of the tank, impotent. Terrified.

Hollie reappeared, looking none the worse for wear. She rubbed the water out of her eyes, taking a handful of deep breaths as she did so.

'I can't find the bottom,' she announced. 'It's got to be four metres at least. And it's too dark to see.' She looked at him worriedly. 'I was hoping the bottom was close enough that you could maybe sink down then kick off it to the surface to breathe. But I'm afraid . . .' Her words trailed off, almost as if she was apologizing. She knew as well as he did that he was running out of time.

Sooner than expected, then. If not by much.

'Help! Somebody help! Please!'

His clothes were getting heavier, pulling at him relentlessly. Too much weight. Too much.

His head dipped beneath the surface, but he brought it up again coughing and spluttering.

'Help! Somebod—'

There was a face peering down at them from the top of the tank. Even though the features were thrown into shadow by the fluorescent lights above, there was no mistaking who it was.

Yemi.

He smiled broadly.

'You guys are very persistent, you know that?' The smile vanished. 'Hey, copper, you still got that bean shooter?'

It took Ethan a couple of seconds to figure out what he was being asked.

'No.' His sidearm had gone to the bottom with his jacket.

'Swell. I'm sending something down to you. If you want to get out of there alive, see, you'd better not thrash or panic or do anything stupid. You get me?'

'Yes.' Ethan's stomach, though, twitched with nausea. He'd already had to deal with a fucking artificial centipede and swarms of tranquilizing mosquitoes. What vile, skin-crawling creation was Yemi going to drop on them this time? His jaw tightened into a firm line. Given that the alternative was drowning, he'd better fucking suck it up.

Yemi's head disappeared from view, only to return moments later. Two short lengths of rope dropped through the air towards them. Rope. Ethan breathed a sigh of relief.

Something wrapped itself around his leg, long and sinuous and alive.

Startled, Ethan lost his tenuous grip on the tank. He had to kick hard to stay above the surface, his breathing coming in quick, panicky gasps.

Not a rope. A snake. He could feel the heat of it through the sodden material of his suit pants.

It's a machine, he told himself. *It's not real.*

His heart wasn't buying it. It thudded thunderously against his ribcage, the rush of blood pounding through his ears, blunting the sound of Hollie's squeals. He kept kicking. Kept his head above water.

The snake was wriggling up his leg now, along the inside of

his thigh and over the front of his groin. Air hissed in and out of Ethan's mouth. Kick. Stay alive. Kick.

The snake kept moving, the heat of it sliding onto his belly, finding the gap between shirt buttons and slithering through, pressing its bulk against the skin beneath. Despite the water, he could feel the dryness of it, the faint irregularity of scales, the ripples of muscular power pulsing through its body.

The mechanism slid around his back, stretched itself upwards along the length of his spine. Ethan could feel the top of it forcing itself through the back of his collar, pressing against the base of his skull. He could imagine a forked tongue whispering in and out of a fanged mouth, a gently lethal flickering at the nape of his neck. There was a prickling of goosebumps.

His whole spine burned, a white-hot iron bar of pain. He threw his head back and screamed: tenor harmony to Hollie's accompanying alto.

And then, as quickly as it had come, the searing heat was gone. Replaced by something akin to euphoria.

He was treading water, seemingly without conscious effort on his part. Like in a dream. No fatigue, no liquid flooding his mouth, just the smooth strokes of a brilliantly accomplished swimmer.

Somewhere beneath him he heard the heavy clunk of a valve, the sound of rushing water.

The tank was filling up, the water surface rising, taking Ethan and Hollie with it. An escort of bubbles eddied around them in a fizzing dance, random cross-currents plucking at their feet.

'Give me your hand,' Yemi said, as soon as he was within reach. Ethan did as he was told. The man – the alien – hauled him onto solid ground with no more apparent effort than if he were a rubber duck. Hollie joined him seconds later, her once flouncy, many-layered skirt plastered wetly against her legs. Ethan looked around, trying desperately to get his bearings.

The tank, if tank was the right term, was sunk into a floor of smooth concrete. So smooth, in fact, that the colourless slick of water spreading out from his drenched clothes made walking on it treacherous, even in socks. Ethan didn't risk it, his body rigidly still under the unsparing fluorescents. His gaze, though, was drawn inexorably across the shadowed abyss of the tank to what could only be the gate he and Hollie had stepped through. Comprehension forced a snort through salt-rimed nostrils.

This gate, significantly bigger than the one in Yemi's South Side basement, was round like a doughnut: a redly bejewelled wreath of writhing cables, scuffed junction boxes, and cooling coils. It was mounted on a sturdy wheeled platform that was presently right at the edge of the tank. Ethan had no doubt it had been nowhere near there when Yemi had stepped through it. He would have wheeled it to the water's edge afterwards, a precaution against the very thing that had happened: someone following him through, his pursuer condemned to death the moment their aching muscles gave way.

Except Yemi had intervened, dragging them to safety.

Comparative safety. The disconcertingly human-looking alien, tall like a basketball player, his stygian skin rippled with muscle, was looking at them curiously. Ethan tried to meet his eye. Couldn't manage it.

The air was hot and humid and smelled of the sea. And not just from the tank. Ethan was sure of it. The tang of it was too strong. The sea – a sea – was somewhere close by.

The tank rumbled and gurgled in protest as the water level dropped again.

'Say, you guys don't know when to stop, do ya?'

Ethan was struck by how accurately Professor MacPherson had captured the alien's strange accent. *A Nigerian imitating Al Capone. Or maybe John Wayne.*

The same way Abidemi spoke. The woman – seeming woman – who'd led them into this.

'What do you want with us?' Ethan asked, glad that his voice sounded stronger and more confident than he actually felt. 'Why'd you rescue us from your Bond-villain shark tank?'

Yemi laughed at that.

'You want to go back?'

'No,' Hollie said firmly.

'And it's not a shark tank, folks. It's a test bed.' He nodded in the direction of the doughnut-shaped mechanism. 'Unlike that one, I needed a gate that would work under water, so I could move the sea from, well, not so far from here to an apartment in Chicago or a living room in Rhode Island. It took me years to figure it out but I managed it. Neat, heh?'

'Outstanding. Give the man a Nobel Prize,' Ethan said. 'Now answer my other question. What do you want with us?'

'I don't want anything from you, except to be left alone to go about my business. But you keep getting in the way, see, and that's gonna stop. You hearing me, lawman?'

'No one's leaving you alone, Yemi. You're a murderer, you're never going to get away with this. Give yourself up. Don't make things worse than they already are.' The words echoed off the corrugated iron roof, metallic and hollow.

'I'm not a murderer, Detective Krol. I'm a dispenser of justice.'

'By killing children and babies?'

'By punishing those who deserve it.'

The matter-of-fact way he said it, the very idea that little Benedict Okoro 'deserved' what happened to him, drained the words from Ethan's tongue. Regardless of his outward appearance, there was nothing human in there, no point of commonality.

When the words finally returned, they took him in a different direction.

'Did Jennifer Okoro kill her family or did you?'

Yemi's eyes flickered with surprise.

'Why would she do such a thing?'

'Well *someone* helped you. She's the only one who could have.'

The surprise morphed into amusement.

'What makes you think that?'

'Jennifer told the doormen to let you in on Tuesday. She also says you attacked her Tuesday evening. But we know for a fact that you left the building hours earlier and didn't return till Wednesday morning, when *she* said you could come up. So, she either killed her family on Tuesday using equipment you left for her, or you helped her do it on the Wednesday.'

Yemi's laugh was rumbling and deep.

'Oh, you poor man,' he said. 'You poor, poor *oyinbo* man. I can see how it might look like that.' He was laughing again. 'I used a gate to go in and out as I pleased. I had to build it first, of course. A very particular design, mind you. Not just a gate but a tank to hold enough seawater for a good drowning. On the Tuesday did you say?'

Ethan nodded.

'On the Tuesday, I wheeled in the equipment, having persuaded the guards at the door that I had permission. I set everything up and left. Then, from the back of my truck, I stepped back in and waited. After *gbese* had been paid, I stepped through the gate and went home. Came back and collected my things the next day. Wheeled 'em right out, easy as pie.'

'But how'd you get in in the first place? We know Jennifer Okoro called to say you were coming.'

'Did she now?'

Ethan found his jaw dropping. The words had come out of Yemi's mouth but the voice . . . the voice was Jennifer Okoro's. Or as near as made no difference.

Yemi grinned at his discomfiture.

'Back home, there's people who ain't exactly human, see? Their voices work different. So we have machines that let us talk to them. Turns out they're pretty good at impersonating actual humans, too. You just need a sample for the files. Easy enough to pick up the phone and pretend to be someone else, you catch my drift?'

'And Rhode Island?'

'That was easier. No guards. I broke in, set up and left. Gated back in and made sure them what needed drowning got drowned. Removed the gear later that night. Same way: just wheeled it out.'

Ethan grunted. There'd been no witnesses to the removal, but it made sense.

'Dorothy Vielfrass was when I realized you were on my tail.' Yemi was on a roll now, more than happy to share. 'I took care of the cop at the end of the drive easy enough but I wasn't expecting his absence to be noticed quite so soon. Had to leave in a hurry, hack a cop car computer to stymie the chase.' He shook his head, his expression wry. 'Man, that was a mess. It didn't exactly go like eggs and coffee, know what I mean? There was no time to reverse the process, to gate the water out, never mind pack up my gear. I had to leave the lot. I set it to self-destruct before I skipped.'

Ethan remembered the torrent of seawater pouring down

the steps of the Vielfrass mansion. The Okoro and Hollander crime scenes had been dry, except for the bodies, because Yemi had had time to clean up after himself, thousands of gallons of seawater magicked away by the same alien process that had brought it in. Dorothy Vielfrass was different. Yemi had been interrupted mid-crime. Had they arrived at the mansion just a minute earlier, he and Gutierrez would have found Dorothy Vielfrass suspended in a cube of water. Exactly like her son.

'And Chuck Vielfrass?'

Yemi's expression darkened.

'That fink? Abidemi threw me a real curve. I'd no idea she was here, see? Had to make tracks, lickety-split, what with the shooting and all.'

Ethan could smell the stench of burning plastic like he was back in the condo. Yemi's equipment self-destructing, its work only half done.

'Where is Abs?' Hollie asked. 'What have you done with her?'

Yemi nodded at the receding waters of the tank. 'Down there somewhere. She can't swim, you know.' He smiled carelessly. 'With that backpack of hers, she sank like a stone before you two even got here.'

'You fucking bastard shit for—'

Hollie's voice twisted into a strangled scream. She'd hurled herself at Yemi but had suddenly stopped, standing instead with a strange, awkward formality. An embassy marine at attention rather than a Goth girl from England. Her eyes were at complete odds with the rest of her, though, darting from side to side and glazed with terror.

'The *ejo*, the mechanism on your spine? It's not going to let you move any way but the way I want you to.' Hollie was dancing now, joyous, graceful movements, utterly at odds with the expression on her face. The movement stopped as suddenly as it began, leaving her once again at attention. 'Me? I'd rather you moved – or stood right where you are – of your own free will. Saves me some brain power.' He tapped lightly at his temple, his voice hardening as he did so. 'But one way or another, your body belongs to me. You too, detective.'

Ethan felt perfectly normal. He couldn't even feel the thing pressed against his back. But he had no doubt the heigh-ho, or whatever Yemi had called it, was in complete control. It explained why swimming in the tank had suddenly gotten so easy. He didn't feel the need to test it out.

'Why'd you let her drown?' he asked evenly. 'Why not pull her out like you did for us?'

Yemi looked at him with something approaching pity.

'Abidemi ain't drowned.' Yemi leaned over the edge of the tank, peering into its depths. For reasons he couldn't quite put his finger on, Ethan was certain he could see all the way to the bottom. 'The machines in her body will keep her alive. For a while, anyhow. Thing is, she's unconscious now, see? Makes her easier to handle.' Yemi nodded, more to himself than Ethan. 'You two first. We'll deal with her later.'

'But why not just attach a heigh-ho like you did to us? Why put her through . . . Through that?'

Again, the pitying look.

'Because she ain't *oyin* . . . she ain't like you. She's like me. The machines in her body would have disabled the *ejo* before it hooked into a single nerve. It would have meant a fight.' Yemi rubbed a hand over his face and Ethan realized that behind the superiority, the physical prowess, the alien was exhausted. 'She'd have tried to ice me and I can't be doing with that. I'm almost done. *Gbese* will have been paid.'

'What's Basie?'

Yemi didn't answer. He was looking once again into the dark waters of the tank.

Ethan tried a different tack.

'What have you done with the Vielfrass kids? The Scotch lady?'

'They're here.' A wry smile tripped across the alien's face. 'I won't say they came willingly, but the *ejos* can be real persuasive. Walked 'em through the gates no trouble at all.'

'Why'd you bother? You killed everyone else at home. Why the change of plan?'

'Chicago was crawling with cops, not to mention Abidemi and her . . . friend.' Yemi spoke that last word with the air of a man who couldn't quite believe he was saying it. '*Gbese* needs to be done right, see? There has to be . . . propriety. Meaning. Wasn't no time to do it right with you guys on my tail. I'd no choice but to take 'em with me.'

'And the Scotch lady?'

Yemi's expression hardened.

'Kirsty Forbes is the last. The biggest, most corrupt fruit of the poisoned tree. She was always gonna be coming here. But now she'll have company.' The alien expelled a long sigh. 'And then it'll be over. *Gbese* will have been paid.'

'It can be over right now, Yemi. All you've gotta do is stop. Right here. Right now. Just walk away. I won't even try and arrest you – like that'd even work. You can have as long a head start as you like. Just . . . don't kill them, okay? They don't deserve this.'

Yemi's laugh had a bitter edge to it.

'Oh but they do, lawman. They really, truly do.' He held up a hand to quiet Ethan's protests. 'I've had enough of your empty talk. You've cost me time and equipment. Thanks to you and Abidemi, I'm all out of mosquito drones. You're wearing my last *ejos*, and I had to destroy a base in Chicago that took me years to get right. I am *not* going to let you burn out my ears with your gum-bumping. Let's go.'

He turned on his heel and started to walk towards a vinyl and steel door that had seen better days. It was clear he expected Ethan and Hollie to follow him. Hollie started to do so until a gesture from Ethan brought her to a halt.

Yemi looked back in surprise.

'You understand I can *make* you walk?'

'Then make us,' Ethan snapped. 'It's not our job to make things easy for serial killers.'

Yemi shrugged.

'As you wish.' He looked irritated, though, and Ethan took a certain amount of satisfaction from that.

Ethan found himself moving forward. In other circumstances it would have been a pleasant experience. The motion felt effortless, like in a dream, and far more fluid than his middle-aged, banged-up body could have managed on its own. It was almost as if he was floating across the room. Curious, he willed himself to stop. Nothing happened: his thoughts were completely disconnected from what his body was doing.

They followed Yemi into what looked like a small warehouse. It was mostly empty but for a forklift truck, an overhead crane, and a couple of wooden crates, stamped HANDLE WITH CARE, and emblazoned with a green and white striped flag. The door at the far side of the space was far more substantial than the one they had passed through. It was built from heavy, grey-painted metal, secured by a series of even heavier looking bolts. As the three of them approached, the bolts slid back of their own accord, and the door swung open, letting in a flood of humid, sea-salted air.

Ethan would have been quietly impressed if he had not been immersed in so much strangeness already. What he noticed instead was a fleeting connection between his brain and body that caused him to stumble a little. When the bolts had shifted, Yemi's grip on his nervous system had momentarily loosened.

The alien was tired, he decided. Or his brain could only handle so many things at a time. Or both.

Ethan tried harder to make himself stop.

'Ain't gonna work, lawman. Quit fighting it. You'll only tire yourself out.'

But the alien's voice had an edge to it.

Good.

They emerged into a tropical night: stars above, a steep hill to one side and, beyond the hill, a looming orange glow that hinted at the presence of a town or city. Ethan tried to look back at the building they'd been held in, the building where Abidemi was slowly drowning at the bottom of a tank. He wasn't allowed to. He could only take in what was in front of him: a rough concrete path, heavily dusted with sand, ragged tufts of grass growing on either side. The sand scrunched under his shoes as he walked.

The path ended abruptly in a set of steep steps that led down to the sea.

And a large, two-masted sailboat, dwarfing the wooden jetty against which it was moored. The vessel rocked gently from side to side, wind and sea squeezing metallic chimes from the rigging.

'What a lovely boat,' Hollie said. She looked slightly embarrassed at having said it out loud.

Yemi looked at her curiously.

'You like boats?'

'Yes,' Hollie admitted. 'I sail a bit.'

'You won't like this one.'

With a dark chuckle, the alien's mind propelled the two of them down the steps. The closer they got to the jetty however, the harder Yemi seemed to be working to keep them under control. Ethan's legs were still moving against his will, but the motion was jerkier now, and Ethan fancied he could feel at least some of the effort they were making. He redoubled his attempts to take back his body. It didn't work but Yemi let loose a grunt of pain as he and Hollie jumped aboard. The woman almost fell, a little squeak of fright forced from her mouth before Yemi regained her balance.

They boarded at the back of the boat, a recessed space dominated by a huge brass wheel and a pair of dormant computer screens. They marched forward into the dark maw of an open hatchway. A few steps down and they were below decks, a luxurious, port-holed cabin of leather and wood.

Yemi stopped, stooped under the low ceiling and gasping for air. A bead of sweat ran down his temple.

Ethan tried to run.

Yemi hissed something in a language he didn't understand.

'You can't hold us like this forever,' Ethan said. 'You're getting tired. And I'm never going to stop trying to break free.'

Yemi gave a short, strangled laugh.

'You think it's *you* doing this, lawman?' He pointed beneath his feet. 'It's *her*, the Scotswoman. Abidemi filled her with . . . machines. They're fighting me at every turn. And this close to her . . . Well, no matter.' A hatch opened in the floor, swinging up on smooth hydraulics. Ethan gagged on the hot stench of miasma and sewage that swirled around the cabin. 'Down you go.'

'No,' Hollie said, her face a mask of revulsion. 'Please, no. I don't like confined spaces. I don't—'

'I don't care.'

Hollie screamed as her body led Ethan's into the bowels of the vessel. The stink of it filled his nose, smothered his lungs. There was no light here. They descended only a little distance before his feet found a slick, sloping surface and he was forced to his hands and knees. A slimy liquid, reeking of seawater and waste, slithered through his fingers.

'Please,' Hollie whimpered. 'I can't do this. I can't breathe. I can't . . .'

The hatch slid silently closed behind him.

Hollie threw up, a wet splatter landing unseen on the floor. Seconds later, he was crawling through what she'd left behind, the mess of it sticking to his hands, soaking hot through the knees of his pants.

He was retching himself now. Once. Twice.

His last meal added itself to the floor in front of him. Yemi kept him crawling.

Somewhere, somewhere very close to him, he could hear crying that wasn't Hollie. A child. Low muffled sobs. The sort that you knew had been going on for hours and hours.

'It'll be all right,' he found himself saying. 'Don't worry.'

He had no time to beat himself up over the stupidity of what he'd just said. He was rolling himself onto a low table, no, *bench*. It was barely the width of his body. The hard wood of it pressed against his shoulder blades and the thing on his spine as he lay face up in the darkness, his breath hitting a ceiling that could be only inches above him.

His hands moved into his lap, as if in repose. All he needed was a sword, he thought incongruously, and he'd look like one of those statues you saw on the tombs of medieval knights.

As if in response, he heard the sudden clank of metal moving towards him.

'No,' Hollie cried. 'No, no, n—'

She stopped too suddenly. Yemi must have had enough, had shut her mouth.

Ethan gasped as cold metal clamped around his wrists and ankles. And then, suddenly, his body was his own again. He could move of his own free will.

Except, of course, he couldn't. His wrists and ankles were bound. He could move his arms and twist his upper body – a godsend of sorts, as lying on his back with a tube fused to his spine was next to impossible. He would even have been able to sit up if the ceiling hadn't been so low. But his ankles, in addition to being clasped to each other, were anchored to the floor somehow. He could feel the clanking tug of a chain when he tried to move his legs. He could bend his knees a little but that was about it.

Hollie was beside him, her head somewhere near his feet.

'I can't breathe,' she said, having been given back her voice. 'I can't breathe. I can't—'

'Hollie,' Ethan said, as gently as he could. 'Close your eyes. Pretend you're in bed. Your own bed. Where do you live again?'

'B . . . Bristol.'

'Connecticut?'

He was rewarded with a small laugh.

'No. England.'

'England, good. Merrie olde England. With pubs and warm beer and country manors. You're in Bristol. In bed. In your own bedroom. It's very comfortable. You're soft and easy, breathing in, and out, in and out, in . . .'

And slowly, ever so slowly, Hollie's breathing fell into the same rhythm as Ethan's voice. He heard her sigh in the darkness. The child's sobbing, he noticed, had also stopped.

Ethan looked around. The darkness, he realized, wasn't quite total. He could make out vague shapes, like people camping, crammed together in a night-time tent.

If only.

'What's going to happen to us?' Hollie asked.

'What d'ye think's gonnae happen?' a woman's voice answered, before Ethan could respond. The accent was thick and Scottish and difficult to understand.

Not difficult enough, though.

'We's aw as good as deid.'

Seventy-One

Monday the 14th: 6.02 a.m. EST

*B*oat. The word for *ọkọ oju omi* was boat. Abi remembered it now, as the amulet kicked her back into consciousness. Words almost never uttered in her own language, except in the recitation of The Story, but common here: she was sure of it. There was so much water.

It was almost all she could see as she opened her eyes. The ocean: grey and startling and scary in the half light, dawn a pinkish glow on the horizon ahead of them. It rippled in a slow, endless heave, incomprehensibly vast. The boat on which she found herself would rise on its shoulders as if intent on climbing into the steely sky, only to drop precipitously between moving hills of water. Sails from two masts billowed fat and taut above her head, pushing the vessel to one side so that the deck rose up from where she was sitting in a steep slant. A large, unmanned wheel turned this way and that, an invisible hand holding the vessel to its prescribed course. Water smashed against the prow, throwing up gouts of spray before racing along the side of the hull with a loud chuckle.

'It's almost like it's alive,' said Yemi.

Abi, who'd thought she was alone in the boat's deep cockpit, started at the sound of his voice and discovered she could barely move. She was lashed in place like cargo. Like . . .

'Let me go,' she snarled.

Yemi just laughed.

'Once it's over. Once *gbese* has been paid.'

'*Gbese* cannot be paid. Not here. Not like this. It's forbidden.' She tried to ignore the pounding in her head, her brain cells waking up from their machine-induced stasis.

'Why?' Yemi asked. 'Because the *masu amfana* say so?' Yemi moved into her field of vision, taking a bench seat on the high side of the boat. Long legs braced themselves with practised ease against the pull of gravity. The wheel squeaked a little as it adjusted course. '*Gbese* is *gbese*, and *gbese* must be paid.' He looked at Abi intently. 'Do you understand where we are? Where we're about to be?'

'I could make an educated guess.'

Yemi gave a tired chuckle.

'Where we began,' he said quietly. 'Where it ends.' His long, elegant hand rubbed at his face, thumb and fourth finger massaging his temples.

'You look awful,' Abi said.

'And whose fault is that?' Yemi snapped. 'Flooding the *oyinbo* woman with hackbots, turning my own augments against me. Did you think it would incapacitate me? Bring me down?'

'One had hopes.' Truth be told, Abi was amazed he was still standing. The hackbots had been her idea, personalized for the man's augments. Contact with Kirsty Forbes, the only one of Yemi's targets she'd managed to dose, should have reduced him to a coma, allowed her to bring him home, her *gbese*, the *gbese* his actions had heaped upon her, finally paid.

'I am sorry to disappoint you.'

Abi probed with her own augments, seeking answers. The *oyinbo*s, restrained somewhere below, Abi guessed, were too primitive, too purely biological to be aware that the entire vessel was an electronic battleground. With the tiny voltages involved, distance mattered. Somewhere below, Kirsty Forbes was close enough for the machines inside her to load Yemi's implants with instructions. Instructions that should have stilled his muscles, flooded his body with anaesthetics, slowed his oxygen supply to a trickle.

But the hackbot signals were being jammed by something Abi had never seen before. An interference pattern generated by Yemi's own augments. The interference itself would be excruciating, like screaming to drown out someone else's voice. It explained Yemi's near exhaustion. The headaches alone had to be agony. But it allowed him to function.

It shouldn't have been possible. Yemi's implants were all logged at the Registry, modified for his biochemistry, to be sure, but standard models, nonetheless. They weren't capable of generating a defence like this. Unless . . .

Abi came to the stunned realization that Yemi must have modified his own hardware. On Earth.

But Yemi was talented, everyone knew that. And the *masu amfana* had badly miscalculated. He'd emerged from the gate far earlier than they thought. Long enough to get everything just right, augments included.

'When did you get here?' she asked. 'How long have you been planning this?'

'Five years ago, almost six.' Yemi laughed at her stunned expression. 'I came through the Kaduna gate.'

'But the Kaduna gate is unstable. It's damaged beyond repair.'

'*Was* damaged beyond repair. I fixed it.'

'No. That's not possible. No one could—'

'I'm an engineer, Abi. There are very few things that can't be fixed once you know what's wrong with them.' He laughed again, despite the pain etched on his face. 'I bet the *masu amfana* didn't even consider it, did they? And once I knew how to fix it, this whole . . . project became possible. I knew it would take years to track them down, particularly the Okoros: no birth records, you see. I had to take DNA samples from a quarter of a million people before I found them.'

Abi could feel her jaw dropping.

'How—?'

'Drones. I designed them to look like mosquitoes. Sent them out across the West African coast collecting blood samples for analysis. Then, once I found what I was looking for, I repurposed them to deliver neurotoxins.' He looked wistful. 'They were works of art, Abi. Truly. But fragile. You and your *oyinbo* policeman destroyed the last of them.' A short, incredulous laugh. 'He used a fire extinguisher.'

Yemi looked away, eastward past the boat's spray-haloed bow. A pink sun was creeping over the horizon.

'Not long now,' he said. He heaved a long sigh. 'And then, finally, it will be over.'

Abi ignored him. The boat was a cacophony of signals, Kirsty Forbes's hackbots tirelessly beating at the walls of Yemi's impenetrable defences. Perhaps, if she were sufficiently quiet, and if Yemi had been sufficiently acquisitive . . .

Yes!

Reaching out with her own augments, she found her phone. Yemi would have removed it from her pockets when he'd dragged her unconscious body out of the water. But he'd brought it aboard with him, somewhere. Quietly, ever so quietly, she reached into its modified innards, caressing silicon and copper, flicking open valves and gates. Suddenly released microcurrents circulated with undetected purpose. Abi prayed to the *orishas* for all she was worth. For this to work, she would need more than her phone.

Abi stifled a gasp as visual telemetry appeared on the inside of her eyelid. Somewhere below decks, stuffed into the darkness of a closed locker, was her backpack.

And in the deeper darkness of the backpack's interior, the eight legs of something that wasn't actually a spider spasmed into an eerie approximation of life.

Seventy-Two

Ethan Krol's body refused to accept that he had nothing left to throw up. He retched again, bruising the delicate lining of his stomach with the force of his contractions.

Ethan had no idea what the name was for the damp, reeking darkness at the bottom of the boat. But he did know he couldn't take much more of it. The boat bucked, and yawed, and rolled without rhyme or reason. The angry roar of water smashing against the hull drowned every waking thought in noise, and there wasn't a muscle in his body that didn't scream out in agony. Between the manacles, the unforgiving rod along the length of his spine, and the narrow confines of the bench, he couldn't find a position that provided even a moment of respite. Exhausted as he was, the blessed relief of even a few minutes' sleep continued to elude him.

Huge, gulping sobs rose into the shadows. Rage. Frustration. Fear.

'It'll be okay, Ethan,' Hollie said gently. 'Please don't cry.'

For a brief moment, a tidal wave of shame washed away every other sensation. He hadn't even realized it was him. He choked it back, feeling an unaccustomed wetness trickling down his face.

'Abi'll figure it out,' Hollie assured him. 'You'll see.'

She's dead, lady. Drowned at the bottom of a tank.

'Abi always figures it out,' she said.

After the first wave of panic had passed, the Brit had endured the hellish confinement far better than he had. She'd even exchanged dark jokes with Kirsty Forbes and one of the Vielfrass children: the girl, Claire, he thought, but both kids were of an age where it was impossible to be sure without seeing them. 'Abi's from outer space. She's bound to have a trick or two up her sleeve. I'll bet she's following us right now in some kind of super-sub.'

Ethan smiled at that, despite himself. The woman was delusional. But if delusions of rescue were helping her keep it together, he wasn't going to be the one to burst her bubble.

'Well I wish she'd hurry up. These chains are killing me.' He was rewarded with a giggle.

As much to distract himself as to make conversation, he asked, 'How long did it take you to figure out she was an alien?'

'She isn't an alien. She's as human as you and me but with bits added on.'

'She told you that?'

'Uh-huh.'

'And you believe her?'

A small hesitation. 'Yes. Absolutely.'

'You know that doesn't make sense, right?'

'Why not? You've seen her. It's not like she's got tentacles or anything, is it?'

'Maybe she does and we just can't see them. Or maybe her people just happen to look like us on the outside. But the one thing she absolutely *cannot* be is human.'

'Why not?'

Ethan, remembering his fifth-grade daughter babbling in the back seat after science class, felt a nostalgic smile tugging at his lips.

'Who was the first man on the moon?' he asked.

'Neil Armstrong,' piped up a small voice before Hollie could answer. If Claire was the joker, this must be the boy, Sebastian.

'Correct. And who was the first man on Mars?'

'That's a trick question,' Sebastian protested.

'Okay, who was the first woman on Mars?'

'It's *still* a trick question.' The boy sounded outraged. 'Nobody's ever been to Mars. Not yet. *Everybody* knows that.'

'Right. No human has ever set foot on any place but the moon. So, if no one has ever gotten past the moon, how can a *human* claim to come from another world? It's not possible. This Abidemi, whatever she is, isn't human. She can't be.'

The rest of them digested the logic in silence.

'Yeah, well, I don't care,' Hollie said eventually. 'So long as she's—' She gave a sudden squeal.

'What is it?' Ethan asked.

'Something crawled over my face!'

'What thing?'

'I don't know! A buggy, creepy crawly thing!'

Ethan tried to ignore the goosebumps prickling his skin.

'At least it's not a rat,' he said.

'There are *rats* down here?'

'*No.* I'm just trying to look on the bright side, is all.'

'There'll be rats here somewhere,' Kirsty Forbes muttered darkly. 'This place is perfect for 'em.' Her voice trembled on the sudden edge of hysteria. 'They'll chew our skin off.'

Sebastian started to cry.

Ethan was about to tell Kirsty to shut the fuck up and stop

scaring the children when he felt it too. Something skittering on the bare leg above his ankle. And then, seconds later, on his wrist.

It's a goddamn spider.

Ethan didn't know how he knew that. He just knew. He found himself closing his eyes, tensing against the sensation of the nasty little monster crawling all over his face. Spider bites, someone had told him once, were an absolute bitch.

Click-click-click.

Ethan barely had time to register the sound before it was drowned out by the rattle and thump of falling chains. The manacles slid from his limbs.

'Hey, Hollie,' he whispered. It seemed important to be quiet now. 'Can you move?'

'Yeah. But don't. Don't move a muscle.'

'Why the hell not?'

'It's Abs. She's here. Somewhere. She has these . . . things. They look like spiders but they're not. She uses 'em to unlock doors and shit. But if you step on one by accident, I'm pretty sure you'll break it. You don't want to be killing them when they're here to help us. Give 'em a few minutes to do their thing and get clear.'

Ethan, remembering how Yemi had bemoaned the loss of his fake mosquitoes to a fire extinguisher, froze in place. Abidemi's 'spiders' were probably as delicate as the real thing.

The children squealed in delight as their chains fell off. Kirsty emitted a teary sigh of relief. A couple of minutes later there was a small, hydraulic hiss. Blinding sunlight forced its way through a crack in the ceiling.

Hollie shifted to lean on one elbow.

'Now what?' she asked.

'I reckon your friend wanted us free for a reason,' Ethan said. 'So I guess we'd better get up there and help her. You, me and her – mostly her – can probably overpower him.'

'What about us?' Claire asked.

'Stay out of sight.'

Contorting his body into a half-crawling, half-squatting kind of walk, Ethan positioned himself beneath the barely open hatch. He pushed tentatively against the underside, then harder, fighting the creaking resistance of hydraulics. It lifted a fraction, allowing him to peer through the gap.

The wood and leather cabin, what he could see of it, appeared to be empty. Bright, tropical sunlight gambolled through brass-ringed portholes, sea-tanged air eddied in his nostrils. Ethan almost wept at the freedom of it. He held himself still a moment longer. Straining ears could pick up no sign of occupancy, no booted foot attempted to stamp down on his head. He pushed the hatch fully open and levered himself into the cabin. Hollie and the others followed.

Casting about for a weapon, Ethan's eyes fell upon a small nook that served as a kitchenette. He cursed inwardly as the drawer he opened did so with a loud squeak.

But there were no cries of alarm, no thumping of feet on the deck above – though Ethan fancied he could hear a murmur of conversation. He pulled out a wicked looking kitchen knife and presented a smaller one to Hollie. She waved it away, her grimy, bedraggled face a picture of revulsion.

Ethan didn't press the point. He doubted the woman would be much use in a fight anyway. Gripping the knife by its comfortable handle, Ethan took a moment to marvel at how normal his right wrist felt. He crept slowly to the steps that led up top.

There were definitely voices. He could hear them clearly now, drifting down through the open hatchway. Yemi and Abidemi, Ethan decided. The musical, pitchy lilt of their native language did little to disguise the intensity of the exchange, the mutual ill temper.

He put a foot on the steps.

Another: his head rising to a point where he had line of sight to the rear of the boat.

He choked back a cry of disappointment.

Abidemi was there all right, trussed up like a chicken in the back corner and no fucking use to anybody. Yemi, who was speaking, was out of sight somewhere. Abidemi's face was tight and disapproving, the entirety of her gaze fixed on the man she was talking to.

But the next time she spoke it was in English, in that weird accent of hers, African laced with something not quite New York.

'I pray to the *orisha*s that in five minutes your prisoners rise out of the hatch at the front of the boat and assault you to within an inch of your life, you no-good crumb. It's no less than you deserve. How can you still not see that what you're doing is all wet?'

'You speak their language even worse than I do. No one talks like that anymore.'

'That's not the . . .'

The rest of it was drowned out by the roar of the sea as Ethan, taking Abidemi's hint, retreated back down the steps and moved forward through the cabin. The cabin, which bellied wide in the middle, following the shape of the hull, narrowed again towards the front, where it ended in a wall of dark, richly grained wood. Set within it was an equally opulent brass-handled door.

The door opened onto a triangular-shaped cabin, narrowing to the boat's prow, dominated by a three-sided bed that fitted snug against the walls. Directly above the bed was a skylight, the hatch Abidemi must have been talking about.

Ethan glanced at his watch, then at Hollie.

'In a couple of minutes we're going to go up through that,' he said, pointing at the skylight. 'We'll get as close to Yemi as we can, and then bum-rush him.'

'Translation, please.'

'Of what?'

'Bum-rush. That's American as fuck.'

Ethan felt a smile twitching at his lips. 'Charge. As in "run at", not "plug in".'

Hollie looked alarmed.

'You can't be serious. He'll kill us. We'll not get within a metre of the guy.'

'Abidemi thinks we can.' He explained what he'd heard on deck. As Hollie absorbed what he was saying, her expression changed to one of frightened resolution. She managed a nod, the clench of her jaw making the movement abrupt and small.

'She must have a plan, yeah?'

'Must do,' Ethan agreed, though he had his doubts. Abidemi was tied down. By a fellow alien, no less. It was unlikely she had any weird tricks that Yemi didn't already know about. Maybe this was one last desperate gamble. Throw the humans at Yemi. And if it didn't work out, too bad for them. He shoved the thought away, jammed the knife through the belt of his pants like a makeshift sword. 'Right then, let's do this.'

Followed by the anxious stares of Kirsty Forbes and the children, Ethan and Hollie opened the skylight and clambered onto the curved roof of the cabins. Ethan was relieved to see that their egress was obscured by the alloy bulk of the boat's masts, their sails billowing fat in the stiff, tropical breeze.

The relief was short lived. The boat was tilted at an extreme angle, rising and falling on a rollercoaster of waves and jerking alarmingly when the prow bit into the water. The roof of the cabins was not only curved but plasticky smooth: it would be all too easy to lose his grip and slide 'downhill', flying off the edge of the roof so fast he'd hurtle straight into the sea. The strip of deck at the side of the boat was too narrow, the spray-soaked guard rail too low to have any say in the matter.

'This way,' he muttered, scrambling up to the high side of the boat. Quietly as he could, he slid off the roof and onto the narrow strip of deck, crouching low in an attempt to keep out of sight. Hollie dropped down behind him. She seemed perfectly at ease with the boat's pitching and rolling.

'Ready?' he asked. If he looked even half as bad as Hollie, he thought, maybe Yemi would be too startled by their appearance to put up a fight. The Goth's dark clothing was badly torn and covered in slime. Her dyed-black hair was matted and stiff with filth, the face beneath so dirty that her eyes and teeth gleamed out of it like beacons. She managed a weak grin.

'Ready.'

Ethan pulled out his knife and moved towards the back of the boat, step by slow, careful step. The warm sea air was fresh in his nostrils, his skin spattered by the occasional drop of spray. He crept past one mast. Then the other. The back of Yemi's head and shoulders came into view, the rest of him hidden by the deep recess in which he was sitting. Next to him, the boat's large and unmanned wheel, shifted eerily as he watched, guided by an invisible helmsman.

One more step. Another. He could see Abidemi, still tied on

the low side of the boat, still speaking urgently in her exotic, sing-song language.

One more step. Another. Ethan's hand tightened its grip on the knife.

Seventy-Three

Monday the 14th: 8.19 a.m. EST

*A*bi had, for the most part, stopped arguing with Yemi. She just wanted to keep him talking. How and when he'd decided to do this thing, the preparations he'd made, the means by which he'd fooled the *masu amfana*.

The more he talked, the more she could figure a way out of this.

In theory, at least, she could seize control of the boat: the steering, the sails. The *oyinbo*s had built it to be sailed single-handed, she realized. Its computers and machinery were all native tech. All Yemi had done was improve the programming, linking it to his own augments. If she could cut the link, corrupt the programming, many things would become possible in the ensuing chaos.

In theory.

She'd have to break his security. She could do it, she figured, with the *opolo keji*'s help. But it would take time. And time was not on her side.

She really needed to get free.

Behind her, unseen, two *alantakun* were gnawing on the ropes. Not a task they were designed for. It was slow going.

Too slow, she feared. How long was five minutes? She had no feel for *oyinbo* units of time. Five minutes had popped out of her mouth unthinkingly, as she'd scrambled to stop the policeman coming up through the hatch and getting himself brained. She needed to be free of the damn ropes first.

'They were too trusting,' Yemi was saying. He nodded sagely, as if agreeing with himself. 'It is their great failing.'

Behind him, the *oyinbo* policeman had reappeared, Hollie at his shoulder, a hunched collage of flesh and ragged clothing glued together by filth.

Too soon.

Even at a distance, she could smell the stink of them. A wicked-looking knife glinted in the sunlight. She opened her mouth to say something, to send them back below.

Yemi's nostrils flared.

'Can you sm—'

He whirled around, just as Ethan and Hollie ran at him, yelling. Startled and off balance, Yemi fell back into the well of the boat, the policeman's slashing blade a finger's width from his throat. Ethan was on top of him before Yemi could get up, knife raised above his head.

The knife plunged down.

Abi screamed.

But Ethan's grip on the weapon suddenly loosened. The blade turned uselessly against Yemi's clothing and fell clattering onto the sea-damp deck. The policeman's eyes widened in alarm as he stood up, stepped across to Abi and sat tamely beside her, hands in his lap. Hollie joined them, the fear on her face a stark contrast to the ease with which she was sitting.

Ejo, Abi realized. Through the crackle and scream of interference, Abi could just about feel the signals coming from Yemi's augments. Designed for treating spinal injuries while nerves were grafted and regrown, it would be easy enough for Yemi to turn them into instruments of control. No wonder he'd been able to travel so easily with his prisoners. She should have thought of it before, the possibility at least.

Now it was too late.

Yemi was looking at her, as if expecting an answer to something.

'What?' she said, her tongue slamming angrily into the *oyinbo* consonants.

'I asked: how'd you set them free, these no-good buddies of yours?' Now he had an audience, Yemi seemed happy enough to speak in words they could understand.

'No idea. They must have done it on their own.'

'Impossible.' Yemi's eyes narrowed. 'Where are your drones?'

At her back, the *alantakun* squeezed under the collar of her jacket and froze in place. She could feel Yemi's augments searching for them, for the tiny signals that linked them to her own.

But the *alantakun* were dormant now, there was no signal to be found. And even if there were, Yemi, blinded by the cloud of interference his own augments were putting out, would have trouble finding it.

He sucked at his teeth in frustration.

'Where are your drones, Abi?'

'I got no idea what you're talking about.'

With a yelp of alarm Hollie jumped abruptly to her feet. She climbed out of the cockpit to the high side of the boat, stood briefly on the deck, and then swung a foot over the rail.

'Abs! Help me!'

The other foot followed. Matted hair flew in the stiff breeze. 'Abs! Please!'

Hollie had her back to them facing the endless rolling blue. Small hands gripped at the rail behind her, splashes of water wetting her legs.

'Even a fool would know to bring drones,' Yemi said. 'And a fool you are not.' Hollie screamed as she took a step over the water before Yemi brought her back. 'Last chance, Abi.'

'What do I care for an *oyinbo*?' she said coolly. 'No skin off my nose.'

Yemi just laughed.

'You cared enough to jump down a flight of steps when you thought she'd been stabbed.'

'I was trying to stop a murder. This time I can do nothing. You have me restrained and I cannot tell you what you want to hear. The drones I had have been lost.'

Hollie jerked forward, so far and so fast that Abi couldn't help herself. She flinched.

'Aha! I knew it. She doesn't need to die. It's not *gbese*. And if she does, it's on your head, not mine. Try and explain *that* to the *masu amfana*. To the elders. What will be the *gbese* then – and who will pay it, I wonder? It won't be you, will it? That would be too easy. Too light a load for those broad shoulders.'

Abi ground her teeth in frustration.

'There's one below deck.'

'Bring it here.'

Abi sent the signal.

'And the others?'

'Destroyed when I fell in the water. Still at the bottom of the tank for all I know.'

Yemi grunted sceptically and stepped across, his eyes working on a number of wavelengths, scanning the ropes, her skin, her clothing for any sign of drones.

Abi held her breath.

Yemi tugged at the ropes. Hard. He leaned over her shoulder, inspecting the far side. Abi breathed in the smell of him and closed her eyes. Baking, and wood, and wisps of smoke. And in her mind's eye the sun, the *real* sun, was hot on her back, and she was atop his shoulders, giggling and gripping too hard as he weaved through the sosumes, long legs racing across golden soil.

A tear seeped out beneath a closed eyelid. Ran down her cheek.

Yemi stepped back.

'The rope is frayed,' he said.

'Can I help it if you use *oyinbo* rope? It will not hold me forever.'

'It will hold you long enough. I have plenty more.' He turned and dropped down the companion way hatch to the deck below.

There were screams of fear. Kirsty. The children.

'Get on deck!' Yemi roared.

'Don't!' Abi yelled. 'Make him make you.'

Yemi swore in two languages. Ethan chuckled. But Hollie shrieked as Yemi's grip on her weakened momentarily and she almost fell overboard. Her grip on the rail became white-knuckle tight.

Soon enough, though, Kirsty and the children trooped up on deck, followed by Yemi with a coil of rope. His skin, Abi noticed, was almost grey with fatigue. Beads of sweat pimpled his forehead. He sat the children down on the high side of the boat. Kirsty, he pushed farther away, made her sit where the rearmost mast came through the cabin roof.

Defences or not, Kirsty Forbes's hackbots were really hurting him. But for the need to keep eyes on her, Abi was sure Yemi would have sent the Scotswoman as far away as possible.

Abi glanced astern. There was still a faint hint of land, a last mountaintop to fall below the horizon. But once it did . . .

She grunted with pain as Yemi secured her wrists with new rope. Blinded and deafened and exhausted by hackbots, Yemi had failed to find the *Alantakun* nestled under her jacket collar. But it almost didn't matter. They would have to start again. And they were not built for such primitive work.

Yemi sat down beside the children. They would have flinched away if they could but Yemi was holding them tight in place, wincing with the effort.

'Don't stop fighting,' she told them. 'Make him hold you.'

Yemi half-laughed, half-growled at her.

'It's not going to work, see? Not in a million years. I'm too strong.'

'Not from where I'm sitting.'

'Says the tied-up gal. I'll be strong enough for long enough. And then . . . then it won't matter.'

On the edge of the boat, Hollie turned to face inward. One leg swung back over the rail. Hollie sighed with relief.

'Fight him,' Abi said.

'Are you fucking joking? We're in the middle of the ocean! Do you think I *want* to be one step away from drowning?'

'Fight him anyway.'

Hollie shot her a murderous look. But from the tightened line of Yemi's mouth, Abi figured she was complying. Not that it stopped him from putting her back beside the policeman.

The *alantakun* dropped down from her collar. Started gnawing on rope again.

Seventy-Four

Monday the 14th: 9.16 a.m. EST

Ethan stared at the hands in his lap willing the fingers to move.

Nothing.

Well, not . . . nothing. Something. A feeling of pins and needles. Maybe. Was the alien weakening at long last, or was he just fooling himself?

Yemi certainly didn't look well. His face had an ashen cast to it, the full lips of his mouth drawn into a too-tight line. He had stopped talking, even in his own language, lost in his own strange thoughts and staring astern as the last hints of land slid below the horizon.

'Don't do this,' Abidemi blurted out. 'I'm begging you. Show some mercy.'

Yemi seemed to find the idea amusing. There was a faint smile on his face as he stepped across to the boat's wheel and laid a hand on it for the first time.

Ethan gasped in surprise as the boat turned into the wind, sails flapping angrily in protest, the hull suddenly ungainly, a stomach-churning yaw and roll and yaw and roll as the sea had its way with it. Ethan desperately wanted to grip his seat for balance but, somehow, Yemi held him steady.

Hidden motors whined, ropes hissed through pulleys, metal rigging clinked and clattered. The sails swung into new positions, seemingly at odds with each other. And then, miraculously, everything was still. The boat levelled out, the spray over the bow died away, and they were motionless, or nearly so. They were no longer moving forward, just rising and falling atop long, lazy rollers.

The wheel twitched beneath Yemi's long hands, keeping the boat balanced. He was no longer steering, Ethan decided. The autopilot was back on. The movements were too abrupt, too unnatural, even allowing for the alien nature of the captain.

He was, however, leaning against the helm. For support.

The asshole's getting tired.

With a visible effort, Yemi made his way to the very back of the boat where he could see everyone at once. He leaned gratefully against the high fibreglass of the stern, blue sky merging with the blue sea behind him.

'We're here,' he announced.

Ethan's heart started to hammer in his chest.

'This,' Yemi continued, 'is where it all began. Where it ends. Where *gbese* is paid.'

'What the fuck are you talking about? We're in the goddamn middle of nowhere.' Ethan spat out the words, more to keep himself distracted than anything else. To avoid the creeping unease unfolding in his stomach. He had a horrible feeling he knew how this was going to end.

'Where I come from we have a story, see? Not just any story. *The* Story. How we came to be.'

'A creation myth?' Hollie was wearing the expression of someone who hadn't meant to speak aloud.

'Not a myth, girl. The Story's all too real. You can begin it any number of ways but I'd like to start it like this.' Yemi turned his tired face to the sky, squinting a little against the glare.

'Up there – *out* there – are a race who call themselves, or like us to call them, anyway, the *masu amfana*.' He smiled wryly. 'They thought the name made sense in our language but they kinda messed up. Anyhow, the name stuck. The *masu amfana*, now, they come from a planet not so far away as these things go. But it's still unimaginably far for the people they'd come to study, the people of Earth. Life ain't that common in this here corner of the galaxy, and maybe not in any corner, and intelligent life is rarer still. So when the *masu amfana* discovered Earth, they got kinda excited, see? Despite the distance, despite the heavy price the volunteers would have to pay, they sent a manned expedition with all kinds of fancy gear. The only one of its kind ever mounted. They brought along tiny drones, robots that looked like humans, orbiting satellites. You name it, they had it. Anything and everything to get up close and personal like, without being caught. Because the last thing they wanted, the very last thing, was to interfere with the natural development of the planet and its people.'

Yemi was leaning against the back of the boat, breathing in the sea air. He looked more relaxed now, Ethan thought. Maybe because, like him, everyone was so busy listening they'd given up trying to break free.

'But that not interfering? Easier said than done sometimes, ain't it? 'Specially if you happen to have a heart. Or four.' Yemi grinned briefly at that. 'Some of the *masu amfana* had been studying trade. And they were following this ship, the *Esperance*—'

'The *Esperance*?' Ethan blurted out. 'But . . . but that's a . . . Wait. When *was* this?'

'Did I not say? This is 1790, 1791 as you guys measure things. Twenty-five, almost twenty-six years into the expedition. I guess the *masu amfana* had seen quite a lot by then and maybe they'd just got worn out by all that watching and watching and doing nothing. Because people here are assholes and studying assholes is exhausting.

'Anyhow, there's two things you need to know about the *Esperance*. First is, her crew were kinda dumb. And second, she was a slave ship.'

Of course she was, Ethan thought. *Of course*. Pieces that made no sense began clicking into place.

Hollie was looking at Abidemi in wide-eyed horror. Abidemi's expression, in contrast, was rigid. Stonelike. Her dark, bottomless eyes were fixed on the hazy line where sky met sea.

'So – in 1791 this would be – the *Esperance* is anchored off the West African coast, quite a ways further east than the *masu amfana* were expecting, given the nature of the trade. The *masu amfana* had been following her on and off for quite a whiles by then. They'd picked her up in Jamaica, in 1790, where she loaded up with sugar and sailed for Newport, Rhode Island. She'd then sailed for Bristol, England with a cargo of rum and then, in February 1791, had set sail for Africa loaded with manufactured goods: linen, mostly, which the ship's captain, Theodore Bradock, then traded for slaves. And now he's loading his cargo of humans from the local barracoons.'

Something in Ethan's expression must have caught his eye.

'Do you know what a barracoon is?'

Ethan shook his head.

'It's a hut or compound where slaves are kept before transport.

They'd been captured inland by their so-called neighbours and sold on to traders at the barracoons who, in turn, sold them on to the master of the *Esperance*. As I'm sure you can imagine, the trip to the barracoons was not an easy one. Several of the women were raped by their captors, one of whom, Monifa, became pregnant, though she didn't know it at the time.

'Monifa is one of three hundred souls loaded aboard the *Esperance*. She's chained below deck and won't see the sun again for fifty days. And when she does, she's begging, *begging* to be taken below again.

'Remember I told you the crew of the *Esperance* were dumb?'

As it was clear Yemi wouldn't go on before he got a reaction, his captive audience answered with various flavours of 'yes'.

'So,' he continued, satisfied. 'This dumb crew sail for Jamaica, intending to sell their cargo to the sugar plantations. But they get lost, see? They overshoot to the west, then sail back east and miss it again. To about where we are right now.' He pointed to the direction they'd sailed from. 'Even though Jamaica is *right there* just below the horizon, they have no idea where they are. And they're running out of water.

'If they'd been carrying sugar, or rum, or linen, they'd have been just dandy. But they were carrying people. And people . . . Yeah, well. People drink water.

'So, late in the afternoon of Friday, July seventh, 1791, Captain Bradock heaves to, just like we did. And he brings his cargo, his human cargo up on deck, lowers the ship's railing and, one by one, shoves them overboard.'

Hollie was white as the sails above her head. Silent tears leaked from the children's eyes. Kirsty Forbes looked sick. Yemi and Abidemi, though, appeared uncannily alike. Jaws tight, nostrils slightly flared, eyes completely devoid of expression.

'We've seen the movies, Abidemi and I. The recordings the *masu amfana* made were real heavy on the detail. The slaves, the Africans, were brought up in small groups, naked mostly, and harried with cutlasses and swords and bayonets until there was no way for them to go but overboard. Oh, they begged and screamed and sometimes fought, but the crew didn't care. The ones who fought were chopped down and the rest went over the side. The crew thought it was great sport. Captain Bradock had broken open the grog beforehand, see, and they were half cut and giggling and joking, and each time a wailing body hit the water they'd raise a cheer and point west. "Swim for Africa!" they'd say. "It's not far." And when some of them did, desperate for any kind of hope, the crew'd collapse against the ship's rail, laughing fit to burst. Knowing they'd now have plenty of water put 'em in a good mood, I'd guess.

'And then they sailed away. In the wrong direction, still, 'cause you can't fix stupid.

'Monifa, now, she's in the water with the others. Two hundred and seventy went in, thirty having died on the journey, see? And eighteen go straight to the bottom 'cause they couldn't swim, or couldn't swim well on account of being ill from the journey. The rest, though, they're hanging on. They come from a land of rivers and lakes and swimming was normal for them.' Ethan was surprised to hear a wistful tone in the alien's voice. 'They don't swim so much as float in the sea, like they had back home in better times, weeping and calling to each other and praying to *orisha*s who will not hear them.

'And then, as the sun starts to go down, the sharks come up.' Yemi's grim expression became grimmer yet. 'A shark attack ain't nothing at first. You don't see nothing, don't feel nothing, don't know they're circling beneath you, closing in nice and slow and easy. And even when you do feel something it still ain't nothing much, a thump against the legs is all. But when you do nothing, *can't*, because you're a creature of the land and helpless, they come back and bite you. Real hard. A chunk of your back, a mouthful of calf. And now you're screaming, and the people around you are screaming, and there's blood in the water – your blood – and it's making red foam as you thrash about and try to get away.

'The sharks, though, they ain't concerned about any of that. They're too busy figuring out if you're good enough to eat. And when they do, well, they turn around and come at you for real.'

Yemi's face was like stone.

'Some are dragged under and torn apart, and some are eaten alive on the surface, the sharks don't much mind which. And the man next to Monifa, he's bitten in two right in front of her, and the young boy whose hand she's holding, he's dragged under, almost taking her with him. And Monifa is praying like she's never prayed before in her life. Not for herself, because she knows she's pregnant now, but for her baby, the baby of the African who enslaved and raped her.

'And all this time, not so very far away, the *masu amfana* are watching.'

Shockingly, to Ethan, at least, Yemi broke into a smile.

'You know how sometimes you're watching a wildlife show on TV and some baby animal, an African wild dog, a gnu, whatever, gets injured and separated from its parents and now it's going to die? But it doesn't want to die and it struggles on and it struggles on because, what option does it have? To just give up? That ain't how those animals is made. And so on they go, limping and dying by inches. And the camera crew follows it for days or weeks until the inevitable is about to happen. You seen a show like that?'

There were reluctant nods all around.

'Well, the crew have a choice, don't' they? Keep making their award-winning show and film the death; or show some gosh-darned compassion and intervene. Mostly, they keep filming and pick up their award. But sometimes, *sometimes* they intervene: take the animal to a rescue centre or a zoo or some such.

'And maybe because Monifa is praying for a baby she has every reason to wish dead, or because the *masu amfana* have seen too much and can't take it anymore, or maybe because of plain dumb luck, Monifa gets her miracle. The moon is shining now, low in the sky. The silver waters ripple and part and a huge turtle, its shell vast as an island, rises to the surface. And there's music and voices calling for people to swim to it and people do. But the sharks do not. They hate the music and flee to deeper, quieter places in the ocean beneath.

'Huge and strange as the turtle is, it gets stranger. Openings appear in the glistening shell revealing warm, golden light within. And there are more voices, different now and impossible to understand, save for their urgency, their welcome, drawing Monifa towards them.

'Monifa, exhausted and bedraggled, reaches the shell and climbs, desperate to get to the golden opening that is higher than she thought and farther away. But she scrambles her way up, and her hand is grabbed by a hand that is not a hand, attached to an arm that is not an arm, and is pulled inside where, for the first time in her life, she gazes into the face of a *masu amfana*.'

Yemi's expression turned wry.

'She screams, of course, and struggles to get away, more terrified of what is in front of her than what she has left behind. And she is strong, even now, after all she has endured since her capture beside a quiet stream. Stronger than her rescuer. But the way she came through is gone and the *masu amfana* is quiet and calm and keeps their distance. Until Monifa begins to see beyond the *masu amfana*'s horrifying outer layers to the creature, the *true* creature, within. The creature that rescued her from death, that wishes her no harm, the creature that is, above all else, *kind*. And she too becomes calm, and uncurls her clenched fists, and allows the hand that is not a hand, attached to an arm that is not an arm, to take her and lead her into the depths of a turtle that is not, in any way shape or form, any such thing.'

'How many?' Hollie asked quietly. 'How many did the *masu amfana* rescue?' She looked stricken.

'One hundred and forty-nine,' Yemi said. 'Of the three hundred that left the barracoons, less than half.

'And nothing was settled, see? The *masu amfana* knew they shouldn't have done what they did: reveal themselves to humans. And they didn't know what to do next, except they weren't going to cast these people back into the sea.

'The *masu amfana* thought about returning them to their homes in Africa but couldn't risk knowledge of their existence being revealed. They thought about marooning them in an isolated part of the world, far from human contact. But the world, even in 1791, was not that isolated. Word would still get out. The story of the miraculous rescue would live on. And one day, someone, perhaps in the time of technology that was surely coming, would tie the incident to the tale of the slave ship *Esperance*, which finally made Jamaica four days later, its holds empty, its profits lost. Except for the insurance claim, of course.'

'So what did they do?' Hollie asked.

'They returned home with them,' Abidemi said abruptly. 'Gave them a new world, not so very far from their own.'

'A whole planet? For a hundred and forty-nine people?'

'A whole planet. My planet. His planet. Ibi Aabo.'

'And they weren't a hundred and forty-nine for very long,' Yemi said. 'The baby Monifa carried was born there, on Ibi Aabo. The first of many.'

'I'm sorry about what happened to your ancestors,' Ethan said. 'But it doesn't really explain why you've come all this way to murder people.'

'It's not murder, lawman. It's *gbese*. *Gbese* must be paid.'

'Basie, basie. So you keep saying. But what does it mean?'

'A debt. An obligation. A need to atone.' Yemi's gaze, hard now, shifted to Kirsty Forbes and the children. 'A punishment that fits the crime.'

Ethan would have moved if he could.

'You cannot be fucking serious. You pick randoes off the street in revenge for something they had nothing to do with? That happened over two hundred goddamn years ago? That's insane.'

'They're not random,' Abidemi said quietly.

Ethan looked at her, painfully aware that his face was graffitied with shock.

'They're not random,' she repeated. 'Kirsty Forbes is a direct descendant of Theodore Bradock, the Captain of the *Esperance*. And not just any direct descendant. She's the closest possible genetic match to the man himself.' A wry smile. 'I know, because I did the same research Yemi did.'

'And the kids?' But even as he was asking the question, his stomach clenched at the answer. The *Esperance* had travelled to Rhode Island; traded American rum for British linen. Textiles. The technology they'd ended up stealing.

'Let me guess. Dorothy Vielfrass, her kids, and grandkids are all descended from a guy called Nathaniel Wolfe, the owner of the *Esperance*.'

Now it was Abidemi's turn to look surprised. Yemi burst out laughing. And, for a moment, it was the real thing: rich and deep and rolling, smoothing the tiredness from his face, sparking his eyes.

The laughter throttled back to an ironic chuckle.

'You are good at detecting, detective. The Vielfrasses – Wolfes back then – traded slaves for sugar, turned sugar into rum, traded rum for linen and traded linen for more slaves and on and on. They kept close ties with the British, even during your so-called revolution, and made a fortune. Which they live off to this day.' The look he directed at Claire and Sebastian was one of pure loathing. More disquietingly, the expression on Abidemi's face was little better.

'But they're just kids. Just . . .'

He thought of Benjamin Okoro, tiny and crumpled and drowned at sea two hundred feet above the ground. His voice faded away to nothing. If Yemi could do that . . .

He tried again.

'This isn't justice, this is . . .'

Something in Yemi and Abidemi's expression made him stop.

'It's *our* justice,' Abidemi said, her voice firm. And Ethan realized he'd been right about them after all. They were aliens. Their bodies might look human, might even be descended from humans, but the minds inside them were not. Not anymore. They'd been away too long, grown too far apart.

As if reading his thoughts, Abidemi said: 'There are thousands of us now, on Ibi Aabo. And what we brought from Earth, we kept: our language, our traditions, our religion. But we were taught to live, to really live, by the *masu amfana*. Their technology is our technology, their justice is our justice, more or less.' A prideful smile. 'We are better at engineering, at spatial visualization than they are. We have taken their technology in . . . *unexpected* directions and they are grateful for it. But when it comes to what is right, and what is wrong, we are as one with our neighbours.

'When the *masu amfana* die, they are absorbed by their off-spring, and with that absorption come the memories of the deceased: incomplete, imperfect for sure, but a window into the past that we can only dream of. Some *masu amfana* have memories stretching back thousands of years. Faint, mind you, but real, nevertheless. And with memory comes guilt, obligation, responsibility for the sins of your forebears. *Gbese.*'

'But you're *human*,' Hollie protested. 'We don't remember like that. No one this . . . this complete fucking *arsehole* has murdered, has any connection to what went on back then.'

'Do you know how many people on the *Esperance* could read?' Yemi asked suddenly.

Hollie shook her head, confused.

'Four. Including the Captain. And do you know what book they all carried on this cursed voyage?'

'The Bible,' Hollie said, with a very English certainty.

Yemi looked surprised.

'Yes,' he said, recovering quickly. 'And part of it says, "I the Lord your God am a jealous God, visiting the iniquity of the fathers on the children to the third and fourth generation." Even today, your people talk past each other about so-called repar-ations, so don't pretend to me that humans are immune to the concept. That woman's ancestor,' he pointed at Kirsty, 'who read his Bible every day, knew these things to be true. The present must atone for the past. She's connected. They're all connected. And they must pay the price for what they did.'

He paused suddenly.

'You understand I'm going easy on you?'

'What?' The word popped out of Ethan's mouth before he could stop it.

'Sure. *Gbese* is only being paid by a few of the guilty. The most direct genetic descendants of those most responsible. Some *masu amfana* would insist on a far higher price. Many thousands. Millions, even.'

'But *all masu amfana* forbade this,' Abidemi said, eyes flashing. 'The elders, *our* elders, forbade this. This is a closed world. Savage. Backward. Our laws don't run here. However much we may dislike it, no *gbese* is owed.' Ethan was shocked to see Abidemi shaking with fury. 'Except, of course, that's not completely true, is it? Because of you and your stupid, *selfish* behaviour, *gbese* – real, lawfully incurred *gbese* – is on *my* shoulders. *Mine. I* must pay for what you did. And I will pay it in full or die trying.'

'Don't say that,' Yemi said, looking genuinely upset. 'I'm sorry you pulled the short straw. Truly, I am. I'd hoped – *prayed* – it would be someone else. But it couldn't be helped. Couldn't be helped.'

For a moment, it looked as if doubt had found a toehold on the cliff face of Yemi's certainties.

The moment passed.

Kirsty Forbes and the children were on their feet, fear etched across their faces. A warm, uncaring wind fluttered at the sails. The ocean rose and fell beneath them, waiting.

'Please,' Kirsty begged, hard to hear above the children's panicked cries. 'You don't have tae do this.'

'But I really, really do.'

Like Hollie before them, the boy, the girl, the woman found themselves climbing over the boat rail, facing out towards the hungry sea. Spray whipped at their legs, making the children scream louder.

'Please, man. I'll give you anything you want. *Do* anything you want. Just—'

'You want those to be your last words, lady? I'd have thought you—'

'*Aseyori!*' Abi snarled.

The boat's wheel, large and brass and polished, spun wildly. Sails cracked in angry confusion. The vessel changed direction. Tilted wildly. The children's high-pitched screaming tore at Ethan's ears. Yemi, who'd leaped to his feet, stumbled and almost fell.

Which was why he didn't see the nearest sail, with the huge beam that held it taut at the bottom, swing crazily across the deck. Ethan flinched as the beam whipped over the top of him and slammed into the back of Yemi's head.

Yemi collapsed face down on the deck and, suddenly, Ethan was free. He grabbed at the back of his neck, ripping the loosened *ejo* from his body, and staggered to his feet, stunned to see Abidemi wriggling out of her ropes, the frayed end of one of them looking like it had been chewed through by rats.

'Grab him,' she ordered. 'We don't have much—'

Ethan launched himself at Yemi's prone body, pinning him down.

And not a moment too soon. Yemi's wiry frame bucked under him, threatening to throw him off. He slammed Yemi's head into the deck.

'Not this time, you fuck!'

The impact would have stunned a normal man. But the moment Ethan removed his hand from Yemi's close-cropped head, the head reared up and smashed into the bridge of his nose. There was a sickening crack of bone, the hot, metallic taste of blood in his mouth, and a blurring of vision as his body, unhinged from its brain, toppled to one side.

Yemi was on his feet again, looming over him. Ethan tried to get away, to scramble upright. He knew, though, with a sickening certainty, that he was moving far too slowly. Some part of Yemi would lace into him, incapacitating him if he was lucky, killing him if he were not. The muscles in his body relaxed, resigning themselves to the inevitable: a savannah animal falling to the lions.

But Yemi was already turning away, climbing out of the bench-lined recess around the wheel. He was heading for Claire, and Sebastian and Kirsty who, miraculously, were still clinging to the rail. The man was determined to throw them into the sea.

Ethan's befuddled brain took a moment or two to figure out why he felt such a stab of surprise. It wasn't simply that Yemi had left him alone, it was the fact that, either because of the collision with the beam or the violence of the subsequent assault, Yemi had lost control of his prisoners. Otherwise, they would have stepped into the heaving blue ocean all on their own.

Yemi reached the side decking. Laid long, elegant fingers on a shrieking Claire Vielfrass.

Ethan felt something move past him in a blur of motion, slamming into Yemi's side.

Abidemi. The force of the collision took both of them to the deck. But it also dislodged Claire's hands from the boat's rail. She screamed as her feet slipped on the wet edge of the hull, toppling off the side.

Only to be held back by Hollie, whose grasp bunched the girl's soiled tee shirt in a small, white-knuckled fist.

Yemi was on top of Abidemi now, raining down punches too quick for Ethan to follow. And yet, somehow, the woman was blocking them. With a sinuous twist of her body, she managed to throw him off and they were both on their feet, their thrashing, intertwined limbs moving faster than any normal human being could hope to follow.

And they didn't *look* human, Ethan decided. There was something about their faces, a slackness of expression, that didn't sit right.

As if they were drugged.

He scrambled to his feet, determined to help. Yemi saw him coming, glanced his way. By the time he glanced back it was too late.

Abidemi landed a vicious chop to his throat. Ethan could hear the cracking of cartilage, the suddenly laboured breathing. Yemi's hands flew to his neck, eyes bulging wide. He staggered backwards against the boat's rail.

Yemi was tall. The boat's rail was only a little higher than the back of his knee. Not high enough to stop him falling.

For Ethan, what happened next seemed to unfold in slow motion.

Yemi toppled backwards over the rail, one foot coming off the deck, arms spreading wide in a vain attempt to regain his balance.

Abidemi rushed forward, reached out to grab him.

Yemi's outstretched arm hit Claire Vielfrass, who was holding onto Hollie and trying to climb over the rail.

Claire lost her grip and fell backwards towards the sea.

Abidemi grabbed and steadied her. Turned back towards Yemi quicker than humanly possible. Grabbed at him.

But still too late. Her slim hand could grasp only air. Yemi fell screaming into the blue, sun-glittered waves. Ethan rushed to the rail, saw a head in the water, drifting away from them at shocking speed. Bobbing.

And then it was gone.

Abidemi was at the rail beside him, face no longer slack, screaming at the water.

'*Baba!*' she cried. '*Babaaa!*'

Ethan didn't need to speak her language to know what she was saying.

Seventy-Five

Monday the 14th: 3.03 p.m. EST

Earth's slow-moving sun was still high in the sky when, with much swearing, Hollie Rogers crashed the boat into the same dock they'd left from. The policeman and the children, visibly shaken by the impact, had jumped ashore. They were tying the vessel down with amateurish loops of rope.

She should have helped in some way, Abi supposed. But she couldn't.

She'd been this way since her father had fallen into the sea, no more able to swim than his daughter. His augments would have done what they could, kept him alive as long as they could, but they would have failed by now.

And the creatures of that awful ocean would have consumed him.

She barely remembered the journey back. How Hollie had taken charge, instructed her to drop the too-difficult-to-understand sails and turn on the engine.

'Can that head of yours get us back to where we came from?' Hollie had asked, and she'd nodded, her mouth too leaden with grief for actual words.

Without sails to balance it, the boat had wallowed unsteadily atop the water, the low-throated burble of its motor barely audible above the sighing of the waves. It bucked and yawed and bucked and yawed until all except Hollie had leaned over the boat's rail and thrown up.

Even that had made little impression on her. A necessary bodily function in the circumstances, the sharp tang of bile gone too soon, a minor distraction from misery.

Later, as she'd lain on the triangular bed at the front of the boat, Hollie had left the machines in charge and come down to see her.

'I'm sorry about Yemi,' she'd said. 'I had no idea he was your father.'

'It never came up, babe. Didn't seem relevant.'

Hollie had grimaced at that but let it go.

'And you got sent here *because* he was your father?'

'Yeah. That's how *gbese* works. Yemi violated our laws. It falls to the family to make it right. Or as right as possible. The family chose me because I had the skills. And the fewest children.'

Hollie's jaw had dropped.

'You're a mum? But you look so—'

'We age slower than you do. I'm a lot older than I look.' Tears had almost leaked into her eyes. 'A lot older.'

'How old are you?'

She'd forced a weak smile.

'A lady never tells, doll. Ain't that what they say?'

Hollie had had the good sense not to push it.

'And how many kids?'

'Two. A girl and a boy.' She'd remembered their hot tears mixing with her own, their desperate, slipping grasp as the *masu amfana* tugged them away. And then she was through the gate, the warm moistness on her face all that was left of her children, washed away in a cold, *oyinbo* rain. 'Ayo and Kehinde.'

'I bet they'll be super proud of you when you get home.'

If she'd had the energy, she'd have balled her hands into fists. 'Maybe. *Gbese* is paid, for sure. Nothing's gonna come down on them. Not now. But . . . I'd hoped to bring him home, you know? Make him face justice. Instead, all I've got is . . . is . . .'

She'd turned on her side then. Stared obdurately at the wooden panelling. Hollie had patted her softly on the hip and left.

Now, with the boat secured by bulging, ungainly knots, and a gangplank laid to the dock, she slouched disconsolately back to land.

The policeman was waiting for her as she stepped off.

Seventy-Six

Monday the 14th: 3.11 p.m. EST

'If you try and arrest me, detective, I will kill you.'

From the expression on her face, Ethan had no doubt that the woman-alien meant every word. He stepped back, hands spread wide in as peaceable a way as he could manage.

'My badge don't run to Jamaica, ma'am. I got no jurisdiction here.' He glanced up at the steep, viridian hillsides; around the small, private cove Yemi must have bought years before; at the chain link fencing that kept it private. Hard to believe, at the shadowed bottom of such deep slopes, that there was a normal, bustling town just a few miles away. Much easier to believe, in fact, that the towering Black woman standing in front of him came from farther away than he had brain cells to imagine. 'This whole thing is out of my jurisdiction,' he sighed. 'Fuck knows how I'm going to write it up.'

He studied her for a few moments, hesitant to intrude.

Screw it.

'I do have a question, though.'

'And what would that be?'

'I get – kinda – how your ... how Yemi targeted the Vielfrasses and Kirsty Forbes. There were records he could look at. Ways to track the descendants. And I get – in theory – how he could analyse the DNA of quarter of a million people like he said. Whatever. But there's one thing I don't understand, and it's busting my noodle.'

'Which is?'

'How'd he know whose DNA he was looking for? If there were no written records in 1791 West Africa, there sure as hell weren't any DNA databases. I'm a cop. DNA is useless unless you have something to match it against. So: what was he using? Or were the Okoros just murdered at random?'

Just for a second, Ethan thought he'd gone too far, that his neck was going to get snapped like a twig. It took real effort for Abidemi to smooth the anger from her face.

'Yemi didn't attack anyone at random, detective. And he went out of his way to keep people like you alive. As for your question: he brought all the DNA he needed when he made the trip. As did I.'

'Really?'

'Yeah, really. Did you listen to the story he told you? About what happened here?'

Ethan nodded.

'The woman, Monifa. The one who was pregnant with the slaver's child. She was Yemi's great-grandmother. My great-great grandmother. As for my great-great grandfather, the rapist-slaver,' she patted her chest, 'his genes are still here. Some of them, anyway. And you don't grow a settlement of a hundred and forty-nine humans into many thousands without paying close attention to genes. Yemi didn't know his great-grandfather's name but he knew nearly every syllable of the man's DNA. The ones that made it into him. The ones that didn't. With an *opolo keji* to fill in the blanks, he could have popped them in a birthing tank and grown a decent enough replica if he'd a mind to.' Despite herself, a grunt of dark amusement issued from Abidemi's lips. 'Perhaps he should have. And made the replica pay *gbese*.'

For the briefest of moments, Ethan's mind slipped from its moorings, saw the drowned father and baby in that high-end Chicago apartment not as innocent victims, but as manifestations of a rapist-slaver who'd escaped punishment. Who needed to be punished in his stead.

He pushed the thought away with a half gasp. What Yemi did was murder pure and simple. No alien mumbo jumbo was going to change that. The bastard deserved what happened to him. And more.

'What happens now?' he asked.

Abi started up the steps dug into the hillside with long easy strides. Ethan scrambled to keep up.

'I guess I have to find some way of getting you back where you belong, seeing as you don't have a passport and all.' She pointed up the hill. 'There'll be enough gear in that building of his to make it happen, I'm sure. Then I have to clean up all the k-balled doohickeys he left lying around this planet of yours. Not least his gosh-darned truck. Now that . . . *that* will be a real cave of wonders. And then . . .' A long, querulous sigh. 'Then I can go home.'

Home for her is so far away, Ethan thought, this place probably isn't even a dot in her sky. It made him feel very small.

And his worries and concerns smaller still. Time to stop being a coward. Time to talk to the people he cared about. Mend some fences.

He reached into his pocket and grunted with exasperation. Abidemi looked at him curiously.

'I was looking for my cell,' he admitted sheepishly. 'Forgot what had happened to it for a minute.'

'You planning on ringing someone?'

'I was, yeah.'

'Borrow mine.'

Ethan took the proffered phone. It felt strangely heavy in his hand.

'Life's too short,' he murmured, tapping out a number. 'For me, at any rate.'

He looked into Abidemi's bottomless dark eyes, felt a sudden need to explain.

'I have a brain tumour. Doc says I've a few months at best.'

Her laughter caught him by surprise.

'Go see your doc again,' she said. 'I reckon they'll have changed their mind.'

Ethan tried to ignore the sudden thudding in his chest.

'The machine that fixed your wrist? It fixed other things, too.' Abidemi's eyes turned vacant, as if she was consulting something. Which, given she seemed to be as much machine as woman, was probably exactly what she was doing. One hand ran idly over the ivory amulet on her wrist. 'A fatty heart. Disgusting arteries. And a growth in your brain that didn't belong there. All cleared out, for now, at least. You have more than a few months, detective. Try not to waste them, heh?'

Ethan couldn't walk anymore. Hell, he could barely stand. His knees threatened to give way and plunge him off the side of the dangerously steep stairway. He gripped tightly to a rocky outcropping for balance.

Thank you.

But his mouth was working no better than his knees. The words failed to get past his stalled tongue.

'What are you two talking about?' Hollie asked as she caught up with them. Kirsty Forbes and the children laboured up the steps behind her.

'Nothing,' Ethan managed to grunt, turning back to face her. Glancing over her shoulder he could feel his expression change. 'You gotta be shitting me.'

Secured at an ungainly angle to the jetty below, the sailboat's stern was clearly visible. The copperplate letters beneath the rail, obscured by darkness when they'd been marched down these very same steps, were now plain to see.

ESPERANCE, it said. BRISTOL, UK.

Abidemi let loose a short laugh. Wiped a tear from her eye.

'How could it not be, given who my father was and why he was here? A filthy name for a filthy boat.'

'True enough,' Ethan said. The phone in his hand was ringing now. He raised it to his ear.

'Cara? Hi. It's your dad. Sorry to call you at work but I'd like to come to the wedding if it's not too late. I'm okay to sit by Devin's parents, Pumpkin, but can you keep me at a safe distance from your mom?'

He started to climb the steps again, a small smile tugging at his lips.

Seventy-Seven

She was standing once more in an ocean of grass. No rain this time, no children's tears on her cheeks. The last stars were fading from the sky, tired of waiting for a slow sun. Abi hefted her backpack more securely on her shoulders, bent down to pick up a suitcase full of reclaimed technology and the odd souvenir.

'So this is it, then?' Hollie was asking. 'This is where you arrived?'

'Sure is.' Abi straightened up, the suitcase heavy in her hand.

'And the gate's here too?' Hollie peered blankly over Abi's shoulder. 'I wish I could see it.' A small giggle. 'I guess the drugs have worn off then, yeah?'

'I guess they have.' Abi smiled down at the pale little Earth woman. She took a last, regretful look at her beguiling blue eyes, capturing them forever in her files. 'Well, babe, this is it. Time to—'

'Take me with you!'

The blue eyes were wide now. Hollie clamped small hands over her mouth. It was as if she was trying to stuff the words back where they came from.

'Hollie, I—'

The hands dropped away, allowing more words to escape.

'I didn't mean that. Okay, yeah, well I did, and I like you and I've only just met you and you're literally the most interesting person in the world and I'd like to know more about you and meet little Ayo and Kehinde and . . . oh, Abs, I didn't mean to make you cry.'

Crying was for children. And the weak.

And yet here she was, eyes blinded by tears, great racking sobs venting from her lungs. Her legs, her legs were giving way. She dropped the suitcase and sat on it with what scraps of dignity she had left. She sat there and wept, hunched and humiliated in front of an *oyinbo*.

Not just an *oyinbo*. A friend. She wiped her eyes and nose on the sleeve of her jacket, tried to regain a little bit of composure. Hollie sat down beside her, took one of Abi's hands into both of hers.

'I'm sorry about your dad, Abs.'

'That's not why I'm crying, babe. Not mostly, anyhow.' Abi adjusted her position so she could look directly into Hollie's face. 'I'm crying because you can never meet my children. At least, not the way you imagine. And it's why I can't take you.'

'You're not making any sense. Not even a little bit.'

'You see those stars up there, the ones that are almost gone?'

'Yeah.'

'They're so far away that the light you're looking at, the light that's almost gone now, is hundreds, maybe thousands of years old. That's how long the information takes to get here.'

'Okay.'

'Ibi Aabo, the worlds of the *masu amfana*, are closer than that, but they're still a long way away. Information from here, from the robots and probes that we now use for our research, travels for many years before it arrives.'

She managed a wry smile.

'Do you know how I learned to speak your language?'

Hollie shook her head.

'By watching the latest movies from Earth. Talkies, I think you call them. The last one I saw was from 1938. Cary Grant, that statue you have of him downtown? Back on Ibi Aabo when I left, he was just starting out.'

'But that means you're like close to a hundred years old and that doesn't—'

'Whoa there, doll. The movies, the information, didn't reach me in 1938. They left *here* in 1938. It just took a long time to get to Ibi Aabo.' She tried and failed to keep the sadness off her face. 'Just like it took me a long time to get here.'

Hollie was fighting what she was being told. Abi could see it in her face.

'But you came through a gate. It's like, *poof*, and you're there.'

'It is. Even when you make a jump between worlds.'

'So it didn't take long to get here then, did it?'

'In a sense, sure. You move so fast that time stops for you. But the rest of the universe? It moves on, same as it ever did.' Her free hand flitted absently across her cheek. 'There's a reason there's only ever been one manned expedition to this place. A heartbeat in the gate is half a lifetime for the people you leave behind. I left my children, my little boy and girl . . . sixteen days ago but they are already in the prime of life, older than I am now. Soon I will return and it will still be sixteen days for me. But they will be old – if I'm lucky. If I'm not . . .' Abi paused, taking in the ocean of grass, the lightening sky, the warmth of Hollie's hands. 'This is *gbese*. This is the price we pay for our fathers' transgressions.'

'But it's so cruel!'

'The punishment must fit the crime, doll. My father wished to kill children. So, in recompense, I must lose mine. Not by murder, of course, but they are lost to me nonetheless by time. By the physics of the universe we live in. It's our way. And it's why you can't come with me. The journey will be short but way too long. I can't – won't – do that to you. Even if I, too, would like to know you better.' She gave Hollie's hands a quick squeeze. Stood up. Breathed in the air, unfiltered, with all its myriad pollutants. Savoured it.

'Time to go, Hollie Rogers. Walk with me?'

Abi walked across the ocean of grass, suitcase in one hand, Hollie in the other, the laggardly *oyinbo* sun tincting the sky pink.

Acknowledgements

I am a lawyer. Feel free to judge.

Before I was a lawyer, though, I was a law student, and at a time when law reports were written in books rather than computers. As a law student with access to a library and a keen interest in history, the temptation to wander away from the curriculum and browse through slices of life from hundreds of years ago often proved irresistible.

So it was that one rainy afternoon, while wrestling with the rule against perpetuities, I stumbled across a marine insurance case from 1783. That case, which I have carried around with me my entire adult life, is the inspiration for *Esperance*. I hope, given the temporal uncertainties involved in the reading of acknowledgements, that you either have enjoyed or will enjoy the results.

Despite the fact that my name appears on the cover, books are a team effort. Especial thanks to my friends from either side of the Atlantic, Shelly Geppert and Lyndsey Ratcliffe; to my agent, the esteemed Brady McReynolds, James Farner, Arielle DeVito and all at JABberwocky Literary; to my UK editor, the super enthusiastic Anne Perry, Gaby Puleston-Vaudrey, Kay Gale for the copy-editing and all at Arcadia Books; in the US, to Madeline Goldberg, Laura Fitzgerald and the entire team at DAW; and last, but not least, to my family: Barbara, Alex, Amina, Alima, Tom, Nadia, Max, Elliot, Henry and Bex (who will be tying the knot around the time this book comes out), Harriet, Angus, Corey and Margot, whose support, be it enthusiastic, disbelieving or otherwise, is always appreciated.

Arcadia